A CASTLE IN THE CLOUDS

A Castle in the Clouds

KERSTIN GIER

TRANSLATED BY ROMY FURSLAND

HENRY HOLT AND COMPANY
New York

Henry Holt and Company, *Publishers since 1866*
Henry Holt® is a registered trademark of Macmillan Publishing Group, LLC

120 Broadway, New York, New York 10271 • fiercereads.com

Library of Congress Control Number : 2019940908
ISBN 978-1-250-30019-5

Our books may be purchased in bulk for promotional, educational, or business use.
Please contact your local bookseller or the Macmillan Corporate and
Premium Sales Department at (800) 221-7945 ext. 5442 or by email at
MacmillanSpecialMarkets@macmillan.com.

First edition, 2020 / Designed by Katie Klimowicz
Printed in the United States of America

1 3 5 7 9 10 8 6 4 2

For Sonja

So there I stood, exhausted, in the snow, as the sound of violins drifted toward us from the ballroom. Around my neck was a thirty-five-carat diamond that didn't belong to me, and in my arms was a sleeping child who didn't belong to me, either.

Somewhere along the way I'd lost a shoe.

People always say that in an emergency you don't feel pain or the cold because of all the adrenaline coursing through you, but it's not true. The wound in my shoulder was throbbing like mad, the blood was running down my arm and dripping onto the snow, and the cold gnawed painfully at my foot. The muscles in my arms and shoulders were burning from carrying the child, but I didn't dare put her down again in case she woke up and alerted our pursuers to where we were.

People also say your brain works best in moments of great danger, arming you with razor-sharp insights. But that wasn't true in my case, either. I couldn't tell who was good and who was bad anymore. And the only razor-sharp insight I'd had recently was that silencers on guns really do what they say they will.

And that there were definitely better moments for a kiss than this one.

I had no idea whether the boy kissing me was one of the goodies or one of the baddies, but either way, I felt my strength returning.

"I've been wanting to do that since the first time I saw you," he whispered.

BIENVENUE. WILLKOMMEN. BENVENUTO.

WELCOME TO

A Castle
IN THE
Clouds

Enjoy your stay.

1

My first day as a hotel babysitter was shaping up to be a complete disaster.

"You are without doubt the worst babysitter in the history of the world, Sophie Spark," was Don's verdict, as I dashed past him yelling, "Boys! This is not funny! Come back here, please!"

"*Yes, please, please, please!*" said Don, mimicking me. *"Or I'm going to get fired!"*

It was entirely possible. But I'd only taken my eyes off them for a minute. In my defense: It's easier than you think to lose sight of children in the snow when they go sneaking off wearing white parkas, white ski pants, and white hats. It ought to be illegal to dress kids like that.

They couldn't have gotten far. Up the hill from where I was standing, the glistening blanket of snow was untouched. But here on the west side of the hotel, there were plenty of hiding places where a pair of very small and devious children could have gone to ground, decked out as they were in camouflage gear. There were lots of snowdrifts they could be crouching behind and various trees, woodpiles, and walls that also offered ideal cover.

I squinted against the light. The weather forecast had said more snow was due to fall tonight and over Christmas, but for now the sky was still bright blue and the snow gleamed as if it were trying to outsparkle the windows and the copper-clad turrets and dormer roofs. The valley below, on the other hand, had been shrouded in thick mist since yesterday morning. Weather conditions like this were what had given the hotel its nickname: *Castle in the Clouds.*

"Strangely quiet, isn't it?" said Don Burkhardt Jr., reminding me that now really wasn't the time to be admiring the Swiss mountain scenery. "I just hope those sweet little boys haven't already frozen to death."

Don was sitting on the big sled that was used to transport firewood to the basement door, swinging his legs and licking an ice-cream cone he must have sweet-talked out of someone in the kitchen. The firewood itself he'd simply tipped out into the snow beneath the WELCOME TO A CASTLE IN THE CLOUDS sign.

The ice cream gave me an idea. "Hey, boys! How about a nice ice cream?" I called.

But I was met with absolute silence.

Don giggled gleefully. "You shouldn't have let that handyman distract you from your duties, Sophie Spark."

"You'd better pick that wood up if you don't want to get in trouble," I said.

Although Don was small and skinny and looked sweet and perfectly harmless with his little snub nose and soulful brown eyes, I was secretly afraid of him. He was always coming up with things you'd never expect to hear from a nine-year-old, and it was doubly disconcerting because of his high-pitched little voice, cute Swiss accent, and equally cute lisp. His odd habit of calling people by both their first and last names, sometimes accompanied by description and age—"You've got a hole in your tights, Sophie Spark, seventeen-year-old high-school dropout"—had something weirdly menacing about it, like in a mafia film when someone murmurs "I know where you live" and later deposits a horse's head in your bed. If you're lucky.

Don and his parents were regular guests at the hotel, and Don knew the place like the back of his hand. He'd spend all day roaming around the building, eavesdropping on people's conversations, and stirring up trouble, behaving as though the hotel and everyone in it belonged to him. He seemed to know everything about everyone, guests and staff alike. It was creepy the way he managed to remember everything, right down to the tiniest detail. Freight elevators, offices, the basement—Don's favorite places to loiter were the ones guests weren't supposed to have access to, but because he was so small and sweet he rarely got in trouble for it. Whenever he came across someone he couldn't charm with his innocent doe eyes, he put the fear of God into them by reeling off their full name and mentioning, as if in passing, his fabulously rich father, Don Burkhardt Sr., and his father's friendship with one of the Montfort brothers, who owned the hotel.

That was what he did with me, anyway. And even if I tried not to show it, his mafia-style methods were pretty effective. Just two days ago, I'd caught him wiping his chocolatey hands quite coolly and deliberately on the embroidered velvet drapes in the little vestibule on the second floor. He met my outrage with a superior smile. "Oh, high-school-dropout Sophie Spark clearly has a *penchant* for hideous curtains!"

That made me even more outraged: All the curtains and cushions on the second floor were made from the same fabric, a beautiful crimson material embroidered with birds and floral patterns in soft gold thread. You didn't have to be an expert to realize how valuable they were, even if the red had faded slightly over the years. When you ran your fingers gently over the velvet, it felt almost as if it were stroking you back.

"Anyway, isn't it your job to keep things clean around here, temporary chambermaid Sophie Spark with the funny freckles?" Don had asked. Two days ago, I hadn't yet started my babysitting duties; I'd still been assigned to the housekeeping team. "How much money d'you think my dad spends in this hotel every year? And who do you think they'd kick out first—you or me? If I were you, I'd be glad it's only chocolate and try to get these stains out quickly before Fräulein Müller reads you the riot act again." (Where on earth did he come up with these expressions? Not even my grandma talked like that.)

"And if I were you, I'd get out of here quickly before I whack you with this duster!" I'd replied, but Don had sauntered away with a grin on his face, knowing full well that he'd won. I was more afraid of Fräulein Müller, the head housekeeper, than I was of him. And as I scrubbed the chocolate stain out of the velvet curtain, I did actually feel a certain relief that it was only chocolate and nothing worse.

"If anyone's going to get in trouble around here, it's you," Don remarked now, licking his ice cream. "You were flirting with Jaromir Novak, thirty-eight, mustache-wearer, instead of looking after the children. I saw you."

"I wasn't flirting," I corrected him at once. "I was just quickly helping Jaromir untangle those Christmas lights. Which happens to be part of my job." After all, I wasn't just a babysitter; according to the job description, the hotel intern was supposed to turn their hand to "a variety of roles" and be "flexible and adaptable at all times."

Don shook his head. "You smiled, tucked your hair behind your ear, and exposed your throat—all key signals in the body language of female mating behavior."

"Rubbish!" I said indignantly. "Jaromir is far too old for me and has a wife and child in the Czech Republic who he loves very much." And even if he'd been twenty years younger and single, I'd never have flirted with him. I didn't flirt with anyone, out of principle. Even the word *flirt* made me cringe. "Anyw—" I broke off. It was obvious from the expression on Don's face how much he was enjoying this, seeing me defending myself so vehemently. It was yet more proof that I took him seriously. And that was the last thing I wanted him to think. "Well? Have you seen the twins or not?" I asked tersely.

Don immediately changed tack. "Yes. I even know where they're hiding." He fixed me with a butter-wouldn't-melt look even Bambi would have been proud of. "I'll tell you if you say 'please, please' very nicely."

"Please," I said, against my better judgment.

"Please, please!" Don demanded.

"Please, please," I said through gritted teeth.

Don laughed delightedly. "I'll tell you why you're such a bad babysitter: You just don't project any natural authority. Kids pick up on that kind of thing."

"And I'll tell you why you don't have any friends: You just don't project any natural niceness." I'd blurted it out before I realized how mean it actually was. I bit my lip in shame. I really must be the worst babysitter in the world, having managed to lose two small six-year-olds just by turning my back on them for a minute and then having felt the urge to hurl personal insults at Bambi himself. And I was pretty sure I'd only gotten the internship at the hotel in the first place because I'd mentioned my experience looking after my two little brothers and given the impression that I was particularly good with, and fond of, children.

"Ouch!" Don had nearly tripped me from his sled, but somehow I made it past his outstretched leg without falling over. Fond of children, my arse. Children were little pests, as far as I was concerned. But that didn't change the fact that I now had two of them to recapture. And the third I would simply ignore from now on.

"Boys! Hello!" I tried to make my voice sound friendly and relaxed, as if we were just playing hide-and-seek. Not a peep. And to think that before this they hadn't been able to keep their mouths shut for so much as a second and had chattered away constantly in rhyming gibberish. If only I could remember their stupid names! They had trendy, wannabe-American names like . . . "Josh? Ashley? Where are you? Don't you want to finish your snowman? I've found an extra-special carrot for his nose!"

Don giggled again. "You don't even know their names, screw-up Sophie. You can stick your carrot where the sun don't shine. Why don't you just give up now?"

I pretended not to hear him. There was no way I was giving up. In the last three months, I'd risen to plenty of other challenges. And this situation was actually nowhere near as bad as it looked. My job was to take the Bauer twins (Laramy? Jason?) out for some fresh air and keep them entertained, leaving their parents free to do their packing and check out of the hotel in peace. If you thought about it, that's exactly what I was doing: These kids were having the time of their lives out here, now that they'd managed to hide from me. In the fresh air.

"Ever heard of culpable negligence, soon-to-be-ex-intern Sophie Spark?" Don licked his ice cream again. "I hope you've got good insurance. If I were you, I'd be praying they don't both fall into a crevasse. If it starts snowing again, soon even the tracker dogs won't be able to pick up their scent."

I resisted the urge to put my fingers in my ears. This child really did have an evil streak. As far as I knew, there were no crevasses around here, but even I could hear how shrill and anxious my own voice sounded when I called to the twins again. "Do you want to pet a squirrel before you go?"

"They're not going to fall for that one." Don flicked his half-eaten cone into the snow. "Oh, go on then, I'll help you: They went that way." He pointed to the new ice rink next to the antique children's merry-go-round, which Old Stucky and Jaromir had conjured up over the past few days. "I think they were planning to hide in the ski cellar."

I wasn't completely stupid. I didn't follow the direction he was pointing but plodded resolutely the opposite way. And sure enough, I'd only gone a few feet when I heard muffled giggles and saw a branch jiggling about in the old half-moon fir tree. Jaromir and Old Stucky had decorated the tree with strings of Christmas lights during an intrepid climbing expedition that November; or rather, Jaromir had climbed the tree and Old Stucky had held the ladder. It had been nicknamed the half-moon fir tree because only the branches facing the hotel had lights in them. The same strings of lights had been in use for thirty years, I was told, but since trees grow over the course of thirty years and Christmas lights don't, they were now only long enough to cover half the tree. This meant that one side of the fir tree twinkled in the darkness as if trying to go one better than the blazing windows of the hotel, while the side facing the valley stayed black and still, blending into the night sky—just like a half moon.

The tree also marked the threshold between the hotel's well-tended, well-lit grounds and the mountainside beyond, where nature was left to its own devices. There wasn't much difference between them at the moment, though, because everything was buried deep under a thick blanket of snow.

The tree really was the perfect hiding place if you were only four feet tall. The branches fanned out in thick, sweeping layers reaching almost to the ground. It was probably soft and dry under there, a bed of moss and fir needles untouched by the snow.

Not wanting to scare the children off, I approached the tree in an unobtrusive, meandering way. "Those clever Bauer twins really are very good at hiding," I said in a stage whisper. "It's just such a shame I can't find them and show them the big surprise I've got for them. And it's not even anything to do with squirrels . . ."

Whispers from beneath the fir tree. I couldn't hold back a grin.

But my joy didn't last long.

"Don't be fooled, Jayden and Ash Bauer!" cried Don from right behind me. He'd jumped down off the big sled and followed me, clearly with the intention of making my life even more difficult. "She doesn't have a surprise for you! And she certainly doesn't have any squirrels! She just wants to catch you, and then you'll have to go home with your parents and all the fun will be over! You should make a run for it!"

"Jayden and Ash are too clever to listen to stupid old Don," I said hopefully, but already the children were scrambling out from under the tree and racing across the parking lot, laughing and hooting as they went. Don clapped and cheered. I had no choice but to set off in pursuit. Unfortunately, my little charges were headed in the wrong direction—away from the hotel and toward the road.

They leapt nimbly over the wall of dirty snow and ice formed by the snowplow, crossed the road, and climbed over another bank of snow on the other side.

"No! That's dangerous!" I called as I clambered after them. And it really was. Although the road ended here at the hotel and there were never many cars on it, the asphalt wound its way down into the valley like a shiny black ribbon in a series of alarmingly steep hairpin bends. Steeper still was the slope they cut across, which was covered in fir trees and which the children now began to slither down, laughing as they went. They grabbed at the low-hanging branches like clever little monkeys, swinging themselves down the mountainside at lightning speed. Unlike the twins, I was too heavy for the thick snow that had thawed and frozen so many times: With every step, I sank into it at least up to my knees, to the sound of loud crunching. It was like trying to walk across the caramel crust of a giant, tilted crème brûlée.

"Stop," I cried despairingly. "Please!"

"Please, sneeze, nibbleknees, nibblechitter, chotter, cheese!" the twins bellowed delightedly. Don was right. I projected absolutely zero authority.

The children had already reached the next bend in the road and were soon scrambling across it.

"You really need to stop now!" I hastily pulled my foot out of a particularly deep hole in the snow and tried taking bigger steps. "There are . . . there are bears around here!"

"Bears, snares, nibblenares, nibblechitter, chotter—oops!" One of the twins had lost his footing—he slid down the hill a little way on his butt and collided with the nearest tree, laughing his head off. His brother thought it was so funny that he sat down and started sliding on his butt, too.

9

"Don't do that!" I cried in alarm, already having visions of them hurtling down the steep mountainside unchecked until they either crashed into a tree trunk and broke their necks or fell into the road and got run over by a car. I was convinced I could hear the sound of a car engine already and redoubled my efforts to catch up with them. But that only made me lose my balance, too. I landed on my belly in the snow and was immediately transformed into a human bobsled. With my increased surface area and slippery coat, I practically flew across the snow. As I went speeding down the mountainside, neither my outstretched arms nor my panicked shouts—something unimaginative along the lines of "Noooooooooo!"—could stop me. I shot past the twins, was flung over the top of the next wall of snow, and landed slap-bang in the middle of the road. It all happened so quickly there wasn't even time for my life to flash before my eyes.

The children came flying over the top of the wall, too, and fell in a heap on top of me. If their exhilarated laughter was anything to go by, they hadn't done themselves any harm. I wasn't so sure about myself, though. But before I could check to see if I was still in one piece, I heard the screech of brakes. And a moment later, a furious voice shouted, "Are you out of your minds? I nearly ran you over!"

I shoved a twin's leg out of my face and tried to lift my head. Just a few feet away from us was the bumper of a car. It was a small, dark green car with a Zurich license plate. The door was wide open and the driver, a boy not much older than me, was standing over us. He looked scared to death, and I could understand why.

Now the shock of it all made my teeth start to chatter. That really had been a close shave.

"Is anyone hurt?" asked the boy.

I picked myself up, surprised to find that my body was still working properly. It had been a hard landing, but my padded coat and thick gloves had saved me from grazes or anything worse. "I don't think so," I said, and gave the twins a quick once-over. No blood, no twisted limbs, and their front teeth had been missing already. They were all shining eyes and rosy cheeks: the picture of happy children.

"Again!" they cried. "That was so much fun!"

Just to be on the safe side, I grabbed hold of them by the hoods of their still snow-white parkas.

"That was incredibly stupid and dangerous," scolded the boy. "You could all have been killed."

God, yes. "You're absolutely right," I stammered, between chattering teeth. "I'm so sorry. It's just that once you start sliding down the hill, it's practically impossible to—"

"And it would have been my fault," the boy broke in. He hadn't been listening to a word I'd said and was clearly speaking more to himself than to me. He stared grimly past us into the distance. "There would have been a trial and all the witnesses would've been dead and I would probably have had to go to prison and I would've lost my driver's license and my dad would have—" He broke off with a shudder.

I cleared my throat. "Well in that case, I guess we should all just be thankful we're still alive!" My teeth weren't chattering quite so hard now, and I ventured a smile. I would have liked to put my hand on his arm, too, to bring him back from his bleak vision of a parallel universe in which we were all lying dead in the road, but I didn't dare let go of the children. "Like I said, I'm really sorry we gave you such a shock. Could you possibly do me a huge favor and give us a lift up to the hotel? That is where you were going, isn't it?" Of course that was where he'd been going. It was the only building for miles around. He was probably one of the six extra waitstaff the hotel had taken on to work in the restaurant over Christmas.

"You guys are from Germany, right?"

"Yes, cress, pinklepress, pinklepankle, ponkle, fess," said Ash. Or perhaps it was Jayden. They were absolutely identical. The boy nodded as if that explained everything. He opened the back door for the two kids. Just to be on the safe side, I didn't let go of their hoods until they were firmly strapped in.

"Phew!" I closed the car door with great relief and gave the boy a grateful smile. "Child lock! The best invention since the printing press."

"Your brothers like running away, do they?"

"Oh, they're not my brothers. I'm not a hotel guest—I'm the intern, here on a one-year placement. And today's my first day on babysitting duty." I laughed. "Not the best first day, as you can see. Me and children are not a good combination. I actually preferred working in the laundry, to be honest, even though I burned myself on the rotary iron the very first day. And ruined a monogrammed napkin." I wasn't usually so talkative with strangers—it must have been the shock I'd just had and my sheer joy at still being alive to tell the tale. And the boy had a trustworthy sort of face. "Just don't tell anyone these kids nearly got run over on my watch, will you? Or I'll definitely get fired." I took off one of my gloves and held out my hand to him. "I'm Sophie, by the way. Sophie Spark." I very nearly added "high-school dropout," so well had Don Burkhardt Jr. succeeded in getting inside my head.

"Ben." The boy took my hand and shook it. My chattiness

seemed to have calmed him down a bit, and he even managed a smile. "Ben Montfort."

"Oh, that's funny," I said. "The owners of the hotel are called Montfort, too. Gordon and Gilbert Montfort. They're brothers . . ."

Oh, God. Oh, God. I stared at him in horror. "Please, please tell me you're not related to them."

Ben shrugged apologetically. "Sorry," he said.

2

I was sorry, too. Sorry for myself, I should say. As if it hadn't been bad enough getting catapulted into the road along with the two little kids who'd been entrusted to my care, it had to be the son of one of the hotel owners, of all people, who'd nearly run us over.

As I walked glumly around the car to get into the passenger seat, I replayed in my head everything I'd said to Ben just now. I'd already provided him with two white-jacketed reasons to fire me, plus a scorched monogrammed napkin. But it could've been worse. If, for example, I'd said *Montfort—like the owners of the hotel? Gilbert and Gordon, or as I call them: Gutless Gilbert and Grouchy Gordon.*

There was a paper bag full of carrots on the passenger seat, which I lifted onto my lap as I sat down.

Ben must be the son of Grouchy Gordon, the elder of the two brothers. I knew Gordon had a son from his first marriage who lived with his mother in Zurich, but I'd pictured the son as a small boy, not a nearly grown-up man. Gutless Gilbert didn't have a family— he lived alone in a small apartment under the eaves on the fifth floor of the hotel. As Denise from Reception had told me, it was common knowledge that he'd lost the love of his life in tragic circumstances when he was young, and since then he'd lived like a monk. What those tragic circumstances were, Denise didn't know, but the story certainly explained Gilbert Montfort's drooping, hunched posture and troubled look. He always nodded in a friendly way when you ran into him around the hotel, though, and had a melancholy smile for everyone.

His brother Gordon's smile, on the other hand, was reserved exclusively for hotel guests. If you were an employee, he'd either completely ignore you (if you were lucky) or go ballistic at you (if you were unlucky). The most trivial thing could set him off. So far, he'd always studiously ignored me, but ever since September I'd been dreading the day I might fall victim to one of his rages.

Perhaps today would be that day. If Gordon Montfort could yell at someone for fifteen minutes just for having a speck of toothpaste on their uniform or fire an employee for leaving cigarette butts outside the back door of the hotel, what on earth would he do to someone who launched the children of hotel guests into the path of his son's oncoming car?

As Ben started the engine, I shot a sideways glance at him. A certain family resemblance was undeniable: blue eyes, high forehead, strong nose, firm chin, thick brown hair—all just like his father. But a younger version. And a nicer version. Even from the side he had a trustworthy sort of face.

In spite of that—or perhaps because of it—I felt I should proceed with caution. I mustn't let myself think he was harmless just because he had a nice face. He might still be planning to rat me out to his dad. Like father, like son and all that . . .

Perhaps he'd forget what had happened if I could distract him with my sparkling conversation. I rustled the bag of carrots. "That was good thinking, bringing a few snowman's noses with you. Especially as there's supposed to be more snow coming this evening."

He promptly smiled again. "The snowman's noses are for Jesty and Vesty."

Oh dear—he really did make it difficult to be suspicious of him. Now it turned out he was an animal lover, too!

Jesty and Vesty were the hotel horses, a pair of friendly Norikers whose full names were Grand Gesture and White Vesture. In the summer months, they galloped across the mountain meadows, their pale manes streaming out behind them. When it came to idyllic Alpine clichés, they gave even the fluffy cows with bells around their necks a run for their money. In the winter, they pulled the vintage sleigh that Old Stucky had polished up to a beautiful shine. They loved taking the guests out for sleigh rides, so I was told. I was still hoping my internship would include some time in the stables because Jesty and Vesty were by far the friendliest horses I'd ever met.

"Oh, they'll like that," I said. "Old Stucky's put them on a diet—he says they've put on too much weight while they've been in the stables." I was probably partly to blame for that. I'd been known to bring them bananas now and then, which they loved. And they loved me, too. They snorted happily as soon as I entered the stables, and I always felt mean if I didn't have anything to give them. "But they're going to have plenty to do over the next few weeks—Monsieur Rocher has already taken loads of reservations for sleigh rides."

"And I always worry hauling a sleigh full of people will be too much for them." Ben sighed. "When I was little, I could hardly bear to watch—I used to wish I could have pushed the sleigh instead of them having to pull it." As we drove up the mountainside, he steered the car around the bends so slowly that the twins in the back called "Faster, plaster, minklemaster, minklebunkle, bonkle, blaster!" and put their heads together, giggling.

"So you're visiting your dad?" I continued, a little more boldly now. "I don't think he's there today." Gordon Montfort didn't live in the hotel but with his girlfriend in Sion, about a forty-five minutes' drive away. (I'd gotten that from Denise, too.) Because he didn't work regular hours, you never knew whether and when he was going to turn up at Castle in the Clouds, or how long he was going to stay. I hadn't seen him yet today. Another reason to be thankful: What if I'd fallen in front of *his* car?

"Doesn't matter. I'm here for the whole holidays," said Ben.

"Here? But not in the hotel!" I exclaimed.

"Day and night." He cast a sideways glance at me. "Is that a problem?"

No, of course not. I just wondered where he was going to sleep. Perhaps in his uncle's apartment? The hotel was completely full for the Christmas season. Every single one of its thirty-five rooms and all the suites were booked. We'd even had to put extra beds in Rooms 212 and 213. And the staff accommodation was full, too, with all the temps who'd been brought in.

"Do you know which room you're in?" I inquired cautiously.

Ben laughed. "Yes, of course. I've booked the Duchess Suite," he said sarcastically. "Don't worry, I've always managed to find somewhere to sleep. And anyway, I'm not here to sleep, I'm here to work—as my dad would say."

"To work?" I echoed.

"Yes, to work—go figure!" Ben sounded rather irritable now. "On my vacation. As usual. This is my last Christmas break before my exams. Everyone else is going to be sleeping late and going to parties and getting spoiled rotten by their parents, while I'll be waking up at five thirty every morning and not even getting paid for it."

"I know the feeling," I murmured, but Ben was so worked up by now that he didn't even hear me.

"You may be here on a one-year contract, but I'm here on

a lifetime one. Uncle Gilbert has me down to cover for Denise at Reception this time, but I can chlorinate the swimming pool and change the beds, too, if necessary. And I know how to operate a rotary iron—even Big Edna."

"Oh," I said, impressed. Big Edna had rollers five feet thick and—along with Tired Bertha, a washing machine dating back to the previous century, whose drum could comfortably have housed a small family—was the inner sanctum of the laundry room. "Pavel must think a great deal of you."

"He does." Ben smiled proudly, and I decided once and for all that I liked him, even if he *was* Grouchy Gordon's son. A warm feeling of friendship came over me. Any friend of Pavel's was a friend of mine.

Pavel was master of the washing machines, dryers, mangles, and folding machines in the basement of the hotel. He was a tall, burly, bearded bald man with arms covered in tattoos of skulls, snakes, and pentagrams. It was easy to imagine him working as a bouncer in some dingy hellhole of a nightclub. Until you saw him lovingly ironing the collar of a chambermaid's uniform, that is, and singing "Ave Maria" at the top of his voice. Pavel had a lovely clear baritone, and his cantatas and operatic arias were legendary. Sometimes I'd just listen; other times I'd sing along. By the end of my time in the laundry, we'd pretty much nailed Papageno and Pamina's duet from Mozart's *The Magic Flute*, accompanied by six washing machines on spin cycle.

Ben took the last bend a little faster, and we came out of the shadowy woods at last. Ahead of us, on the sunlit plateau, lay Castle in the Clouds in all its glory, with its many high windows, its turrets and stone ledges and balustrades. As always, the sight took my breath away for a moment, and I got the feeling it was the same for Ben. Or perhaps there was another reason for his deep sigh.

He drove past the entrance to the underground parking lot, and, instead of taking the winding road to the doorway, he stopped in the lot at the side of the hotel. "I can drop you right outside the front door if you want, of course." He shot me a sideways grin.

I grinned back. "That's very kind of you, but we can walk from here, can't we, boys?"

"Look, there's stupid Don." The twins were pointing to Don Burkhardt Jr., who was standing in the sun in front of the half-moon fir tree with his arms crossed, seemingly waiting for something.

For us, to be precise.

I groaned. "You have my permission to stick out your tongues at him," I said, and the twins did so immediately with great gusto. They also took the opportunity to lick the windows of Ben's car.

"You've got this babysitting thing down to a T." Ben squinted at Don. "Is that the Burkhardts' little brat?"

"The very same."

Don had spotted us now and was ambling toward us, looking inquisitive.

"They've been here nearly three weeks already while they have some work done on their house. I just keep wondering how they managed to take their child out of school for so long. It wouldn't be easy to do that in Germany."

Ben shrugged. "Old Burkhardt probably bribed the headmaster. And if that didn't work, he'd probably have just bought the whole school. He buys anything he can get his grubby little hands on."

He sounded rather bitter, and I would have loved to ask why, but the children had already undone their seat belts and were now climbing out of the car. I hurried after them and instinctively grabbed hold of their white hoods.

"*Don* rhymes with *prawn* and *yawn*, by the way," I said.

I heard Ben laugh out loud. "You really do love children, don't you?"

I stuck my head back inside the car. "Maybe not. I do have a knack with Tired Bertha, though. Just ask Pavel!" I would have liked to shake Ben's hand again, but my fingers were buried in the twins' hoods, so I just lowered my voice and said, "Thank you. For not running us over. And for not telling your dad."

For a moment he looked back at me just as earnestly. "Of course I won't. We interns have to stick together."

I beamed. I knew it: Anyone Pavel trusted with Big Edna couldn't possibly be a bad person.

"I'm glad you're so nice even though you've got such an awf—" I began effusively, but then bit my tongue. However nice he was, perhaps it was still a bit too soon to tell him I was glad he didn't seem to take after his awful father. "Even though you must have gotten a shock just then," I finished rather lamely, as I closed the car door.

"Oh, look. It's Sophie Spark and the children she was meant to be looking after, getting out of some stranger's old rust bucket of a car with no car seats." Don had caught up with us now. He watched Ben's car as it turned onto the road that led to the stables. Ben clearly wanted to hand over the carrots right away.

Don turned back to me. "I wonder what Mr. and Mrs. Bauer will think about this. Do you want to ask them, or shall I? Here they come now, look."

With a malicious grin, he pointed to the Bauers' snow-white Mercedes, which was pulling up as he spoke and soon came to a stop beside us. Mrs. Bauer got out and waved her white Dolce & Gabbana handbag cheerily. "Yoo-hoo! There you are, my little snowflakes. What perfect timing! Did you have fun with the nice babysitter?"

"Nice babysitter indeed! Just be glad your sons are still alive," said Don, but Mrs. Bauer couldn't hear a word he said because one of the twins was crowing loudly, "Don, yawn, pitterpawn, pitterpatter, potter, prawn!" and the other was shouting, "Agaaaiiiin!"

Mr. Bauer had also gotten out of the car and now pressed a rolled-up banknote into my hand with a jovial smile. "Thank you for looking after our little monsters so well."

"Ha ha ha," scoffed Don. "That's like thanking a shark for only eating your little toe instead of biting your whole leg off."

Luckily, Mr. Bauer wasn't listening because his sons were both hanging on to his legs and gabbling something about a supersteep mega-slide.

"It was a pleasure," I assured Mr. Bauer, and at that moment I actually meant it. I watched fondly as—damn it, what were their names again?—climbed into the car with their parents and drove off, waving to us as they went.

Once they'd disappeared around the first bend, Don let out a disappointed sigh. "You've got a pine cone in your hair by the way, Sophie Spark, and it looks really weird," he said.

I forced myself not to put a hand to my hair, and instead unrolled the banknote Mr. Bauer had given me. It was a hundred Swiss francs. I gasped.

"No way," said Don.

Yes way. Ha! "Well, my first day as the worst babysitter in the world hasn't turned out so badly after all," I said. Although I knew it was stupid to take so much pleasure in this little moment of triumph, I couldn't resist giving Don a patronizing pat on the head. "Don't you agree, little Donny?"

Don pursed his lips (he made even that look cute) and smiled. "Luckily, the holidays are only just beginning," he said, his lisp a little more pronounced than usual. Against my will, I felt goose bumps rising on my arms. Don's smile broadened. "You know what? I'm going to tell my parents that starting tomorrow I want to come to day care, too. I'm sure you're going to play some great games with us." And then he fixed me with his best butter-wouldn't-melt look and added: "Somehow I get the unmistakable feeling that something bad is about to happen to you, Sophie Spark."

It was infuriating, but somehow I got that feeling, too.

3

I slipped through the ski cellar into the hotel and scurried up the back stairs to my room, hoping not to meet anyone who might take exception to my disheveled state. The last person I wanted to run into was Fräulein Müller. Her old-fashioned title—the German equivalent of *Miss*—didn't fit with her imposing, angular, immaculate appearance at all, and being in her early forties she was much too young to remember a time when all unmarried women got called *Fräulein*. But she absolutely insisted on being addressed that way, and what you might have thought would sound ridiculously old-school actually inspired great respect and was even a little intimidating when applied to Fräulein Müller.

She'd once sent me back to the laundry just because the hair bands in my braids were different colors. "Whatever will the guests think?" she'd said with distaste. "This is a respectable establishment."

I'd been overcome by a burning sense of shame, and so as not to sully the hotel's honor and reputation any further, I'd immediately thrown out every hair band I owned apart from the black ones.

I guessed I must have lost one of those hair bands during my trip down the mountainside just now because my neat ponytail had come undone and my hair was loose over my shoulders, tangled and full of pine needles. I didn't have to look in the mirror to know that even an easygoing type of person would probably have tutted disapprovingly at the sight of me.

But I was in luck. The only creature I came across was the Forbidden Cat, who stretched herself out on the floor in front of me so I could tickle her tummy. Pets in general were not allowed in the hotel, but cats in particular were forbidden—Gordon Montfort couldn't stand them. Nobody knew where the Forbidden Cat had come from. Monsieur Rocher, the concierge, who knew all the hotel's secrets, said she'd always lived there. And she acted like it, too, as if the whole hotel belonged to her. She herself, on the other hand, didn't appear to belong to anybody. When she was hungry, she'd wander into the kitchen for some food, and when she wanted attention she'd go and find somebody to pet her, as she'd done with me just now. The rest of the time she spent sitting about or lying in a highly decorative fashion on windowsills, steps, and armchairs, harmonizing beautifully with her surroundings.

Oddly enough, even though she roamed freely around the hotel and often chose to sleep in some pretty public places, Gordon Montfort had never set eyes on her. Sometimes—as I'd seen to my astonishment—they missed each other by just a few seconds, as if the Forbidden Cat knew exactly when the hotelier was going to appear and when she needed to make her exit. Guests would occasionally mention something to Gordon about the pretty ginger cat they claimed to have petted on the third floor or seen sleeping on the grand piano in the ballroom, and this would reignite his suspicions that one of the staff might have flouted his ban and secretly acquired a pet cat. Whenever that happened, he'd turn up unannounced in the staff quarters and threaten whoever had dared to disobey his cat ban with "something much worse than being fired." (There were numerous theories about what this might be.) But given that he'd never actually *seen* a cat anywhere in the hotel, he must also have felt slightly paranoid.

In his shoes, I'd definitely have thought my employees were

leaving stuffed cats around the place just to annoy me and drive me insane. Either way, it was a miracle that in all these years none of the staff had ever thought to turn the Forbidden Cat in to their boss; they'd almost certainly have gotten a promotion for it.

After a couple of minutes petting the Forbidden Cat, I went around the back way and made it to the staff quarters in the south wing without encountering Fräulein Müller.

There were all sorts of back ways and back stairs—even hidden elevators—in Castle in the Clouds. It had taken me weeks to discover them all, and although I knew my way around very well now, I was sure there was still plenty of uncharted territory in the hotel—particularly in the basement, which was built into the rock like a multistory labyrinth. Legend had it that the hotel was haunted, and I could well believe it. I'd listened with bated breath to every ghost story I'd been told since I'd arrived there. As well as a questionable "moontin ghoarst" that Old Stucky claimed to have seen whenever he'd drunk too much of his brother-in-law's home-made pear brandy, there was the Lady in White, who was said to float around the hotel at night in search of a kindred soul, making the chandeliers tinkle as she passed. The Lady in White had been a guest at the hotel, or so the story went—an unhappily married young woman who'd thrown herself out the window of the highest turret with a broken heart. And now there were two versions of the legend: One said the Lady in White would never be at peace until she'd lured another unhappy soul into jumping off the turret just like her; the other (much nicer) version had it that she simply wanted to comfort anyone else who was lovesick and to dry their tears. No one is worth jumping out a window for, after all.

Denise from Reception swore that once, just after she'd had an argument with her boyfriend, she'd seen something white and translucent floating through the lobby in the middle of the night, and it had waved at her. But she admitted she'd dozed off shortly before it happened. Other people only ever said they knew somebody who knew somebody who'd seen the Lady in White.

Only Monsieur Rocher maintained that the legend was complete nonsense. Nobody had ever jumped out of a turret window in this hotel or any other window for that matter. Broken heart or no broken heart.

He was probably right (Monsieur Rocher was usually right), but it was a bit of a shame, if you asked me. I'd have preferred to run into a real ghost than some of the living inhabitants of this place.

The corridor leading to the staff quarters was deserted. Relieved, I pulled the door marked PRIVÉE, STAFF ONLY, and NO ENTRY shut behind me and hurried through to my room. Officially I now had three hours off before I had to be back for my evening shift in the spa. If I was quick getting changed, I could run down to the laundry and take Pavel a slice of his favorite apple and cinnamon cake, then be back in the lobby in time for an afternoon coffee with Monsieur Rocher in the concierge's lodge. This would also be a good opportunity to find out as much as possible about the various guests who were due to arrive. I spent my breaks with Monsieur Rocher whenever I could. Not only did he keep me supplied with a constant stream of wonderful anecdotes and useful information, but I also always came away from our meetings feeling full of confidence and the joys of life. I have no idea how he did it.

To me, Monsieur Rocher was the heart and soul of Castle in the Clouds. On my very first day, he'd comforted me, treated the burn on my hand, and reassured me that I wasn't a failure and that

Pavel and I would soon be best of friends. Anything he said in his soft, quiet voice you couldn't help but believe. And I was more than happy to take advantage of his seemingly boundless knowledge of the hotel and the guests.

The guests I was most curious about were the aging British actor (everyone but me, on hearing his name, had exclaimed "Oh, *him*!") and the family of a business mogul from South Carolina who'd booked six rooms and suites with a total of twelve beds (or thirteen if you counted the cot in Room 210). That evening we were also expecting a famous figure skater, a gold medalist who'd been invited to host the hotel's annual New Year's Ball. It was her first time at Castle in the Clouds, and she'd insisted on bringing her two toy poodles with her.

"Oh, there you are, Work Experience!" a shrill voice rang out. I'd celebrated too soon. True, it wasn't Fräulein Müller who now came charging out of the bathroom, blocking my path before I could get to my bedroom door, but Hortensia was almost as bad. Probably worse, in fact. She'd only been here two days, but she'd clearly made up her mind to hate me from the moment she'd arrived, for reasons I couldn't fathom. She and her friends Camilla, Ava, and Whatsername were students at the hotel-management college in Lausanne. Fräulein Müller had taken them on as extra chambermaids over the holidays. So far, I hadn't been able to work out whether their work counted toward their studies or whether they were simply being well paid for this temporary job. They seemed to think they stood way above me in the hotel pecking order, at any rate, and that this entitled them to push me around.

"See this, Work Experience?" Hortensia thrust a long copper-colored hair in my face. "I just found this in the sink. It's disgusting."

She pronounced it *dizgusting*. "It's bad enough having to stay in this horrible old dump, in these appalling conditions. So if you want to carry on sharing this *prehistoric* bathroom with us, then please clean up after yourself! Understood?"

I gulped. Nobody else around here had long red hair, so it must be one of mine. I didn't like finding hairs in the sink, either, and I always tried not to leave any behind. But there was a reason I hadn't managed it this time.

I took a deep breath. "You actually threw me out of the bathroom this morning, remember, so that you four could all come in and brush your teeth together? So I didn't get a chance to—"

"Blah blah blah! I never want to have to pick another one of your dizgusting hairs out of the sink again, all right, skank?" Hortensia flicked the hair off her finger and gave me a revolted look. "Oh my god, are those pine needles in your hair?"

I gulped again. It was the first time anyone had ever called me a skank and really meant it, and for a moment it floored me. My friend Delia and I had made up a game to be used in difficult situations. It was called "What would Jesus do?" but the idea was that you could replace Jesus (we'd gotten the idea for the game during a very boring religious-studies lesson) with anyone you liked. Jesus wasn't ideal as a practical example, because it was pretty difficult to emulate him—not only could he walk on water and turn water into wine, but in this instance he'd probably also have just laid his hand upon Hortensia and miraculously cured her of her bitchiness. I could give that a go, of course. She'd probably be a bit taken aback if I laid a hand on her head and murmured something like *Pass out of her, demon!* She'd probably also give me a slap. And then, of course, I'd have to turn the other cheek.

"What's wrong, Work Experience? Cat got your tongue?"

I pondered. What would . . . er . . . Mahatma Gandhi do in my situation? Oh, damn it. I really wasn't very good at this today. On the other hand, wasn't it Gandhi who'd said "Let us never negotiate out of fear. But let us never fear to negotiate"?

All right then. Smiling benignly, I straightened an imaginary pair of Gandhi-style glasses on my nose. "Let's talk about this like adults, my dear Hortensia. If you want me to clean up after myself, all you have to do is not throw me out of the bathroom until I'm finished. Can we try that tomorrow?"

But I could see straightaway that Hortensia was not impressed; on the contrary, Gandhi seemed to have put her in a more aggressive mood than ever.

Perhaps I should just do what she *would have done*, I thought, as she said it again: "Blah blah blah!" I knew mirroring people's behavior was supposed to be a good way of defusing tension. So I put my hands on my hips, narrowed my eyes menacingly, and said, in an unpleasantly nasal voice: "Blah blah blah yourself! And don't you dare call me a 'skank' again. Or 'Work Experience.' Got it?"

"Or else what?" Hortensia stuck her chin out even farther than mine. "You'll go and rat us out to Müller? You're welcome to try, but I'm afraid she likes us more than she likes you, Work Experience." With a triumphant smile, she added, "Camilla happens to be Müller's niece. Her favorite niece!"

Ah. That certainly explained a few things.

It was definitely a sign that I'd been spending too much time around the little brat, but at that moment I actually wondered what Don Burkhardt Jr. would have done in my situation. And then I heard myself say: "For your information, Hortensia Haughtypants, temporary cleaner from Lausanne, I've been here longer than you and I have quite a few friends in this hotel." Oh, that was good! I sounded just as ominously friendly as Don when he mentioned his dad's relationship with Gordon Montfort. But without the Swiss accent and cute lisp, of course. "Friends who would be very unhappy to see me being treated unkindly," I went on, "or to hear someone referring to this venerable building as a 'horrible old dump.'"

Hortensia opened her mouth to retort, but at that moment a gust of wind swept along the corridor and the bathroom door fell shut with a loud bang.

We both jumped, but as Hortensia looked around, startled, I felt in some strange way that my words had been borne out.

"I'm glad we understand each other," I said, and strode past Hortensia to my room at the end of the corridor. It was a little worrying (and I felt bad for Jesus and Gandhi) that I'd adopted the questionable tactics of a nine-year-old delinquent, but you had to admit they worked like a charm.

I closed the bedroom door behind me emphatically, took off my coat, and started picking the pine needles out of my hair.

When I'd arrived at Castle in the Clouds that September, I'd had my pick of the free beds—for most of the year, the staff accommodation wasn't even half full. There were no single rooms, and certainly none with en suite bathrooms, but the little bedroom I'd chosen was so small it could almost have been classed as a single. Nobody had wanted it because the radiator was broken and there was an old water pipe in the wall that, I'd been told, emitted a spooky moaning sound. (Or perhaps, said Denise from Reception, it wasn't the pipe at all but the Lady in White, trying to lure souls up into the turret.) I didn't care; the main thing was that I had my own room. And I still thought I'd made a good choice. I liked the faded lilac striped carpet and the dormer window in the pitched roof that looked out over Obergabelhorn, Dent Blanche, and Zinalrothorn, the mountains that could be seen from the hotel. It was exactly the same view for which the guests staying in the Panorama Suite on the floor below had to pay a small fortune. (Although they did get a panoramic window for their money, along with a panorama terrace.)

Even though there was no heat in my room, I still liked to sleep with the window open. Snuggled up under a thick down comforter and two woolly blankets, I hadn't felt the cold yet even on the chilliest of nights. And as far as the spooky moaning noises were concerned, I'd only been woken up twice in the night by a sort of gentle sighing, and both times I'd been having a bad dream anyway and was positively grateful for the interruption.

I used the second bed under the pitched ceiling as extra shelf space, and I'd been afraid I'd have to clear it over the Christmas holidays to make room for one of the temps. That really would have been a tight squeeze, because apart from the beds there was no space for any other furniture in the room, and there were only two shelves on the walls. I'd piled up a few of my clothes on these shelves, but the rest of my stuff was still in my suitcase under the bed (including a bathing suit that I'd packed in the misguided—and very naive—belief that hotel staff would be allowed to use the pool during their time off).

So far, though, it looked as if I'd be allowed to keep my little room all to myself. There were a lot more male temps than female, so it must have been even more crowded in the men's quarters than it was here.

As I stripped down to my underwear to try to get rid of all the pine needles, I checked my phone for messages.

My mum, as she did every day, had sent me a smiley face. "Dad, Finn, Leon, and I hope you have a lovely day in the mountains. Hopefully you'll get some time to relax and enjoy the great outdoors."

Sure, Mum—scrubbing skid marks off toilets, working your way through mountains of dirty laundry, running after naughty children, and getting harassed by snooty chambermaids from Lausanne is the perfect way to relax. It's practically like being on holiday.

The message from my friend Delia wasn't much better, though. "Holidays at last! I'm not even going to pick up a textbook or think about finals for at least a week. I'm going to binge Netflix all day and drink and go out dancing—that's the plan anyway." I couldn't help thinking of Ben's bitter words about his friends' vacation plans and grinning. "How are things at your fancy hotel?" Delia went on. "What are the cocktails like? And have any cute guys checked in yet? Perhaps a couple of young millionaires looking for a lovely intern to marry? I get first dibs on the brother, remember. Thanks. Hugs and kisses, D."

I sighed. Delia and I had been best friends since kindergarten; we'd always done everything together, and we'd even picked the same classes at school so we could spend all day every day in each other's company. When I'd failed junior year and gotten held back, being separated from Delia was the worst thing about the whole situation. She said it didn't make any difference because I'd still be sitting next to her in spirit and it really didn't matter whether I did my college entrance exams a year earlier or a year later. But that simply wasn't true. I'd never felt lonelier than when I had to repeat junior year. Just the thought of being stuck in town with another bleak year ahead of me, after all my friends had left school and gone out into the world, was too depressing for words. So I'd beaten them to it.

Okay, so ideally I would've liked to do something a bit cooler and more spectacular than an internship in a hotel, but in order to get a job at a cheetah sanctuary in South Africa or work with whale sharks in the Maldives or spend a year as an au pair in Costa Rica, I would have had to be eighteen. In the end, I'd been glad to find something I could get my parents to agree to, which didn't cost any money and which was still a decent distance away from home.

A quiet tap on the windowpane interrupted my train of thought. Two black button eyes peered in at me, and I hurried to open the window.

This was yet another reason why I loved my little bedroom. The windowsill was a favorite perching place for the mountain jackdaws, probably because whoever had slept here before had been secretly feeding them. It was a habit I'd wholeheartedly embraced as soon as I'd moved in, even though it was technically forbidden. But it wasn't like we were talking about huge flocks of pigeons here. (Apparently there were so many pigeons in Saint Mark's Square in Venice that they eventually were going to cause the whole city to collapse because they pooped on everything and corroded the marble.) We were only talking about seven jackdaws, and they weren't doing anyone any harm. To be honest, I'd never even seen them poop. They were exceedingly well-mannered birds that presumably flew off into the woods when they needed to do their business. I'd christened them all Hugo, because at first—with their yellow beaks, shiny jet-black feathers, and intelligent black eyes—they'd all looked utterly identical to me.

Over time, though, I'd learned to tell them apart. So now there was Melancholy Hugo, Unbelievably Greedy Hugo (they were all greedy, but Unbelievably Greedy Hugo was just . . . unbelievably greedy), One-Legged Hugo, Kleptomaniac Hugo (he'd already stolen two of my hair clips and the lid off a plastic bottle, and had nearly made off with my phone charger cable, too, but secretly he was still my favorite), Chubby Hugo, Hopping Hugo, and Suspicious Hugo.

"Hello, Hopping Hugo! Have you come to visit Super Sophie?" It was a good thing no one could hear me, because I always spoke to the Hugos in baby talk—and what was more, I referred to myself in the third person to help them learn my name. I'd heard that jackdaws were so clever they could actually learn to talk, and I patiently awaited the day when one of the Hugos would look at me and caw "Hello, Super Sophie. I'm very well thanks, and how are you?" That day was probably some way off, though. Hopping Hugo only hopped up and down and gazed at me expectantly.

The sun was shining less brightly now. The wind had come up, and the bank of clouds drifting across the mountaintops from the west was already starting to break up into scraps of mist that gleamed with a milky light.

"What do you think? Is it going to snow before it gets dark?" I asked, crumbling up a milk roll and scattering it over the windowsill. According to an online ornithologists' forum I'd consulted, milk rolls were easy for jackdaws to digest in comparison to normal bread, and unlike sunflower seeds, oats, and nuts, which I'd also tried offering them, the Hugos couldn't get enough of milk rolls.

While I carried on getting changed, One-Legged Hugo and Suspicious Hugo landed on the windowsill and helped Hopping Hugo polish off the crumbs. I took a few photos of them on my phone and sent one, of all three Hugos gazing adoringly into the camera, to Delia with the caption: "Yep, this place is full of cute guys. I just didn't tell you about them before because I couldn't choose between them. But you can definitely have the brother."

I sent the same photo to my mum. "The great outdoors begins right here on my windowsill. And just think, Mum: These birds didn't go to college and they're still perfectly happy."

Even after they'd vacuumed up all the crumbs, the three Hugos stayed sitting on the windowsill and watched as I wriggled into one of the ten pairs of opaque black support tights I'd recently acquired. Fräulein Müller insisted that we wear black tights with our black uniforms. I'd persevered for a while with thinner tights that didn't make me look quite so much like a grandma, but they'd all ended up with so many runs that I got sick and tired of having to replace them. To say nothing of their other disadvantages. Woe betide anyone Fräulein Müller caught pulling up a pair of tights that were falling down! So I had to resort to the support tights. Passion-killers they may have been, but once you'd gotten them on, they were super-comfortable and stayed put all day without falling down. And they made my legs look good. Although there wasn't much leg to be seen, since the black uniform, which I now slipped on under the curious gaze of the three Hugos, came down to just below the knee.

This so-called "front of house" uniform was a phenomenon: On the hanger it looked like nothing more than a buttoned cotton smock with a white collar, but the moment you did up the buttons at the front it was transformed into a decidedly stylish piece of clothing. High-necked and close-fitting at the top and flaring slightly from the hips, the dress looked as though it had been tailor-made for me, and although it was very simple, the snow-white collar, starched cuffs, little gold buttons, and embroidered crown emblem of the hotel made it look really quite elegant, even when I had a feather duster in my hand. I automatically stood up straighter when I was wearing it. However mad (and sad) it might sound, I'd never been more elegantly dressed than I was in this housekeeping smock and a pair of support tights.

I glanced in the mirror that hung on the back of the door. Satisfied with my appearance, I pushed a final hairpin into my bun, now free of pine needles, and turned to the three Hugos. "This would be a good moment to whistle appreciatively."

They didn't whistle, but they did manage an appreciative look before flying off when I went to shut the window. I had to, if I didn't want to come back and find a snowdrift on my bed. I always found it fascinating how suddenly the weather could change here. The sky was a little darker now, and the outlines of the mountains outside my window looked hazy. The bank of clouds had moved a little closer and the wind was picking up. The weather forecast said we were going to have "prolonged snowfall even in low-lying areas" all week, and although that was bound to make it more difficult for the guests to get to the hotel, I couldn't help but be pleased.

This was going to be by far the snowiest Christmas I'd ever had.

And the first Christmas away from my family.

I'd been expecting to feel homesick at the thought of having to work on Christmas Day and spend it with complete strangers, but in fact all I felt was an excited tingling in my stomach.

Because one thing was for sure: This Christmas was going to be anything but boring.

lthough pets were expressly forbidden at Castle in the Clouds (*in the interests of all our guests in need of rest and relaxation*), we checked in no fewer than three dogs that day. Together with the pug belonging to Mr. and Mrs. Von Dietrichstein in Room 310, who'd arrived the day before, that made four exceptions to the rule. They had all been personally approved by Gordon Montfort himself, however.

"There are guests and there are guests," he would say. "And for *certain* types of guest there are no lengths we won't go to."

The Von Dietrichsteins were definitely *certain* types of guest. Not only were they bona fide aristocrats, but they also worked in the media—he was a photographer; she was a freelance journalist—and for years they'd been granted exclusive coverage of the New Year's Ball and the various celebrity interviews that went with it. To be fair, the Von Dietrichsteins' pug wasn't really an issue when it came to guests in need of rest and relaxation. He was so quiet and placid that the first time I saw him I thought he was a stuffed dog, or an eerily lifelike candy box where you had to unscrew the head to get to the chocolate inside. He didn't even slobber, which was most unusual for a pug.

The two poodles belonging to Mara Matthäus, the figure-skating gold medalist, were a lot more lively, but even they behaved themselves impeccably while their owner was checking in. And this was despite the fact that Gordon Montfort, who'd arrived at the hotel a short time before, wouldn't leave them alone and kept ruffling their ears like there was no tomorrow.

I'd watched the ball hostess arrive from my hiding place in the concierge's lodge. From here, I had a perfect view of the whole of the lobby and the forecourt beyond the revolving doors. I could hear what was being said at Reception, which was diagonally opposite, but I felt safe behind the wood-paneled counter. If necessary I could disappear from view entirely by taking one step to the left, which I'd done with all possible speed when the hotelier had appeared. Though he tended to ignore me whenever he saw me anyway, to be fair.

"Champion little dogs, these, just like their champion of an owner," he said jovially to Mara Matthäus, laughing at his little play on words.

His son, Ben, at the reception desk, grimaced very briefly, but his face soon regained its bland expression.

Clearly Ben hadn't had any time to unpack after he'd fed the horses but had started his shift at Reception straightaway. Either he was unusually conscientious, or his father terrorized him the same way he did his other employees. Still—if it was true that Ben worked for free, then at least Gordon Montfort couldn't exactly threaten to fire him or dock his wages.

From my hiding place I'd also witnessed the rather chilly greeting between father and son. Gordon Montfort hadn't smiled at his son half as warmly as he'd smiled at the two poodles, and Ben hadn't smiled at all, just looked anxious. He'd walked in to find his father laying into Anni Moser for having had the audacity to cross the lobby.

"What have I told you?" he'd hissed at her.

"That you don't want to see my wrinkly old face anywhere I

might alarm the guests?" Anni Moser was the oldest chambermaid on Fräulein Müller's team—perhaps the oldest chambermaid in the entire world, to judge by the wrinkles on her face and the liver spots on her hands. Anni Moser would never tell anyone how old she was, only that she had no intention of leaving Castle in the Clouds until she was too old to wield a feather duster. Which certainly wasn't the case yet: Nobody, not even Fräulein Müller, wielded a feather duster as energetically as Anni Moser, nobody climbed ladders more fearlessly to clean curtain rails and cornices, and nobody knew more tricks for getting stains out of carpets and furniture.

"I'm sorry—it won't happen again," she'd muttered, and hurried away under Gordon Montfort's scowling gaze as he turned to greet his son.

I hadn't heard what Ben had said to Gordon, but whatever it was he hadn't seemed to like it much. He'd continued to scowl, and instead of hugging his son, he'd given him a brief, awkward clap on the shoulder, which Ben had returned just as awkwardly. Then Gordon Montfort had spotted some greasy fingerprints on the glass of the revolving door and flown into one of his frequent rages, complete with bulging veins at the temples. (The fingerprints, incidentally, to judge by how low down they were, belonged to a certain diminutive nine-year-old boy.)

Ben must have been used to his father's temper tantrums—he hadn't batted an eyelash at any rate, when Gordon had started yelling his head off. The new bellhops, on the other hand, had fled in terror to fetch a cloth for the glass. One of them was trembling even now.

Standing behind the reception desk in his black suit, Ben looked older than he had before, and I was fairly sure he hadn't had a side part in his hair when I'd first met him, either. He handed Mara Matthäus her room key with a nonchalant smile.

Castle in the Clouds still hadn't arrived in the age of digital magnetic key cards—in fact, when it came to locks and keys, it was stuck in the nineteenth century. Some guests found this outlandish and outdated, but most thought the ornate wrought-iron keys, just like the heavy gold tassels that served as key rings, were all part and parcel of the hotel's ingenious nostalgic decor.

"Please allow me to personally escort you to your room so I can make sure everything is to your satisfaction," purred Gordon Montfort, snatching up the key before the (very attractive) Ms. Matthäus could reach for it. "Jakob here will see to your bags."

"Jakob here" was in fact Jaromir, an unfamiliar sight in his doorman's uniform with top hat and braided frock coat. You'd never have guessed it from his stoic expression, but I knew he felt exceedingly uncomfortable in this getup because he'd spent most of the past two days complaining about it. As a result, I'd learned some Czech vocabulary I was fairly sure didn't appear in any Czech textbooks, as well as the wonderful phrase: "I'm a bloody handyman, not a bloomin' ringmaster!"

Jaromir had actually gotten off quite lightly in comparison to Jonas and Nico, two young temps who'd been recruited for the holidays, like Hortensia and her friends, from the hotel-management college in Lausanne. Their bellhop uniforms consisted of funny little waist-length jackets and ridiculous caps. But that was little consolation to Jaromir.

Only when I'd reminded him of the big tips he was likely to get thanks to his new uniform had he cheered up a little. And that was probably why he tipped his hat to me now and winked as he wheeled the luggage cart toward one of the staff elevators.

For most of the year, the hotel didn't employ bellhops, doormen, or porters. When guests arrived, whoever happened to be working at Reception at the time was responsible for greeting them and helping them with their luggage. But over the holidays, when the hotel was full of illustrious visitors, these traditional posts were filled again and the old uniforms were brought out of storage. Weeks ago, in the laundry room, I'd helped Pavel take these precious treasures (most of them old enough to be in a museum) out of their cloth bags. Together we'd steamed the heavy wool fabric and polished the brass buttons. As we worked, I'd learned the aria "Il Mio Tesoro" from *Don Giovanni* and the lovely word *epaulet*—which was the name of the fancy shoulder decorations that were stitched onto the uniforms. I'd been waiting for an opportunity to impress somebody with it ever since.

Once the antique grille and doors of the elevator had closed with their usual clank and rattle behind Gordon Montfort, Mara Matthäus, and the two well-behaved poodles, a collective sigh of relief went through the lobby. I was finally able to emerge from my hiding place.

Monsieur Rocher winked at me over the top of his glasses. "As long as they don't bark or chase cats, I have nothing against dogs," he said. "I just always think it's such a shame about the nice white snow."

I giggled. "That's true! That's the first thing my mum ever taught me about snow: Avoid the yellow patches. But in the valley where I live, the snow doesn't usually last long enough to get peed on."

Monsieur Rocher looked at me sympathetically.

"Especially at Christmas," I said. "It always rains at Christmas."

"That's terrible! Another marzipan truffle?" As if to console me for my snowless childhood, Monsieur Rocher held out a silver bowl full of chocolates whose outer shells the hotel pâtissière had deemed not perfect enough for the guests.

"Yes, but this really is the last one!" I closed my eyes in rapture as the chocolate melted on my tongue. Luckily for the staff, who got fed all the chocolates she wasn't happy with, the pâtissière Madame Cléo was a pedant and a perfectionist. A snippet of grated orange peel in the glaze was enough for her to declare a petit four a failure, and she'd once rejected an entire tray of éclairs because she said they looked like penises.

"Was your first day as a babysitter as bad as you thought it would be?" inquired Monsieur Rocher.

"It exceeded even my worst fears." I rolled my eyes dramatically. "And I only had two kids to look after. But from tomorrow on, I'll have a trained teacher with me, and I'm sure she'll know what to do when the children would rather run away and fling themselves in front of cars than build a snowman." Childcare at Castle in the Clouds worked in the same way as the bellhops and the doormen—for most of the year it wasn't offered (unless somebody expressly requested a babysitter, and then the hotel would arrange it for them). But during the holiday season, a kindergarten teacher came every day from the nearest village to entertain all the guests under the age of twelve, from nine in the morning until four thirty in the afternoon, including Sundays and public holidays. And this year she'd have me as an assistant.

"Hmm." Nobody said *hmm* as kindly as Monsieur Rocher.

He always sounded so encouraging, never disapproving or doubt-ful. "If this weather keeps up, you'll probably have to stay indoors tomorrow anyway. And we can open up the game room if necessary. The key's just inside, on the ledge above the door. In case anyone tries to escape."

"Or break in," I said, thinking of Don Burkhardt Jr.

We fell into a companionable silence as we sipped the cappucci-nos I'd brought with me. The drinks had gone a bit cold by now but it was such good coffee that it still tasted nice and I could feel myself relaxing as I drank it.

Monsieur Rocher was like balm for the soul. I had no idea how he did it, but in his presence I always felt calm and confident. Prob-lems didn't completely disappear, but they suddenly seemed a lot more manageable. And my argument with Hortensia and the nas-tiness in the bathroom that morning felt so insignificant now, so unimportant, that I didn't even feel the need to tell him about it.

It was hard to guess at his age: His long, pale face had hardly any wrinkles, apart from a few smile lines, but his gray hair and grand-fatherly wisdom and kindness made me think he was older than his smooth skin would suggest. I'd asked him once how old he was, and he'd looked at me with a rather bemused expression and said, "Oh, you people! You're always so fixated on numbers." Which had con-firmed my suspicions that he was older than he looked.

After all the noise and chaos of a few minutes earlier, a sooth-ing sense of peace had descended upon the lobby, and the fact that it was the calm before the storm made me appreciate it even more. Ben was sorting through some papers; Mr. and Mrs. Ludwig from Room 107 sat on the sofa by the crackling log fire, rustling their newspapers now and then; and the two bellhops stood around in the lobby looking slightly lost. In those ridiculous outfits, they looked as though they might be about to launch into "March of the Tin Soldiers" from *The Nutcracker* at any moment.

We were expecting most of the guests this evening or at some point tomorrow, although some had arrived already. A nondescript-looking older man, traveling alone, had checked in shortly before Mara Matthäus—and I'd immediately have written him off as boring if it wasn't for Monsieur Rocher.

"That gentleman is anything but boring," he'd murmured. "Just look a little closer. Perhaps you can't see it very well under that coat, but he's extremely fit and well-built, as if he's been in training. Watch the way he walks, his tailored clothes, his practiced eye as he subtly checks out his surroundings—and do you see that bulge under his arm? That's a shoulder holster with a pistol in it."

"Oh," I'd whispered excitedly, as I briefly caught sight of the bulge, too. "A hit man? Or a . . . er . . . romance scam artist who's . . . er . . . carrying a gun for some reason? Shouldn't we let someone know there's a man wandering around with a pistol? What if he's planning to raid the hotel?"

But Monsieur Rocher had just smiled. "Given that he's checking into Room 117, right next door to the Panorama Suite, I think we can safely assume he's a bodyguard employed by the Smirnov family."

"Oh, right." That was rather less exciting, but a lot more reassuring than a hit man. The Smirnovs—the Russian family who'd booked the Panorama Suite—seemed to be very unusual indeed: unusually rich, at least. They were definitely a *certain* type of guest. On top of the six-hundred-franc deluxe welcome package they'd ordered, consisting of a bouquet of roses plus champagne, truffles, caviar, and Japanese strawberries, they'd also paid for an extra flower arrangement made up of thirty-five white amaryllis and a quarter pound of steak tartare made from Charolais beef. This last item must have been for the dog. Dog Ban Exception Number Four, along with the Von Dietrichsteins' pug and the two poodles. (At least the Smirnovs' dog must only be a little one—very little, judging by the amount of steak tartare they'd ordered. Or perhaps he was on a diet.)

I set my empty cup down on the counter. Dusk was falling now and, as if she'd simply been waiting for a quiet moment, the Forbidden Cat came sauntering down the stairs to keep us company. She settled herself between the bell on the counter and my propped-up elbows, graceful as a Ming vase. Well, as a purring Ming vase that licked its paws occasionally.

Mr. and Mrs. Ludwig nudged each other conspiratorially at the sight of the cat and smiled. I'd secretly decided that the white-haired old couple from Room 107 were my favorite guests. They were always holding hands and reading poetry to each other and generally being adorable. He called her "my beautiful" and she called him "my love," and they both looked a little dowdy with their old-fashioned haircuts and clothes, which were probably supposed to be elegant and chic but which actually just looked a bit dated. It was clear they weren't used to being waited on and found it embarrassing to have other people doing things for them. Every day they left five francs on the chest of drawers in their room and a note saying: "This is for you, dear Chambermaid!" I always left two complimentary choco-lates on their pillows instead of one and placed the money virtu-ously in the tip jar in the staff office, even though it was definitely meant for me. After all, the other chambermaids were not actually very nice, and the Ludwigs were always showering me with praise for doing perfectly ordinary jobs, like bringing them a firmer pillow or waterproofing their shoes.

Ever since she was a young girl, Mrs. Ludwig had dreamed of dancing the waltz at Castle in the Clouds' New Year's Ball, wearing a beautiful gown and a tiara. For years, she'd been studying the photos in the glossy magazines showing crowds of rich, famous, and beautiful people dancing, laughing, and drinking champagne in the huge ballroom.

"I could just *hear* the violins," she'd confided to me one day.

"She could, you know," Mr. Ludwig had added and gazed lovingly at her.

When she'd met Mr. Ludwig, at the age of twenty-one, there'd been no doubt in her mind whom she wanted to dance with at the ball one day, and the pair had married just four months later. Because the Ludwigs were neither rich nor famous, there was no way they could afford to stay at Castle in the Clouds, but that didn't stop them from being happy. The years passed and they brought up three children, built themselves a small house, and worked hard to pay off their debts.

"But she never stopped dreaming of Castle in the Clouds," Mr. Ludwig chimed in at this point in the story (I've shortened it a bit), and Mrs. Ludwig added, "Dreaming is good—it keeps you young."

And so for thirty years, Mr. Ludwig had put money aside and secretly taken dancing lessons until, at last, he'd saved up enough to afford a room at Castle in the Clouds.

"He even wanted to buy me a tiara for the ball," Mrs. Ludwig said, laughing as she patted Mr. Ludwig's hand. "But I said that would just be too much. I'm going to be the oldest but also the happiest girl ever to dance at this ball, isn't that so, my love?"

"You'll be the most beautiful girl of them all," Mr. Ludwig replied, and I secretly wiped away a tear. If that wasn't romantic, I didn't know what was.

The fact that the two of them were now sitting reading the paper in the lobby, keeping a close eye on the revolving doors, was no coincidence. They were at least as curious as I was and keen to catch a glimpse of any celebrity guests. They'd been delighted to see Mara Matthäus arrive, as well as the millionaire businesswoman and patron of the arts known as the Ball Bearings Baroness, who'd checked into Room 100 along with her much younger boyfriend. With any luck, the British actor, the American textile mogul with his extended family, and the extravagant Russians from the Panorama Suite would also show up before dinner.

I looked over at Ben. Now that his father was gone, I plucked up the courage to speak to him.

"Would you like a chocolate?" I called softly.

"Oh God, yes, toss them over here," said Ben. "I'm half starved."

For a second, I was tempted to take him at his word and hurl the truffles across the lobby. But, first, the reception desk was quite far away; second, I'd have had to somehow throw them around a pillar decorated with garlands of fir tree branches; and, third, the truffles were far too precious to risk dropping on the floor.

"Go on," said Monsieur Rocher, as if he'd read my mind. "I've eaten enough marzipan truffles today to last me a hundred years."

And because it was still so quiet and peaceful, I took the bowl and left the concierge's lodge. If I didn't want to climb over the counter (which would have been much quicker, naturally, but not really appropriate) I had to go through the back door into a little staff room with no windows but plenty of doors, and from there into the lobby.

It had started snowing outside. The snowflakes danced gently in the light of the lamps. From the bar on the east side of the hotel, the soft sound of piano music drifted over to us as I offered the chocolates to Ben, the Ludwigs ("Oh, how lovely! What wonderful service you get here!"), and the two bellhops.

One of them, Nico, hesitated for a moment. "We're not allowed to eat while we're on duty," he said.

"Hmm," I said, and my *hmm* didn't sound nearly as forgiving as Monsieur Rocher's.

Nico was about to scratch his head indecisively but couldn't because of his silly bellhop's hat. "If Mr. Montfort catches us, he'll fire us on the spot. You heard him yelling about those fingerprints just now. And I think his brother's back there in the office." He pointed to the door behind the reception desk. "They say he's not as strict, but still, I don't want to get on the wrong side of both my bosses on my first proper day at work."

Ben and I exchanged a glance. Clearly Ben hadn't made his relationship with the two hoteliers public yet.

"They might have put hidden cameras up there." Nico pointed at the ceiling. "Though most of this place is hopelessly out of date when it comes to technology. I've never seen elevators like that anywhere except movies. And the boilers in the staff bathrooms—"

"In the time it's taken you to make your mind up, you could have eaten the whole bowlful," I broke in, and made to take the bowl away from him. "And FYI, *Food and Travel* magazine has rated

Madame Cléo's truffles the best in the world." (Well, they would have done so, if they'd ever been here).

Nico hastily shoved a chocolate into his mouth. "You're Work Experience, right?" he asked with his mouth full. "The intern. Camilla and Hortensia told me about you."

Work Experience! I was so fed up with being called that, no matter by whom.

"We don't say *work experience* here. Or *intern*. The technical term is . . . *epaulet*." Sometimes these crazy notions just came over me, and I couldn't help myself. Delia called these my "mental moments."

"Epaulet?" echoed Nico. "I've never heard it called that before."

I raised my eyebrows. "What's it called again, the degree you're working on?"

"Bachelor of Science in International Hospitality Management," said Nico like a shot, and you could see him swelling with pride for a moment. Until he remembered his bellhop's uniform.

"Well, I'm sure you'll be learning all the terminology soon," said Ben, grinning as he leaned forward with his elbows on the desk. "Are there any chocolates left, Epaulet?"

"Two," I was about to reply. But at that moment, the peace of the afternoon was shattered, and all hell broke loose.

5

It all started with Don Burkhardt Jr. sauntering out of the restaurant holding a slice of chocolate cake. I had no time to wonder why he was grinning so deviously in my direction because suddenly, lots of things happened at once: Outside it started snowing heavily; several cars pulled up in front of the hotel; the phones at Reception, in the concierge's lodge, and in the office all started to ring; the elevator grilles rattled; and the Forbidden Cat jumped down off the counter. It was as if someone had flicked a switch from slow motion to time lapse, and suddenly everything was moving at double speed. Jaromir pushed the empty luggage cart out of the service elevator, and the Forbidden Cat's tail whisked through the door into the staff room just as Gordon Montfort appeared on the stairs and stood there with his arms folded.

The crystals on the chandeliers tinkled softly and the flames in the fireplace leapt higher as someone pushed the revolving door from outside, and an icy breeze swept through the lobby.

"Well, what are you waiting for?" bawled Gordon Montfort at the two bellhops. "I don't employ you to stand there looking pretty! You should be helping the guests with their luggage without having to be asked!" His gaze rested on me for a second—I felt myself freeze—then settled on Ben, who was just finishing his phone call. "I hope that wasn't a personal conversation," Gordon barked as he came down the stairs. "Where's your uncle? We need all hands on deck. The Barnbrookes are here, and I want . . . for heaven's sake! Am I surrounded by idiots?"

In their hurry to get outside, Nico and Jonas had caused the revolving door to jam. It always stopped moving if you pushed it too hard; it had its own slow, leisurely rhythm. A girl in a checkered coat was now stuck inside it, tapping on the glass with annoyance.

"Unbelievable!" Gordon Montfort strode furiously across the carpet, headed straight for me. I stepped back and, in a moment of quick thinking, opened the door beside the revolving door so that he could rush past me and out into the snow. At the same moment, Nico and Jonas managed to get the revolving door moving again and stumbled out into the forecourt, while the girl in the checkered coat was catapulted into the lobby. She was pretty, about my age, with enviably smooth skin and shiny long blond hair falling loose over her shoulders.

"That's a few points off right away," she said in English, with an American accent—clearly not to anyone in particular but in a stage whisper. With a theatrical sigh, she turned slowly on the spot, looking around her. "Nothing's changed at all here." She sniffed the air. "And it still smells exactly the same. Of wood fires, furniture polish, and dust."

With that she lost my sympathy. Dust! What nerve. As if the tiniest speck of dust would survive in this place under Fräulein Müller's watchful eye! It was true about the wood fires and the furniture polish, but I happened to think the furniture polish smelled amazing—of oranges, turpentine, linseed oil, and honey. (I always got a slightly heady feeling when I was dusting.) And anyway, all those smells were being drowned out right now by the aroma of freshly baked brown bread drifting up from the kitchen.

"You almost expect the butler from *Downton Abbey* to come shuffling around the corner," the girl went on, yawning pointedly. But then she caught sight of Ben, and her eyes grew wide. "Oh! My!

Gosh!" She strode across to the reception desk and threw her achingly chic caramel-colored handbag down on top of it. "Ben? Ben Montfort?"

Ben smiled, a little awkwardly it seemed to me. "Welcome to Castle in the Clouds." I'd meant to seize this opportunity to hurry back to the concierge's lodge and safety, but now, afraid of missing something, I moved as if in slow motion. My English was quite good thanks to all the British and American TV I'd watched with Delia, and this girl could easily have been a character in one of those series. The bitchy blond one.

"I can't believe it!" She rested her elbows on her handbag and went on staring at Ben. "Oh my God! I literally *can't even*! Forget what I said about how nothing's changed around here. I take it all back! Last time we saw each other, you were five inches shorter than me and you had acne all over your face and this weird hunchback way of standing."

Ben's smile was noncommittal. "I hope that you had a pleasant journey and an easy flight," he said in perfect English.

I'd crept past the reception desk now and was heading toward Monsieur Rocher, who was on the phone. But I was still moving in slow motion, as if I had no control over my own limbs.

The girl didn't answer. "I still can't get my head around how broad-shouldered you've got all of a sudden." She went on, in a dreamy tone, "When we were little, we used to play hide-and-seek together and you taught us how to skateboard and you always smelled of chlorine. If I'd known . . . But who could have guessed you were going to grow up to be so hot!" She fluttered her long eyelashes. (I saw her do it, because by this point I'd actually started walking backward, much to my own astonishment.) "Do you remember who I am?"

52

Ben shot a sideways glance at me. I might have been mistaken, but it looked as though he was on the verge of rolling his eyes.

But then. "Of course! You're one of the Barnbrooke girls," he replied, in a studiously friendly tone. "We're very glad to be able to welcome you to the hotel again this year."

"Oh, no, no, no! I'm not one of the Barnbrooke girls. I'm *the* Barnbrooke girl." She looked at Ben expectantly, then sighed. "Gretchen! I'm Gretchen! You always used to say my name was so cute."

Really? I wasn't so sure. The way she pronounced it—"Grr-*retch*-in"—it sounded more like a sneeze gone wrong.

"Welcome, Gretchen." Ben was still smiling his noncommittal smile, and I accidentally walked into a pillar, which finally shook me out of my reverie and brought me back to my senses. I really didn't have any time to lose if I wanted to stay out of sight. I ran the last few feet to the staff room, facing forward this time. I only just managed to close the door behind me before Gordon Montfort entered the lobby again from outside, along with the rest of the Barnbrookes.

Monsieur Rocher was putting the phone receiver back on the hook as I slipped into the concierge's lodge. (This phone really did have a receiver and a hook. The rest of the hotel had modern phones, but this one was from the forties or fifties, and I'd taken countless photos of it. I couldn't get enough of its old-fashioned finger wheel and elegant shape.) "The airport in Sion is closed because of the snowstorm. The Smirnovs' private jet will have to land in Geneva now, so I've postponed Mrs. Smirnov's herbal stamp massage until tomorrow, just to be on the safe side."

"Oh—they have their own jet, too?"

"A whole fleet, if I'm not mistaken," Monsieur Rocher replied, but I was only half listening. I still had one ear on what was going on at Reception.

Chaos had erupted in the lobby. It turned out to be more difficult than expected to allocate the various Barnbrookes and their luggage to the six rooms they'd booked, especially since they were all talking at once and Ben could hardly keep up. There was still no sign of his uncle.

The two Ludwigs were watching all the commotion from their sofa with evident enjoyment. Don, on the other hand, seemed to have made himself scarce—I couldn't see him anywhere.

Above the general tumult of voices, Gretchen's voice rang out very clearly. "Ella! This is Ben Montfort! Was he this hot last year and you just forgot to tell me?" She clearly couldn't get over the fact that Ben didn't have acne anymore. "I didn't come last year because I had mono, remember?" Her voice rose even more. "Or the kissing disease, as Grandma calls it."

"Humph," I said quietly. Could she *be* any more crass?

"Big family, isn't it? And very lively." Monsieur Rocher smiled indulgently at me. In my eagerness to see what was going on, I was leaning possibly a little too far over the counter. "It's been a while since you met anyone of your own age, hasn't it?"

He'd got me there. Both the guests and the staff at Castle in the Clouds tended to be somewhere between middle age and old. Little kids were few and far between, and until now there hadn't been anyone else my age at all. Since the holidays had started, though, the place was suddenly full of young people—and I wasn't quite sure what to make of it.

"It's just that they all look so alike. It's hard to remember who's who," I murmured, embarrassed.

"Oh, it's not all that complicated," said Monsieur Rocher in a chatty tone, pointing to the older gentleman with the big white mustache talking to Gordon Montfort (who was now smiling genially once more). "That's Mr. Barnbrooke Sr., also known as Big Daddy, head of the family and owner of Barnbrooke Industries. His parents used to spend the holidays at Castle in the Clouds, too, and Big Daddy—who was a sweet little boy, I must say—is so attached to the family tradition that he's threatened to disinherit anyone who dares to make alternative plans for Christmas. He won't accept any excuses, apart from illness. And there must be a lot to inherit, because so far the whole family has turned up every year without fail, unless they really are at death's door."

"I can think of worse places to spend a holiday than a luxury hotel in the Swiss Alps," I said.

Especially since Big Daddy picked up the bill for the entire family, according to Monsieur Rocher, and bought each of the female members of the family a new ball gown every year. The Duchess Suite on the second floor had been set aside for him and Mrs. Barnbrooke (who staunchly refused to be called "Big Mama"), while their sons, Hank and Tom, would be staying with their wives, Lucille and Barbra, in Rooms 208 and 209. Room 210 was reserved for Harper, Hank and Lucille's eldest daughter, who was already married with a baby—here Monsieur Rocher floundered for a second, but then remembered that the husband was called Jeremy, had a degree in textiles and clothing technology, and was allergic to nuts. The baby's name was Emma. Gretchen was Harper's younger sister and was in her second-to-last year of high school, as was Ella, Tom and Barbra's eldest daughter. Ella had three younger sisters. Amy was fifteen; Madison, ten; and Gracie, eight. We'd put an extra bed in the Theremin Suite for the five girls. Room 212 opposite was reserved for the three boys in the family: Gretchen's twin brother, Claus; their twelve-year-old cousin, Jacob; and eighteen-year-old Aiden, who was deaf. Big Daddy and his wife had adopted him as a baby.

With a drawing or a family tree it probably would have been easy to keep track of who was who, but all I had was Monsieur Rocher's whispered explanations, and I struggled to assign names to faces. As I went through them all again—adopted son Aiden was the only one with dark hair and a long, straight nose; all the others were blond and snub-nosed and looked ridiculously alike—an argument broke out at Reception.

"But we wanted a rear-facing room this time," complained the girl who'd been handed the key to the Theremin Suite. Ella, if I wasn't mistaken. "Just for me and Gretchen. We're too old to still be babysitting the little ones. And anyway, one bathroom between five of us—it's like summer camp."

"Ella!" her mother, whose name I'd already forgotten, reprimanded her. "Let's not have any more of your whining."

"And we don't need a babysitter anyway, Ella, you buttnut," said little Gracie.

"And if we did, we'd rather have Amy," Madison added. "She's much more fun than you two."

Amy, the fifteen-year-old sister, was standing on the edge of the group. She looked exactly like Ella, who in turn looked exactly like Gretchen and Harper, but her hair was shorter and she wore glasses. This was very considerate of her, I thought. At least I could tell her apart from the others.

"As I recall, the Theremin Suite has two separate bedrooms," she said in an irritated voice. "And the bathroom is massive."

"And there's a separate toilet, a dressing room, and an open fire in the master bedroom," Ben added cheerfully.

"Which Ella and Gretchen are obviously going to lay claim to," Amy cut in.

"That can be the buttnut room, then," said Gracie.

"Good heavens, Gracie," cried her mother. "Wherever do you get these words from?"

"I make them up," said Gracie proudly, and Madison giggled.

"But I wanted a rear-facing room," Ella whined, on the verge of stamping her foot. "With a panoramic view. And a balcony. Why don't me and Gretchen swap with Harper and Jeremy? They're always busy looking after the baby anyway and they don't have time to have sex, so it's not like they'd disturb the kids."

"Ella Jane Barnbrooke!" Their poor mother clearly didn't know which of her children was more embarrassing. She cast an anxious glance at her parents-in-law, but they were still deep in conversation with Gordon Montfort and his perma-smile. The scraps of conversation that came our way were all about golf, the weather, and the strength of the dollar. "You need to start behaving. Otherwise you can spend the rest of the holidays upstairs in your room! Is that clear?"

"It's all so unfair," Ella wailed.

Her mother looked as though she had a migraine coming on. "I mean it, Ella. If I have to speak to you again, you're not going anywhere near that ballroom."

The older sister with the baby had already snatched up her room key and led her husband over to the elevator, where she was whispering something in his ear. The Barnbrooke boys were already on their way upstairs. And bellhop Jonas and ringmaster Jaromir were wheeling two fully loaded luggage carts into the service elevator.

Under her mother's stern eye, Ella reached for the key, looking as if she was about to cry.

"A lot of our guests actually prefer the front-facing rooms—you get a wonderful view of the sunrise," said Ben consolingly. "And the chamois on the rock faces." (I wasn't sure what a *chamois* was, but I thought it might be some kind of goat. Or perhaps a sort of moss or lichen; although in that case, Ben probably wouldn't have advertised it as one of the highlights of a front-facing room.) "And the Theremin Suite is steeped in history. Not only did Leon Theremin, the man it's named after, stay there in the late 1920s on his world tour, but Rainer Maria Rilke actually wrote some of his famous Valais poems there."

"Well, technically, they were some of his lesser-known poems," Monsieur Rocher whispered. "'*Pays silencieux dont les prophètes se taisent.*' He wrote them in French."

"Either way," I whispered back, "I'll bet neither of them have ever heard of Rilke." (Let alone Leon Theremin—even *I* hadn't the faintest idea who he was.)

And it was at that moment I saw it. The dog poop. It was a big brown mound, lying on the marble floor by the pillar in the middle of the lobby, and it was a miracle no one had spotted it yet. The only reason I hadn't noticed it before was because there'd been a suitcase in front of it. Now, as I stared at it in horror, I was sure I could smell it, too. How on earth had it gotten there?

Had one of the two poodles done its business without anyone noticing? And if so, why hadn't we smelled it straightaway? It couldn't have been the Von Dietrichsteins' pug because they always carried him everywhere, and it didn't seem very likely that Mr. or Mrs. Von Dietrichstein would have snuck into the lobby on purpose

to let their dog poop. While Monsieur Rocher went on merrily recit-
ing French Rilke poems beside me and the older Barnbrookes carried
on chatting with Ben's father, I wondered frantically what was to be
done. Gordon Montfort was unlikely to hold the un-house-trained
dog or its master or mistress responsible—no, he'd find someone else
to blame, someone who'd have to pay for the fact that there was a
stinking pile of dog turd in the middle of the lobby. Even though,
strictly speaking, it was Montfort's own fault for allowing exceptions
to the no-dog rule in the first place. But that was irrelevant. Dog
poop in the lobby was very bad for business, and heads would roll for
this—one head, at least. The question was, whose?

"Come on, Ella!" Gretchen linked arms with her cousin. "Let's
go and freshen up. We can take a few photos from Harper's balcony
and pretend it's ours."

"Gretchen is superfamous on Instagram," said Gracie to Ben,
who couldn't see the dog turd because the pillar was in the way.

"Oh, superfamous is going a bit far," Gretchen protested modestly.

"Yes, but really only a bit." Amy rolled her eyes. "She has an
incredible one hundred and thirty-one followers, and she knows them
all personally."

"Yes, one hundred and thirty-one! And I'm only just starting
out." Gretchen flicked her hair, and she and Ella sashayed off toward
the staircase. They were going to pass right by the poop. I had to do
something—anything.

"Perhaps Ben would like to follow you on Instagram." Amy
grinned at Ben, lifted her little backpack onto her shoulder, and
followed Ella and Gretchen. "It really is a very cool account. It's
called Grumpy Gretchen. Grumpy Gretchen explains to her followers
why blond girls shouldn't wear yellow, when you can get away with

wearing lots of eyeliner, and how to take cute selfies with pets without them stealing your thunder."

"Gritty Gretchen." Gretchen stopped in her tracks, and Ella glared at Amy. "It's called Gritty Gretchen, and as you can tell from the name, it's about much more than makeup and fashion. It's about giving advice. Helping people with their problems. Helping gutsy girls navigate the rocks in the sea of life."

That was my cue. This dog poop was a rock in the sea of life, and I was the gutsy girl who was going to navigate it.

Much to his astonishment, I plucked Monsieur Rocher's snow-white handkerchief out of the breast pocket of his jacket and swung myself up and over the counter.

"The ultimate advice for life: how to use contouring to make your nose look smaller and the only proper recipe for rainbow cupcakes," scoffed Amy.

"Come on, Gretchen." Ella drew her cousin away. "Amy's just jealous. As usual."

I slid out in front of the two girls, missing them by a hair, knelt down in front of the pillar, and draped Monsieur Rocher's handkerchief over the turd. It was just about big enough to cover it. But it looked a bit weird, hovering a few inches above the floor like some kind of magic handkerchief.

"Whoa," said Gretchen—as loudly as she could, of course. Amy, Ella, Madison, Gracie, and their mother also looked at me curiously.

"Sorry." I tried to block their view of the handkerchief-covered mound with my body. "That was . . . er . . . is a little puddle of melt-water. Very bad for the floor." I reached courageously for the handkerchief; for a brief moment, I hoped I'd merely been taken in by one of those trick plastic dog turds, but unfortunately the stuff felt soft and—here I had to stifle the urge to retch—positively creamy. And there was too much of it to scoop up all at once in the handkerchief. I'd have needed two or three handkerchiefs. Or something else to wrap this unspeakably disgusting mess in. I was temporarily immobilized, at a loss as to what to do.

To my great relief, though, the Barnbrooke women soon went on their way toward the staircase. And the grandparents were now being escorted toward the elevators by Grouchy Gordon. I lowered my eyes and held my breath, trying to stay invisible until they'd all gone past me. Hopefully Gordon Montfort would go up to the second floor with them, then I'd have enough time to sort this business out.

Annoyingly, though, I realized when I looked up again that little Gracie hadn't moved and was still standing there staring at me. I must have looked very strange, kneeling by the pillar with my hand over a little cloth-covered mound that was supposed to be melted snow. Monsieur Rocher, in the concierge's lodge, was also looking over at me in bewilderment.

"I like your dress," said Gracie, and you could see she was trying to find something nice to say to me. She probably felt sorry for me. "I like the buttons and the crown."

"Thank you. I think it's pretty, too," I replied. "And your cat hat is great. I love the little fluffy ears." Then I was struck by an audacious thought. "Hey, Gracie—would you mind lending me your hat until tomorrow morning?"

Gracie's eyes widened with curiosity.

"My name is Sophie," I added quickly. "I'm the babysitter here, and I promise I'll get your hat back to you by tomorrow." Washed and perfumed. "I need it for an important mission."

Gracie didn't hesitate for a moment. "Of course!" She pulled the hat off her head and handed it to me. Then she turned and ran up the stairs after the others. Oh, if only all children could be so generous and uncomplicated! I waited till I heard the rattle of the elevator grille closing and then, hurriedly, without looking (or breathing through my nose), I shoveled the dog poo into the hat with the aid of the handkerchief. It was a sticky business, but by some miracle I managed to keep my fingers clean. Gracie's hat, on the other hand . . .

"What are you doing, Sophie Spark?" I felt someone tap me on the shoulder from behind. It was Don, who naturally had to appear at this precise moment—out of nowhere, as usual.

"What does it look like I'm doing?" I snarled.

Don folded his arms. "Well. It looks like you're stuffing a disgusting brown glob of something into a hat you just nicked off a little girl. Clever idea, by the way. I wouldn't have thought of that." He giggled softly.

The suspicion suddenly dawned on me that he'd been here the whole time, watching me. I clearly wasn't the only one who was good at hiding.

"Did you . . . is this *your* doing, you little . . . ?" I stared at him, aghast.

"Quick on the uptake, aren't you, Sophie Spark?" Don grinned, managing to look fiendish and outrageously cute at the same time. Then: "Oh dear, oh dear!" he said, in a stage whisper even Gretchen couldn't have bettered. And in a lilting childish voice that was most uncharacteristic of him, he added: "Is that little Gracie Barnbrooke's favorite hat? What are you doing with it?"

"I . . . cut it out, would you?" I hissed, but it was already too late.

"What's going on here?" Gordon Montfort came striding toward us. He hadn't gone up in the elevator with the Barnbrookes.

That was it, then. It was clear now whose head was going to roll. All the way back to my parents' front door, just in time for Christmas.

I leapt to my feet, clutching the cat hat against my chest. "N-nothing," I stammered.

Gordon Montfort looked at me through narrowed eyes. "Are you one of Fräulein Müller's temps?"

"No." I swallowed hard. *I'm the intern, don't you remember? You shook my hand when I arrived here in September*, I was going to say, but Don beat me to it.

"That's Gracie Barnbrooke's cat hat," he said, sounding deeply perturbed. "The lady put some strange brown stuff inside it. Why did she do that, Uncle Gordon? I'm sure Gracie still wants that hat."

"I beg your pardon? What strange brown stuff?" The dreaded vein on Gordon Montfort's forehead was bulging. Close up, it looked even more terrifying than usual. I realized my teeth were about to start chattering.

"Give it here," he yelled at me.

I kept the hat pressed to my chest. "It's . . . I can explain," I stuttered. "Don . . ." Yes, what had the scheming little Bambi done? Collected a dog turd and placed it right in the middle of the lobby out of sheer malice, just to see what happened? Nobody was going to believe that. And they definitely weren't going to believe anyone was stupid enough to try and dispose of said dog turd in a child's woolly hat.

A wave of self-loathing washed over me.

"Poor Gracie," lisped Don. "That's her favorite hat."

Gordon Montfort grabbed me by the elbow. "Why have you stolen this hat?" he asked, very slowly and clearly, as if talking to a deaf person. "And what's this brown stuff you're hiding in it? Drugs?"

Oh, crap—now I could feel a highly inappropriate fit of the giggles bubbling up inside me. And at the same time I felt like crying. I clutched the hat without saying a word, wondering frantically what I should do. What would Jesus do?

Gordon Montfort turned his head without letting go of my arm. "Hello? Could somebody please tell me who this person is? What is this madwoman doing working in my hotel?"

I heard the door to the concierge's lodge opening, and I knew Monsieur Rocher was hurrying to my rescue. At the reception desk, at the same moment, Ben opened his mouth to speak. But Nico the bellhop got there first.

"That's the epaulet," he said, nodding smugly.

"The *what*?" Gordon Montfort snatched the cat hat off me in one rapid movement.

"Epaulet," Nico repeated, pleased with his own knowledge.

"She's the intern," Ben chimed in. "And she's doing a brilliant job. She's been down here helping us out even though her shift hasn't started yet."

"I'll second that," said Monsieur Rocher, slightly out of breath. He smoothed his suit. "Sophie Spark is the best intern we've ever had."

"And what is she hiding in the favorite hat of one of our guests?" spat Gordon Montfort, but in a slightly hushed voice. I knew he would have liked to shout, but he didn't dare because of the guests on the staircase.

I looked on in horror as he opened up the hat. "What the hell is this?"

Everyone stared into Gracie's hat. It wasn't a pretty sight.

Don was the first to speak. "It looks like squashed chocolate cake," he said, dipping his finger in and licking it, to my horror. "Yep. It's chocolate cake. The only question is, how did it end up in Gracie's hat?"

I felt as though my knees were about to give way beneath me. I'd been taken in by a piece of chocolate cake, sculpted by skillful little hands to look exactly like a dog turd. I'd even convinced myself it *smelled* like a dog turd.

"I don't think we really want to go into that, Don, do we?" Ben said. He must have realized who the culprit was, too—Don's mega-cute, ultra-innocent look didn't seem to impress him in the least. "I saw you with a piece of cake just now, standing right there." He turned to his father. "Sophie was just trying to cover up Don's little mishap. That's all."

"With a hat?" growled Gordon Montfort, still glaring at me but looking less sure of himself now. I stared back, my teeth chattering. Then, luckily for me, another car pulled up outside.

"I'll be keeping an eye on you, young lady." Gordon Montfort thrust Gracie's hat at me. "Sort this out. We don't tolerate trouble-makers in this hotel."

He didn't wait for my reply; instead, he turned on Nico. "And what are you doing standing around like a lemon, you idiot? Look, more guests have just arrived."

6

That night I dreamed I was riding an air current, circling high above Castle in the Clouds with the seven Hugos as if I were one of them. It was strange to see the hotel from above. It looked like a magical, jagged rock formation jutting out of the snow like a piece of the mountain. The lower we flew, the more details I could make out: the steep turret roofs, the wrought-iron roof rails, the big skylight above the staircase—like a Victorian greenhouse. On the ground, Monsieur Rocher was standing in the snow outside the entrance to the hotel with the Forbidden Cat, and when he saw me he smiled, pulled his handkerchief out of his breast pocket, and waved it at me.

But you'd better wake up now, Sophie, he said. *The early bird catches the worm . . .*

And at that point, I did indeed wake up, just like that, for no apparent reason. My phone told me it was only quarter to five, and I wanted to roll over and carry on dreaming my lovely dream. I didn't need to get to the playroom on the third floor until nine o'clock, after all, and it couldn't hurt to be well rested when I got there, especially if Don was going to make good on his threat and turn up at day care, too.

But no sooner had I closed my eyes again than I heard a soft sighing sound coming from the wall, tentative at first but then more forceful, until it sounded more like an angry man clearing his throat. After five minutes, I couldn't stand it anymore and sat up. Clearly, the old water pipe in the wall had decided that today was the day to catch up on all the noises it had refrained from making over the past few months. I switched my bedside lamp on and stood up. I was only imagining it, of course, but the noise from the pipe almost sounded pleased.

And to be honest, I felt pretty well rested already. "The early bird gets a free bathroom, at any rate," I said to myself. It was pitch dark outside and I couldn't see whether it was still snowing, but the whistling and wailing of the storm had dropped as I crept along the corridor as quietly as I could.

It was a lot more relaxing taking a shower when I knew Hortensia, Camilla, and co. were still fast asleep.

When I'd gotten back to my room after my evening shift yesterday, I'd put my hand in a big glob of gooey stuff that someone had smeared all over the door handle, and Hortensia and her three friends, who'd obviously been waiting for me in the doorway of their own room, had been beside themselves with laughter.

Toothpaste on the door handle—ha ha. Very original.

"Someone's clearly been reading too many boarding-school books," I said as I walked past them to the bathroom to wash off the toothpaste. Unbelievable—they were all wearing exactly the same set of frilly polka-dot pajamas. "What's your next trick? A whoopee cushion?"

"Oh dear, Work Experience is sulking!" As they followed me in their spotty pajamas, laughing idiotically, they both looked and sounded uncannily like a pack of spotted hyenas I'd once seen in a wildlife documentary. "Can't you take a joke?"

No. I'd had quite enough practical jokes for one day. I was no more in the mood for joking than the wildebeest the hyenas had chased down and eaten for dinner in the documentary.

I grimly proceeded to wash the toothpaste off my hand while Camilla stood at the sink to the left of me and admired her reflection in the mirror. Ava, Hortensia, and Whatsername positioned themselves to my right. Ava started braiding her shoulder-length, dark-blond hair, Whatsername batted her eyelashes coquettishly at herself in the mirror, and Hortensia ran cold water over her wrists and dabbed it on her temples.

I turned off the tap. "I'm really tired, and I want to go to bed. So if you're going to beat me up and stick my head down the toilet then could you please just get on with it, or else leave it till tomorrow."

The four of them looked at me in bewilderment.

"Huh? What are you talking about?" said Hortensia in her nasal voice. "It was just a harmless little joke. You're the one who's not following the rules around here."

"What?"

"You used the bathroom at the same time as us," Ava explained.

"And then you started being rude to us." Whatsername looked at me reproachfully.

Camilla nodded vehemently. "And now you're lying and saying we want to beat you up and stick your head down the toilet."

"Have you completely lost your minds?" I cried indignantly. "You pushed me and insulted me. And put toothpaste on my door handle."

"Yes, because you threatened Hortensia with your so-called *friends*," said Camilla. "My aunt said we shouldn't let you intimidate us."

"What?" Who was intimidating who here? I was definitely the wildebeest in this situation.

"And you left your disgusting hair in the sink," added Whatsername.

"And you're ugly," said Ava.

At that moment, the tap in her sink went haywire. It seemed to suddenly explode, spitting a jet of water right onto Ava's pajamas.

All four hyenas jumped backward, screaming, but by that time the tap had already settled down again.

Since it didn't look like anyone else was going to, I turned off the tap and moved toward the door. Nobody stopped me; they were all staring suspiciously at the sink.

In the doorway, I turned back. "As my so-called friend the tap just told you: Leave me alone."

Hortensia didn't answer me but muttered to Camilla: "Something must be wrong with the pipes. This hotel really is in a shocking state. Even if your aunt does seem to think it's on a par with the Ritz-Carlton."

Yes, and she was right, damn it. Though I was willing to bet they had nicer chambermaids at the Ritz-Carlton.

One of the four hyenas was now snoring loudly as I crept past their room, freshly showered and dressed and with my hair already done. That must be Hortensia; the snoring had a nasal quality to it.

I didn't run into anyone on my way downstairs to the kitchen, which was located in the basement below the restaurant, but that didn't mean everybody else was still asleep. There was always someone awake somewhere in the hotel. Or, as Monsieur Rocher often said: *Castle in the Clouds never sleeps.*

Because there were no fixed mealtimes for the staff, food was left out for us all day in a room just off the kitchen. When I arrived, Pierre (one of the two junior chefs permanently employed at the hotel) was laying out a cheese board, and the smell of fresh bread filled the air. The breakfast buffet down here was almost identical to the one served to the guests in the restaurant upstairs. Granted, we didn't get summer fruits arranged in concentric circles, freshly squeezed juices, or trays full of little glasses of mango lassi, but we got almost everything else, and around the clock, too. From midday onward, there was hot soup. In the afternoons, there were little pastries; bowls of apples, oranges, and carrots; and often casseroles on hot plates. There were always cold meats, fresh bread, cakes, and tarts—nobody had to go hungry here.

"You're up early," said Pierre.

"So are you." I bit happily into a slice of crusty buttered bread and lowered myself onto one of the few chairs. "The early bird gets the best breakfast. And a seat."

Pierre laughed. "You've got to have some of this salmon. I made the marinade myself, with lime and sea salt and juniper and dill and . . . oh, just try a bit." He laid out a big piece on a plate for me. I really liked Pierre. He was the one who supplied me with the milk rolls I fed to the seven Hugos. He always put a few aside for me. And when I'd first started working here, he'd helped me understand the regional dialect that most of the staff spoke. I'd probably never be able to speak it myself, but I found it easy enough to follow a conversation now. Old Stucky was the only person I couldn't understand at all. Pierre said that wasn't my fault but was due to the fact that Old Stucky had no teeth.

The salmon was absolutely delicious. And it went perfectly with the bread. And the egg. And the cheese. I always ate as much as I could for breakfast because I didn't usually get to eat again until the afternoon. It was nice not to have to rush for once and to get a chance to chat with Pierre. There'd been fourteen inches of fresh snow overnight, he said, and snowdrifts several feet high.

The mountain pass roads had been closed, and only cars with snow chains could manage the road to the hotel. The next bout of wintry weather was already on its way, and from Christmas Day on, the snow was supposed to be even heavier. Where I lived, weather like this would have triggered a state of emergency, but here it was nothing special.

"And what's morale like in there?" I asked, pointing to the door that led to the kitchen. There were more extra kitchen and waiting staff than any other kind of temp, and two thirds of the people working in the kitchen and the restaurant were new.

"It's going very well. Except that the newbies still haven't realized how serious Chef is about the ban on cell phones. I've done what I can, but I'm afraid they won't really get the message until the first phone gets melted on the grill. Or minced. Or thrown in boiling water." Pierre grinned, and I couldn't help laughing. The head chef was very creative, in more ways than one. "One of the new waiters is really cute. I think I might be a little bit in love." He winked at me. "And how are things upstairs?"

"Gordon Montfort has got it in for me, the students from Lausanne are evil creatures with a warped view of life, and little Don Burkhardt has taken it upon himself to make my life hell. But apart from that, everything's fine, thanks. Oh, good morning! Where did you spring from?"

The Forbidden Cat wound herself around my legs and then Pierre's, purring. Then she mewed loudly.

Pierre put down a plate of cold meats chopped up into little pieces—he'd obviously prepared them for her specially. "Do you know the one thing that puzzles me?" he asked, as the Forbidden Cat dug into her breakfast with relish. "Chef says this cat was already here when he started working in the kitchen." He left a short, dramatic pause. Then he added quietly, "In 1989."

Math wasn't my strong point, but even without a calculator I knew that couldn't be right. "Perhaps there was a different cat here then that looked like this one. A ginger forebear."

The Forbidden Cat started washing herself. We looked thoughtfully at her.

"Yes, that must be it." Pierre picked up the cat's plate. "Shall I save you a mini raspberry cheesecake for this afternoon? Madame Cléo wasn't happy with the glaze, so I managed to nab us twenty-four of them, believe it or not."

I heard footsteps on the stairs, and Nico appeared in his bell-hop's uniform. He had his funny little cap clamped under one arm.

I greeted him in a friendly way and offered him my chair.

"Good morning," he said rather stiffly, as if he felt a bit embarrassed about running into me. "Oh! A cat! I didn't think pets were allowed here. In the house rules we got given, that was underlined three times."

"What cat?" said Pierre and I simultaneously.

"That one there!" Nico pointed to the Forbidden Cat, who was now making her way up the stairs in a leisurely fashion.

Pierre narrowed his eyes. "Do you see a cat around here, Sophie?"

I shook my head. "Where?"

"Ha ha, very funny." Nico glared at us. "I'm not falling for it this time like I did with the epaulet thing."

As he shoveled his breakfast indignantly onto his plate, I said good-bye to Pierre and followed the Forbidden Cat up to the ground floor. I'd been planning to go back upstairs again to brush my teeth before those stupid sheep from Lausanne woke up. But the cat padded on ahead of me, purring, and kept turning around as if to check I was still there, so I did what she seemed to want and followed her. We walked right across the empty lobby and past the corridor that led to the conference room, toward the bar and the library. It was a very roundabout way of getting to my room but one that appealed to me because there was a door in the library that opened onto a hidden back staircase leading down to the basement or up to the third floor.

The library was one of the most beautiful rooms in the hotel. It had ceiling-high shelves full of books, upholstered window seats where you could sit and read, an old-fashioned tiled fireplace with a bench in front of it, comfy armchairs, side tables piled high with coffee-table books, and a library ladder on rollers that glided all the way along a twenty-foot-long and twelve-foot-high bookshelf. Thanks to this ladder, dusting the books was great fun.

If I'd been a guest, I would have spent all day in here. The wood-burning stove in the fireplace gave out a cozy warmth, and it smelled irresistibly of old books and furniture polish. If you wanted, you could even order a cup of coffee or a port or whatever you fancied to be brought to you in the library. In spite of this, not many of the guests found their way here. Most of the time the big room was deserted.

"It's all the books that put people off," Monsieur Rocher had said with a wink, when I'd told him how surprised I was to see the library so empty. "It makes them feel guilty when they see how many books there are out there that they haven't read."

The Forbidden Cat clearly wasn't interested in finding a cozy corner in here, either; she planted herself by the door to the back staircase and meowed until I opened it. The door was set discreetly into the bookcase where the thrillers and crime novels were kept, and featured the usual NO ENTRY—STAFF ONLY signs in three languages. On the first floor, the staircase opened onto a long room full of nooks and crannies that lay between the Small Tower Suite and Room 102 and had space for storing vacuums and cleaning equipment; on the second floor, you went through a big room full of built-in cupboards for bed linens and towels, and through a door into the corridor that passed the entrance to the Large Tower Suite, where Don Burkhardt Jr. had been staying with his parents since early December. On the third floor, the stairs opened onto the men's staff quarters.

From the corridors on the first and second floors, the doors to the back staircase and the rooms branching off it looked like perfectly ordinary hotel room doors—none of the guests would have guessed there was anybody staying in Rooms 103 and 203. Unless they happened to be particularly brazen and inquisitive, like Don Burkhardt Jr., who presumably found NO ENTRY signs too tantalizing to resist. Don Jr. had already scared me half to death once when I'd opened a cupboard in the laundry room to find myself staring straight into his cute little face. My cry of alarm had alerted Fräulein Müller, who had initially scolded him but ended up believing his story (told with his usual doe-eyed look and adorable lisp) that he'd been playing at being a pirate and had completely lost track of where he was. Ridiculous! As if Don Burkhardt Jr. would ever indulge in innocent children's games!

The cat seemed to be in a hurry; instead of ambling along at a leisurely pace as she had been doing until now, she suddenly went bounding up the stairs. When I got to the first floor she was nowhere to be seen. Typical. First, she led me on this huge detour as if she had something to show me, then she just vanished.

On the second floor, one of the cupboards in the linen room had been left open. I knew how much this would annoy Fräulein Müller, so I was just about to close it when the door to the main corridor swung open and somebody came in. Afterward I couldn't explain why I'd done what I did, but by that time it was too late anyway. I slipped inside the cupboard as quick as lightning and pulled the door shut behind me, and then I stood there in exactly the same spot where I'd come across Don two weeks earlier and held my breath in astonishment. Something was clearly wrong with my reflexes. Why on earth had I leapt inside a cupboard to hide just because somebody had walked in? I hadn't been doing anything wrong. And I looked immaculate—not even Fräulein Müller could have found fault with me this morning. But I couldn't exactly come strolling out of the cupboard now as if nothing had happened—I'd have to wait until whoever it was that had come into the room went out again.

The problem was he didn't go anywhere. And it wasn't just one person, either—it was two. Right outside my cupboard, they started having a conversation.

"I can't understand why you're being so stubborn, Gilbert," said one, and I almost fainted with shock. That was Gordon Montfort! He must have slept here at the hotel last night because of the snow-storm, instead of going home.

"I'm not being stubborn—I just want to find another solution," replied the other person, and I recognized the voice of Gutless Gilbert, Gordon's younger brother. "Just give us a little time."

Gordon sighed. "We've been over this a hundred times. More

time is not a solution. And if we wait any longer, this offer will be off the table. We won't get a better one."

"But we can't do this," said Gilbert, sounding even more depressed than usual. "We have a responsibility to this hotel with all its traditions and to the people who work here. And just think of your—"

"Oh, don't give me all that guff about tradition and responsibility," Gordon broke in. "This clapped-out old pile of bricks with its clapped-out old traditions and staff have been a millstone around our necks for long enough now. Christ, you know the numbers better than I do. You know how long we've been in the red. We're about to go under."

"Things might seem rather hopeless just now, but the hotel has so much potential and an excellent reputation still, and if we try another relaunch—"

"With *our* debts? Who the hell is going to give us another loan for all the modernization this place would need?" Gordon cut his brother off again. I was amazed he wasn't shouting: By his standards, he was practically whispering. But that made his words all the more powerful. "Christ, Gilbert, just accept it. We're finished—it's the end of an era. The hotel is slowly but surely dying of old age, our guests are dying of old age, and so are the staff—like that senile old caretaker you insist on keeping on the payroll even though he should have been put in an old people's home years ago. All he does is scare the guests!"

"Old Stucky has always been an excellent worker," said Gilbert. "The hotel is his home, he doesn't have any other, and it would be cruel to send him away just because he's old. And he still looks after the horses very diligently and makes himself usef—"

"That's just your problem," Gordon hissed. "You're incapable of thinking about the bottom line—you're far too sentimental. Use your common sense! Burkhardt's offer is our only option. We'll get out of this mess with all our debts cleared and a bit left over for us to make a fresh start."

"But the man is an unscrupulous crook! He'll destroy everything our great-grandparents built. And he's a philistine. Have you even looked properly at his plans?"

"I like them. I like clear lines and modern decor. This ornate kitsch is way past its sell-by date."

"A hundred rooms instead of thirty-five? The music room split up into three separate bedrooms? Jascha Heifetz and Elisabeth Schwarzkopf gave concerts in that room!"

"That was before we were born!" I could almost hear Gordon shrug.

"But we were there when Roald Dahl gave a reading in our library! The same library Burkhardt wants to turn into a golf shop. How can you be so blasé about it? When I hear him talking about parking lots, cable cars, chairlifts, and apartment buildings, it sends a shiver down my spine."

I, too, felt a shiver run down my spine. I'd thought before that the hotel couldn't possibly be making much of a profit—it'd had so few guests during the months I'd been here—but I was shocked to realize how bad the situation actually was. No wonder Don Burkhardt Jr. went around acting as though the hotel belonged to him, if his father was planning to buy it and turn it into goodness knows what.

"Burkhardt is a hard-nosed businessman," said Gordon. "We should be glad he sees some potential in this godforsaken corner of the earth. Our great-grandparents are dead, and so are our grand-parents and our parents who lumbered us with this responsibility without asking us whether we wanted it. Personally, I'm done. If you keep standing in the way of this deal, I'll just sell my share to Burkhardt and you'll have to see how you get on with your half of the business once I'm gone."

"You can't do that," Gilbert pleaded.

"You bet I can," Gordon retorted. "Go ahead and sue me, if you can afford a lawyer."

There was silence for a few moments. Inside the cupboard, I held my breath.

"Of course, I'd prefer it if we brothers could work together," said Gordon at last, in a surprisingly soft voice. "Let's end this with dignity, Gilbert, before it's too late."

"What's dignified about selling our souls to Burkhardt for a suitcase full of dirty money?" said Gilbert bitterly. "And what about your son? Have you even thought about him?"

"I'm thinking about *him* more than anyone!" Gordon protested. "He'll be free, unlike us! Free to choose a job he actually enjoys, free to live wherever he wants—without this millstone around his neck, without debts, without responsibility. He won't understand it yet, but I'm doing the boy a huge favor."

They both fell silent again for a few moments.

"But he loves this place," Gilbert whispered then. "Just like I do."

Gordon groaned. "Sentimental nonsense. Nothing but sentimental nonsense. There's more to the world than this godforsaken mountain, you know. What have you got against change and progress?"

It sounded as though he was walking away as he spoke—I heard a door opening, and then his footsteps on the stairs.

"Wait!" Gilbert sighed as he followed him. "We could cut a few more costs. It would break my heart, but Madame Cléo, for example, is a luxury we could manage without. And what about Mr. Odermatt from the bank? Wasn't he going to go over all the numbers one more time?"

I couldn't hear Gordon's answer. I stood stock-still in the cupboard for a few more minutes after their voices and footsteps had died away. Only now did I realize how hard my heart was beating. And I started to get the feeling I was running out of air.

Very carefully, I pushed the cupboard door open and emerged from my hiding place. Too late, I realized there was someone standing right in front of it.

Someone who looked just as surprised to see me as I was him. Except that he recovered much more quickly.

"Well I never," he said in English. "A chambermaid in a cupboard."

7

The person standing in front of me was a complete stranger. He was young, very slim, athletically built, slightly tanned, with short black hair combed back from his forehead. He looked to be of Asian heritage, and his eyes were so dark that in this light I couldn't tell where the pupil ended and the iris began.

He had by far the most attractive face of any boy or man I'd ever seen (he was probably somewhere in between a boy and a man), and that was including all the actors in all the TV shows and movies I'd ever watched.

His full lips curved into a mocking smile as he looked at the cupboard. "Were you alone in there?"

"That's none of your business." I was glad to find that my voice was still working and that I was even able to find the right words in English. Attack was the best form of defense, after all. "Only hotel staff are allowed in this room. So I hope for your sake that you work here."

He smiled more broadly, revealing his perfect, bright white teeth. He probably found the idea of someone as good looking as him working as a waiter highly amusing. "Or else what?"

"Or else you'd be trespassing," I said sternly. "And I'd have to report you. I didn't hear you come in." Probably because I'd been in the cupboard straining my ears to catch all of the Montfort brothers' conversation.

The stranger was wearing black jeans and a dark sweater. And his posture was incredible—straight-backed, graceful, and languid all at the same time. He couldn't be the British actor we were expecting: he, according to Monsieur Rocher, was over sixty. Perhaps this boy was a ballet dancer. Or a prince.

"Well?" I asked, crossing my arms.

The boy started laughing. "No, I don't work here. Perhaps I'm a hotel thief, casing the joint?"

Sure. And the Forbidden Cat was a unicorn.

"Well if that's the case, then you *definitely* shouldn't be in here."

He bit back a laugh in a rather endearing way. "Okay then. Let's rewind. There's no sign on that door saying it's off-limits. I thought it might be a shortcut."

"But there's a room number on it, so you couldn't have known there'd be a way through." I pushed past him to the door and opened it. "See?" Perhaps he'd seen the Montfort brothers going in without using a room key and been curious about where the door led to. That was understandable.

He came over and stood beside me, so close that I could detect the faint scent of freshly washed cotton and something lemony. It made me remember that I'd had fish for breakfast and hadn't brushed my teeth yet. I pressed my lips together.

"Yes, at first sight it looks like an ordinary door to a room," he said. "But this thing here puzzled me." He pointed to the small, luminous green emergency exit sign above the light switch, showing a little man running and an arrow pointing unmistakably in the direction of the back stairs.

I'd never noticed it before.

"Hmm," I said. "But it's only to be used in the event of a fire. And I don't see anything burning around here, do you?"

Now he was looking me directly in the eye, and I could see that his irises were not jet black but dark brown. "I'm not sure," he said quietly. "And I like to be prepared. Just in case." Then he took a step back. "I'm Tristan Brown. I'm spending the holidays here with my grandfather, Professor Arthur Brown. We arrived last night in the middle of the snowstorm."

"Brown, Room 211," I murmured, mentally running through Monsieur Rocher's list of guests. No special requests for Room 211, no horse-drawn sleigh rides, no spa treatments, no skiing lessons, no allergies or intolerances, no dog, no VIP note made by Gordon Montfort; nothing that could tell me anything more about this guest. Room 211 was right at the other end of this floor, next to the room where the Barnbrooke boys were staying and opposite the couple with the baby.

And he was trying to tell me he'd thought this was a shortcut. Nice try! To get here from Room 211, Tristan—I liked the name, it suited him, somehow—would have passed both the main staircase and the elevators. He could easily have taken either of those. What sort of guest went wandering around the hotel at this time in the morning opening random doors, emergency exit sign or no emergency exit sign?

"Do you have a name?" he inquired. "And are you really a chambermaid?"

"No, I just put this uniform on as a disguise."

Of course, it was completely inappropriate for an intern to speak to a guest like this. Fräulein Müller had already had to reprimand me for smiling too familiarly at the guests. In her opinion, the staff were part of the movable fixtures of the hotel and should neither display any emotion nor elicit any. Guests shouldn't have to be reminded of the fact that the staff were human beings or even feel obliged to smile back.

"You should be discreet, polite, and stay in the background at all times. You don't see sofas grinning at people, now do you?" she'd asked. My smile had quickly been wiped off my face.

If she could hear me now, she'd probably have chased me all the way back to my hometown with her feather duster made of Egyptian ostrich feathers. (She swore by them.)

I'd better think about getting out of here ASAP.

"Are you going to tell me what was in that cupboard that was so important?" asked Tristan from Room 211.

I didn't answer him, but pulled the door shut behind us and looked quickly along the deserted corridor. The bag with that day's newspaper, which Burkhardt Sr. had ordered, was still hanging on the door handle of the Large Tower Suite, which meant that a) the newspaper man had managed to get his car up the mountain last night despite the chaos caused by the snow, and b) Don Jr.'s father might open his door and reach for his newspaper at any moment.

Another reason to make myself scarce.

Tristan Brown did not give up, however. He followed me doggedly down the corridor. "Have you lost the power of speech?" he asked.

Ha! He'd like that, wouldn't he? "If you really want to know, I was in the cupboard on the phone with my boss. I'm actually an undercover FBI agent, Special Division for Overseas Hotel Crimes. But that's top secret, obviously."

Tristan kept pace with me. "I see," he said, laughing. "But you could still tell me your name. I'd even be happy with your code name."

"Shh. The other guests are still asleep." I sped up a little. "Why aren't you?"

"Jet lag. I flew in from New York yesterday. Manon? Lilou? Lola? You look French."

From New York. Wow. "But you sound British," I said.

We'd reached the main staircase. To get to the staff quarters in the south wing, you had to turn left, while Tristan's room was straight ahead at the end of the corridor opposite us. I stopped by the alcove that housed an oil painting of a lady in a pearl necklace. She was so lifelike that at first glance you might easily have mistaken her for a real person, standing there behind the embroidered red velvet curtains with her elaborate hairstyle and her plunging evening gown. One of her elegant hands rested on the back of a chair, and in the other she was holding a pair of opera glasses. I felt her glaring at me reproachfully. And with good reason!

"I *am* British," Tristan explained. "I was in New York on business."

"On business?" I echoed sardonically, violating all the rules of Fräulein Müller's code of conduct. This conversation with Tristan was like a game of ping-pong; I couldn't help returning the ball. "You can't be more than nineteen."

"We hotel thieves start young." Tristan laughed. "Back to the French. Are you?"

"No," I said, annoyed by the note of regret in my voice. Okay, this guy was incredibly cute. And he smelled nice. And he was fun to talk to. But that was all. No reason for me to start acting so weird.

At least I wasn't the only one of us acting weird.

"Someone's coming up the stairs," whispered Tristan, and before I could look around to see who it was, he'd pulled me into the alcove with the stern pearl-necklace lady and closed one of the velvet curtains behind us. I clearly wasn't the only one with bizarre reflexes.

The single curtain didn't hide us completely, so I hurriedly closed the other one and we both peered out through the gap toward the staircase.

There was a man in a suit coming up the stairs, as light-footed as he was purposeful, and I recognized him straight away as he walked past our alcove and carried on up to the third floor. It was the unremarkable-looking man from Room 117, the one Monsieur Rocher thought must be the Smirnovs' bodyguard. What was he doing heading up to the third floor? The Panorama Suite was in the south wing, on the first floor. The main staircase and the elevators ended on the third floor, where Rooms 301 to 305 were located, along with the game room, the men's staff quarters (off-limits to guests), and access to the two other top floors. We heard a door close softly upstairs. If I wasn't mistaken, it was the door to the staff quarters. That was definitely a little odd.

I turned to Tristan—he was standing so close to me that he made me jump. A tiny sliver of light filtered through the closed curtains into our hiding place. "Could you please tell me why exactly we're hiding in here?" I said in a low voice.

"Why? Because it's fun." He grinned and reached past me to open the curtains again. "After all, you're an undercover FBI agent and I'm a hotel thief; we do this sort of thing all the time. Who was that guy?"

He'd checked in as Alexander Huber, but that might not be the name his gun was registered under. *If* it was registered. And what on earth was he doing in the staff quarters? Was that one of the security checks bodyguards had to carry out—investigating the hotel staff?

And why was Tristan's face so close to mine?

"I like your freckles," he said.

Under his steady gaze, I remembered I still hadn't brushed my teeth. I turned away and stepped out of the alcove. "Sorry, I'm not allowed to talk about ongoing investigations. And I really have to go now or . . . er . . . I'll blow my cover."

"That's a shame," said Tristan, completely serious all of a sudden. That suited him pretty well, too. I stared at him, trying to tear myself away.

Then a door opened at the end of the corridor and before I knew it I was back in the alcove beside Tristan, pulling the curtain closed behind us again.

He laughed softly. "Good reflexes, Agent . . . What was your name again?"

"Shh," I whispered. Damn it! Was I going to spend the rest of my life jumping into alcoves and hiding whenever I heard a noise? What was wrong with me?

"If the water's anything less than seventy-five degrees, I'm going nowhere near that pool!" I recognized the voice at once; it was Ella Barnbrooke, the girl who'd been complaining yesterday about having to stay in the Theremin Suite.

"It's real glacier water, and the colder it is the more calories you burn when you swim," replied another voice, which I identified as that of her cousin Gretchen. The pair of them came quickly toward us, making no effort to keep their voices down. "Possibly even enough to eat one of those divine croissants they have here. Oh my God, why can I not stop thinking about food? I've thought about nothing else for *hours*."

"It's this stupid jet lag," said Ella. "When you go to bed at five in the afternoon, it's no wonder you feel wide awake again in the middle of the night." They walked straight past our alcove, and I held my breath for a moment.

"I think I'm going to sneeze," Tristan whispered.

I stared at him in horror. But it seemed he was only joking. I saw the flash of his teeth in the half darkness.

Outside, Ella went on, "And you weren't *only* thinking about food—you were thinking about Ben, too. Admit it!"

Gretchen giggled. Like Ella, she was wearing her white hotel bathrobe and matching terry-cloth slippers, and she had her long blond hair tied up in a ponytail. "Man, he's cute. And I was afraid this vacation was going to be boring!"

They stopped in front of one of the elevators.

"You get first dibs on Ben, then, do you, cuz?" Ella put her hands on her hips. "And what about me? Do I not get a chance?"

Gretchen giggled again. Or rather, she carried on giggling—she'd never actually stopped. "You can try your luck with him if you want; I don't mind. That just makes it more exciting."

The elevator made a soft *ping* sound and the grille rattled open. "Okay then—may the best woman win," said Ella as they stepped into the elevator. "The main thing is not to let Amy get her hands on him."

"I don't think we need to worry about that," said Gretchen. "No man in the world would look twice at Amy when he had the option of Gretchen or Ella."

At that moment, Tristan actually did sneeze. Quite loudly, I thought. I glared at him, but Gretchen and Ella obviously hadn't heard anything. Still, it felt like an eternity before the elevator doors slid shut.

I quickly pulled the curtain aside and stepped out of the alcove.

"You did that on purpose," I said reproachfully.

"Sorry." Tristan smiled contritely. "Nearly blew your undercover mission there, didn't I? So what are these American cheerleader types up to, then? No, don't tell me. I want to guess. Cinderella's wicked sisters are at the head of an international drug cartel, right? They're on their way down to the swimming pool to meet with an Italian mafia boss. Shouldn't you go after them, quick, and arrest them?"

I sighed. Suddenly all this didn't seem so funny anymore, just a bit silly. My "mental moment" was over. "I have to go," I said.

"Oh please! At least tell me your name. Like I said, it doesn't have to be your real one. Something French, perhaps?" The way he was standing there in the alcove with his arms crossed beside the severe-looking lady in the pearl necklace, he looked almost like a painting himself.

"Fine." Time for the unglamorous truth. "My name is Sophie Spark, and I'm the intern here. I'm currently working as the hotel babysitter."

If Tristan was disappointed, he didn't show it. "Shame I'm not a baby anymore, then."

"How old *are* you?" I blurted out. I'd already taken a few steps away from him. Still facing him, though.

"Nineteen, as you quite rightly guessed. And you? I mean your cover identity, of course?"

"Seventeen. It was nice to meet you." I finally succeeded in turning around. Now I just had to move my legs and walk away. It really wasn't all that hard.

"Enjoy the rest of your stay at Castle in the Clouds," I said over my shoulder. As I strode down the corridor between the two elevators, I felt his eyes on my back. Well, I thought I did, anyway. Why I had to choose that moment to remember that Delia always said I walked like a boy, I don't know. At the door to the women's staff quarters, I turned to look back. But the alcove was empty. Tristan was nowhere to be seen.

I blinked, bewildered. Perhaps I'd just imagined him. Perhaps I'd just imagined everything that had happened in the past hour. Perhaps I was actually still lying in bed and I'd dreamed the whole thing. I didn't have a fishy taste in my mouth, the hotel wasn't bankrupt, there was no suitcase full of dirty money, and I hadn't behaved like a complete idiot in front of probably the hottest guy on the planet.

But then the door opened from the inside, and the door handle banged into my hip so hard that I was pretty sure I wasn't dreaming.

I was most definitely awake.

"Sorry, didn't mean to." One of the temps from the kitchen squeezed past me with an apologetic smile.

"My bad," I replied, slipping through the door.

And all before 7 a.m.! Unbelievable, the things you see as an early bird.

8

You already knew?" I looked at Monsieur Rocher in amazement. I'd been wondering all day whether and how I should tell him about the conversation between the two Montfort brothers, and now that I'd told him he wasn't even surprised. Nor was he outraged or horrified. He just listened quietly and attentively till I'd finished, and looked as though *he* felt sorry for *me*. And I'd been so worried about how he would react and how I was ever going to console him. This was *his* hotel. For him, Old Stucky, Anni Moser, even for Fräulein Müller and all the others, Castle in the Clouds wasn't just their place of work; it was their home. I'd been expecting more of a reaction.

"I know I'm just the concierge, but it's obvious from the dwindling number of guests that the hotel isn't making a profit anymore," said Monsieur Rocher calmly. "It's been spending more than it can afford to on staff and maintenance for a long while now, and the loans it's taken out are no longer enough to cover its costs. The idea of bringing in an investor has been in the cards for a good few years." He straightened his glasses. "A very sensible idea, if you ask me. If the right investor could be found."

"Yes, and Burkhardt certainly isn't the right investor! He wants to set up a golf shop in the library. Which wouldn't make much sense without a golf course. And they were talking about chairlifts, parking lots, and cable cars, too." In my indignation, I forgot to keep my voice down.

But Ben, who was standing at Reception talking to a late arrival (the British actor—I wouldn't have recognized him, incidentally), didn't seem to have heard me. I'd have loved to ask him whether he knew about his father's plans and what he thought of them. So far, I hadn't had the opportunity, and, to be honest, I didn't really know how to go about it. I'd run into Ben in the laundry room earlier when I'd popped in to deliver Pavel's apple and cinnamon cake and pick up Gracie's cat hat. Thanks to Pavel, the hat now looked as good as new. Ben had been sitting cross-legged with a sandwich in his hand on top of Bertha, who was merrily rumbling away. It had all looked wonderfully cozy. Pavel had been singing the bass aria from Bach's *Christmas Oratorio*, and I—momentarily overcome with Christmas spirit—had taken the part of the solo trumpet. The machines were making such a racket that all our musical inhibitions melted away. Ben had thought my impromptu trumpet impression was hilarious, and without further ado he'd turned Tired Bertha into a giant drum. For a few minutes we'd sung, drummed, and trumpeted with joyous abandon. But then Ben had jumped down off Bertha, excused himself, and dashed out of the room. Lifelong interns didn't get proper breaks in their contracts, it seemed.

"Joyful shepherds, hurry, oh hurry!" Pavel had sung after him.

"Yes, the plans do sound rather worrying," said Monsieur Rocher now, smiling at me reassuringly, "but they're still only plans."

I didn't know how he could be so calm.

"In the late seventies, there was talk of using the mountain as a ski resort and building a cable car. But people soon went off the idea."

"But Gordon Montfort seems to be hell-bent on selling the hotel as quickly as possible. And he doesn't care what Burkhardt does with it." I lowered my voice a little. "They mentioned a suitcase full of dirty money."

Even this didn't seem to surprise Monsieur Rocher. "The waste disposal industry appears to be a shady but very lucrative business." He sipped his cappuccino, which I'd managed to wangle out of the kitchen staff even though it wasn't officially coffee-break time. I hadn't wanted to turn up at the concierge's lodge empty-handed when I was the bearer of such bad news.

My babysitting shift had finished at four thirty and, apart from the half ton of glitter I'd had to shake out of my hair afterward, it had been uneventful and drama-free. This was probably due to the fact we'd seen neither hide nor hair of Don Burkhardt Jr. all day, not even when we'd gone around the hotel showing off the unicorns the children had made. I'd started to hope the Burkhardts might have checked out and gone home, but it turned out Don was just suffering from a stomach bug. If it was anyone else, I'd have felt sorry for them. But this was clearly karma in action.

"It's not the first time Mr. Burkhardt has closed a deal with a suitcase full of cash, incidentally," Monsieur Rocher confided after a moment's pause.

"Seriously?" I whispered.

Monsieur Rocher nodded. "But until now, as far as I'm aware, he's only ever invested in incineration plants, recycling firms, landfill sites, and nuclear-waste repositories—a hotel would be a completely new line of business for him. He obviously wants to try his hand at something different."

But this hotel wasn't a millionaire's plaything! If Burkhardt was so set on getting into the hospitality business and if he was so keen on modern facilities, then why, of all the hotels he could have bought, had he chosen this one with all its nooks and crannies, alcoves, bay windows, turrets, and architectural flourishes? Couldn't he start off with a simpler project? "Gutless . . . er . . . the younger of the Montfort brothers said Burkhardt wants to make a hundred rooms out of the thirty-five we've got now."

"That would be possible, in theory, if you factored in all the empty rooms in the attic and if you didn't provide staff accommodation at the hotel anymore."

"But that's terrible!" I said, far too loudly. This time, Ben looked over at me and raised his eyebrows inquiringly. I shot him a quick smile. Poor Ben. If my suspicions were correct, his time as a lifelong intern at the hotel was almost at an end.

"He loves this place," his uncle Gilbert had said.

I loved this place, too, and I'd only been here since September— how much more must Ben love it, having known it his whole life?

"Those are the Smirnovs, by the way, from the Panorama Suite." Monsieur Rocher cocked his chin at the couple now walking toward us. Having missed their arrival the night before, I was particularly curious about the Smirnovs. I gazed at them as I pushed our cappuccino cups discreetly out of sight behind the little postcard rack and took a few steps backward to blend unobtrusively into the rear wall.

Mrs. Smirnov looked to be in her early thirties, a strikingly attractive woman with smooth skin and meticulously styled shiny brown hair that tumbled over the fur collar of her fitted jacket. She was wearing a pair of incredibly high heels that she didn't seem to have any trouble walking in. She crossed the lobby with the long strides of a catwalk model, flicked her hair off her shoulder with her right hand, and elegantly swung a handbag in her left. Her fingernails were painted a deep red to match her lipstick. Not until she put the handbag down on the desk did I realize there was a small dog inside it. The smallest dog I'd ever seen. It looked like a fluffy white teddy bear with black button eyes, and even its bark sounded artificial, like a cartoon dog.

"Is emergency," the dog's mistress declared in English, with a strong Russian accent. "My husband says zere is no boutique here, no shop, no perfumery. Is zis true?"

"That's right, Madam," Monsieur Rocher replied. "But we do try to get hold of anything our guests require as quickly as possible. What can I do for you?"

"Clive Christian." Mrs. Smirnov waved her hand in an extremely dramatic fashion. "I cannot live wizout."

That sounded bad. But who was Clive Christian? Monsieur Rocher didn't seem to know, either, and sounded slightly confused as he asked, "I beg your pardon?"

Now Mr. Smirnov approached the desk. He was considerably older than his wife, in his late forties or early fifties at least, and unlike her he was dressed quite plainly, in a gray sweater and loose-fitting trousers. He was slim and very good-looking in a melancholy, long-nosed, bald-headed sort of way. On his shoulders sat a little girl of perhaps three or four, who was holding onto her father's bald head with both hands and staring at us in wide-eyed silence. She had cute curly hair and was wearing a little two-piece dress that looked a bit like a waistless version of her mother's outfit (fur collar included).

"This man does not understand me," said Mrs. Smirnov accusingly to her husband, and then added something in Russian that sounded irritable and not entirely complimentary.

The man smiled at Monsieur Rocher in a friendly way. "I'm

sorry! She dropped a perfume bottle in the bathroom and is very upset about it." His pronunciation was much better than his wife's.

"Yes, is emergency!" she cried. "As I say! Clive Christian No. 1. If I cannot wear, I feel naked. How soon can you get for me?"

Monsieur Rocher opened his mouth to reply, but Mr. Smirnov beat him to it. "No, Stella," he said softly but firmly. "It's the weekend, tomorrow is Christmas Eve, and out there it is chaos with the snow. You saw yourself how far away we are from the nearest town, and for this special perfume they might have to travel even as far as Geneva. And since you do not want to put anyone to such trouble, you can use one of your other perfumes."

Mrs. Smirnov looked at him in consternation. She said something in Russian that sounded very sulky, something about "Chanel," and turned on her heel. "And he is ze one who always says my ozzer perfumes give him headache! What have I done to deserve zis? All our friends are in Saint Moritz or the Caribbean, but we must come to zis strange place far away from civilization. Zis year of all years!" She flounced off angrily in the direction of the staircase. The handbag barked in agreement.

"Please excuse my wife's behavior." Mr. Smirnov smiled sadly at Monsieur Rocher. His daughter chirped something and stretched her hand out toward the gold stars and little birds hanging from the garland of fir branches above the desk. "She sometimes needs a little time to get used to a situation."

"I'm sure the peace and quiet and the fresh mountain air will do her good," Monsieur Rocher replied.

Mr. Smirnov went up on tiptoe to help his daughter reach the garland. Instead of grabbing at them, as I'd feared she might, she gently stroked one of the little birds.

"I came here once as a boy, you know, and I have wonderful memories of this place. You might even say it saved my life. I was twelve years old then," said Mr. Smirnov. He paused and looked expectantly at Monsieur Rocher, but Monsieur Rocher said nothing. I could hardly bear the suspense, and in his shoes I'm sure I would have blurted out the question: How could this place possibly have saved a little Russian boy's life?

But Smirnov went on without being prompted. "I am very glad to see how little has changed here. As if time has stood still. For thirty years. Even the telephone is still the same. And you—you haven't changed at all. Although that can't be right. It must have been your father who helped me?"

Helped him with what, for goodness' sake? Couldn't he be a little more specific? I was dying of curiosity here.

Monsieur Rocher laughed softly. "Anyone over thirty probably looks ancient to a twelve-year-old. But thank you for the compliment, Mr.—er—Smirnov." The hesitation before the name, and the pointed emphasis he placed on it, were very unusual for Monsieur Rocher. Usually all the guests' names, along with their details and personal information, were engraved completely and indelibly upon his memory as soon as he'd added them to his list.

Smirnov smiled wistfully. "Of course you don't remember me. I'm sure I was just one child among the many you had to comfort over the years. But I will never forget you. You told me nobody can take away your home if you are at home within yourself. And that we have everything inside us that we need to be happy, wherever we are."

Yes, that sounded like Monsieur Rocher. He was always coming out with pearls of wisdom like that. It often made me want to run off and fetch a notebook so I could write down what he'd said.

"There was a big change ahead of me in my life back then, which I was very afraid of," Smirnov went on. "I hated everything and everyone, and I'd had enough of the world. But by the time we left this hotel, in some strange way I was ready for the changes and for anything else life might throw at me."

And today he was a multimillionaire with a fleet of private jets, a beautiful little daughter, and a bodyguard. His life was going pretty well, I'd say. It was only his choice of wife that left a little to be desired.

"Yes, this place can work wonders, sometimes," said Monsieur Rocher lightly, and turned briefly to me.

Smirnov nodded. He patted his little daughter's legs, which were dangling on his chest, one over each shoulder. The girl stroked the stars on the fir garland contentedly. "That's why I was determined to bring my family here so they could get to know the hotel, too. I hope they'll feel something of the magic I felt back then. And take something of the strength of this place away with them."

"Oh, I'm sure they will." Monsieur Rocher glanced at his list. "And I'm sure they'll enjoy the sleigh ride tomorrow. Dusk is always the loveliest time for a sleigh ride. I can have the kitchen prepare you a flask of hot chocolate to take with you and perhaps a few cookies."

The little girl clapped her hands and cried, "*Loshadka!*" or something along those lines, and Smirnov laughed. It made him look ten years younger.

"That's right, Dasha, horses! Horses pull the sleigh. I always think she doesn't understand any English, then she goes and surprises me."

"I hope you all have a wonderful stay at Castle in the Clouds," said Monsieur Rocher.

"Thank you," Smirnov replied. "Thank you so much for everything." As he reached the staircase, he turned back. "It's incredibly reassuring to see that time hasn't changed you or this hotel."

Time hasn't, I thought as I watched him go. *But people with suitcases full of dirty money and crazy refurbishment plans certainly will.*

My eyes met Ben's—he'd clearly been listening from his post behind the reception desk. For a couple of seconds, we looked at each other earnestly, and I was almost sure he was thinking the same thing I was. Then his phone rang, and he smiled apologetically.

I'd try and talk to him later.

"Can you really not remember Mr. Smirnov as a little boy, Monsieur Rocher?" I asked.

"Oh, Sophie." Monsieur Rocher looked at the clock on the wall behind me. Strictly speaking, it was three clocks. But only the one in the middle showed Central European Time; the other two showed the time in New York and Tokyo. "Doesn't your evening shift in the spa start at six?"

"Yes," I exclaimed in surprise and headed straight out the door. It was 5:59. I would just about make it.

9

Officially, of course, double shifts were not allowed, but unofficially everyone at the hotel worked many more hours than the legal limit and didn't always take all the breaks they were entitled to. Pierre, for example, not only worked the early shift in the kitchen but was also on the bartending rotation, meaning he worked almost nonstop from six thirty in the evening until eleven thirty the next morning. Pavel practically lived in the laundry room—he always wanted to be on the spot in case anything went wrong with the machines—and Monsieur Rocher was at his post in the concierge's lodge from early in the morning till late at night, seven days a week. Even Fräulein Müller seemed to be constantly on duty. In all the months I'd been here, I'd never seen her out of uniform. Which was why it would never have entered my head to complain about my work schedule.

Anyway, my shift in the spa was so easy it could scarcely even be called *work*. All I had to do was keep the shelves stocked with clean white towels, pick up any used towels I found lying around, and fill up the drink dispensers and fruit bowls. As well as discreetly cleaning up after the guests, mopping up puddles of water, and popping my head into the sauna occasionally to check no one had locked themselves in or fallen asleep there (both of which I presumed must have happened before).

The only really challenging aspect of the job—apart from surviving the tropical heat in my chambermaid's uniform and black support tights—was keeping Mr. Heffelfinger happy.

Mr. Heffelfinger was new here, and the first time he'd set eyes on the spa of which he'd just become manager, he'd been plunged into a deep depression. Admittedly, the spa area didn't have much of the belle epoque charm that characterized the rest of the hotel, which had been built in the late nineteenth century. In fact, the spa didn't really have any charm at all. The one thing that set this section of the hotel apart was its complete lack of beauty and style. The spa had been built in the basement of the south wing in the 1980s and hadn't been altered since. Only the rooms on the west side had windows to let daylight in; the rest was just basement, and there was no pretending otherwise. The downlights set into the ceiling gave off a bright, harsh light, and the massage and beauty treatment rooms had the ambience of a dentist's office. The walls were covered floor to ceiling in beige tiles with dark beige streaks, and underfoot were dark beige tiles with light beige streaks. There was only one sauna, the twelve-by-thirty-foot pool was distinctly average and rather on the small side, and the showers were a bit like those old-fashioned locker rooms you find in school gyms. Everything was kept meticulously tidy and sparkling clean, but with the best will in the world you couldn't have called it pretty.

"I've seen abattoirs with more atmosphere. This is not a spa; it's a catastrophe," said Mr. Heffelfinger as he arranged semiprecious stones, scented candles, and an artificial magnolia branch on a silver platter. He glanced nervously at the door as he did so. Any minute now, Mrs. Smirnov from the Panorama Suite would be coming in for her herbal stamp massage, and since last night when I'd foolishly told him about the deluxe welcome package, the bodyguard, and the private jet, Mr. Heffelfinger had convinced himself that he would never be able to meet this lady's expectations. There was clearly a great deal of professional pride at stake.

"I'm so ashamed I just want the ground to open up and swallow me," he'd wailed. "Any elite guest who sets foot in this spa is going to go straight back out again and tell the world how low Manuel Heffelfinger has sunk. This is the end of my career."

If I'd mentioned that Mrs. Smirnov would much rather be spending the holidays with her friends in the Caribbean or Saint Moritz, he would surely have burst out crying.

"That's not true, Mr. Heffelfinger!" I'd said, trying to cheer him up. "Just look at this place! You've only been here three days and already you've done wonders with it. Mrs. Smirnov is going to love these luxurious drink dispensers with lime and cucumber slices. And the way you used a mirror to cover up that crack in the wall by the pool was genius!"

"Thank you—that's kind of you," Mr. Heffelfinger said, sniffing. He was probably in his early forties, a small, attractive man with short, neatly trimmed hair and perfectly manicured hands that trembled when he was nervous. "And I got rid of that ugly old tanning bed, don't forget, which I'm sure nobody would ever have used again unless they wanted to look like a piece of dried meat." He looked from the clock on the wall to the door and back again. There were only two minutes to go until Mrs. Smirnov's appointment. "Heaven knows I've done all I could to dim that hideous lighting that showcases everyone's cellulite and to make the tiles look a little less ghastly. But those are just superficial improvements! What good are scented candles and orchids when our guests are expecting a spa like the ones they're used to from other luxury hotels? Have you seen a steam room anywhere around here? A chromotherapy sauna?" The words came rushing out faster and faster: "A gemstone sauna? An herbal sauna, a panorama sauna? An ice fountain, a plunge pool, a cascade shower? A Jacuzzi, an outdoor pool, a seawater pool, a thermal pool?"

He probably could have gone on like this indefinitely, so I interrupted him. "But you have made it very . . . very stylish and comfortable." Well, compared to an abattoir, anyway. "Putting that daybed in the alcove was a great idea. I don't know what you said to Fräulein Müller to get her to give you all this—all these cushions and vases and mirrors and jugs and silver trays." Fräulein Müller had even rustled up a gilt-framed oil painting by an unknown artist to help decorate the alcove. The voluptuous woman in the painting, reclining on a chaise longue by a pool full of water lilies, had presumably been consigned to a junk room several decades ago because of her semi-nakedness. But here she fit in perfectly—and anything that covered up a few of these beige tiles was a blessing.

"Oh, Fräulein Müller is a true kindred spirit." A smile crept over Mr. Heffelfinger's face. "She even managed to unearth these bamboo screens in a storage room."

The door opened, and his smile froze into a grimace of fear. I immediately felt guilty again. I really shouldn't have told him about the bodyguard. He probably thought that if Mrs. Smirnov wasn't happy with her spa treatment he was going to be taken out and shot.

But it was only Mrs. Ludwig from Room 107, who walked in wrapped in her bathrobe and looked around hesitantly. She smiled with relief when she saw me.

"Ah, my dear, I'm so glad you're here. Now I can ask you what the etiquette is." She pointed at her feet, looking rather embarrassed.

"Am I allowed to wear the hotel slippers in the spa? I forgot to bring my own flip-flops from home."

"Of course you are," I assured her. "I can give you a new pair of slippers if yours get dirty or wet. Just say the word."

"You're a treasure, as always!" said Mrs. Ludwig.

Mr. Heffelfinger watched her as she walked past the sauna and the relaxation room and disappeared in the direction of the swimming pool. "At least I can be sure *that* lady doesn't know me from Arosa or Saint Moritz."

Then the door opened again, and Mr. Heffelfinger clutched at his heart. But it wasn't Mrs. Smirnov (who was by now five minutes late). It was Tristan Brown. Since our meeting early that morning, I *might* perhaps have thought about him once or twice—okay, maybe more—but it still took me by surprise just how incredibly good-looking he was, as if I'd forgotten in the intervening hours. In Mr. Heffelfinger's cellulite-friendly lighting, his skin was a gleaming golden brown and he made the horrible hotel bathrobe look like designer clothing.

"Good Lord," whispered Mr. Heffelfinger, awestruck.

I thought that was a *little* over-the-top.

When Tristan saw me, he smiled, "Ah. Agent Sophie. Have I wandered into the playroom by mistake?"

"No, sir. This is the spa." It wasn't that I couldn't think of a good comeback, it was just that our game wasn't any fun with somebody else there. And I was also afraid that little beads of sweat were forming on my upper lip. I could only hope the lighting was as flattering to my complexion as it was to his. "You'll find the Finnish sauna through here, and the pool at the end there. The water temperature is eighty degrees."

A moment ago, his smile had been the smile of someone who knows exactly how irresistible he is. But now Tristan seemed positively amused. He shot a glance at Mr. Heffelfinger. "Eighty degrees happens to be my favorite temperature," he said, strutting off down the corridor like a catwalk model for bathrobes.

"Did he say the *playroom*?" Mr. Heffelfinger looked horrified. "Does he think the decor looks childish?" He wrung his hands. "It's too colorful, isn't it? I knew it: *Less is more*, that's usually my motto. It's just that this place is so ugly I thought *the more, the better* . . ." He broke off as the door opened again.

All five Barnbrooke girls now entered the room: Ella and Gretchen first, followed by Gracie and Madison and, finally, Amy.

Mr. Heffelfinger gurgled something that sounded like "ChChCh," his eyes wide with dismay. But I had no time to find out what was wrong with him because Madison immediately called out "Sophie!" and Gracie came rushing up to me and threw her arms around me.

I should point out that very close friendships can develop when you spend the whole day making glittery unicorns with somebody and inventing a secret language that only unicorns and their friends can understand. Which was what I'd done with Madison and Gracie and the three other children in the playroom that day, including Anton and Elias, the sons of a well-known thriller writer who was giving a reading in the hotel over the holidays. Anton had christened his unicorn Sparkleslasher and Elias's was named Stabbyhorn, but apart from that they seemed to be perfectly ordinary children. Together we'd founded the top secret Unicorn Club.

"Ella and Gretchen say only real unicorns can grant wishes," cried Gracie, and Madison added: "Rhubarbish swamp cows." (The secret language wasn't quite perfected yet.)

Mr. Heffelfinger, who still looked horrified, gasped out something in Swiss German that I couldn't understand.

Ella and Gretchen paid no attention to the two younger children or to me. They were busy looking around and whispering to each other.

I knew at once what they were looking for. Or rather, whom.

"The pool is along there, right at the end," I informed them.

"We *know*," replied Gretchen snootily.

"We're just having a little look around," said Ella.

"Yeah—looking for Tristan Brown," Madison explained. "We met him at dinner and he's supercute and now Ella and Gretchen are fighting over which one of them gets to go out with him."

"Nonsense," said Gretchen. "We're not fighting." Then, under her breath but not quite quietly enough, she murmured to Ella, "And even if we were, it wouldn't be any of that weird chambermaid's business!"

Ella giggled.

Rhubarbish swamp cows, the two of them. I tried to keep my facial expression as neutral as possible.

"They've got waterproof mascara on," Madison told me. "And Ella's wearing a bikini with only one strap. And they don't want us to come swimming with them. For obvious reasons."

"Because you're annoying and embarrassing," said Ella. "You're a pain in the butt, both of you."

"I'm going to ask Tristan whether he'd rather go out with Amy instead of Gretchen or Ella," said Gracie. "She's so much nicer and smarter. I don't know why boys always have to be so stupid."

Amy blushed. I could see that even in this dim light.

"Can't you just leave us alone?" Ella rolled her eyes. "Why can't you just go to bed like normal kids?"

"No . . . no. . . . *no children*!" Mr. Heffelfinger spluttered, pointing to a sign on the door. At last I understood what he'd been trying
to say the whole time.

CHILDREN UNDER 16 ARE NOT ALLOWED IN THE SPA said the
sign, in four languages. (There was another sign on the outside of
the door saying the same thing, which made more sense really, provided the children could read.)

Ella and Gretchen were delighted. "Ha!" Ella gloated. "Children
and dogs are not allowed. At last, some sensible rules."

"Come on, Mr. Heffelfinger, surely you can turn a blind eye
just this once. They only want to cut through to the pool quickly." I
looked pleadingly at him. Gretchen and Ella had already sauntered
off and were waving gleefully back at us over their shoulders. They
hadn't realized children were allowed in the swimming pool, just
not the spa area.

"No! Out of the question!" Mr. Heffelfinger had recovered the
power of speech. "They will be so kind as to go around the other
way." He jabbed his index finger at Gracie. "The last thing anybody
wants to see when they're coming out of the sauna naked is a . . . is
a . . ."

"Child?"

"Exactly. A child is the last thing you want to see. Children have
an unsettling way of staring at you without blinking. And a ten-
dency to ask awkward questions when you're naked. This is a place
of relaxation! An oasis of calm! It's no place for children." He flapped
his hands around violently as he spoke, as if trying to shoo away a
swarm of bees. "Send them away before Mrs. Smirnov sees them and
my fate is sealed."

Although he was speaking in German, Gracie, Madison, and Amy had understood enough to know that Mr. Heffelfinger was less than pleased to see them. They'd already retreated to the door.

"Don't worry, he's harmless." I smiled reassuringly at them and opened the door. "Come with me! You can get to the pool this way, too, and to be honest it's a nicer route—no naked people."

"Tell them adults don't want children hanging around gawping at them," Mr. Heffelfinger hissed after us.

I was definitely *not* going to tell them that.

"And tell them no jumping in the pool! No screaming! No lying on the loungers without a towel! No peeing in the water . . ."

I shut the door. "He's a nice guy really," I murmured apologetically. "He's just feeling a little flustered right now."

In the pool, Tristan was swimming laps—if you can really call thirty feet a lap. Ella and Gretchen had already taken their bathrobes off. They looked extremely peeved when I came around the corner with Amy, Gracie, and Madison, and Gracie belly-flopped into the pool right beside Tristan.

I couldn't help grinning as I returned to the spa. Whatever Ella and Gretchen were planning to do to impress Tristan, Madison and Gracie were going to make it mighty difficult for them.

When I rejoined Mr. Heffelfinger, I found Mrs. Smirnov had finally arrived for her treatment (more than twenty minutes late) and was complaining volubly about what a complete disaster her day had been. When she realized Mr. Heffelfinger understood hardly any English, she switched to Russian, which immediately made everything she said sound a lot more dramatic.

Trembling, Mr. Heffelfinger led her into the massage room,

watched closely by Mrs. Ludwig, who was now back from the swimming pool. She was sitting on the new daybed leafing through one of the glossy magazines Mr. Heffelfinger had put there.

"Good heavens," she murmured.

"I know," I said rather anxiously. "I hope his hands won't still be trembling during the massage."

"Oh, I was talking about the lady," said Mrs. Ludwig. "She looks so familiar."

"Mrs. Smirnov?"

"Is that her name? It must not be her, then." Mrs. Ludwig sat up straighter. "But she looks just like the wife of that Russian oligarch who just gave three million to a marine conservation project—Viktor Yegorov. They say he's richer than Bill Gates. Wait, I think there's a photo in here of a charity event in Cannes, attended by Caroline of Monaco." She started flicking through one of the magazines. "Oh, I do love these magazines. Though I never buy them myself, of course, because they're too expensive. You don't see many photos of Viktor Yegorov—he tends to stay out of the public eye—but his wife is often spotted at film premieres, celebrity parties, and charity events. And she's always being invited to stay on the yacht of that real estate tycoon and his wife. Before she married Viktor Yegorov, she was a very rich supermodel." She laid the first magazine aside and picked up the next one. "It must be somewhere in here. Ah—you see, my dear? That lady in the backless dress: Isn't she just the spitting image of Mrs. Smirnov?"

I stared at the photo. It was true. Either Mrs. Smirnov had a clone, or . . .

"Stella Yegorov, thirty-four, turns heads in a gorgeous red Dolce

& Gabbana dress as she parties without husband Viktor," said the caption.

Stella was Mrs. Smirnov's first name, too. It had to be more than a coincidence.

"Perhaps they're here incognito," Mrs. Ludwig mused. "It must be tiresome to be photographed all the time. And the press has been speculating recently about Viktor Yegorov's uneasy relationship with the Russian government." She beamed at me. "This is all terribly exciting! I think I'll stay down here for a little while. Perhaps I'll try out the sauna. It's supposed to be very good for you. Do you have anything I can just pop my jewelry in, my dear? And what should I do about towels? Am I allowed more than two? Mr. Ludwig will be wondering where I've got to, but when I get back and tell him who I've met, he won't believe his ears. Oh, this really is a wonderful place!"

Yes, and full of surprises.

While Mrs. Ludwig delighted in trying out the sauna and waiting for the massage room door to open again, I poked my head around the door of the pool area to check that everything was all right. Tristan was sitting on a lounger surrounded by Ella, Gretchen, and Madison. He didn't look bothered by all the attention—quite the opposite, in fact. He seemed to be rather enjoying it.

Gracie was floating in the pool on her back. She spat a stream of water at the ceiling and called, "Look, Tristan! I'm a whale!"

The only person missing was Amy. I found her outside in the corridor, leaning against the wall and looking rather unsure of herself.

"I should have brought a book with me," she said awkwardly when she saw me.

I put down the basket of freshly laundered towels and began folding them and rolling them up. "There are much nicer places in the hotel to sit and read."

"I know." Amy sighed. "My favorite place is the window seat in the library. I've spent whole afternoons there with a book, watching the snow fall and stroking the cat. And I like the little vestibule on the second floor, too, behind the curtains. And the bay window in the bar in the early mornings, when there's no one around. Nobody can find you there."

"Who do you not want to find you?"

Amy shrugged. "Take your pick. My mom, who's always telling me to *stand up straight, Amy, you've always got your nose in a book, Amy, you need to learn to have a little fun, Amy*. My dad, who always looks at me with this surprised expression as if he's forgotten I even existed. That's what happens, I guess, when you've got five kids. And Gretchen and Ella, who . . . well hey, you've met them. You know what they're like." She bent down to pick up one of the towels. "Can I give you a hand?"

I looked at her in surprise, but she seemed to be serious about the offer and asked me to tell her what to do.

"Mr. Heffelfinger wants them rolled up like this, see. He says it looks more elegant. And then we have to stack them up, six to every shelf. Yes, just like that."

For a while we folded, rolled, and stacked in silence, and then Amy said suddenly, "Gretchen and Ella told Aiden I'm learning sign language. And now he thinks I'm in love with him."

Thanks to Monsieur Rocher I knew exactly who she was talking about. Aiden was the boy the Barnbrooke grandparents had adopted as a teenager, which meant he was Amy's adopted uncle and not a blood relation. So I guess it was okay if she was in love with him.

"Hmm," I said, hoping I sounded as understanding and supportive as Monsieur Rocher always did.

It seemed to encourage Amy to go on, anyway. "Aiden's been really weird with me since they told him that. He hardly looks at me. And . . ." She sighed. So deeply it almost made me want to sigh, too. "We always used to get along so well. Even without being able to talk to each other. The only time I've ever been annoyed with him was two years ago, when Ella and Gretchen used him as a guinea pig and he went along with it."

"As a guinea pig?" Now I definitely didn't sound like Monsieur Rocher, just like myself.

"Yes—they wanted someone to practice kissing with." Amy snorted angrily. "Apparently Aiden is particularly good at kissing. Gretchen thinks it's because of his . . . because he can't hear, so he's unusually sensitive and perfect for practicing with. I gave her a slap when she said that. Well, two slaps. One on the right cheek and one on the left. I slapped her so hard I actually hurt my own hand."

"Good for you," I couldn't help saying.

Amy gave a wry smile. "I was grounded for three weeks and banned from watching my favorite TV series."

"It was worth it," I said.

"I agree." Amy gave me a grateful sideways glance. Then she sighed again. "That's why I don't understand why Aiden's being so weird with me. He knows I never . . . and even if . . . after all, you can learn sign language without being in love . . . I mean, I'm the same person I was before."

Gradually, a clear picture was emerging from the confusion.

"My friend Delia had a good friend called Paul," I told her. "Paul lived next door to her and when they were kids he rigged up this miniature cable car between his bedroom and Delia's, that little Playmobil characters could ride in. They used it to send messages to each other. Their families went on vacation together, and they got along superwell and told each other everything. Until one day Paul started acting weird. He basically stopped talking to Delia, and whenever they ran into each other at school he just blanked her and looked the other way."

Amy looked at me wide-eyed. "But why?"

"That's what Delia asked him, which wasn't easy given that Paul kept avoiding her. But in the end, he admitted he'd fallen in love with her."

"Oh," said Amy. "And what happened then?"

The truth was that Delia had felt flattered but sadly didn't feel the same way about Paul. It had been the end of their friendship. Paul hadn't spoken to Delia again for a whole year. We still called him Sulky Paul. I decided not to tell Amy about this sad ending to the story. "The reason I brought it up was that it just shows you can know someone for years and then suddenly realize the other person's not a kid anymore and you want them to be more than just a friend. Perhaps it's the same for Aiden as it was for Paul."

Amy chewed thoughtfully on her lower lip. "And what if it isn't? What if he just thinks I'm in love with him and it's making him feel really awkward?"

"*Are* you in love with him?" I asked, then stopped short. That was probably a bit too direct. But Amy didn't seem to mind.

"Maybe," she said hesitantly. "If your heart starts beating faster when you look at them and you go weak at the knees, does that mean you're in love?"

It wasn't like I'd ever been in love, but I'd read enough books and seen enough movies to answer "Yes!" with profound conviction. Or rather, I would have if Mr. Heffelfinger hadn't appeared around the corner at that very moment. Amy immediately put down the towel she'd been folding and fled in the direction of the swimming pool.

"I couldn't understand a word of what she said, but I think Mrs. Smirnov enjoyed her massage," Mr. Heffelfinger whispered happily.

"Has she gone?" I whispered back.

"No. She wants to look around the rest of the spa." He wrung his hands again. "I couldn't stop her. I've got another massage client now, so please could you make sure the children behave themselves while Mrs. Smirnov is down here? And could you do something about that old lady who keeps staring at the poor woman as if she's Beyoncé?"

"That's because she thinks Mrs. Smirnov is actually called Mrs. Yegorov," I said.

"Like the Russian oligarch?"

Of course, everyone knew the name apart from me. "Isn't an oligarch always Russian?" I asked. "Like a raven is always black?"

But Mr. Heffelfinger was already hurrying off to his next appointment.

I found Mrs. Smirnov, or whatever her name was, at the pool. Mrs. Ludwig had followed her there; she wasn't letting this unexpected celebrity guest out of her sight for a moment. Mrs. Smirnov, on the other hand, only had eyes for Tristan, who was currently drying himself off and putting his bathrobe back on. The scene was a bit like a body-spray commercial; all that was missing was music and some slow-motion camerawork. Everyone, myself included, gazed appreciatively at Tristan until he'd finished wrapping his perfect torso in white terry cloth. Gretchen even ran her tongue around her lips.

Mrs. Ludwig, however, was far more interested in Mrs. Smirnov. She hurried over to me in great excitement.

"It's definitely her," she whispered to me, perhaps a touch too loudly.

Mrs. Smirnov, aka Yegorov, gave Mrs. Ludwig a puzzled look for a moment but then smiled graciously, leaving Mrs. Ludwig beaming with joy.

Tristan set off toward the exit, and naturally the two elder Barnbrooke girls now saw no reason to stay in the pool any longer. Gracie and Madison followed hot on their heels, and the presumed oligarch's wife left via the spa, although not before booking five more massages and a facial for the coming week. Only Amy lingered—I guessed she wanted to continue our conversation from earlier. But we didn't get the chance because when Mrs. Ludwig returned to the sauna she realized she'd lost her ring. Her beaming smile vanished, to be replaced by a look of despair.

"I put it in the bowl you gave me, along with the rest of my jewelry," she said with tears in her eyes. "But now I can't find it anywhere. It's my engagement ring, you see. It's of great sentimental value to me." Her lower lip trembled, and I felt so sorry for her that I could have cried. Her engagement ring from Mr. Ludwig, of all the things to lose!

Amy and I searched every nook and cranny for the ring, but in vain. After he'd finished his appointment Mr. Heffelfinger came to help us. He turned on the bright lights so we could see better, but still the ring was nowhere to be found. We looked in all the beige-tiled corners and turned the pockets of all the bathrobes inside out, and I rifled through the laundry basket and shook out all the towels one by one. No matter hard we searched, the ring stayed lost. Eventually we gave up in frustration. It was already past eleven o'clock.

"Perhaps one of the children hid it," Mr. Heffelfinger mused once a thoroughly dejected Mrs. Ludwig had left the spa accompanied by a sympathetic Amy. "Children love playing tricks."

Either that, or the ring had been stolen. But why would anybody do such a thing? Mrs. Ludwig had said herself that the ring wasn't worth much and was purely of sentimental value.

"I don't think so," I said firmly. "I'm sure it's just fallen on the floor and rolled somewhere where we can't see it. First thing tomorrow, I'll get Jaromir to take the drain covers off so we can search the filters. We'll find it."

"I hope so." Mr. Heffelfinger blew out the scented candles with a sigh. "Otherwise that old lady is going to report us for theft—and then we'll all be suspects."

10

I was completely worn out by the time I finally left the spa that night. I was so hot you could have fried an egg on my forehead, and I felt as though my tights had melted onto my legs. And I was worried about Mrs. Ludwig. I hoped the poor woman wasn't going to lie awake all night fretting.

The Forbidden Cat was sitting in the middle of the corridor. She stood up when she saw me, as if she'd been waiting for me, then curled herself around my legs, meowed, and padded over to a narrow cellar door from which a few steps led outdoors.

The key was in the lock, so I obliged and opened the door for her. Mr. Heffelfinger used this spot for his cigarette breaks, so the first few feet of snow, although not properly cleared, were neatly trodden flat. A welcome blast of cold air rushed in through the open door. I grabbed the key—the door tended to close on its own and lock you out—then stepped outside and breathed in deeply. As the icy night air flowed into my lungs, I immediately felt better.

Snow had been falling steadily until late that afternoon, but now the sky was clear. Stars twinkled between the scattered clouds, and the almost-full moon peeked over the tops of the fir trees, bathing everything in a cool white light. The Forbidden Cat sat in the snow and stared up at the wall of the hotel. As my body temperature gradually returned to normal, I followed her gaze. We were standing on the lowest side of the hotel, seen from the outside; the only rooms on this level with windows were the spa and the kitchen below the restaurant. On the other three sides of the building the basement floor was set deep into the mountainside. Above the spa, the moonlight was reflected in the huge arched French windows of the ballroom. And above them were the rooms of the south wing. But all the windows on that floor were in darkness now except the third one from the left. That must be Room 117, where the Smirnovs'/ Yegorovs' bodyguard was staying. The last two windows on the right were the bathrooms of the Panorama Suite.

And right there, between the window of Room 117 and the bathroom windows of the Panorama Suite, there was something moving—that was what the Forbidden Cat was staring at. My heart stood still for a moment when I realized it was a human silhouette moving up there, twenty or thirty feet above me on a narrow ledge that jutted out of the wall. Quickly and very nimbly, the figure slid past the illuminated window. As the light from inside fell on his face, I recognized Tristan Brown. It was him, no doubt about it.

All sorts of thoughts raced through my head, but none of them made any sense. What kind of person went clambering about on tiny little ledges at dizzying heights in the middle of the night?

Bored circus performers. Superheroes. People contemplating suicide. Santa Claus, a day early. And hotel thieves, of course.

At that moment, the light went out in Room 117 and Tristan, who'd almost reached the window of Room 118, froze against the wall. A cloud passed slowly in front of the moon, but I could still see him quite clearly against the pale facade. A moment later, someone opened the window of Room 117. It was too dark now to see whether it was the Yegorovs' bodyguard standing there, but I could see the red glow of a cigarette and smell the smoke from it. I wondered whether Tristan and the smoker could see me when they looked down or whether I just looked like a dark patch in the snow to them.

Either way, I had no reason to feel guilty. I wasn't the one standing on a ledge where I had no business being or smoking in a nonsmoking room. Nevertheless, I stayed perfectly still. The Forbidden Cat, too, sat motionlessly as if rooted in the snow.

After what was maybe a minute—it was hard to say, though, the seconds seemed to pass so slowly—the cigarette came sailing down into the snow and fizzled out, and the smoker closed the window.

Tristan immediately continued on his way.

The most sensible thing for me to have done would probably have been to stay quiet, keep watching him, and make a note of where he climbed to. And then report the incident.

But instead of doing that, I decided to clear the matter up there and then. Otherwise I knew I wouldn't be able to sleep because of all the unanswered questions running through my head. When he was directly above me, at the window of Room 119, I meowed—loudly, and without even trying to sound like a real cat.

Tristan froze again, his body pressed to the wall. He was probably staring down at me just as I was staring up at him, but I couldn't tell in the dark.

I waved at him, then heard a soft laugh and watched, flabbergasted, as he leapt down onto the gutters and swung himself down the wall at lightning speed, like a real-life Spider-Man. When he was a few feet from the ground, the moon came out again and now I could see more clearly how skillfully he was moving, hand over hand, down the ornate stone facade. He was wearing fingerless gloves. He let himself drop the last six feet and landed softly and smoothly on his feet, like a cat.

The real cat then turned and trotted away through the snow, and for a brief moment I thought perhaps I should do the same.

"Hello," said Tristan. His teeth gleamed in the moonlight.

"Well, yes. Hello," I replied. "Sorry to disturb you, but I did just want to at least say hi. It's not every day you meet Spider-Man."

"I thought you were going to arrest me." To judge by his tone of voice, Tristan was finding this all wonderfully amusing. He was standing with his back to the moon, so his face was in shadow. I couldn't make out his expression.

"Why—were you up to no good?"

"Not as far as I know. Do you still think I'm a hotel thief?"

No! Of course I didn't! I wasn't falling for that trick. On the other hand . . . "Yes," I said sharply. "I can't think why else you'd be climbing up the side of the building in the dead of night, all in black and wearing special gloves."

Tristan laughed. "And what am I supposed to have stolen?" He looked down at his slim form.

"I have no idea," I admitted. "Perhaps I spotted you before you had time to steal anything." Then I added in a softer tone: "That's why I . . . er . . . meowed at you. So you wouldn't do something you might regret."

"Oh." Tristan's voice was serious all of a sudden. "That's very kind of you, Sophie. You seem to be not only an exceptionally pretty person but an exceptionally nice one, too."

Yes, I was. Or an exceptionally stupid one, because I found myself feeling deeply flattered.

"I can assure you," he went on, "that I haven't stolen a thing. I solemnly swear to you that nobody in this hotel is missing any of their belongings."

"Well what exactly are you doing climbing the walls, then?" I pointed to the facade. "Is this your standard evening workout after you've been for a swim?"

"Sort of," he replied. "Climbing walls is something of a hobby of mine. But people always get so terribly agitated when you do it during the daytime. Especially my grandpa. He's got a weak heart. I had to promise him years ago that I'd stop doing dangerous things." He paused for a second. "Unfortunately, I have a *penchant* for dangerous things."

I could easily believe that last bit. As for the rest, I wasn't so sure. But I half believed it.

"Mrs. Ludwig is missing her engagement ring," I said slowly, wishing he'd turn his head so I could see his face better. Was he standing with his back to the moon on purpose?

"The old lady who was in the swimming pool earlier?" he asked. "The ring with the pink stone?"

"You know what the ring looks like?" There really was only one explanation for that. A wave of emotions washed over me, a mixture of disappointment and anger. "You *did* steal it! How could you?! We've been looking for it for over an hour, and Mrs. Ludwig is crying her eyes out. And why did you take it, anyway? The ring isn't even worth anything!"

"Hey!" Tristan grabbed my arm and shook me lightly. "Sophie! I haven't stolen anything. I just noticed she had a very nice ring on, that's all."

"A boy who's interested in old ladies' jewelry?" A likely story. "Is that another hobby of yours?" I crossed my arms. I was gradually starting to notice how cold it was. Standing around in the snow when it's 5 degrees below zero and you're drenched in sweat must be a surefire way of catching pneumonia. My arm felt warm where Tristan was holding it, though. It was practically on fire.

"I like looking at people's hands," he said quietly. "You, for example, have cute little hands with slim fingers and short fingernails. You don't wear any jewelry, and you sometimes bite the skin around your nails when you're nervous."

That was true, unfortunately.

"I'm sorry the old lady lost her ring," he went on, gently. "I can help you look for it, if you like."

I took a deep breath. "You really didn't steal it?"

"No." Tristan loosened his grip on my arm, and I could hear from his voice that he was smiling again. "I swear on my grandpa's life. And apart from that, I can assure you I'm far too well educated to be a hotel thief."

I couldn't help sighing at his arrogance. But this time I believed him. Eighty percent of me did, anyway. The other 20 percent was just exhausted and wanted to go to bed. "It would have been a bit silly, seeing as the ring isn't worth anything." My teeth started chattering with cold.

Tristan let go of my arm. "Exactly! If I was going to be a hotel thief, I'd at least be a clever one. You're freezing cold! Do you want my jacket?"

"No. I'm going inside. I need to get to bed—it's been a very long day." I pointed up at the roof, my teeth still chattering. "But I'm too tired to climb. I'm going to take the stairs just this once."

"Well I had a four-hour nap this afternoon. I need a bit of exercise," said Tristan. In the blink of an eye, he'd leapt up onto the wall again and was suspended six feet above me. "I hope to see you tomorrow, Sophie."

"Unless we have to send out a search party and find you lying frozen stiff in the snow with a broken neck."

"I appreciate your concern for my welfare." He was already

another few feet higher. This time he headed left and, hanging from the gutter by one hand, he launched himself out over the buttress below the restaurant window and around the corner of the building. At least he wasn't as high up now as he had been before. I waited until he'd swung himself up over the railing onto the restaurant terrace, then I went inside.

Tristan didn't seem to take anything or anyone seriously. Maybe not even himself. I just couldn't work him out, and it was driving me up the wall.

I locked the door behind me with a sigh. I was shivering with cold by now. Yawning, teeth chattering, I climbed the stairs to the second floor. I could have taken one of the elevators, of course, but I didn't really trust the juddering, rattling old things, and taking the stairs gave me the chance to talk to Ben. He was sitting on the staircase with his long legs stretched out in front of him, thermos in hand. He must be having a midnight feast.

"Sophie!" he exclaimed in surprise. "Have you only just got off work?"

I nodded. "Mrs. Ludwig from Room 107 lost her ring. And then I spent a bit too long outside in the snow cooling off."

Ben held out the thermos. "Then I've got the perfect remedy."

I shook my head. "I'd better not if it's coffee."

"It's tea. This'll warm you right up." He unscrewed the lid of the flask to use as a cup, poured in some of the steaming liquid, and handed it to me.

I sat down beside him hesitantly, took a big gulp from the cup, and immediately started coughing. "Didn't you say it was tea?" I spluttered, once I'd regained the power of speech.

He grinned. "Tea with a dash of rum."

Eighty-proof rum, by the taste of it. I took another, much more cautious sip, and the tea ran down my throat like fire. I handed the cup back to Ben.

We eyed each other. "You don't look very lively, either, I must say." He had dark circles under his eyes. Again, I was struck by his resemblance to his father. The same well-formed facial features, the blue eyes, the firm chin—and yet they were so different. In Ben's eyes I could see intelligence, trust, and genuine interest, while his father always came across as cold and disdainful.

Ben looked away before I did and sipped at his tea. "I made the mistake of not taking a nap while I was off-shift and doing some studying for biology instead. We've got a test as soon as we get back after the holidays. I need to try and do well on my exams now that I'm . . ." He broke off and took another sip. Then he grinned at me. "I think there's more than a dash of rum in here."

"Now that you're what?" I asked gently.

Ben sighed. "You know, I always thought my life was all mapped out for me. That I'd finish school and go on to study hotel management and eventually take over the running of the hotel my great-grandfather built." With a little smile, he filled up the cup again. "But things can change. And suddenly you find you're a free agent."

I couldn't help thinking of what I'd overheard Gordon Montfort saying that morning from the linen cupboard. "And is that good or bad?" I asked.

Ben looked pensively at me. "Good question," he said. "I have no idea what it means to be completely free. How did it feel to drop out of school?"

"Have you been reading my personnel records?"

Ben blushed slightly. "Um. Yeah. I'm sorry."

He didn't need to be sorry; I'd have done the same in his shoes. "It didn't feel great." I was surprised to find myself admitting it so openly. Until now I'd always avoided talking to anyone but Delia about it. To be honest, I'd avoided even thinking about it. "My parents freaked out. They couldn't imagine how you could survive in this world without having a degree. Or a carefully laid life plan. It's like they knew they wanted to be teachers from the day they were born. But all *I* know is what I *don't* want to do. And sometimes not even that."

Ben patted my arm sympathetically. "It was different for me," he said. "It was just always there. It was my past, my present, and my future."

It was clearly the hotel. I decided to put all my cards on the table, so he didn't feel he had to speak in riddles anymore. "I know about your dad wanting to sell the hotel."

"Really?" For a moment Ben looked wide awake again. "Does the whole staff know?"

"I have no idea," I said truthfully. "Probably not. I just happened to overhear . . ." (just happened to, while I was hiding in a cupboard) ". . . your dad talking to your uncle about selling the hotel to Burkhardt."

"Who is going to destroy it." Ben grimaced. "I'm afraid this place will be unrecognizable by the time he's finished with it." After a short pause, in which I visualized again the golf shop in the library, he added sadly, "It seems to be the only way to stop the hotel from going bankrupt."

"But if your dad sells, you'll be free to choose whatever job you like and live wherever you want," I said, quoting what his dad had said that morning almost word for word.

Ben filled the cup again, handed it to me, and took a gulp from the thermos. "But what if *this* is where I want to live?" He looked at me earnestly. "Has anyone ever told you you've got very . . . lovely eyes? They're not brown or gray or properly green; they're somewhere in between. So pretty. And so bright. Like you're lit up from the inside. When you look at me, I feel like I want to tell you all my secrets."

He did? Embarrassed, I took another sip of the tea and rum cocktail. And then another. "Mr. Smirnov from the Panorama Suite is actually called Mr. Yegorov," I said at last. I could share secrets, too. It was my way of telling Ben that I thought his eyes were lovely, too.

But it didn't win me any brownie points.

"I know," he said, unimpressed. "He wanted to come here incognito because of the press. And all the commotion he'd have caused otherwise because of the diamond."

"Diamond?" I sat up straighter.

"That huge rock he bought at auction at Christie's. It was a present for his wife on their wedding day. Worth as much as a small island, apparently. It used to belong to Catherine the Great, then it went missing for a long time and everyone thought it was lost. And they say it's cursed, just like any respectable diamond."

"And it's here in the hotel?" I asked, my eyes wide.

"Not yet," Ben replied. "But someone's going to bring it here in the next couple of days because Mrs. Yegorov wants to wear it for the New Year's Ball. Why? Are you afraid the curse is going to get you?"

"Of course not." It was just that I happened to have come across someone scaling the walls of the hotel only a few minutes earlier, and he'd been coming from the Panorama Suite. Perhaps he was getting

125

in a bit of practice ahead of time. "Aren't you worried there might be jewel thieves here, posing as guests or staff?"

Ben laughed. "The press thinks the Yegorovs are spending the holidays on their yacht and in a luxury villa belonging to one of their fashion designer friends in the Lesser Antilles. So the jewel thieves are more likely to be hanging out there. And anyway, almost all our guests are regulars . . . Oh!"

I jumped, too. The Forbidden Cat had come slinking down the stairs behind us and now barged her way in between us, purring loudly.

"Where did you come from? You were outside a minute ago." I stroked her back. Of course, she could have come back into the building through a different entrance. Or perhaps there were several ginger cats at Castle in the Clouds. That would explain why people had been seeing them here for decades. I mustn't forget to tell Pierre about this theory.

The Forbidden Cat rubbed her head against Ben's shoulder.

"Yes, yes, all right," Ben murmured. "I'm coming." He stood up and gave me an apologetic smile. "She sleeps in my bed, you see. It's very useful, given that there's no heating up there." He looked at his watch. "Midnight exactly. The witching hour. Don't let the Lady in White get you."

"I thought she only went after people who were unlucky in love." I stood up, too, and stretched my stiff legs. The cat walked a little way up the stairs and then turned expectantly to Ben.

"It was nice talking to you, Sophie," he said emphatically. "We should do it more often, intern to intern."

"Yes, we should." I passed him the empty cup. "Sleep well."

He'd already climbed three steps when something else occurred to me. "Ben? The people in Room 211—are they regulars, too?"

"The English professor and his grandson? Not exactly regulars. But Professor Brown has been here once before, twenty years ago. Monsieur Rocher remembers him. The grandfather is an expert in antique jewelry and his grandson is studying at Oxford. Why do you ask?"

"Oh, no reason," I murmured.

11

The twenty-fourth of December began for me with the shrill beeping of the alarm clock on my phone. I'd slept like a log—if the old pipe had made any noises again in the night, they certainly hadn't made their way into my dreams. But I would have needed at least another two or three hours' sleep to get rid of the dark circles under my eyes, and that was never going to happen. I was on the early shift today, and even if my alarm hadn't woken me up, my mother would have. It was six thirty in the morning and already she was sending me texts and photos clearly designed to make me feel bad that I wouldn't be home for Christmas. One photo showed my grandma's Christmas cake in front of the organically grown Christmas tree in the living room, hung with my brothers' homemade Christmas decorations.

She couldn't have chosen a better photo to make me feel glad to be spending Christmas at Castle in the Clouds. I couldn't stand my grandma's Christmas cake because of all the raisins she put in it, and I'd always hated the forced family Christmas-tree-decoration-making sessions that took place in our house every year. My mother was an art teacher. Every Christmas, she came up with a new crafting project, and we had to implement her vision. However much she said *Be as creative as you like!*, we knew that what she really meant was *You must follow my instructions to the letter!* At least she was always creative when it came to crafting materials.

I squinted at the homemade stars in the photo. Just as I'd

thought: It looked like this year's Christmas tree decorations were made of wholegrain pasta.

"Dear Sophie!" her message said. "Mum, Dad, Leon, and Finn wish you a Merry Christmas and hope that in between the festivities up there in the mountains you also find time for some quiet reflection."

"Quiet reflection. Honestly!" I said to the Hugos on my return from the bathroom. (I'd run into the four hyenas from Lausanne there, but they'd obviously decided to ignore me as punishment for my previous behavior. It was wonderfully relaxing.) The seven jackdaws had arrived promptly on my windowsill at dawn, ready for their breakfast of milk-roll crumbs. As usual, Unbelievably Greedy Hugo ate the most, while Chubby Hugo behaved as if he was on a diet.

I loved this time just before sunrise, when it wasn't light yet but it wasn't completely dark, either. The moon had gone down a long time ago, but above Obergabelhorn a single bright star—the morning star?—shone in an almost cloudless sky. Sunshine was forecast for today, but another cold snap was coming and there was supposed to be lots more snow on its way.

"By reflection, she means she wants me to reflect on all my failings." I was so angry I forgot to talk to the Hugos in a baby voice. "She just can't accept that the higher-education ship has sailed. All the hard work I'm doing here doesn't seem to count."

Hopping Hugo and One-Legged Hugo fought over the last crumb, then they all flew away. Only Kleptomaniac Hugo carried on pecking around in the snow on the windowsill as if he were looking for something else.

"It'd be nice if they could just be proud of me for a change," I said.

Kleptomaniac Hugo hopped closer and gazed at me with his head to one side. He looked as concerned as a jackdaw can.

"I'm sorry! Super Sophie didn't mean for her bad mood to rub off on you," I said contritely. "It's Christmas, after all! What's that you've got in your beak?"

Kleptomaniac Hugo hopped a little closer, solemnly deposited a button in front of me on the windowsill and looked at me expectantly.

"Thank you!" I was quite touched. It was a shiny round gold button that must have come off a chambermaid's uniform. Perhaps I'd lost it myself. But I preferred the idea that Kleptomaniac Hugo had stolen it from Hortensia or Camilla. And all of a sudden, I felt almost festive. "That's a brilliant present. It's really cheered me up."

Kleptomaniac Hugo cawed softly, then hopped off the windowsill and flew away to join his brothers.

A few hours later, the jackdaws were still circling on the thermals high above the castle, as if keeping a close eye on everything going on below them. And there was lots for them to look at because the sunny weather had brought everybody outdoors.

Jaromir had been shoveling snow since early that morning. (He no longer had to go around dressed as a ringmaster-doorman now that all the guests had arrived—Gordon Montfort evidently thought a good first impression was enough.) Now the forecourt, the driveway, the sun terrace outside the restaurant, and the ice rink were all clear. Old Stucky had also cleared a path with the snowplow, a long circular walk that snaked its way through the snowy woods. The Von Dietrichsteins had taken their pug for a walk there right after breakfast, and Mara Matthäus's two poodles could now be seen dragging Nico toward the trees at a breakneck pace.

I'd already ushered my little flock of children outside. My prediction that there'd be enough to see out here to distract them from their excitement about their Christmas presents turned out to have been quite correct. This time I'd been smart enough to put on ski pants and snow boots myself, just in case any of the kids took it into their heads to run off into the woods.

Jaromir had started up the carousel next to the ice rink and, as it turned, barrel-organ music floated across the glittering white landscape and mingled with the soft sounds of the horse-drawn sleigh. Waiters carried tables and chairs out onto the sun terrace and started constructing an ice bar, and Gutless Gilbert supervised the setting out of loungers draped with woolen blankets. If it snowed again tomorrow all this effort would be for nothing, but for the moment all the hard work was definitely worth it. I'd never seen so many happy faces at the same time. Especially not among the adults. People went for walks in the snow, took photos of the snowy fir trees, and found nice spots to sunbathe in. The sunshine grew warmer and warmer as the day wore on.

On the ice rink, Big Daddy Barnbrooke, his son Aiden, and Gretchen's twin brother, Claus, were playing ice hockey. There was lots of whooping and yelling. Monsieur Rocher and Jonas had fetched two trunks full of ice skates (from the past four decades at least) out of the basement along with some ice hockey sticks, a puck, and two human-sized penguins with runners for feet and handles on their backs; these were for beginner skaters to hold onto so they didn't fall over. The thriller writer was talking animatedly to the old British actor, while the thriller writer's wife lay on one of the loungers reading a romance novel.

For once Tristan Brown wasn't scaling the walls of the building but was sitting at one of the little tables engrossed in a game of chess with his grandfather, who, with his white hair and tweed jacket, looked like a British aristocrat. On the terrace, Gordon Montfort shared a bottle of champagne—first with Don Burkhardt Sr. and his wife, then with the Barnbrooke grandparents. Viktor Yegorov built a snowman with little Dasha and gave it his cashmere scarf to wear. Madame Cléo ushered the waiters back and forth to the guests with trays of canelés, cream puffs, and tiny glasses of Irish coffee.

The most photographed object of the day was the horse-drawn sleigh, pulled by Jesty and Vesty with Old Stucky perched high up on the driver's seat. The Ball Bearings Baroness from Room 100 went for several extra rides in the sleigh, to make absolutely sure that Mr. Von Dietrichstein got a photo of her smooching passionately with her young lover. I'd even managed to persuade Mr. and Mrs. Ludwig to book themselves a sleigh ride. That morning before my shift, I'd gone down to the spa, where Mr. Heffelfinger had already had somebody search all the filters. But the ring seemed to be gone for good. Mrs. Ludwig had been very dejected all morning, but the sleigh ride worked like magic on her. She held hands with Mr. Ludwig and waved cheerfully as they drove away.

I was still hoping that the ring would turn up somewhere or that there was a perfectly mundane explanation for its disappearance—but I didn't have much time today to wonder where it might have gone. It was Carolyn the kindergarten teacher's day off, and I was on my own with the children. Today my faithful band of unicorns consisted of Madison, Gracie, the thriller writer's two sons, and Faye, the five-year-old daughter of a pharmaceutical executive who was staying with his family in the Fabergé Suite on the first floor. There were also four newcomers—including Don, now recovered from his stomach bug. Although I feared the worst and kept a particularly close eye on him, he behaved impeccably. He didn't spoil anyone's fun and didn't tease the other children (or me). Even his strange habit of addressing people by their full names didn't bother me today; on the contrary, it helped me remember the new children's names.

I found it surprisingly easy to keep the kids occupied all day, especially once Amy joined us later that afternoon. From here, she could watch Aiden playing ice hockey from a safe distance and she didn't have to listen to any of Ella's and Gretchen's catty comments. We still weren't sure whether Aiden's weird behavior was a good or a bad sign, but Amy was reluctant to take my advice and just ask him. "I'd rather die of a broken heart," she said. She didn't seem particularly unhappy, though—quite the opposite, in fact. She had a great day, and so did the children and I. In the morning, we had a snowball fight, fed carrots to the horses, and ate sausages and potato salad together at a big table on the terrace.

In the afternoon, we watched the squirrels, played at curling, rode on the carousel, and built a giant snow dragon out of the snow that had piled up around the edge of the ice rink when Jaromir had cleared it. We got plenty of help from the adults, and our building project gradually developed into a real team effort. By the end, it really looked as though a glittering white dragon had landed in front of Castle in the Clouds and wrapped its jagged tail around the ice rink. It was a shame this magnificent creation would soon be buried under a fresh layer of snow. But it had been photographed from all sides and so preserved for posterity.

As the sun began to sink behind the mountains, the hotel grounds emptied out as the rosy-cheeked guests went back inside to get warmed up. The children got more and more excited as Christmas Eve drew nearer, and one after the other they said good-bye to us and went off with their families. Aiden came strolling over from the ice hockey rink to accompany Amy, causing her cheeks to turn pink, too. She looked like all her Christmases had come at once.

Only Don and Faye were left. As I wiped little Faye's nose (the poor thing was suffering from a horrible cold; it was unbelievable how much snot such a tiny little nose could produce), Don started taking photos of us on his phone.

"What are you doing?" I said indignantly.

"Oh, it's just for my documentary about school dropouts," said Don. "*Choose Your Career with Care.* And I need material for my photography project, *Fifty Shades of Snot.*"

I was almost a little relieved to find him back to his old self. "You'd be really funny if you weren't so mean," I said. I snatched the phone off him and hurriedly deleted the photos.

"They're already in the cloud, anyway." Don grinned deviously, managing to look inexplicably cute at the same time. "You must have realized by now, Sophie Spark, that it's best not to mess with me. Don't count your chickens."

I wasn't. Nobody around here was safe, not if Don's father really was going to buy the hotel.

"I watched you very closely today, and do you know what I saw?" I said slowly. "A little boy having a good time without being mean to everyone. Perhaps you just forgot to be horrible, or perhaps you've had enough of it."

Don was silent for a moment. A whole range of emotions that I couldn't interpret flashed through his big brown eyes. Then he crossed his arms. "It's such a shame you can't do a degree in psychology without having graduated from high school, Sophie Spark, hopeless loser." He turned to leave. "But since tonight is Christmas

Eve, I'll give you a piece of advice for free: Don't stop looking over your shoulder. You never know what's about to happen."

He really was back to his old self. "Thanks for that," I murmured as he walked away. I hoped Santa Claus brought him back that stomach bug.

I dropped off little Faye with her mother, the only one still lying on her lounger watching the sunset, and heaved a sigh of relief. Work was over for the day, and I had the whole evening before me. The spa was closed for Christmas Eve—probably because once the guests had finished their delicious twelve-course Christmas Eve meal they'd be too full to do anything other than collapse into bed in a food coma. But most of the staff wouldn't have a minute to themselves until then. From six o'clock on, the pianist would be in the bar playing international Christmas songs for the guests to sing along to, and at nine o'clock Jaromir was taking a handful of guests to Midnight Mass at the church in the next village. The poor man would surely rather have been spending Christmas with his family in the Czech Republic.

Pierre had invited me to come and celebrate with him and the other kitchen staff in the basement after their shift was finished, but I wasn't really in the mood for a party. Not yet, anyway. Perhaps I could retire to the laundry room for a bit and hang out with Pavel; I could sing "Silent Night" with him and hear his interpretation of the line "Round yon virgin mother and child." Perhaps Ben and his thermos would join us, too. I liked that idea.

Before that, I was going to have a good long shower—Hortensia and co. were on cleaning duty until eight o'clock—and put on my nicest clothes. I didn't have any really fancy clothes with me, but I did have a smart yet comfy pair of black velvet pants that I had once worn to the opera, and I could wear my favorite green sweater with them. And perhaps I'd wear my hair down . . .

But unfortunately my transformation would have to wait a while because at that moment I happened to run into Ben's father escorting the Yegorov family to the horse-drawn sleigh. Old Stucky was waiting for them with Jesty and Vesty, and he'd lit the torches that were attached to the sleigh by iron brackets. The sun had almost set, the full moon was on the rise, and the sound of distant church bells drifted up from the valley below.

Monsieur Rocher was right: Dusk was the best time for a ride in the horse-drawn sleigh—and even more so on Christmas Eve. I'd have loved to snuggle up under the fur blankets myself and be driven around the peaceful mountainside.

The Yegorovs' excitement was dampened, however, by the fact that Viktor Yegorov had dressed Dasha in the wrong hat. She was supposed to be wearing one that matched her little sable coat. To judge by the fuss Stella Yegorov kicked up over this fashion faux pas, it was an even greater catastrophe than the loss of her perfume bottle the day before. She made it crystal clear that there was no point in them going on the sleigh ride at all without the sable hat, and nothing her husband said could persuade her otherwise. So Viktor Yegorov gave in and agreed to go and fetch the hat from their room, to put a stop to his wife's whining—and that was where I came in.

I'd been trying to slip past them unnoticed, without making eye contact, but Gordon Montfort spotted me. He grabbed my arm and cried, "No, no, dear man. No need to fetch it yourself. You and your family go and make yourselves comfortable in the carriage and pour yourselves a glass of champagne, and my colleague here will run up to the Panorama Suite and fetch the little lady her hat." He plucked the heavy room key out of Yegorov's hand, passed it to me, and hissed, in German, "You have two minutes."

I took the key hesitantly. "But I have no idea what a sable hat looks like," I stuttered. By that point, however, Gordon Montfort had already shoved me through the revolving door and into the lobby.

Okay then. Two minutes. I could manage that. Although it would mean breaking Fräulein Müller's Rule Number Four: "We never run! We walk briskly, discreetly, and quietly through the corridors, in a dignified manner." Oh well, I wasn't in uniform right now, so I could probably get away with breaking the no-running rule. And it was impossible to walk in a dignified manner in snow boots anyway, let alone run. It made you look like a duck on speed. But I had no time to think about that now. I just had to keep looking straight ahead, not left or right. Especially not left because that was where Ben was standing at Reception.

The shortest way to the Panorama Suite was across the lobby and straight through the ballroom. I sprinted over to the stage, and from there a flight of stairs took me up to the first floor and onto the corridor where the Panorama Suite was. I was panting by now and my heart was beating like crazy, but I'd made it to my destination in well under a minute. Only now did I lose precious seconds because I couldn't get the key in the lock at first. But once I entered the room and switched on the light I spotted the sable hat at once, lying there on the bed. It was clearly made of fur and had the same mottled brown pattern as the coat Dasha was wearing. That was lucky.

Relieved, I hurried over to the bed and scooped up the hat. "And now we have to run like the wind, little sable, so that you didn't die for nothing," I said. But as I was saying it, I realized I wasn't alone in the room.

omeone was hiding behind the curtain. And not very well, either: One black-clad shoulder was clearly visible poking out the side. For a second, I thought about just taking off with the sable hat and pretending I hadn't noticed anything. But at that moment, the intruder emerged from his hiding place and grinned at me.

It was Tristan, and he laughed softly as I let out a gasp.

"Thank goodness it's you," he said. "I thought it might be a hotel thief."

I was paralyzed with shock and the effort of running up all those stairs in my snow boots, so all I could do was whisper in horror: "Please tell me I'm wrong and you didn't break into this room!" Which was, of course, the stupidest thing I could possibly have said under the circumstances.

"Well—I wouldn't call it breaking in," said Tristan in a conversational tone. "The window was open. So I thought I might as well test my theory. But what are you doing here?"

"I have to take this sable h— What theory?"

I couldn't think straight. What on earth were you supposed to do when you caught a guest red-handed breaking into someone else's room? What . . . help! What would Jesus do? What would . . . Fräulein Müller do? Retreat discreetly to the hallway and call, in a hushed voice, "Stop, thief!" Even if the intruder wasn't actually a thief but just someone who enjoyed climbing up buildings, saw everything as a big joke, and seemed to be hell-bent on driving the poor intern insane?

The two-minute deadline for bringing back the hat was almost up; I could hear the last few seconds ticking away as if in slow motion while all sorts of useless thoughts ran through my brain and I stared at Tristan, my eyes like saucers.

"Okay," I snapped, "I have to take this stupid sable hat downstairs, and you need to get out of here right now before you get shot by the bodyguard. I'll meet you in five minutes, in the same place where we met the first time, and if you don't have a very good explanation for this then I'm afraid I'll have to report you."

Without waiting for Tristan's reaction, I ran out of the room. It was probably completely the wrong thing to do, but at least it was better than just standing there like an idiot trying to decide what to do while time was running out.

One step at a time. Just take things one step at a time.

I slammed the door shut behind me, ran down the stairs and through the ballroom, raced past the concierge's lodge and the reception desk, and burst out onto the forecourt. Although I felt as if I'd aged years in the past few minutes, nobody seemed to have missed me. Miraculously, only three minutes had passed. The Yegorovs had only just climbed into the sleigh and snuggled up under the fur blankets.

"There, you see!" Gordon Montfort snatched the hat out of my hand and handed it to Mrs. Yegorov with a little bow. "Here's the hat. Now all that remains for me to do is to wish you a most enjoyable evening."

"You are a treasure," cooed Mrs. Yegorov, and although it was directed at Gordon Montfort, I felt as if she were speaking to me. I was a treasure—albeit a treasure who'd just let an intruder escape from their suite scot-free.

The sable hat was placed on little Dasha's head, Old Stucky clicked his tongue, and Jesty and Vesty set off for their last ride of the day. The sun had dropped well below the mountaintops by this time, and the light from the torches cast mysterious shadows on the snow. The sound of church bells still floated up from the valley, mingling with the tinkle of the little bells on the horses' harnesses and Dasha's rapt childish laughter.

"What are you doing, standing there like a lemon?" demanded Gordon Montfort. "Get back to work."

Before I could explain to him that my shift was already over for the day, he'd gone striding off. Lemon himself. The spirit of Christmas had obviously passed him by this year.

I strode off behind him, at a safe distance.

As I crossed the lobby, I noticed Ben's worried look. "Everything all right, Sophie?"

"Everything's fine," I murmured, without slowing my pace. "I just need to get to . . ." Since I didn't finish the sentence, he'd have to complete it automatically in his head, and surely not with: ". . . the linen closet on the second floor to meet Tristan Brown, who's just broken into the Panorama Suite." He must have thought I was desperate for the toilet.

When I got to the second floor, Tristan wasn't there yet. What if he didn't turn up? If he simply claimed he'd never been in the Panorama Suite at all? What if the bodyguard had caught him? Or he'd fallen off the wall of the building? Perhaps I shouldn't have said five minutes—it must take a lot longer than that to climb all the way around the hotel, past all those lighted windows.

But just as I was about to drive myself mad with "what ifs," the door to the hallway opened and Tristan came in.

"Ah, how lovely—this brings back memories," he said, grinning broadly. "This is where we first met—you stepped out of that cupboard there looking so charming in your chambermaid's uniform, with your hair done up like a schoolteacher."

A far cry from tonight, when I'd stood before him sweating like a pig in snow boots, ski pants, and a parka. I hadn't looked in a mirror since eight o'clock that morning, so I could only imagine what a frizzy mess my hair must be and how red my face was. Whereas he—of course—looked perfect as usual, dressed all in black, not a bit out of breath, with not even the tiniest drop of sweat on his golden-brown skin.

"I didn't choose this meeting place for romantic reasons, you . . ." Unfortunately I couldn't think of a single English insult. "*Dummkopf*," I added lamely in German. "It was just that I was in a hurry and this was the first place that came to mind. What were you doing in the Smirnovs' room? And don't lie to me, or I'll scream the place down."

"Fine." Tristan smiled benignly at me. "Perhaps we should go somewhere else? Where no one can eavesdrop on us?"

I opened the cupboard door and, with a theatrical sweep of my arm, showed him its empty interior. "Nobody there, see? So spit it out."

"Okay," he said. "But first of all: Those people are not called Smirnov; they're called Yegorov." He paused for an instant and smiled. "Ah, I see—but of course you know that already. I recognized them straightaway, too, when I saw them at dinner yesterday. As did everyone else who's opened a magazine in the past few months, no doubt. If you ask me, Stella Yegorov likes being recognized. She doesn't seem the type to enjoy going incognito."

"And you thought there was bound to be a good haul in the oligarch's suite," I breathed, furious. "I swear, if there's anything missing . . ."

"There is." Tristan put his hands in his pockets and leaned against the wall. In this pose, he could easily have passed for a model in a fashion magazine. "Shouldn't we continue this conversation elsewhere? Somewhere we could sit down, for instance?"

"What's missing, Tristan? What did you steal?" I was practically whispering, but I still sounded hysterical. "Stop playing for time."

"You ought to know better, Agent Sophie. A thief steals things in order to get rich. Which is something I never do."

"Oh really? Who are you, Robin Hood or someone?"

Tristan laughed out loud. "Yes, you could say that. I was only trying to help, I promise. After you told me yesterday that the old lady's ring had gone missing, it was obvious to me what had happened. I just needed this little bit of proof." He paused for a moment and then, with a flourish worthy of a stage magician, plucked something out of his pocket and placed it in my hand. It was a silver ring with a big pink stone.

I gasped. "Mrs. Ludwig's ring."

Tristan nodded. "And before you go accusing me of stealing it, all I'm doing is returning it to its rightful place. Which is certainly not in the drawer of Stella Yegorov's nightstand."

"But . . . how . . . ? Why . . . ?" I stammered.

"Why would Stella Yegorov want to steal a ring from a poor old lady when she's dripping with jewelry as it is?" asked Tristan. "Well, some of these spoiled rich people are like magpies. They see something sparkly, and they just can't resist."

"I don't believe you." I narrowed my eyes, looking from Tristan to the ring and back again. "The ring isn't even worth anything—why on earth would she steal it? And more important, when? And how? Mrs. Ludwig was following her around wherever she went, gazing at her like a teenage fangirl."

Tristan shrugged. "It calls for a certain amount of skill and cunning. But for a kleptomaniac that's all part of the thrill."

"A kleptomaniac?" This was getting increasingly bizarre.

Tristan nodded. "At Tiffany's a few years ago, a thirty-five-thousand-dollar sapphire bracelet ended up in her handbag—quite by accident, of course. It's always an accident with these people. The shop assistant who gave the story to the press was fired."

I was silent for a moment. Slowly, the whole implausible story was starting to make sense. Though perhaps only because I wanted to believe it.

"So you're telling me Mrs. Yegorov stole Mrs. Ludwig's ring and hid it in her nightstand? Because she's a kleptomaniac?"

"She might be a kleptomaniac, or she might just be a bored, greedy person who can't resist a valuable piece of jewelry."

"But that's just it. The ring isn't worth anything. Mr. Ludwig bought it at a flea market. The stone is a beryl, Mrs. Ludwig said, and the metal probably isn't even real silver."

Again, Tristan laughed softly. "You're right about the metal, anyway. Because it's not silver: It's platinum."

"What?"

He tapped the stone gently. "And to call this a beryl is a terrible insult to this wonderful, almost flawless emerald-cut pink diamond. Don't look at me like that, Sophie. I know about these things. My grandpa is an art historian and a certified gemologist. He specializes in antique jewelry. He's always getting called in to value things for Christie's and Sotheby's, and he works for museums all over the world. I could tell a diamond from a crystal by the time I was five. You don't see many pink diamonds around, especially not ones this size. This little fellow must be nearly fifteen carats, I'd say. It gave me a bit of a shock, too."

I felt like I needed to sit down. But for now I'd have to settle for undoing the zip on my parka. I was so hot I could hardly breathe, let alone think.

"Are you okay, Sophie?" Tristan slipped the ring back into his pocket.

I shook my head. "So let's say your story is true, and Mrs. Yegorov is a kleptomaniac who stole Mrs. Ludwig's ring, which Mr. Ludwig bought at a flea market thirty-five years ago for forty marks, even though it's actually worth about a hundred times that . . . or a thousand times?" I stared at Tristan in bewilderment.

"Stick another two zeroes on the end," he said. "Give or take a million."

"Oh my God." I gulped. "The Ludwigs are going be able to spend their holidays at Castle in the Clouds for the rest of their lives." If it still existed, that is. "They've been saving up their whole lives just to be able to stay here for two weeks. Imagine all the things they'd be able to do if they sold the ring. Pay off their house, go on cruises, leave some money to their children . . . I can't wait to see their faces when they find out what a treasure they've had in their possession all these years. Come on, let's go and give it back to them!" I grabbed Tristan's hand.

"Wait, Sophie, wait!" Tristan held me back. "Do you really think that's a good idea? It's bound to cause a stir if the ring suddenly reappears."

That was certainly true. Mrs. Ludwig had told pretty much anyone who would listen (and some people who wouldn't) about the disappearance of her beloved ring. "Everyone will just be happy for Mrs. Ludwig, won't they? Apart from Mrs. Yegorov, of course. She'll be kicking herself."

Tristan shook his head. "What are you going to tell them? That I found the ring in Mrs. Yegorov's nightstand?"

"Oh." He was right. It wasn't that easy. "I could say I found it somewhere. And then you just happened to see it and realize it's worth millions . . . What? Why do you look so skeptical? Mrs. Yegorov is hardly going to admit she stole it."

"No. But she'll know you found the ring in her room and took it," said Tristan.

"So? She'll be furious, but she can't exactly say anything about it without outing herself as a thief."

"But she'd know who took the ring from her, don't you see? It's best not to get on the wrong side of somebody like Stella Yegorov."

I remembered the bodyguard in Room 117 and the holster he carried around, and I couldn't help but agree. "The same applies to you, though," I said to Tristan. "What was your plan? If you say you found the ring somewhere, the Yegorovs will know *you* were in their room." Well, Stella Yegorov would know, anyway. I doubted her husband had any idea what she was up to.

"That's true," Tristan replied. "And annoyingly, I haven't yet resolved that particular detail. But we'll find a way of getting the Ludwigs' beloved ring back to them, don't you worry, Sophie." Tristan was still holding onto my wrist, as if he was afraid I might go running off to tell the whole world about the ring. "Even if I have to climb into their room myself and leave it on their nightstand."

"Don't you dare," I said, but I couldn't help giggling.

At that moment, we heard a rumbling sound outside the door, and then it swung open and Hortensia and Ava came in pushing a cleaning cart.

"I hate it when he leaves his chewing gum stuck to the bin," said Hortensia in her nasal voice as she closed the door behind her. "He does it on purpose."

Ava didn't reply; she'd spotted me and Tristan and was staring at us openmouthed. Tristan must have let go of my wrist a second too late.

"As I said, this cut-through is for staff only, sir." I smiled at Tristan. "You're welcome to take the main stairs or the elevators."

"But this is a shortcut to the library." Tristan frowned. "And there's no sign on the door to say it's out of bounds."

"All right then. You can cut through here just this once. As it's Christmas. I hope you have a lovely Christmas Eve."

"Thank you, you too," Tristan replied and moved toward the stairs. I squeezed past Hortensia and Ava and their cleaning cart and opened the door to the corridor.

"Oh, just a minute, Miss!" Tristan called, and I turned. Hortensia and Ava kept looking from me to Tristan and back again. Ava's mouth was still hanging open. She'd clearly forgotten she was supposed to be ignoring me. "The lady with the pearl necklace was asking for you," said Tristan. "She asked me to remind you that you've got an appointment with her."

"Oh yes." I knew immediately which lady he was referring to. The one in the painting in the alcove outside the Duchess Suite, where we'd hidden yesterday. "I'll go and . . . er . . . look in on Mrs. Barnbrooke as soon as I've changed."

As Tristan left, grinning, I said to Ava: "You'd better close your mouth before you start catching flies."

"You're so ugly," Ava retorted. That seemed to be her go-to response when she couldn't think of anything else to say. "I don't get it."

"Don't get what?" There were a lot of things I didn't get, too, but I was sure I'd be able to give Ava a helping hand.

"Why is Mrs. Barnbrooke asking for *you*?" Hortensia had waited till Tristan's footsteps had died away.

I shrugged. "It's probably about little Gracie or Madison. I've been looking after them at day care. Anyway, I'd better get a move on. I'm sure Fräulein Müller wouldn't want me to keep the guests waiting."

With that, I pulled the door shut behind me and sprinted down the corridor (hopefully for the last time that day in snow boots).

I knew it. This Christmas was going to be anything but boring.

13

I got to the alcove with the painting of the stern lady in the pearl necklace later than planned because I'd had to shower and change and also reply to a message from Delia. She'd texted: "Christmas hasn't even started yet and I'm already losing it. My mum and my grandma are arguing about the turkey, my stupid brother has diarrhea and is throwing up so loudly he's almost made me be sick, too, twice; and my dad has decided today is a great day to install a new router. Which means we now have no internet. Which means I can't watch any good shows, only 'It's a Wonderful Life' for the three-hundred-thousandth time. Oh yeah, and I've got a sneaking suspicion my parents are giving me a ceiling fan for Christmas. All because I might have happened to mention that my room was too hot this summer. What kind of sadistic parents give their child a ceiling fan as a present? In the middle of winter! Please tell me that Christmas at your fancy hotel is amazing and full of cinnamon parfaits, kisses under the mistletoe, and dates with hot millionaires, otherwise I'm going to stick my head down the toilet and drown myself."

"Sorry, no time for hot millionaires, now going to meet hot cat burglar to clear up theft of ring which oligarch's kleptomaniac wife stole from old lady who has no idea ring is worth a fortune," I hastily texted back. I'd never kept secrets from Delia. And at least this message would keep her from drowning herself in the toilet. "Long story. If you don't hear from me I've either been caught by the kleptomaniac's bodyguard or the hot cat burglar decided to keep the ring for himself and has disposed of my corpse in the snow."

While I was showering, however, I'd had an idea about how Tristan and I could resolve the problem of giving back the ring without anyone knowing who'd taken it.

When I emerged from the staff quarters, I could see him waiting for me on the stairs. He was leaning on the banister near the alcove with the painting of the pearl-necklace lady, peering down the stairs.

The first guests were already on their way to the restaurant. They probably thought it was just as well to be on time for that evening's twelve-course dinner; the delicious smell of it was already drifting through the hotel. Apart from the "veal sweetbreads on smoked cucumber," everything on the menu sounded amazing.

Whatsername and Camilla were wheeling their cleaning cart into the elevator as I passed, and our eyes met for a moment. I felt them staring after me.

"Would you look at that—Sophie out of uniform!" Tristan whistled admiringly. "And all dressed up, too. Definitely worth waiting half an hour for."

"Sorry I took so long," I said apologetically. "I had to dry my hair." And put some eyeliner on. And a bit of blush. And mascara. And lip gloss. "And do some thinking."

Tristan nodded. "Well, I've been doing some thinking, too, and there's actually a very simple solution to our problem. We just need to get the ring to one of the managers, and then they can pass it on to Mrs. Ludwig. And nobody will know we had anything to do with it."

That was exactly what I'd been thinking. I beamed at Tristan. "We'll give the ring to Monsieur Rocher. That way we can be sure it'll get back to Mrs. Ludwig safe and sound."

Tristan looked distinctly unenthusiastic. "I was thinking of wrapping it up in a package addressed to Mrs. Ludwig and dropping it off at Reception when nobody's looking. Otherwise this Monsieur Rocher would know it had come from us."

"But it would attract a lot more attention if Mrs. Ludwig were to open a mysterious package from some anonymous person and find the ring inside it." I really didn't think it was a good idea. "And Monsieur Rocher would never say anything to anyone."

"And he wouldn't ask any questions?" Tristan looked at me, eyebrows raised.

"Well, yes," I had to admit, "he would ask questions." The faint sound of piano music drifted up the stairs toward us; the Christmas sing-along must be getting going in the bar. They were starting with "O Holy Night." "Perhaps we need an even simpler solution. I'll just wait for a quiet moment and tell Mrs. Ludwig her ring has been found. By . . . Manfred."

"Who's Manfred?"

"There is no Manfred. That's the point," I burbled with increasing enthusiasm. "Manfred found the ring while he was cleaning the swimming pool and then went off on a well-earned holiday for three weeks. So Mrs. Ludwig won't be able to thank him. But she can go around telling everyone that Manfred found her ring if she likes. Manfred doesn't exist, so nobody can do him any harm."

Tristan grinned. "That's quite a good idea. But it needs work."

"You're not trying to find an excuse to keep hold of the ring, are you?" I narrowed my eyes suspiciously. "You'd better give it to me."

Tristan raised his eyebrows again—he was very, very good at that—but obligingly reached into his pocket. I felt a bit queasy. Surely he hadn't been walking around with a ring worth several million dollars in his pocket for the past few hours? But before he could hand me the ring, the door of the Theremin Suite opened, and Ella and Gretchen came out. They had matching outfits and hairstyles. Ella was wearing a red velvet vintage-style dress, and Gretchen had the same dress in blue. They both wore their curled blond hair held off their faces by a braided strand. I didn't like to admit it, but they looked stunning.

And they seemed to know it, judging by the appraising looks and condescending smiles they gave us. I was sorry I hadn't had any sort of reflex this time to make me leap into the alcove and hide. Suddenly I realized how Amy must feel. Until that moment, I'd been feeling pretty good about myself, but without even saying a word, Gretchen and Ella had managed to make me feel unattractive and frumpy. And totally out of place.

"Hi, Tristan," Gretchen whispered.

"Merry Christmas, Tristan," said Ella in honeyed tones. "Are you coming down to dinner?"

"I'm waiting for my grandpa." Tristan smiled politely.

"Then we'll see you later." Gretchen and Ella breezed elegantly down the stairs. If they hadn't giggled and whispered, too loudly, "That was that *weird chambermaid*, wasn't it?" and "Do you think he's got a thing for the staff, like Great Uncle Jeremiah?" I would just have thought how beautiful they looked and how their hair gleamed like gold in the light of the chandeliers. But as it was . . .

"Silly cows," said Tristan.

"They are, aren't they?" I was truly relieved that he hadn't been blinded by the gleaming golden hair. "But the other Barnbrooke girls are lovely. Smart, funny, and kind. It would be good if you could maybe . . . just flirt with Amy a little bit, you know. Then those two would stop thinking they're so irresistible, and Aiden might see Amy in a new light."

Tristan frowned reluctantly. "Don't we have more important things to discuss right now?"

"True. Manfred. And you were about to give me the ring."

But that was clearly not going to happen. From the floor above we heard two sets of short, sharp yaps followed by a door closing, and then Mara Matthäus came down the stairs. She too was wearing a stunningly beautiful dress. It was half covered with rhinestones, and I wondered how she was going to top that when it came to her outfit for the New Year's Ball.

Tristan didn't wait for Mara Matthäus to reach us—he grabbed my hand and pulled me into the hallway where his room was. "Come on. Let's go somewhere we won't keep getting interrupted."

He was right. If we weren't careful, someone was going to see us with the ring, and then all our efforts would have been for nothing. We went past the Theremin Suite and Rooms 212 and 211 (where Tristan was staying with his grandpa) and into the vestibule at the end of the hall. The same vestibule where Don had wiped his chocolatey fingers on the velvet curtains and which Amy had said was one of her favorite places. There were two upholstered seats inside it, facing each other, and on the wall was a gilt-framed oil painting of a sad-looking girl in a sailor dress stroking a cat. The cat bore a striking similarity to the Forbidden Cat, which was perhaps why it often chose this spot to sleep in. The window faced west, looking out over the twinkling half-moon fir tree. Beyond the tree you could see the stables, where Old Stucky was currently taking Jesty's and Vesty's harnesses off, and where he would rub them down and brush them before knocking off work for the night, Christmas Eve or no Christmas Eve.

"Sophie." Tristan still hadn't let go of my hand. He turned it so that my palm was facing upward. Then he solemnly placed Mrs. Ludwig's ring in it. Now that I knew how valuable it was, the stone seemed to positively glow.

I stared at it for a few seconds, awestruck.

"Pretty, isn't it?" Tristan laughed softly. "It really isn't very often you see a pink diamond. They're extremely rare, especially ones of this shade. Fancy Intense Pink, almost flawless."

"And so heavy," I murmured. The thing felt as though it weighed several pounds. My hand started trembling slightly. But that might have had something to do with the fact that Tristan was standing very close to me. So close that I could smell his distinctive scent of freshly washed cotton and lemon. I hoped I smelled even half as good. "I'm not sure how I feel about carrying it around with me. Perhaps you'd better keep it till we've figured out what we're going to do."

"You're sweet," said Tristan. "Are you afraid it might burn a hole in your pocket? Or that you might be tempted to keep it and go on the run with it?" He took the ring from the palm of my hand and slipped it onto my finger, then turned my hand over again. "Well? How does that feel?" he asked, in a soft voice. "Not bad, eh?"

"Get your hands off her," snapped a voice from right beside us. I jumped backward in shock and nearly collided with the sad girl in the sailor dress.

It was Ben, standing between the velvet curtains, frowning darkly. The thick carpet must have muffled his steps so we hadn't heard him coming.

"I beg your pardon?" Tristan crossed his arms and eyed Ben rather arrogantly.

"I said get your hands off our intern. Who, by the way, is a minor." Ben seemed genuinely outraged.

"It's . . . ," I began, but then broke off because I'd been about to say *It's not what it looks like*, which is possibly the corniest phrase in the history of corny phrases.

Tristan laughed out loud. "Or what: You'll beat me up?"

"If I have to," said Ben stonily. "Are you okay, Sophie?"

"Too late." Tristan was still laughing. "I've already bitten her, and next time there's a full moon she'll turn into a vampire just like me."

"Just because you're good-looking and you've got a bit of money doesn't mean you can do whatever the hell you want." Ben was clearly on the point of launching himself at Tristan.

I quickly stepped in between them. "Ben! Nobody's bitten me. And his hands weren't *on* me . . ." Oh my goodness, what on earth was I saying? But Ben's grave expression was making me nervous. I felt exactly like I'd felt that time when I was in my first year of high school and a couple of elementary school kids had sprayed "School is krap" on the wall of the bus shelter, and Delia and I couldn't help being anal about it and changing the *K* to a *C*. Of course we'd got caught; the elementary school kids were long gone. They were probably still laughing about it to this day.

"We're just discussing a little problem we've got," I tried again. "Which you may even be able to help us with."

"Sophie," said Tristan in a warning voice. "Isn't he your boss's son?"

"Yes, but he's all right," I replied.

Ben folded his arms now, too. "What is this problem?" he growled.

I ignored Tristan's warning glance. "I told you about Mrs. Ludwig losing her engagement ring in the spa."

"You did," said Ben. "We had the whole filtration system taken apart and all the filters searched."

"But you never would have found the ring because Stella Yegorov had stolen it. She's a kleptomaniac. Google it." Which was exactly what I'd done while I was blow-drying my hair earlier. Tristan had been telling the truth. In the archives of several online magazines and search engines, I'd found reports of the sapphire bracelet that had ended up in the dog handbag "by accident."

I felt it was to Ben's credit that he stayed silent and didn't say "Huh?" or "What?" like I would have done. No, Ben was very cool in comparison. He just let me carry on talking. But I was getting to the point where I was going to have to be a little creative with the truth.

"I happened to spot the ring lying on the nightstand in the Panorama Suite when I went to get Dasha's sable hat just now."

On the nightstand, in the nightstand—it was pretty much the same thing.

Tristan grinned approvingly.

"So I just grabbed it. I mean, it belongs to Mrs. Ludwig. And she's been crying her eyes out. I couldn't just leave it lying there." I looked expectantly at Ben. He was welcome to break his silence now.

"Is that why you looked so distracted in the lobby just now?" he asked, and I nodded eagerly.

"And you're sure it's Mrs. Ludwig's ring and not just one that looks like it?"

Hmm. That was opening a whole new can of worms. But no—I was absolutely sure. The ring that had disappeared in the spa was the same one that had reappeared in Stella Yegorov's nightstand. I nodded vigorously.

"Okay," said Ben slowly. "So you took the ring from the night-stand to give it back to Mrs. Ludwig. What's the problem, then? And what does *he* have to do with it?" He pointed to Tristan.

"Sophie can't give the ring back herself because then Stella Yegorov might find out how the ring disappeared from her suite," said Tristan impatiently. "And I'm sure you'll agree with my gut feeling that it might be best not to make an enemy of that woman. Do you really think the hotel management is likely to accuse Viktor Yegorov's wife of theft? Or report her to the police?"

Ben didn't answer.

"You see? And there's your problem," said Tristan, and I added hastily, "That's what Tristan and I have been doing this whole time— trying to figure out the best way to give the ring back. We thought we might be able to get a package to Mrs. Ludwig anonymously."

"The whole time—I doubt it," murmured Ben. Then he cleared his throat and went on more loudly, "Why didn't you come straight to me, Sophie? Why would you discuss such a delicate matter with this . . . guest?" He shook his head. He looked disappointed now, and that was even worse than his outrage a moment ago. He put out his hand. "Give me the ring."

I pulled it off my finger and laid it in his hand. I immediately felt about twenty pounds lighter. And I felt like I could breathe again.

Tristan rolled his eyes.

"Come on," said Ben, and I could hear the disappointment in his voice now, too. "We'll make sure Mrs. Ludwig gets her ring back."

"Yes, but there's just one more thing you should know. This ring is . . . ouch!" Tristan had given me a dig in the ribs and a slight shake of his head. Perhaps he was right—perhaps we'd told Ben enough for now.

"This ring is what?" asked Ben.

Worth a few million euros.

"Very special," I whispered. I just couldn't lie any louder. "Mr. Ludwig bought it decades ago, at a flea market."

"I know," said Ben.

Tristan stretched and yawned as if he'd just woken up from a nap. "If you don't need me anymore, I think I'll go and find my grandpa and head down to dinner." He slid smoothly past Ben and out into the corridor. "Merry Christmas to you both."

"Screw you," muttered Ben in German.

14

On our way downstairs, Ben maintained a stubborn silence. And I felt guilty for not having told him the whole truth. Although he couldn't know I'd lied, so he couldn't exactly be angry with me about it.

I shot several sideways glances at him, but he pretended not to notice. His jaw was clamped tight shut as if he was grinding something between his teeth. When Anni Moser, who was stuffing dirty sheets into the laundry chute, wished us a merry Christmas, Ben growled "Merry Christmas to you, too" in such a grumpy tone of voice that she looked quite taken aback. I gave her an apologetic smile.

This was the time of day when Fräulein Müller did her evening rounds with the chambermaids, getting the rooms ready for the night. The evening round had always been my favorite, firstly because it was the last thing you had to do before the end of your shift, and secondly because it involved lots of nice jobs: drawing the curtains, folding back the bedspread, placing a little rug and a pair of slippers on either side of the bed, plumping up the pillows, and leaving a little wrapped square of chocolate on each pillow. As you went out, you tidied up the room a bit and took any dirty cups or rubbish away with you. When the guests returned to their rooms after dinner, everything was all neat and cozy, ready for bedtime.

"I could really go for a bit of chocolate right now, couldn't you?" I said, but Ben didn't answer. He seemed to be taking this very seriously.

When we reached the ground floor and entered the staff room

behind the concierge's lodge, I plucked up all my courage and asked him: "Are you angry with me for taking the ring?"

Ben stopped. "No." He looked me in the eye at last. "I'd probably have done the same thing. I'm angry because you didn't tell me. Instead you went and told that . . . Tristan Brown."

Which of course I would never have done if I really had taken the ring. Oh, crap.

"I thought we were friends," Ben went on. "I thought you trusted me."

Now I felt even worse. Especially because I really did feel I could trust him—last night on the stairs, when we'd been drinking tea and rum together, I'd certainly gotten that impression.

"And I *would* have come to you." If I really had taken the ring, that is. Which I hadn't. "It's just that Tristan . . . he was . . . he just happened to be around at the time."

Half-truths, I was coming to realize, were no good at all. In the end, they just added up to an outright lie. But now, for better or worse, I had to stick to my story, even if I hated it and felt terrible for lying to Ben. "I had to let Tristan in on it, otherwise he would have thought I was a thief and reported me to management."

"I see," said Ben.

No. He didn't, unfortunately. For a moment, I felt genuinely angry with Tristan for putting me in this situation. After all, I was only lying to Ben to cover for Tristan, to make sure nobody found out about his habit of climbing up walls and in through strangers' windows to go rummaging around in their nightstands.

On the other hand, if it hadn't been for Tristan, Mrs. Ludwig's ring would probably have been lost forever. And the old lady really didn't deserve that.

"It's not a great idea to make friends with the guests." Ben looked at me gravely. "Especially not with that British pretty boy who thinks all he has to do is smile and girls will just fall at his feet."

"Which they probably will," I said, then added quickly, "Not me though, obviously."

"That's not how it looked just now. The two of you seemed pretty close. Like it wasn't the first time you'd held hands."

"We weren't holding—" I broke off. This was stupid. Why did I keep having to justify myself? I hadn't done anything wrong. Not even in the untrue version of the story. "What were you doing up there in the vestibule anyway?" I asked, looking Ben straight in the eye.

Ben stared back at me for a few seconds, then looked away. "You mean, how did I know I'd find you there? Ariane told me. Several people saw you on the second floor making . . . er . . . doing whatever you were doing with that English boy."

"Who the hell is Ariane?"

"One of the students from Lausanne who's working for Fräulein Müller, the one with blond hair and bangs. You must know her—her bedroom is right next to yours."

"Ah, you mean Whatsername." I started chewing on my lower lip. Little by little, this was all starting to make sense. It was also starting to make me angry. "So Whatsername came to see you at Reception and told you I was holding hands with Tristan Brown on the second floor, did she? And you believed that stupid little snitch?" I didn't know why I suddenly had such a bitter taste in my mouth.

Ben looked at me, frowning. "She and the other girls were worried about you. They said they'd seen you with that guy before. In the linen room." He took a deep breath. "Which is off-limits to guests."

"Yes, I'm sure they were terribly worried about me. The *girls*." I snorted. Hearing him talk about them so nicely had really made me see red. "How thoughtful of them to bring their concerns to you. What with you being so trustworthy and all. And how very chivalrous of you to come rushing upstairs to . . . do what, exactly?"

"To stop you doing something stupid, perhaps? Or—for all I knew, the guest was pressuring you." Ben pressed his lips together for a moment. "But clearly he wasn't doing anything you didn't want him to."

"You can tell your friends from Lausanne that my private life is absolutely none of their business," I hissed.

"Well at least they know the hotel rules, unlike you," Ben retorted. "This is not the kind of place where employees make out with guests in linen closets and dark corners."

Now he'd gone too far.

I felt my eyes fill with tears. This always happened to me: Whenever I got really angry, I started welling up and I couldn't get a sensible word out. Had I really been feeling guilty a minute ago for having lied to him?

"It's my duty to make you aware of inappropriate behavior that might damage the hotel's reputation."

Ben clearly couldn't see the effect he was having on me. My eyes were burning from the effort of holding back tears. "If I were you, I'd be grateful to Ariane for coming to me with this and not my dad," he said.

"And you expect me to trust you?" I wanted to yell at him, but my voice was strangely quiet and choked. "I think you're behaving just like your dad right now. And as for us being friends—that's a joke! I'd ten times rather be friends with that British pretty boy, as you call him. At least Tristan can recognize a silly cow when he sees one."

Without waiting for his reply, I pushed past him into the concierge's lodge and slammed the door as hard as I could.

"Oh, good," said Monsieur Rocher. "It was getting so quiet around here I'd almost nodded off."

I leaned back against the door, breathing heavily. Monsieur Rocher must have heard every word of our argument, which at least saved me repeating all the sordid details and inevitably bursting into tears.

Ben had gone out through the other door and was now crossing the lobby with long, angry strides. He withdrew behind the reception desk and started tapping loudly and pointedly at his computer keyboard.

"I should have given him a slap," I said between gritted teeth. "Or shoved him against the wall. Or done something else very painful to him."

"A good slap is sometimes better than a bad kiss." Monsieur Rocher took a stack of postcards out of a cardboard box and started arranging them in the postcard rack. "I read that somewhere."

The British actor and his wife, who must have been out for a last little Christmas Eve walk, came in through the revolving doors bringing a blast of cold air with them. Ben handed them their room key and glanced in our direction. I would have liked to grab one of the polished apples from the bowl on our desk and throw it at him.

"He basically accused me of hiding in dark corners and making out with a guest," I exclaimed, as soon as the actor and his wife had gone upstairs. "And all because those *buttnuts* from Lausanne . . ." I could hardly breathe, I was so furious. But using Gracie's insult had made me feel better. And it had helped me hold back my tears.

"That wasn't very nice of Ben." Monsieur Rocher handed me a pile of postcards, and I started arranging them on the rack. "You look very pretty this evening, by the way, Sophie. Even prettier than usual."

"Thanks."

"Which guest did he say you'd been . . . stepping out with?"

"Tristan Brown from Room 211," I said readily, and despite how upset I was, I couldn't help smiling a bit. What a lovely quaint phrase *stepping out* was, compared with "making out."

"And we weren't 'stepping out' together; we were just trying to solve a problem, that's all. And we were doing it for the sake of this hotel, incidentally. The same hotel Ben basically accused me of bringing into disrepute!"

Monsieur Rocher looked at me with an understanding smile. "Tristan Brown from Room 211 is a very attractive young man," he said. "It's just a thought, but perhaps Ben misjudged the situation a little because he feels jealous?"

"No, he misjudged the situation a little because he listened to that snitch Whatsername." I looked darkly over at Reception, where Ben was still pounding the keyboard as if trying to avert a dangerous hacker attack. "He even knows her name. He said it so many times I can't really call her Whatsername anymore."

"*Love looks for roses; jealousy sees thorns*," said Monsieur Rocher. "Or the other way around—was it love that sees roses while jealousy looks for thorns? Either way, I don't envy you people your jealousy. Here's a few more cards, my dear."

For a while we arranged the postcards in silence, listening to the Christmas songs that drifted faintly over from the bar and watching the stragglers making their way into the restaurant, dressed in their festive finery. The oligarch's family (mother and daughter were in matching outfits again, and the dog seemed to have been left upstairs for once) were now coming down the stairs.

"Have you eaten yet?" Monsieur Rocher asked me, once everyone had gone inside the restaurant and the pianist in the bar had launched into a jazzy version of "Let it Snow."

"Nothing since a potato at lunchtime."

"Aha," said Monsieur Rocher, as if that explained a great deal.

At that moment, the Ludwigs entered the lobby. They too were all dressed up. Mr. Ludwig was wearing a suit (the sleeves on the jacket were slightly too short) and Mrs. Ludwig was in a voluminous lilac dress with a matching stole.

Ben sprang into action. "Excuse me, please," he called, coming out from behind the reception desk. Aha! Now things were heating up. My heart was pounding in excitement. I was intrigued to see how Ben was going to explain the business of the ring. Not wanting to miss a thing, I leaned out over the concierge's desk so far that I almost fell off the other side. Unfortunately, the Ludwigs were standing with their backs to me so I couldn't see their faces. And to top it all off, the Ball Bearings Baroness and her young lover chose that moment to come tripping down the stairs and stand right in front of us debating whether to go straight in to the restaurant or have an aperitif in the bar first. By the time they'd finally finished their conversation and wandered off toward the bar, Ben must have handed over the ring because Mrs. Ludwig had flung her arms around his neck and was kissing him animatedly on both cheeks, saying, "You are an angel, young man. A Christmas angel."

Ben blushed slightly and said something I couldn't quite catch.

Mr. Ludwig slid the ring onto Mrs. Ludwig's finger, and I almost shed a tear. He did it with such solemn seriousness, gazing at her so devotedly, that they could have been standing at the altar. Then he kissed her just as tenderly, and eventually the two of them walked away with their arms around each other and disappeared into the restaurant. Where, I hoped, they would be sitting at a table as far away from Stella Yegorov as possible.

Ben stood still in the middle of the lobby and watched them go. All sorts of emotions flitted across his face, as if he'd just come out of a very moving film. When he turned to look in our direction, I quickly picked myself up off the desk, but it was too late—he'd already seen what knots I'd tied myself in to get a good view of him and the Ludwigs. And that I was still leaning over the desk staring at him, even though the Ludwigs were long gone. He'd better not go thinking I'd forgiven him! I tried to adjust my body language to better reflect my emotional state and folded my arms across my chest as grumpily as I could. I also tried to get my eyes to flash dangerously, the way people's eyes do in novels. I was determined not to be the first one to blink.

What did he expect? A round of applause? I could have given the ring back to Mrs. Ludwig myself if I'd wanted to. I'd have found a way. The Manfred plan, for example. Anyway, the real difficulty lay not in giving the ring back but in explaining to the Ludwigs that they could buy this whole hotel, if they wanted, with that flea-market ring of theirs.

Ben wasn't in the least fazed by the dangerous flashing of my eyes. He walked slowly toward us without averting his gaze, seemingly just as determined as I was not to blink first.

"I don't think Ben's had anything to eat this evening, either," said Monsieur Rocher, when Ben finally reached us.

So what? He could starve to death for all I cared.

Neither of us said a word.

"I imagine one or the other of you might be feeling sorry for the things he or she said just now, hmm?" Monsieur Rocher looked at Ben, eyebrows raised.

"Yes, I imagine we might," Ben murmured, lowering his eyes for a second.

"I didn't say anything I have to apologize for." I sniffed, and Monsieur Rocher silently handed me a tissue.

"But I did." Ben sighed. "I don't know how to . . . I'm so sorry, Sophie. I really didn't mean those things."

"The thing about my inappropriate behavior damaging the hotel's reputation or the thing about making out in dark corners?" I blew my nose loudly into Monsieur Rocher's tissue. I had no idea why my nose was suddenly running so much.

"Both." Ben looked genuinely contrite, as I could see when I snuck a quick glance at him, my nose still buried in the tissue. "It was unfair of me. And very . . . rude and offensive. I . . . Please forgive me. I just lost it, thinking about you and that obnoxious English guy . . ."

"Stepping out together?" I said, lowering the tissue.

Ben grinned. "Yes, exactly." Then he grew serious again. "Sophie? Will you accept my apology and come and have dinner with me?"

He looked at me so disarmingly that I had trouble keeping my composure. I decided to stay silent for a little while longer. But at least I didn't need the tissue anymore.

"What a good idea! Just what I would have suggested." Monsieur Rocher took a little package from the mail rack and handed it to Ben. "And if you get the chance, you two, would you be so kind as to give this to Pavel when you go downstairs? It came in the mail yesterday from Bulgaria, and I think we should make sure he gets it for Christmas Eve."

I stuffed the tissue in my pants pocket and gnawed hesitantly at my lower lip.

"Sophie?" Ben leaned over the counter. "Can't we just be friends again?"

I took a deep breath. "Friends no, dinner yes," I said, standing up. "Maybe I'll get a chance to give you that slap you so richly deserve."

"I'm glad we've cleared that up," said Monsieur Rocher happily.

We could tell before we got to the laundry room that Pavel wasn't alone: not even he could sing two parts of "Angels We Have Heard on High" in the original French. It sounded so beautiful and poignant—much more Christmassy than the plinky plonky international Christmas music upstairs in the bar—that I almost reached for Ben's hand as we walked along the dimly lit basement corridor.

But I couldn't do that, of course. I was still pissed off at him.

The acoustics in the basement were impressive, thanks to its vaulted ceilings. (They always made my voice sound at least twice as loud.) But even without that, this was a truly magnificent performance. Pavel was confidently singing the tune, as usual, in his powerful baritone, and over the top was a tenor voice, clear as a bell.

I stood still in the doorway, amazed. The tenor voice belonged to none other than Old Stucky, who was sitting with Pavel at the table that was usually reserved for little mending jobs like sewing on buttons or turning up hems.

A bottle of clear liquid stood between them, the bent, wizened old man and the tall, strapping younger one who was dressed, as always, in jeans and a vest. A couple of machines hummed in the background, and a candle stub cast a flickering light on the walls.

The sight of them, and the crystal-clear tones that filled the room as they sang "Gloria in Excelsis Deo," brought tears to my eyes. How could such an old man have such a youthful, angelic singing voice?

Ben shot me a sideways smile. He was obviously familiar with the caretaker's hidden talents.

"Comes as a bit of a surprise, doesn't it?" he said as the last notes of the chorus faded away. "Old Stucky used to be a soloist with a boys' choir."

"Boowys' chwayre," Old Stucky corrected him, then added something else in his strong Swiss German dialect. The only word I could make out was "but."

"But he decided to leave the city and come and live in the mountains. With the animals. Surrounded by nature," Ben translated. "You can sing no matter where you live."

"No matter where, no matter when!" Pavel had kissed us energetically on both cheeks and taken his package from Ben. Instead of opening it, he poured some of the liquid from the bottle into two large glasses and handed one to each of us. "Old Stucky is worrying about bad omens."

"What bad omens?" I sniffed the liquid in my glass suspiciously. It smelled like my antibacterial face wash.

Old Stucky said something I couldn't quite decipher.

"The moon is wearing a shroud." Ben provided the translation again, but he couldn't help rolling his eyes in amusement as he spoke. "And the mountain ghost visited Old Stucky in a dream and warned him that something bad was about to happen."

Old Stucky narrowed his eyes in agreement. "Tha moontin' seynses et."

"Oh." I felt goose bumps creep up my arms.

"Please no superstitions on Christmas Eve. We drink pear brandy instead," said Pavel. He smiled indulgently, but as he raised his glass there was a solemn sternness in his eyes. When it came to matters of religion, Pavel wasn't one to joke around. Although his thick, brawny upper arms were covered with tattoos of pagan symbols, he was actually a devout Catholic; the tattoos were clearly just there to fool people (and make him look tough). "We raise glass to birth of Jesus Christ, who brought light to world and people's hearts."

Nobody dared refuse this toast.

"To Jesus Christ," we all said. I only took a small sip. I'd have trusted Pavel with my life, but when it came to mysterious liquids in unlabeled bottles, I was a little more wary—and with good reason. The brandy burned my throat as it went down, making me cough. But then I tasted a hint of pear, and a pleasant warmth radiated through my stomach.

"Is good, no?" Pavel looked from me to Ben and back again. "Homemade, by husband of Stucky's sister." He refilled the glasses.

"I think if I drink any more the moon won't be the only one wearing a shroud," I said, holding my hand over the top of my glass just to be on the safe side. Thank goodness Ben and I had made a little detour via the kitchen on our way here and helped ourselves to a pastry each. We hadn't stayed long because neither of us had felt very hungry after our argument, but now I regretted not having had more to eat. It might have soaked up the alcohol.

Old Stucky cleared his throat. "Twalve naights."

"I'm sorry?"

"Durin' tha twalve naights, anythin' ken happn," murmured Old Stucky, fixing me with his piercing gaze. Instead of his usual roguish grin, his weather-beaten face had crumpled into a web of anxious lines and his clear eyes were wide in their sockets. "Earvul creeches, deemins an' ghoarsts walk abrooard, an' peepul foll prey ter their davlish skeeyems."

Now I knew how Pavel must feel when he listened to opera lyrics in German. What on earth were "earvul creeches"?

"During the Twelve Nights, anything can happen," Ben whispered from beside me. "He's talking about the twelve nights between Christmas Day and the sixth of January—local legend has it that on those nights, evil creatures, demons, and ghosts walk abroad." He paused for a moment, and I felt more goose bumps rise on my skin. Why was Old Stucky staring so intently at *me* in particular?

"And people fall prey to their devilish schemes," Ben went on. He couldn't suppress a little chuckle. "I think he's talking about Tristan Brown from Room 211."

"Ha ha, very funny," I whispered. "Don't you find it creepy, the stuff he's saying? And the way he's saying it?"

Ben shot me an amused glance. "You may not understand Old Stucky, Sophie, but he understands you perfectly."

"Aye do," said Old Stucky.

"Sorry," I said, "but you really are scaring me a bit."

"Yes—we stop now with ghost stories." Pavel raised his glass. "We drink!"

"Old Stucky just want you to be on your guard," Old Stucky replied, in almost perfect English. "Earvul forces are at work."

"Then we'll drink to being on our guard against evil forces," said Ben, as he too raised his glass.

"And to little Christ child in manger," Pavel added. He downed his drink in one gulp again, as if it was water. "Where is dear Petrus?" He pronounced it *Petroose*, with the emphasis on the second syllable.

"Monsieur Rocher said he was going to wait and see if any of the guests had any special requests for Christmas." Ben was finding the brandy a little harder to stomach than Pavel. Like me, he was only taking tiny sips of it. "He'll be along later."

"Monsieur Rocher's name is Petrus?" I asked in surprise. Somehow it had never really occurred to me that Monsieur Rocher had a first name.

"We always sing as trio at Christmas," Pavel explained. "And when Jaromir back from church, we sing as quartet."

Old Stucky said something that Ben translated as "the right music keeps the devil away." "That's what his father always used to . . . Oh no!"

"What's wrong?"

"I completely lost track of time! Is it ten o'clock already?" Ben rummaged frantically in his jacket pocket, trying to find his phone.

"I think so. Why?"

"My dad always gives his Christmas speech at ten o'clock, and if I'm not there nodding along when he does his spiel about the next generation being ready to carry on the hotel's proud traditions, he'll be seriously pissed off . . . Oh my God!" He'd located his phone. "It's five past. Come on, Sophie!" He grabbed my hand. "We might pop back later and listen to your quartet, Pavel! Merry Christmas to you both!" And without further ado, he hustled me out of the laundry room. I wondered whether to remind him that our unresolved friendship status meant he probably shouldn't be holding my hand, but he didn't even seem to have noticed he was doing it.

As he rushed me along the winding corridors to the staircase that led to the library, he quoted from his dad's speech and commentated on it at the same time. "Every year, it's the same sentimental shit, *Dear guests, no, dear friends, old and new—it fills me with happiness and pride to see you all here* . . . And his smile is so fake you want to throw an ornament at his head. Sometimes he even wipes an imaginary tear out of the corner of his eye. So ridiculous! *What could be more fitting, at Christmas, than to talk about love?* My dad, talking about love! Ha! He doesn't even know the meaning of the word. *I don't know if you know the story* . . . Yes, they all know the story, Dad, you tell it every fricking year . . ." With his free hand, Ben pushed open the door to the staircase. "*Our esteemed great-grandparents . . . ideals, duty, tradition,* blah blah blah, and then the bit about *my beloved son, Ben, to whom I will one day hand over the keys to this hotel. Ben*—and then he puts his hand on his heart, seriously, every single time—*you are my great pride and my great hope.*"

Ben galloped up the stairs so fast that I had trouble keeping up with him. He flung open the door to the library. "And then everyone applauds, and I go bright red. I've always hated that stupid speech, ever since I was five years old. I wish I could tell them all that the old hypocrite is planning to sell off this venerable place he supposedly loves so much to some shady waste-disposal magnate who couldn't care less about the ideals of his great-grandparents. There is one good thing about the hotel being sold, though: At least I'll never have to listen to that phony speech again." We'd come through the library by now and were standing in the corridor outside the bar. Only now did Ben seem to realize I was still attached to him. Puzzled, he looked down at our clasped hands. "It's really nice of you to come with me," he said, gradually loosening his grip and tucking his hand rather awkwardly into his pants pocket. "But if you'd rather not . . ."

"It's fine. I'm quite curious to hear this speech now, after all that." I smiled at him, and he smiled back with relief.

"Well then . . ." He took a deep breath before we entered the room. There was a big crowd of guests assembled in the bar, many

173

of them holding glasses of champagne. I could see the whole of the Barnbrooke family (apart from Amy, Gracie, and Madison) as well as the Ball Bearings Baroness with her young lover, Tristan and his grandpa, the Burkhardts (Don Jr. was wearing a dark-blue velvet bow tie, which suited him perfectly), the British actor, the thriller writer, Mr. and Mrs. Von Dietrichstein, and Mara Matthäus in her glittery dress. Mrs. Ludwig had laid her head on Mr. Ludwig's shoulder, and the engagement ring sparkled conspicuously on her finger. Tristan must have noticed it by now.

Gutless Gilbert was the only one who saw us arrive; he was standing by the wall next to the door, and we slotted ourselves in as discreetly as possible beside him. Ben's father had positioned himself next to the grand piano and was obviously a fair way into his speech. "I don't know if you know the story, but in 1898 when the hotel was being built, our great-grandparents commissioned a stonemason to carve the family motto above the main door. The motto was *mens agitat molem*, which can be roughly translated as *mind over matter*. But when they came to check on how the work was going, they found that the engraving read *tempus fugit, amor manet*, which means *time flies, but love endures*. Of course they took the stonemason to task, but he claimed he hadn't even started work on the engraving yet. To this day, we don't know who was responsible for the mystery motto. All her life, however, our great-grandmother was convinced that it was the spirit of the mountain who had chosen that motto and placed this building under its protection." He smiled and the guests laughed politely. "Needless to say, *tempus fugit, amor manet* not only became the motto of the hotel, but our family motto, too." Again he paused for a moment. "And it fills me with gratitude and pride to know that my brother and I will one day pass on the guardianship of this building with all its traditions and values to my wonderful son Ben, just as our grandparents passed it on to our parents." He placed his hand on his heart, and both Ben and his uncle gave a quiet sigh. "Ben, where are you?" Gordon scanned the room, spotted Ben standing by the wall, and smiled tenderly. All the guests turned to look at us and smiled, too. "And on that note," Gordon Montfort concluded, in an extremely self-satisfied tone, "I wish you all, old friends and new, a merry Christmas full of love and laughter."

Everyone applauded. Then they raised their glasses of champagne and fell into animated conversation. The pianist slipped back onto his piano stool, and somebody somewhere opened a window to let in the cool night air.

"Unbelievable," I whispered to Ben.

Gutless Gilbert had extricated himself from his spot by the wall and was heading for the bar, along with the British actor, while Grouchy Gordon went over to join the Barnbrookes and called loudly for another bottle of champagne. "It was exactly like you said. Except that you didn't go red this time."

"Inwardly I did." Ben gave a tortured smile. "Oh no! He's coming over. Let's get out of here." But it was too late. Gordon Montfort was already standing before us. He had Gretchen's arm in his; she lowered her eyes and whispered "Hi," as if overcome by shyness.

"Here's my wonderful son," said Gordon Montfort. "I thought for a minute just now that you were not in the room." He glanced over me, and I detected something like confusion in his eyes. I tried to shuffle backward, but unfortunately the wall was in the way.

"Great speech, sir," Ben replied. "Something completely different for a change. And more sincere and moving than ever this time, in light of upcoming events."

His father completely ignored him. I wasn't sure he'd even heard what Ben had said. "Today is your lucky day, son. The lovely Gretchen Barnbrooke here has told me she'd love to dance the first waltz with you at the New Year's Ball. But she's too shy to ask you herself."

Yeah, *right*. I almost snorted aloud. As if sensing this, Gretchen raised her eyes and looked at me with undisguised curiosity. I could practically hear what was going through her head. *That weird chambermaid again. She always seems to pop up wherever the hot guys are.*

"I told her you would be honored," Gordon went on.

"Of course," said Ben. He sounded rather weary.

"But I don't want to impose," Gretchen piped up in a soft voice. Her blue dress shimmered in the light of the chandelier as if trying to outshine her silky golden hair. "So if you'd prefer to dance with someone else . . ." She smiled meaningfully in my direction.

Gordon Montfort followed her gaze, and this time he looked at me more closely.

"It would be an honor to dance the first waltz with you, Gretchen," said Ben quickly, as I tried desperately to make myself invisible. Gordon Montfort was clearly racking his brains to think where he'd seen me before.

Ben stepped forward. "We can even do some lifts if you like; we'll be the king and queen of the dance floor." Was this just a diversionary tactic or was he really flirting with Gretchen?

"We definitely will." I heard Gretchen's self-assured laugh, and I was sure she must be flicking her shiny hair. But I couldn't see her because I was staring as if paralyzed at Ben's father, and he was staring at me. His look changed from one of confusion to one of recognition and finally (once Gretchen had remembered she was supposed to be shy and walked away whispering "I should get back to my family, but I'll see you later") to one of outrage and contempt.

"Staff are not allowed to mix with guests outside of working hours," said Gordon icily. "I'm shocked at your impertinence."

"She's here with me. As my guest." Ben looked darkly at his dad. "Come on, Sophie, let's go. I've played the dutiful son for long enough tonight." He took my arm. To his dad he said, "You can make a scene if you want—and believe me, it will be a very ugly scene!—or you can just leave us alone and go back to celebrating with your friends, *old and new*. Mara Matthäus is looking over here very longingly."

His dad grabbed my other arm, and I broke out in a cold sweat. The vein on Gordon's forehead was bulging the way it always did when he was about to start screaming at somebody. How I wished I was back in the safety of the basement with Pavel! But Gordon Montfort didn't start bawling at me. "You are either extremely naive or extremely smart," he said quietly. "But either way, you clearly need to be reminded of your place—"

He didn't get any further, however, because at that moment there was a loud cracking sound, followed by an almighty crash. As we were standing closest to the door, we were the first to see what had happened: Out in the hallway, right outside the door to the billiards room, a chandelier had fallen from the ceiling. The crystals had shattered into a thousand tiny pieces and were scattered all over the floor. The electric cable dangled forlornly from the ceiling rose, and a little dust trickled down from the plaster. Luckily, nobody had been standing underneath when it fell.

While the guests crowded excitedly toward the door to gape at the scene of the disaster, and Gordon Montfort tried to reassure everyone—"Nothing to see here, ladies and gentlemen! Nothing to see here. Please could everybody stay inside the bar until the staff have swept up the broken glass?"—Ben and I seized our chance and disappeared around the corner and into the library. We took the back staircase again, but this time we headed upstairs, in wordless agreement.

"What just happened?" I panted, once we'd reached the second floor. "Do you think Old Stucky was right about his demons, ghosts, and evil creatures?"

"Absolutely," said Ben drily. "And my dad is the evilest of them all. I'm sorry he's such a . . ."

"It's fine. He was right, really. I had no business being there."

"It was my fault. I practically forced you to come with me." Ben fell into a gloomy silence as we climbed the steps.

"Where are we going, anyway?"

"No idea. Just somewhere far away from my dad." Ben gave me a lopsided grin. "But perhaps we could . . . have you ever been up to the roof?"

"Right to the top?" I shook my head. I'd been meaning to go up there for a long time, but I'd never gotten around to it.

You could get to the roof via the men's staff quarters, but instead of going that way, Ben led me along the corridor to his uncle's apartment. Beside the apartment door there was a hidden door that looked like a built-in cupboard but actually concealed a steep wooden staircase. The steps ended in another door, which Ben opened for me. Fresh, cool air enveloped me as I stepped out onto the roof. I marveled as I looked around. We were standing on a kind of terrace above the skylight to the main staircase, which from up here looked even more like an antique greenhouse. The soft light of the chandeliers shone through the panes of glass between the metal beams, bathing everything around us in an ethereal glow.

"Careful, it might be slippery," said Ben.

During the day, the view from here must be spectacular. I leaned cautiously over the railing and looked out over the edge. Far below, beside the ice rink, lay our snow dragon. It looked as if it were sleeping. "We're so high up," I said, skating across to the other side of the terrace, but the roof of the south wing blocked my view of the ground. I leaned with my back against the railing and tipped my head up. The sky was starless and full of clouds.

Ben came to stand beside me. "I'm so sorry for—for everything," he said.

I looked at him in astonishment. "What do you mean?"

"That you had such a stressful day. That I said such horrible things. And then my dad winning the prize for the world's worst human being. And on Christmas Eve as well. Your first Christmas away from home."

"Hmm," I said. By this time on a normal Christmas Eve I'd be helping my mum tidy the kitchen while my dad drove my grandparents home, and my little brothers, instead of going to bed like they were supposed to, would be busy stuffing their mouths from the candy bowl until my mum noticed, and by then it was usually too late. Either Finn or Leon or both would throw up, and I'd have to finish cleaning the kitchen on my own, and afterward my parents would argue about whose fault it all was. I couldn't say I was terribly sorry to be missing out on it.

Ben misinterpreted my silence and gently patted my arm.

Downstairs, the commotion caused by the falling chandelier seemed to have died down. The sound of piano music drifted up to us through the open window of the bar. And somewhere nearby I could smell tobacco smoke.

In my mind, I went back over the events of the day, from feeding the seven Hugos, to playing with the children in the snow, to my shock at finding Tristan in the Panorama Suite, to the wonderful moment when Mr. Ludwig had slipped the ring back onto Mrs. Ludwig's finger. And then Pavel's and Old Stucky's singing in the laundry room. It was hard to believe it had all happened in the space of one day. Admittedly, the argument with Ben hadn't been very nice, nor had my encounter with Gordon Montfort just now, nor Ella's and Gretchen's scornful looks. If I thought about it long enough, I was sure to remember quite a few other moments that hadn't been completely perfect—but that didn't really matter. A day didn't have to be perfect to be memorable.

"It's definitely been the most exciting Christmas Eve I've ever had." I looked around. "Can you smell that?"

Ben nodded. "It's Fräulein Müller. She's smoking a cigar."

"What?" Not Fräulein Müller!

"Shh." Ben laughed. "No one's allowed to know. It's her secret vice. And I think it's her only vice. Every evening, Monsieur Rocher gives her a fine Havana out of the humidor. She insists on paying for it, of course."

"Of course." I felt almost sad to imagine Fräulein Müller standing at the open window of her bedroom after work every evening, smoking alone and in secret. "It actually smells quite nice from a distance. Almost makes me want a cigar myself. And I've already sampled some pear brandy today."

"If your parents only knew what you've been getting up to," said Ben. "We're corrupting you."

For a while, we just stood there listening to the music from downstairs. The pianist had run out of international Christmas songs by this time and had switched to pop songs. I was starting to get cold out here without my coat. But I didn't want to go in yet.

After a few minutes, we both broke the silence at the same time.

"Are we friends again?" asked Ben, and I said, "Do you even know *how* to waltz?" Then we both answered "Yes!" and started laughing.

"Shall I prove it?" asked Ben, offering me his hand. The pianist had just started playing a slow song.

Dancing wasn't exactly my favorite thing. Delia and I had been thrown out of the dance class we'd signed up for last winter after just five lessons, allegedly because we kept disturbing the class with our giggling fits, but actually because there were a lot more girls than boys.

The sound of the piano drifted through the air, and not until Ben placed his right hand below my shoulder blade and started to spin me around did I realize that "When I Need You," the song the pianist was currently playing, was a slow waltz. In three-four time.

At the dance lessons, I'd never understood what was so great about waltzing, but with Ben it was different. I felt myself standing taller and straighter in his arms. It was a wonderful feeling, gliding around the roof in time with the music without having to think about which foot was supposed to go where. It was completely effortless, almost weightless.

In my head, I sang along. *When I need you, I just close my eyes and I'm with you . . .*

"Right on cue," Ben whispered, pulling me a little closer to him. I felt something wet land on the end of my nose, then on my hand and my cheek. It was snowing—fat snowflakes that swirled around us as if they wanted to join in the waltz, too.

This was just too much.

We stopped dancing and started giggling.

"Oh my God, this is cheesy," said Ben. "Plus I'm freezing my butt off out here."

"And I *hate* this song," I said, feeling like I might burst with laughter. "I don't even know where I know it from. It's terrible."

"Yep, it's horrendous." Ben propelled me toward the door, and we slipped inside, into the warmth. "And the worst thing is: This is going to be *our song* from now on."

elia, as I'd predicted, had decided not to drown herself in the toilet and was absolutely delighted to hear that I'd danced a waltz on the roof. With the hotelier's son. In the falling snow.

For days afterward, she kept sending me smileys with hearts for eyes.

"It's just a shame you didn't lose your glass slipper, Snow White," she wrote.

"Snow White is the one with the poisoned apple, you Rumpelstiltskin," I wrote back. I wasn't all that keen on the idea of me and Ben as Cinderella and Prince Charming (aka the intern and the heir to the hotel). But it did chime with Gordon Montfort's comment that I needed reminding of my place. And in his mind, presumably, my place was by the hearth, sweeping out the grate.

Either way, Gordon Montfort was (to stick with the metaphor) a good fit for the wicked stepmother, and Monsieur Rocher was the perfect fairy godmother. The bossy stepsisters could either be Hortensia and those other idiots from Lausanne or—even better—Gretchen and Ella Barnbrooke. And the Hugos were ideal substitutes for the helpful doves; you just had to imagine them with white feathers instead of black. Perhaps I could teach them to caw: "You *shall* go to the ball!" That would be awesome.

But every time I ran into Ben over the next few days, I realized I'd gotten a little ahead of myself in my fairy-tale fantasy. (Thanks, Delia!) Sure, Ben and I had waltzed together on the roof, but it hadn't gone any further than that. Internella and the Hotel Prince (who would soon have no hotel to inherit) were just friends. Friends who were so overworked that whenever they met during the day, all they had time to do was exchange a harried smile.

The snow that had set in on Christmas Eve went on for days, and the day after Christmas a thick fog descended on the mountainside. For the staff, this meant even more stress and overtime than usual because the guests wanted to stay inside in the warmth all day. On the odd occasions when we managed to take our dinner breaks at the same time, I'd see Ben for half an hour in the evenings, and we'd sometimes meet for a quick chat with Monsieur Rocher in the concierge's lodge or with Pavel in the laundry. But the rest of the time we had to be content with smiling and waving.

I would have been quite happy with this state of affairs if it hadn't been for Delia WhatsApping me every few hours to ask me whether I'd kissed Ben yet. After the third message—"Cinderella can make the first move and kiss the Prince herself if she wants, you know. She's a liberated modern woman"—I started thinking with alarming regularity about what it would be like to kiss Ben. Whenever we met, I had to force myself not to look at his lips. A liberated modern woman I might be, but I definitely didn't want him to know what was going on in my head.

But despite all these annoying thoughts about kissing and my heavy workload, I spent the next three days on cloud nine. Everything seemed to have turned out for the best: My argument with Ben was water under the bridge, old Mrs. Ludwig had her ring back, and Stella Yegorov was laid up in the Panorama Suite—allegedly with a migraine, though I hoped what she was actually doing was wondering how the ring had found its way from her nightstand back onto Mrs. Ludwig's finger and feeling thoroughly ashamed of herself.

And Tristan and I had also thought of a good solution to the problem of telling the Ludwigs about the ring's true value. Or rather, Tristan had thought of it. He'd come to find me outside the playroom on Christmas morning to talk to me about it. The conversation was remarkably civilized by our standards—no hiding behind curtains, no silly jokes about secret agents or hotel thieves, no climbing up walls. The embarrassing end to our last meeting was probably still too fresh in both of our minds.

We agreed that we wouldn't mention the ring to the Ludwigs for a few days. Then we'd break it to them gently that their flea-market find was actually worth a fortune. We were going to delegate this task to Tristan's grandpa—he was an expert gemologist, so the Ludwigs were bound to believe him. I thought it wasn't a bad plan, especially when Tristan explained that he'd already told his grandpa the whole story. His grandfather had been angry with him for climbing the wall and trespassing in someone else's room, but he'd also realized we had to help the Ludwigs.

"Did you tell Ben Montfort how much the ring is really worth?" Tristan had asked me, and he'd smiled with relief when I shook my head. "Good. My grandpa says the fewer people who know about this the better."

I had no time to ask why because at that moment the first few children turned up at the playroom, but I was glad Tristan had put his grandpa in the picture. The Ludwigs would leave the hotel as very wealthy, probably extremely confused, but happy people. And the fact that Tristan, under his grandpa's watchful eye, wouldn't be able to climb the walls anymore was also a welcome development. That was one less thing to worry about. I did feel almost sorry for Tristan, though, when I saw him gazing wistfully up at Jaromir perched at a great height on a metal beam below the skylight. Despite all appearances, this was not a circus act; Jaromir was just inspecting the brackets of the chandelier. He and Old Stucky had been told to check all the chandeliers in the building, because Gordon Montfort wanted to make sure no more of the heavy antique things were about to fall down (possibly burying one of the guests beneath them next time).

I found myself thinking about kissing when I was with Tristan, too. Even if it was only for a few seconds as I stared at his curved lips, which he didn't notice because he was too busy looking at *my* lips. What on earth was going on? It was as if Delia had opened the door to some kind of psychological torment where the only thing anyone could think about was kissing. (Plus, there was only one Prince Charming in "Cinderella.")

Luckily, I was so busy with work for the next few days that I hardly saw Tristan. I was either looking after the children or busy in the spa, which was also a hive of activity. But I saw him several times, from afar, hanging out with Ella and Gretchen. Perhaps he needed them to compensate for all the adrenaline he was missing out on, or perhaps, out of sheer boredom, he'd finally succumbed to the gleam of their golden hair. Gracie and Madison told me Ella had let everyone know Tristan was going to be her partner for the first waltz. You had to hand it to the pair of them—they'd certainly managed to land themselves the best-looking boys in the place for the New Year's Ball.

The ball was a big deal for all the Barnbrooke girls. Even Gracie and Madison had ball gowns to wear for the occasion—pink ones, with lots of tulle.

Amy, on the other hand, had insisted on a simple black dress with a high neck. The way she described it, it sounded like a cross between my chambermaid's uniform and a nun's habit. But Amy wasn't planning to do anything at the ball other than stand by the wall glaring at everyone. (And maybe not even that—she was of two minds about going to the ball at all.) On Christmas Eve she'd plucked up her courage and asked Aiden whether he wanted to be her dance partner. Aiden had replied that she'd be better off finding a boy who could actually hear the music he was dancing to. Amy was so mortified by this rejection that she'd wanted the ground to open up and swallow her. She said she'd never be able to look Aiden in the eye again, and over the next few days, she went to great lengths to avoid him. But it wasn't easy.

Since all the normal scheduled activities—walks in the snow, sleigh rides, trips to ski resorts or nearby towns—had been canceled because of the heavy snow, Amy's usual haunts were now occupied twenty-four seven. People played cards in the library, held darts and billiards tournaments in the billiards room, and attended whisky tastings in the bar (even before lunch). Mara Matthäus organized an impromptu tango class in the ballroom, and the Swiss politician from Room 206 commandeered the music room for a reading from her autobiography, *Politics is Not for the Fainthearted*, which she happened to have brought with her. Amy couldn't even hide in supposedly secret places like the vestibule on the second floor without finding Mrs. Von Dietrichstein there conducting a celebrity interview or Mr. Von Dietrichstein looking for a picturesque spot for a photo shoot.

So every morning after breakfast, Amy came along to the playroom with her two little sisters and stayed all day. Carolyn the kindergarten teacher kindly turned a blind eye. She was a friendly, maternal person who understood that the lovesick Amy needed a safe haven. And someone to comfort her.

"If we don't help her, the poor thing will end up being visited by the Lady in White," she said.

"I thought the Lady in White only came at night."

Carolyn shook her head. "No, no! My mother met her once in the middle of the day. Right here in this very room. She was tidying up some toys when she felt a breath of icy cold air on the back of her neck. And when she turned around, there was the Lady in White standing in the doorway smiling sadly at her. My mother said that in that moment she felt an overwhelming urge to open the window and jump out."

I gulped. "But why did the Lady in White visit her?"

"My mother was in love with man named Claudio. But unfortunately he didn't love her back."

"And what happened then?" As always when someone told me a spooky story, I had goose bumps.

"The light flickered," said Carolyn. "And then the Lady in White disappeared. My mother drove home as fast as she could and accepted my dad's marriage proposal. And she's never looked back."

I sighed with relief. This Lady in White didn't seem to be all that bad after all. "What did she look like?" I asked. Just to be on the safe side.

Carolyn shrugged. "My mother says she looked a bit like a chambermaid."

Okay, that was my fault. I did ask.

Carolyn was a lovely person, but she had an unfortunate penchant for ambitious arts and crafts. If she'd had her way, we would all have sat there from morning till night making unicorns, New Year's crackers, and paper snowflakes—using plenty of glitter, which Carolyn loved and bought by the bucketload. In the evenings, I'd find it everywhere: in my pockets, between my teeth, even in my ears.

Apparently it was nontoxic and biodegradable glitter, which was a good thing, too, because Elias, the thriller writer's younger son, had once eaten about half a pound of the stuff mixed into some of Madame Cléo's marzipan balls. It turned out Don had talked little Elias into this "dare," as he called it. I warned Elias's parents not to be alarmed if their toilet was a bit glittery for the next few days, but other than that there wasn't really much I could do about it. Don didn't tend to get rough with the other children—the little delinquent preferred to wreak havoc using words alone. It was astonishing, the way he managed to identify the other children's weak spots and use them against them. Only the Americans—Amy, Gracie, and Madison—were safe from his machinations, simply because they didn't have a clue what he was talking about. They only knew one word of German, and that was *danke*. Whatever Don said to them, it rolled off them like water off a duck's back, and his primary school English was no match for their South Carolina accents.

On the twenty-seventh of December, the weather was so bad that we had to call off our usual trip outdoors with the children. We'd spent half an hour bundling them into their snowsuits, ski pants, and parkas and putting on their snow boots, hats, scarves, and gloves, only to unwrap them all ten minutes later. It was pointless trying to play outside. The icy wind whipped the snowflakes straight into our faces, and our eyelashes, eyebrows, and hair were immediately coated with a layer of snow crystals. You could hardly see your hand in front of your face. We hadn't even gotten as far as the ice rink when we decided to turn back before one of the children got blown away or lost in a snowdrift. The snowflakes were pricking our skin like hundreds of tiny arrows.

We were all relieved to get back to the warmth of the playroom, but nobody except Carolyn was in the mood for sitting around quietly doing arts and crafts. It wasn't long before a scissor fight broke out between Don and Gracie, in which Gracie lost a lock of hair and Don one of the tails of his untucked shirt. Gracie used all sorts of swear words I was sure her mother had no idea she knew.

Once we'd finally managed to separate the two brawlers (and confiscated the scissors), Don came out with one of his ominous threats. "Gracie Barnbrooke shouldn't think she's going to get away with ruining my shirt like that. She's going to wish she'd never been born." He glared at me. "Tell her that!"

I turned to Gracie. "Don says he's glad he came to the playroom today, otherwise he'd never have got to know you. And he's very sorry about your hair," I translated rather freely.

Gracie crossed her arms. "Fine. Tell him I accept his apology. Because he's got nice eyes, and I think good boys are boring anyway."

Amy rolled her eyes. "This is where pink tulle and purple glitter gets you. You fall in love with a bad boy, you get your heart broken, and you end up in the place where feminism goes to die." She really was in a bad way.

I turned back to Don. "Amy says Gracie may look cute, but in the playground this summer she broke a boy's shoulder when he tried to pick a fight with her. And then there was that time she broke a little girl's nose. But Gracie says that was an accident."

"Really?" Don gulped, visibly affected by this news, as Gracie batted her eyelashes.

"He can teach me some swear words if he wants," she offered. "My mom can't stop me saying words she doesn't understand. Ask him how you say 'horseshit' in German."

I turned to Don again. "Her mum's afraid she'll never be able to manage her temper and will end up killing someone one day, but Gracie says she's got it under control. And she asked me to ask you how to say 'horseshit' in German."

There was nothing more I could do for Gracie. But that was probably enough to put Don off his revenge schemes for the time being. He was looking at Gracie with a lot more respect now, anyway. And he was clearly confused by the way she was smiling at him with her head on one side, coquettishly twiddling a lock of hair around her finger. Lost in thought, he rubbed his shoulder.

"It's all a question of communication," I told Amy contentedly. "Perhaps it's just a misunderstanding between you and Aiden."

But I didn't get a chance to explain my theory because at that moment Gordon Montfort appeared in the doorway, together with the Yegorov family. Their bodyguard wasn't with them; he must have been waiting outside somewhere. I'd noticed he was extremely discreet—he was so good at staying out of sight that I'd never even seen him with the Yegorovs. But presumably that was all part of the job description for a bodyguard.

Ben's dad entered the room without saying hello, while Viktor Yegorov gave us all a friendly nod as he came in. Stella Yegorov positioned herself decoratively in the doorway.

I hadn't seen Ben's dad since Christmas Eve, not even from a distance, so I was rather alarmed to suddenly find myself in the same room as him. The things he'd said on Sunday, and the profound contempt with which he'd said them, came flooding back to me. I realized I was instinctively trying to make myself smaller in the hope he'd ignore me, as he'd always done before.

"This," he said in English, with a sweeping gesture around the room, "is our little playroom. Liz Taylor's offspring played here, you know."

Really? Or had he just made that up? Stella Yegorov didn't seem particularly impressed. She still had her little dog with her, this time stuffed into a silver crocodile-skin handbag that matched her silver stilettos. Together with her elegant backless jumpsuit, it was the perfect outfit for the red carpet at the Oscars.

The little dog gave a shrill yap, and Faye and the thriller writer's sons, who had been chasing one another around the table, stopped abruptly and stared at it in fascination.

"Does it have batteries?" Elias asked, but Stella Yegorov clearly felt it beneath her dignity to reply. To be fair, she hadn't understood a word he'd said.

Little Dasha gripped her father's hand as hard as she could and pressed her curly head against his leg.

"This rocking horse dates back to 1898," Montfort explained in his booming voice. "It was made especially for the hotel." The playroom was indeed a treasure trove of vintage toys: the doll's house, the carved wooden Punch-and-Judy puppets, the out-of-tune piano, and the various tin toys were all antique. Collectors would have been horrified to see our children actually playing with them.

"Hello." Carolyn had stood up from her child-sized chair and was brushing glitter off her pants. "What can I do for you?"

Gordon Montfort turned toward her for a moment. "This is our brilliant education professional, Ms. . . ."

"Imhoff," said Carolyn. "We always say hello, by the way, when we come into the playroom."

"Quite right." Gordon Montfort cleared his throat and then, turning to Viktor Yegorov, continued: "Ms. Imhoff is a qualified kindergarten teacher and highly experienced. She has excellent credentials."

Viktor Yegorov nodded and smiled, and carried Dasha over to the rocking horse. His wife gave a deep sigh and drummed her long fingernails on the wood of the door frame.

"The thing is, Ms.—er—Imhoff," said Gordon Montfort. "The . . . um . . . *Smirnov* family needs a qualified education professional to look after little Dasha. One-on-one."

Carolyn frowned. "Does the little girl have a physical disability or learning difficulties?"

"What?" Gordon Montfort sniffed. "No, of course not! She is just a very special child of very special parents, and she needs very special care. Which you can provide."

"She can come and join our motley crew," said Carolyn amiably. "I'm sure she'll like it here."

"No, no, no." Gordon Montfort was clearly getting frustrated with Carolyn's failure to understand him. "First of all, the girl can't speak any German—she only speaks Russian—and secondly she's not used to other children."

"I wouldn't be any use when it comes to Russian, I'm afraid," said Carolyn politely. "And from a pedagogical perspective, it really isn't advisable to isolate a child in that way. At her age, she needs to be spending time with other children. Fortunately, children have a universal language among themselves, so they can understand each other no matter where they come from."

"I'm afraid you are missing the point!" cried Montfort. "You will be working with the girl on a one-on-one basis. Naturally, Mr.—er—Smirnov will pay you extra for your services. You will make yourself available to the family as a private nanny from nine in the morning until, let's say, ten at night. Is that so hard to comprehend? You should feel flattered and be grateful to the Smirnovs."

But nothing could have been further from Carolyn's mind. "What about the other children?" she wanted to know.

The dreaded vein of rage on the hotelier's head began to swell. But at this point, Viktor Yegorov, who was pushing Dasha on the rocking horse, shot us a puzzled glance, and Gordon Montfort's face smoothed out as if by magic, his mouth twisting into a benevolent smile.

"This is not your own private kindergarten, Ms.—er—," he went on, in such an effusively friendly voice that anyone who didn't speak German would have thought he was paying Carolyn a gushing compliment. I had no idea how he managed it. He certainly was a very accomplished actor. "You don't make the rules here. I do. And if I say you will look after Dasha one-on-one, I don't expect you to argue with me in front of the guests, but to nod politely and be grateful for the extra income."

Carolyn raised both eyebrows and was about to reply, but Gordon Montfort lifted his hand and said, "I'm not finished. As for as the other children, the intern can take over here for the time being." He cocked his chin at me, and I flinched as if he'd hit me.

Carolyn's eyebrows had almost disappeared into her hair.

In the meantime, little Faye had also gone skipping over to the rocking horse. "I want to ride, too!" she chirped. With a smile, Viktor Yegorov lifted her up behind his daughter, and both girls squealed with joy as the horse started rocking.

"Do you understand what I'm saying, Ms.—er—Imhoff?" Montfort had lowered his voice even further. Although he was still smiling, the look in his eyes was chilling. I had to clamp my teeth together to stop them from chattering.

"Yes, I understand." Instead of recoiling from Montfort, Carolyn leaned forward slightly and looked him straight in the eye. "But I don't think *you* understand what *I'm* saying. On no account will I work as a private nanny for people who stuff dogs into handbags, no matter how much they're paying me." She spoke quietly but firmly, and the smile slowly faded from the hotelier's face. "You employ me to work in the playroom from nine till four thirty, and I'm not willing to do any more than that. In fact, the only reason I'm doing this job over the holidays is because my mother worked for your mother, and she'd be sad to think I wasn't carrying on the tradition. She loved Castle in the Clouds."

At the other end of the room, the oligarch was lifting Dasha and Faye off the rocking horse and kneeling on the floor with them, but everybody else in the room was following the exchange between Montfort and Carolyn with great interest. Only Stella Yegorov looked deeply bored as she examined her fingernails.

"You really want to start an argument with me? Do you know how many kindergarten teachers would jump at the chance to work here?" Grouchy Gordon couldn't control himself any longer. The vein of rage was bulging on his forehead again.

"Go on, then! Fire me."

Carolyn was my new idol. She was without a doubt the bravest person in the world. I wanted to be like her when I grew up.

Gordon Montfort was absolutely stunned. His hands grabbed the empty air in front of him as if throttling an imaginary neck. I had no idea what he would have done next in his fury if Viktor Yegorov hadn't appeared at his side. Smiling, he pointed to his daughter, who was sitting on the floor with Faye, feeding a doll with an imaginary spoon. Would it be all right to bring Dasha here tomorrow to play with the other children for a couple of hours, he inquired politely, since she was having such a lovely time?

Don spoke for all of us who'd been following the showdown between the hotelier and the kindergarten teacher when he let out a short "Ha!" Stella Yegorov muttered something in Russian that I assumed was "Can we *go* now?" Meanwhile, Gordon Montfort had somehow managed to get the vein of rage to subside and had plastered on a beaming smile. "That was going to be my next suggestion!" he cried enthusiastically. "I'm sure these little rascals will be only too glad to welcome Dasha to the playroom and help make her feel at home."

The little rascals—those of them who understood English, anyway—nodded eagerly. Carolyn smiled obligingly, and the Yegorovs left with Dasha, who waved good-bye happily as she went. Gordon Montfort followed them. But just as I was about to breathe a sigh of relief, he turned to face us again.

"You may think you've won, Ms. . . . er . . . But this is not over," he said quietly. "I won't tolerate rebelliousness in my staff." His icy gaze fell on me. "And you! What are you thinking, turning up to work in your own clothes? Go and get changed immediately, or you can pack your bags." With that, he went on his way at last, and I slumped into my chair, exhausted.

17

The next day, when things truly began to go wrong, I would have remained calm, I really would have. After all, it wasn't the first time I'd mislaid a pair of children while on day-care duty. Anyway, Monsieur Rocher had told me lost things always turned up again sooner or later at Castle in the Clouds—and everybody knew Monsieur Rocher was always right. Plus, it wasn't as if the children had run away from me personally. They'd just disappeared under rather unfortunate circumstances that nobody could possibly hold me responsible for. Nevertheless, I *was* the one who'd suggested the game of hide-and-seek, and the fact that we hadn't found them yet was probably thanks to the excellent tips I'd given them. There were hundreds of hiding places in this hotel, even for adults. When it came to small children, the possibilities were endless.

Like I said, I would have remained calm. If it hadn't been for that thriller writer piping up with his kidnapping theory and sending me into a total panic.

The day had started badly. As usual, the hyenas had gone into the bathroom before me and taken showers of epic proportions—not only had they used up all the hot water but they'd also left the window open so that I literally had icicles forming on my nose while I was brushing my teeth. I hadn't thought I'd ever get tired of the snow, but now even I was starting to feel like it had gone on long enough.

On the first day, we'd still been able to see the outline of our beautiful dragon alongside the ice rink, on the second day it was just an undulating bulge in the snow, and today you'd never know there'd been anything there at all. Everything was blanketed in snow. Jaromir and Old Stucky had a job just keeping the entrances to the hotel clear and the main pathways to the stable and the road at least passable. The cars in the lot had turned into huge white mounds, gradually melting into one another and looking rather like the meringue decorations on Madame Cléo's *tarte au citron*.

Every day—and sometimes twice a day—the skylight and the roof space (which I'd secretly nicknamed "the waltz terrace") had to be cleared because the snow covered the glass structure like a blanket, blocking out what little daylight there was. Until now, the road up from the valley had also been cleared every day so that the postman, delivery drivers, and hotel staff who drove in from the next village (like Carolyn) had always been able to get through. But during the night of the twenty-eighth of December it had snowed so much that even the dogged newspaper delivery man hadn't shown up. This only ever happened about once every ten years, according to Monsieur Rocher.

Because of the weather, the pace of life at Castle in the Clouds had slowed right down after Christmas. Most of the guests had relished this at first, but their enjoyment of the enforced peace and quiet was gradually giving way to nervous tension. Many of them seemed to have developed cabin fever from having to stay indoors all the time. At breakfast, the pharmaceutical executive and the Ball Bearings Baroness's lover had got into a fight over the last few raspberries on the fruit platter, and Gracie said one or the other of them certainly would have drawn blood if Gutless Gilbert hadn't stepped in. The politician's husband sent back his soft-boiled egg because it wasn't the perfect shape, causing the chef to chase poor Pierre all the way across the kitchen. Don's mother alerted the staff because there was a horrible smell in the Large Tower Suite, at which Fräulein Müller set out at once with three cleaning carts, practically with blue lights flashing.

Shortly afterward, Don came shuffling into the playroom in a bad mood, probably frustrated that he had nothing left up his sleeve but unimaginative stink-bomb tricks.

Myself and Carolyn (who'd made it to the hotel by following the snowplow, thank goodness, just in time to receive little Dasha from the arms of her anxious father) were similarly at a loss as to how to keep the children entertained. We'd done so many arts-and-crafts projects that you could have filled an entire auditorium with our creations; the Punch-and-Judy show we'd written had had its premiere in front of seventeen attentive stuffed animals; and we'd gone through pretty much all the children's games Carolyn knew, from Simon Says to I Spy to Duck Duck Goose.

But what the children needed more than anything was a bit of exercise and a change of scenery. Which was why Carolyn had agreed to my request that we all go out into the corridor to play hide-and-seek. The children were under strict instructions, though: The rooms were out of bounds, as were the elevators, and they all had to stay on the third floor and make sure they didn't disturb any of the guests or the staff.

The children were incredibly creative when it came to choosing hiding places. Faye was the only one who made it easy for us; she thought she was invisible as soon as she closed her eyes. Little Dasha, on the other hand, turned out to be a cunning hider, and her frilly red knitted Dior dress proved surprisingly useful. It blended in perfectly with the velvet curtains, so that all Dasha had to do was crouch down behind them and wait contentedly to be found.

The children crawled under the tables, wedged themselves into the gap between the piano and the bookshelf, buried themselves in the toy chests, and laid down flat on the shelves. Gracie somehow managed to squeeze herself inside the dolls' carriage, pull a doll's lace bonnet over her face, and cover herself up with a blanket, thereby winning second prize for Most Original Hiding Place. The first prize had to go to Don: He succeeded in climbing inside the laundry bag on Anni Moser's cleaning cart, where he would probably never have been found if he hadn't started giggling.

Viktor Yegorov, who stopped by every now and then to have a quick peek at what we were doing, was amazed to see his daughter playing so happily with the other children.

At lunchtime, everything was still hunky-dory. Apart from Elias spilling his glass of lemonade, as he did every day, and Don balancing a meatball on Gracie's head, the children were less trouble than the adult guests, who were keeping Ben, Monsieur Rocher, and the kitchen staff very busy with all their special requests.

But after lunch, one thing led to another, and the disaster began to unfold. It all started when little Faye banged her head on the edge of the table and wanted to be taken to see her mummy. Although we offered to kiss it better and Carolyn even managed to rustle up a Band-Aid with ponies on it, Faye was adamant that she wanted her mum, and by this time her nose was running more than ever. Amy offered to take her down to the first floor and drop her off at the Fabergé Suite. Dasha was determined to accompany her new friend, so we let her go, too. Gracie joined the little group, saying she needed the toilet. Don announced that he wanted to go with them; Faye was a fascinating case study for his long-neglected photo project *Fifty Shades of Snot*.

I only had Amy's account of what happened next, although I didn't doubt the truth of it for a second. At first, the five of them had gone down to the Fabergé Suite as planned, but there was nobody there. So Amy had the smart idea of going down to the lobby and asking Monsieur Rocher if he knew where Faye's parents might be. Monsieur Rocher happened to know that Faye's mother was currently having a back, neck, and shoulder massage with Mr. Heffelfinger. At this point, Amy realized it wasn't going to be easy to take Faye to see her mother, but Faye was not to be deterred—she wanted her mummy, and she wanted her *now*—so Amy had no choice but to take everyone down to the spa. I'd probably have done exactly the same in her shoes.

Remembering Mr. Heffelfinger's aversion to children, she told Gracie, Don, and Dasha to wait outside the door with the forbidding sign until she'd taken Faye to her mother. Which took longer than expected because during the day Mr. Heffelfinger was assisted by a beautician who'd clearly been given the task of guarding the massage-room door like Cerberus. And the fact that Cerberus spoke no English didn't help matters. Amy said it had taken all her diplomatic skill to persuade the beautician that it would be best for all concerned if she let her take the snotty, quietly whimpering child into the massage room to see her mom. At long last, however, Amy had managed to deliver Faye (under Mr. Heffelfinger's scandalized gaze) into her mother's arms, where she cheered up immediately. Amy was feeling pretty pleased with herself, but the feeling evaporated instantly when she left the spa to find that the other children were gone.

Gracie, Don, and Dasha were simply nowhere to be seen. She called their names and searched the corridor that led from the spa to the elevators, but there was no sign of them. By this time, of course, Carolyn and I were starting to wonder what had become of them all, but it wasn't until Amy returned to the playroom and asked whether the three children were back already that we started to worry. Not seriously, but a bit: Dasha's dad was bound to pop in any minute to see how Dasha was getting on. The idea of having to tell him we weren't entirely sure of his daughter's whereabouts was not a very appealing one.

"Don's probably showing them around the hotel," I said, but at the same time I remembered, with a sinking feeling, his bad mood earlier that day. What if he'd come up with a better trick than the stink bomb? "I'm sure he just wants to show off to Dasha, introduce her to his contacts in the kitchen. Someone down there keeps giving him ice cream."

"Quite right—I'm sure they'll be back any minute," Carolyn agreed. "But perhaps you two should go back out there and have a look for them. I'll stay with the other children and make sure we don't lose any of *them*." She gave a little laugh, but it didn't sound as carefree as usual.

Amy and I had only just left the room when Gracie came trotting up.

"There, you see," said Carolyn, relieved, but unfortunately there wasn't much cause for relief. Gracie was alone. And she was very surprised to hear that Don and Dasha weren't back yet. Gracie had last seen them down in the basement. They'd gotten bored waiting for Amy, so they'd decided to go back upstairs without her. Because Ella and Gretchen had happened to come out of the spa just then, along with Tristan, Aiden, and Claus, Gracie had followed them upstairs and spied on them for a bit while Don and Dasha had gotten into the elevator. Gracie had tailed Ella and Gretchen for a few minutes (they'd gone to play darts in the billiards room), then, after a detour to the toilet, she'd come back to the playroom.

"We've got one child back already, and the other two will turn up soon." Carolyn stroked Gracie's head and attempted a breezy smile. "But it can't hurt to speed things up a little. Perhaps just go and have a quick look in the elevators."

Amy, Gracie, and I searched all the elevators. But there was no trace of Don and Dasha.

"I should never have left them alone," Amy lamented. "If they don't turn up soon, Carolyn's going to get into trouble, and it'll be all my fault. And Mr. Montfort is going to be furious."

She was right there. Ben's dad was going to flip his lid when he found out about this.

"I'm sure they're just playing hide-and-seek again," said Gracie.

I wasn't so sure. Don, as we knew, had been in a foul mood. And bored. Not a good combination.

"Did Don say anything else?" I asked Gracie, but of course that was a completely pointless question because even if he had said something, she wouldn't have understood it.

Gracie shrugged helplessly. Then she remembered that Dasha and Don hadn't been alone in the elevator—there'd been a nice white-haired lady there, too, who'd spoken German.

"That must have been Mrs. Ludwig," I said, relieved. At least this gave us something to go on. "Perhaps she might know where they were headed."

But unfortunately Mrs. Ludwig couldn't help us, either. We found her in the corridor on her way down to the restaurant, where she was due to meet Mr. Ludwig for a cup of coffee and a slice of

Havana cake. She confirmed that she had seen the children in the basement earlier. "I did wonder what they were doing just standing around in the corridor like that," she said. "Then the boy and that darling little Russian girl got into the elevator with me. I don't really trust those rickety old things, but I just can't manage the stairs anymore with my old bones. And I was in my bathrobe." She lowered her voice. "Which, by the way, is the softest, most comfortable bathrobe I've ever come across. What do you think, my dear, do you suppose I might be able to purchase one before we leave?"

"Yes, I'm sure you can," I said impatiently. "But back to Don and Dasha. You don't happen to know where they might have gone next?"

Mrs. Ludwig shook her head slowly. "I got out here on the first floor, and the children were going up to the third floor. They'd pressed the button for the third floor, anyway. Have the little scamps gone missing?"

I nodded. "But please don't tell anyone." Especially not Dasha's parents. "I'm sure they're just playing hide-and-seek somewhere."

"Of course," said Mrs. Ludwig with an encouraging smile. "As soon as they get hungry they'll come out from wherever they're hiding, you mark my words. I've seen it often enough with my own children and grandchildren."

I was sure she was right. And yet . . .

"Do you have a weird feeling about this?" Amy whispered to me.

I nodded. Yes, damn it, I did. The hotel was a vast maze of corridors and staircases. Who knew what dangers it held for a sheltered four-year-old? There were probably all kinds of hazards I hadn't even thought of yet. Dasha was so small that she'd fit through pretty much any gap. I could see Don now, helping her climb inside a ventilation shaft. And at that moment, I couldn't help thinking of what Old Stucky had said on Christmas Eve. That something bad was about to happen. That evil creatures were going to walk abroad and people would fall prey to their devilish schemes. And Don didn't need any help in that department—he came up with plenty of devilish schemes all by himself.

I decided the only sensible course of action was to tell Monsieur Rocher. And since Ben was standing nearby at Reception, we filled him in, too. I felt better as soon as we'd told them. They did a wonderful job of calming me down and assured me it was quite common for children to disappear for a little while, especially on departure day. Monsieur Rocher inquired casually as to how long the children had been missing, and Ben said it would be a good idea to check with the parents. The kids had probably just gone back to their respective rooms.

Naturally we'd wanted to avoid asking their parents, but I could see it was the right thing to do. Ben rang the Burkhardts on the hotel phone, while Monsieur Rocher dialed the number for the Panorama Suite.

Amy, Gracie, and I held our breath and hoped against hope, but unfortunately neither Don nor Dasha had turned up at their rooms. Don's parents weren't particularly alarmed to hear Don was missing (which wasn't surprising given that their son knew "his" hotel like the back of his hand and was allowed to go roaming the hallways and poking about wherever he liked at any hour of the day or night). Burkhardt Sr. and his wife didn't even bother coming downstairs.

The Yegorovs, on the other hand, appeared speedily in the lobby. Stella Yegorov was practically hysterical.

My heart grew heavy. I could imagine how worried she must be.

After all, her little girl was only four years old, and she'd probably never been allowed to go off on her own before. Any minute now, Mrs. Yegorov would demand we call the police and a team of sniffer dogs and say she was going to sue the hotel.

But in fact she had something else on her mind, as I realized when she started wringing her hands and wailing at Monsieur Rocher in broken English. She was inconsolable. Because of the weather, nobody had been able to drive her to Geneva to go shopping and get her hair cut, and now she was demanding to be taken there by helicopter to make up for lost time. She refused to accept that there was no way a helicopter would be able to fly through the snowstorm. Her daughter's disappearance, on the other hand, didn't seem to bother her much at all.

But her husband was clearly finding it hard to stay calm. "Nothing bad will have happened to her, will it?" he said to Monsieur Rocher. "Nothing bad ever happens here at Castle in the Clouds, does it? And she's got Don with her . . ."

"Exactly." Monsieur Rocher smiled optimistically at us. "We'll soon find the little runaways. As long as they haven't gone out in the snow, there's nothing to worry about. I've never known anyone to go missing inside the hotel for long."

Carolyn, of course, had been the first to suggest checking whether the children had put on their snowshoes and parkas. But none of their clothes were missing, and nobody had seen them go outside, so they must still be somewhere in the building. We were bound to find them eventually, as I assured Viktor Yegorov over and over again so emphatically that he clearly felt *he* had to calm *me* down and not the other way around.

As his wife tottered away in a huff because nobody would order her a helicopter, he told me Dasha loved playing hide-and-seek. She'd often given them a scare at home, especially the time she'd fallen fast asleep in the laundry basket under a pile of towels.

"This is a special place," he said with complete conviction. "Children can feel safe here."

Yes. Certainly they could. Unless they were lost in the company of a nine-year-old psychopath.

Monsieur Rocher brought Viktor Yegorov a cup of tea and looked after him while we continued the search. Luckily, Gordon Montfort wasn't at work today. I dreaded to think how many of us he would have yelled at and fired on the spot if he'd been here. He'd have been only too happy to serve Carolyn's head on a plate to the Yegorovs and the Burkhardts.

Half an hour later, there was still no sign of the two children, even after Gracie, Amy, Ben, and I had turned all the chamber-maids' cleaning carts inside out and searched the cupboards in all the linen rooms. Don certainly wouldn't have had any qualms about going through a door marked PRIVATE.

Meanwhile, Carolyn was holding down the fort in the playroom in case the children came back of their own accord, and Pavel and Pierre were systematically trawling the basement. It wasn't as easy as I'd thought, thank goodness, to climb into the ventilation shafts because the grilles in front of them were all firmly screwed on. But I still called "Hello?" down a few of the shafts as I passed, just in case.

Perhaps Mrs. Ludwig had been gossiping, or perhaps people had simply noticed what was going on and were glad of a bit of excitement, because several of the guests now came and joined in the search effort. Almost all of them had some anecdote about how, as a child, they'd once found such a good hiding place where nobody could track them down. And Viktor Yegorov was bearing up well, which might have had something to do with the fact that Monsieur Rocher had slipped some rum into his tea. It was obviously having a calming effect.

But just as I was starting to be infected by the general optimism and had almost stopped feeling anxious (I knew Don, after all, and I knew that to him all this fuss and attention must be like all his Christmases coming at once), along came the thriller writer with his kidnapping theory.

He caught up with me and Ben on the second floor and grabbed the sleeve of Ben's jacket. This was the first time I'd had a proper look at the thriller writer. Despite already having several bestsellers under his belt, he only looked to be in his midthirties: a short, slim man with neatly trimmed dark hair, a little snub nose, an impish smile and rather wild eyes, as I now noticed.

He didn't want to panic anyone, he said, and he was sure the children would turn up soon, but he'd never forgive himself if he didn't at least mention it.

"Mention what?" asked Ben, and the thriller writer's eyes flicked from Ben's face to mine as he whispered, "The grand hotel kidnapper."

And that was all it took. The panic he didn't want to cause had already gripped me.

Ben looked distinctly unimpressed. "The grand hotel kidnapper?" he echoed drily.

"Some people call him the luxury hotel abductor," said the thriller writer. "But that's never caught on—too unwieldy. I came across him while I was doing some research for my last book. Over the past thirty years, he's abducted six children. And he's still at large."

"Six children in thirty years?" Ben frowned skeptically.

The thriller writer nodded gravely. "Two in Germany, one in

Austria, one in France, and two in Italy," he murmured. "And always from luxury hotels."

"Six children kidnapped from hotels in four different countries over the course of thirty years?" Ben sounded like a publisher the thriller writer was trying (and failing) to interest in a new book. "That seems a bit far-fetched to me. How do they know it was the same kidnapper every time, if he's never been caught?"

The thriller writer was momentarily flummoxed. "It's—er—detectives have never been in any doubt—every case had his fingerprints all over it."

"They found fingerprints?" asked Ben. "Well in that case, why didn't they—"

"No!" The writer clicked his tongue in annoyance. Ben was being so obtuse that I almost did the same. "I was speaking metaphorically. The crimes bore all the hallmarks of the same perpetrator. The child would disappear, then five or six hours later there'd be a ransom demand by telephone, tailored very precisely to the parents' circumstances and not limited to cash, either. When the child of a world-famous conductor was taken, for instance, the kidnapper didn't just ask for money—he also wanted the Stradivarius that happened to be in the family's possession. Another time he demanded a Van Gogh painting that nobody else could possibly have known about."

"That's terrible," I whispered, breaking out in goose bumps.

Ben looked at me, shaking his head.

But the writer was pleased to have at least one attentive listener. "The ransom was always handed over via a middleman or middlewoman," he went on. "And as long as the police didn't intervene, there'd be a phone call afterward to say where the child was being held. There was only one time when it all went wrong. The son of an Italian businessman was abducted, and as soon as the police got involved . . ." He let out a deep sigh. "Well, you're too young to remember it—but the little boy was never seen again."

"Oh my God!" I exclaimed. "Ben, we have to tell Yeg . . . Smirnov to call in his bodyguard right away." I wondered why he hadn't shown up already.

Ben groaned. "Seriously, this kidnapping thing is ridiculous. How stupid would a kidnapper have to be to abduct someone on a day like today? There's a blizzard raging outside, no cars have been able to get in or out for hours, and the only road out of here goes on for four and a half miles without anywhere to turn off—it's hardly ideal for making a quick getaway with a kidnapped child. And anyway, why did the kidnapper suddenly decide to abduct two children at once? Did he get greedy? Or have his fingerprints changed?"

The thriller writer pressed his lips together, offended.

"I don't think you should just dismiss the idea out of hand, Ben," I said, earning myself a grateful look from the writer. "Don and Dasha are both prime targets for abduction. Just think of the sui—" I just managed to stop myself from saying "suitcase of dirty money." "Of the S.O.D.M," I went on in a lower voice. "And what about the D. that Y. bought for his W. at C.? Hmm?"

"Huh?" Ben stared at me and furrowed his brow, then grinned. "Oh, I see. I suppose both families might be targets for a ransom demand. But the D. that Y. bought for his W. at C. isn't even in the H. yet. And who is this kidnapper supposed to *be*? We know everyone here."

"That's not true," said the thriller writer quickly. "Allow me to point out that with the number of temps you've taken on over

Christmas, it's impossible to keep track of everybody. And according to my sources you haven't performed any background checks . . . So actually, every one of those temps is a possible suspect."

"And you know all this because . . . ?" Ben crossed his arms.

"I've been speaking to some of your employees," said the thriller writer, "while doing research for my next book, provisionally titled *The Bleeding Room*. It's about a serial killer who boards up his victims in the walls of hotels and lets them bleed to death."

I had to look away at this point because the gleam in his eyes was genuinely scary. And he also had a bit of a squint.

"But back to the grand hotel kidnapper," he went on eagerly. "Naturally, the guests are also potential suspects."

"Like you, for example," Ben countered, rolling his eyes.

The thriller writer nodded approvingly. "Yes, that would be an excellent red herring. If I'm the first person to mention the kidnapper, the reader won't see me as a suspect. But for one thing, I'm too young— I'd only have been six years old at the time of the first kidnapping— and for another thing, this isn't a novel. Not yet, anyway."

Ben muttered something that sounded like: "And if it was, it would be the second-worst novel ever written, right after *The Bleeding Room*," but his words were drowned out by shouts from the first floor.

"They're here!" That was Amy.

"We've found them!" And Gracie.

Thank God! I could have cried with relief. Instead, I grabbed Ben's hand and squeezed it tight.

"Well, that puts an end to your kidnapping theories, doesn't it?" I said to the thriller writer. "Which I never believed for a second, by the way."

"Me neither. Not seriously, anyway," he quickly replied. "I just thought I'd better mention it. So nobody could say they hadn't been warned."

"He is such a poser," Ben muttered as we headed downstairs. "I read his last book, and it was crap. Full of implausible coincidences. And at the end of every chapter, there's some fake moment of suspense that all gets resolved two pages later."

We weren't the only ones making a beeline for the music room where Grace and Amy had found the two runaways. Viktor Yegorov was there before us, relief etched all over his face.

"I knew it; I knew it," he murmured, more to himself than to us.

Gradually everyone else arrived and marveled at the children's hiding place. It was simple but very effective. Don and Dasha were lying curled up on the built-in shelves to either side of the huge fireplace, hidden behind boxes of sheet music, piles of heavy books, and plaster busts of famous composers, and they were fast asleep. Well, Dasha was—Don, I was certain, was just pretending.

"If he hadn't been snoring, we'd never have found them," said Gracie proudly.

"And if the cat hadn't scratched at the door we'd never have come back in here," Amy added quietly. "We'd already searched this room."

Viktor Yegorov solemnly shook both the sisters' hands and thanked them in at least three languages. Then he knelt down in front of the shelf and carefully cleared everything off it. Ben and I helped him.

"There you are, little one." Very gently he lifted his daughter out and cradled her in his arms. She didn't wake up, just nestled against him and smiled.

The gaggle of onlookers sighed at this touching scene, and we watched him carry Dasha out of the room.

"That little rascal!" All of a sudden, Don Burkhardt Sr. came marching in. He was a tall, burly man with sharp, pale blue eyes, a low forehead and an unpleasantly booming voice. Don had clearly inherited his cute little voice, pretty face, and doe eyes from his mother. Don Burkhardt Sr. looked at his son and shook his head, but with a certain amount of pride. "Well, in that case I suppose I won't have to sue anyone for negligence, eh?"

Don let out a little snore, and everyone laughed. Ben offered all the helpers a drink on the house and ushered them downstairs to the bar. Carolyn was finally free to leave her post and set off home through the snow.

But Amy, Gracie, and I stayed with Don and his dad in the music room, intrigued to see how Don was going to talk his way out of this one. He was still pretending to be asleep—very convincingly, too—and his impression of an innocent little boy waking up without any idea what had been going on was even more realistic. When his dad shook him awake, he opened his eyes very slowly and looked around as if completely disoriented. "Where am I?" he asked. "How did I get here?"

His dad laughed. "Trust you, Junior! You had everyone going! Just what we needed on such a dull afternoon."

Hmm. Personally, I'd rather have spent the afternoon sticking glitter on cardboard unicorns. No wonder Don didn't know the difference between right and wrong, if his dad actually praised him when he should have been telling him off.

Don rolled slowly off the shelf and rubbed his eyes. It was a shame he was destined to take over his dad's waste-disposal empire.

He could have had a career on the stage. "How . . . ? What am I doing here? The last thing I remember is taking little Snot Nose down to see her mother. What happened then? And why do I feel so tired?"

"Because you're my little rascal, and you've worn yourself out making mischief," said Burkhardt Sr. "Come on, I'll carry you, just this once, okay?"

But however tired Don supposedly was, there was no way he was going to let his dad pick him up, especially not in front of Gracie. He did consent to lean on his arm, though. Burkhardt Sr. may have been an unpleasant character with shady plans and suitcases full of dirty money, but he did seem to genuinely love his son. I just couldn't bring myself to spoil this sweet little father-and-son moment by going into responsible adult mode and giving Don the telling-off he deserved.

But in the end, Gracie did it for me. As the Burkhardts passed us on their way to the door, she said sternly: "That really was horseploppish of you, Don. Everyone was worried sick. And plus it was totally against the rules. We were supposed to stay on the third floor and not go into the rooms . . . But I still found you, you horseplop."

Don, of course, didn't understand a word, though he could tell Gracie was insulting him. But to my surprise, he didn't insult her back (which was very unlike him)—he just smiled wearily and murmured, "See you tomorrow, beautiful Gracie Barnbrooke from South Carolina."

And then it suddenly struck me that perhaps he wasn't acting after all and that he really *didn't* know what had happened to him.

18

P lease don't tell me you believed that idiot's kidnapping story," said Ben.

Unfortunately that was exactly what I *was* telling him, only not in so many words. I just couldn't shake the idea that Don might really have been asleep. Of course, we were talking about Don here, and there was no denying Don was a devious little so-and-so who knew every trick in the book. And yet . . . I leaned over the polished countertop of the reception desk and whispered, "But what if he wasn't pretending? What if he really was asleep and woke up all confused because he didn't know what had happened? What if someone *drugged* him and Dasha?"

Ben looked at me, aghast. "What, drugged them and then hid them on a shelf? Why would anyone do that, for heaven's sake?"

Yes, that was the problem. I didn't know why anyone would do that, either. It didn't make any sense. But I still had this niggling feeling that . . . oh, I don't know.

"Sophie?" Ben smiled at me. "Would I be right in thinking you've had a very long day?"

I nodded at once. "Yes, definitely." It had been such a stressful and exhausting day, in fact, that I hadn't even thought about kissing once. But I was making up for it now, as I gazed at Ben. He was so cute when he smiled. And it sounded so good when he said my name.

"Maybe you should just tell Heffelfinger you're not feeling well today and take the evening off," he suggested. "I think you're working way too hard. And I finish at nine. We could have dinner together."

That was tempting, extremely tempting, but I couldn't leave poor Mr. Heffelfinger alone with the guests. He was on the verge of a nervous breakdown as it was. And I was the only one who understood that you couldn't burn jasmine-and-patchouli-scented candles in the same room as vanilla-and-orange-blossom candles; it created an unholy olfactory mess.

"You know what?" Ben picked up the phone. "I'm going to call in sick for you. I know you won't do it yourself. And I—er—*we* have a responsibility for your well-being. Ah, Mr. Heffelfinger?" He ignored my wild gesticulations. "Ben Montfort at Reception here, good evening. I'm just calling on behalf of Sophie Spark, the intern. She's not very well, I'm afraid, so she won't be able to come in this evening. But I'll try and organize a replacement for you."

"Poor guy," I said when Ben had hung up. But secretly I felt rather relieved. It was ages since I'd had an evening off.

"Pff—he's not a poor guy," Ben scoffed. "He caused a crisis in the kitchen today—ordered a whole tray of banana, arugula, napa cabbage, and chia seed smoothies this morning. When it got to lunchtime and the chef realized he didn't have any arugula or napa cabbage left, he was furious with Heffelfinger and the sous chef who'd made the smoothies. He was about ready to stab them both with his best vegetable knife. He said the only alternative was to fire them on the spot. It took me a lot of time and energy to get everyone to be friends again."

"You're a pretty good manager, aren't you?" I smiled at him, trying not to look at his mouth so he wouldn't realize what was going through my head: . . . *and I bet you're pretty good at kissing, too.*

Luckily, he misinterpreted my expression. "You look really tired. How about you chill out for a bit while I finish up here, and then we'll go and get something to eat?" he asked, putting his hand over mine for a second. He quickly withdrew it when a guest came over with a question about Wi-Fi access.

I went to join Monsieur Rocher. He was going through a list of all the chandeliers in the hotel and putting elegant ticks in fountain pen beside the ones Jaromir and Old Stucky had already inspected.

"Were they all okay?" I asked.

"Of course they were." Monsieur Rocher added one last tick to his list. "None of them would even dream of falling down. The chandelier outside the old study, on the other hand . . . let's say it has a habit of putting on dramatic performances. And an unfortunate penchant for self-destruction." He eyed me over the top of his glasses. "Is there something on your mind, Sophie?"

I glanced quickly over at Ben. "Have you ever heard of the grand hotel kidnapper?" I asked quietly.

Monsieur Rocher shook his head. "I can't say I have."

"The writer from Room 106 was telling me about him. Over the last thirty years, the grand hotel kidnapper has abducted six children from luxury hotels and demanded huge ransoms. He's never been caught."

"Hmm," said Monsieur Rocher, drawing the right conclusions as usual. "And today, when the children went missing, you thought this kidnapper might have struck again?"

I nodded. "Old Stucky said recently that something bad was about to happen. What if that something is the grand hotel kidnapper?"

"Hmm," said Monsieur Rocher again. "There certainly are plenty of children here to abduct, and plenty of rich parents to pay ransom demands."

"Exactly!" I was very grateful that Monsieur Rocher didn't seem to think I was being foolish.

"Although—Don and Dasha did turn up again, didn't they?" he said kindly.

I sighed. "Yes. But . . . Don was behaving really weirdly. What if somebody drugged the children, intending to kidnap them . . . and then the weather threw a wrench in the works?" Even I realized how utterly ridiculous that sounded. It wasn't as if the snow had come out of the blue. "It's just that I've got a really funny feeling about it all," I added lamely.

Monsieur Rocher gave me a benign smile. "I think it's perfectly natural to take funny feelings seriously," he said. "Most of the time, our instincts are trying to tell us something, even if it's not always what we *think* they're trying to tell us." He looked over at Ben, who was talking on the phone. "Perhaps you should call in sick tonight and spend the evening with a cup of peppermint tea and a good book. Or a good friend."

I sighed again. "Yes, that's what Ben said, too. He called Mr. Heffelfinger and told him I wasn't coming to work tonight."

"Very good. And don't you go fretting about Old Stucky and his gloomy predictions. He's always been rather prone to exaggeration." Monsieur Rocher straightened his glasses. "Of course bad things do happen sometimes, Sophie, even here at Castle in the Clouds. This is an honest place. It can bring out the worst in people but also the best." He smiled warmly at me. "When I look at you, for example, I'm not worried about the bad. Because as long as there are people like you in the world, good will always triumph in the end."

All of a sudden, I found I had a big lump in my throat. Only Monsieur Rocher could say sappy things like that without sounding silly. He always knew how to make me feel better.

I went up on tiptoe and gave him a kiss on the cheek. "I think you're lovely, too," I said quickly, then ran up the stairs with a new spring in my step. For the time being, I was simply going to ignore the queasy feeling in my stomach. Perhaps it was just hunger after all.

In the bathroom in the staff quarters, someone had left the window wide open again. Whoever it was clearly didn't understand the principle of ventilating a room; my hand nearly froze to the window latch as I closed it. But I hadn't had a shower that morning, just a quick scrub with a soap and flannel, and if I wanted to transform myself into someone really worth kissing, then I had to have a proper wash. As I shampooed my hair and rinsed it hurriedly under the lukewarm water—which seemed to be all the boiler could stretch to today—I wished for the first time that I wasn't one of the hotel staff but one of the guests. How wonderful it would be to stay in one of those spacious rooms: Room 110, for example, which had not only a balcony but two windows (one south-facing, one west-facing) and an open fireplace as well as a big bathtub. I could have ordered a hot chocolate and perhaps a little slice of apple and cinnamon cake from Room Service, and after a long bubble bath I could have wrapped myself in the fluffy bathrobe, sunk into the soft sofa cushions, and listened to the crackling fire . . .

A surge of cold water put a brutal stop to my reverie. I must have used up the last of the lukewarm water, and I had to rinse the rest of the shampoo out of my hair with water straight from the glacier.

Back in my bedroom, I crept into bed to warm up and covered myself with all the blankets I could find. Straightaway my body went into sleep mode—it never took me long to fall asleep once I was horizontal. But I tried to keep myself awake by checking my messages.

Naturally Delia had sent me some more hearts and kissing emojis, this time accompanied by links to articles such as: "Worried about the

First Kiss? Try These Top Tips," "Can Your First Kiss with a New Man Ever be Perfect? Ten Tips for Lowering Your Expectations," and— particularly insidious—"Missed Opportunities—the Art of Finding the Right Time." As I scrolled through the articles, my eyelids began to droop and my last thought before I fell asleep was that this must be exactly how Don had felt lying on his shelf in the music room.

I'd probably have slept until morning if the old pipe in the wall hadn't made a loud harrumphing sound just after 9 p.m. I woke with a start and, when I realized what time it was, I leapt out of bed. As I hurriedly pulled on some clothes, I reeled off Gracie's entire repertoire of swear words. So much for making myself look pretty. There was no time for that now. The hair on one side of my head was sticking out all over the place while the other side was still damp and flat. And my little nap had left my face looking sadly asymmetrical, too: the cheek that had been resting on the pillow was bright red, while the other cheek was still its usual pale color. The eye on the red side was all small and puffy; the other eye was wide open and stared reproachfully back at me from the mirror. I could only hope my face would go back to normal before I saw Ben. I drew my hair into a loose braid, applied some eyeliner and mascara, and brushed my teeth again (you never knew what might happen), all in record time. But when I eventually got down to the lobby, Ben was gone.

Gutless Gilbert had taken over at Reception. He was very surprised to see me. "I thought you were having dinner with my nephew," he said, his face glum as usual. "He's just gone to fetch you."

That was the downside of all the staircases in this place—you could never be sure which way someone had gone. It wasn't until I was back on the first floor that I realized it would probably have been more sensible to wait for Ben downstairs. We could spend all night chasing each other around the hotel. One of us would get to the top of the stairs just as the other one arrived in the lobby, and vice versa. So I spun round—and promptly bumped into Viktor Yegorov, who'd just come striding around the corner.

We both started apologizing at the same time and couldn't help smiling.

"I wanted to say thank you, too," he said, serious again now, "for your patience and help earlier and for allowing my daughter to have such a lovely day with the other children. She's been talking about it nonstop, and she can't wait to come back to the playroom tomorrow."

"Then we'll have to think of something else to play rather than hide-and-seek." His words made me feel a little uneasy. We'd lost his daughter—that wasn't something you'd usually thank a babysitter for. Without warning, the queasy feeling in my stomach returned, even queasier than before. "I'm so terribly sorry about what happened today," I said. "We'll keep a closer eye on her tomorrow, I promise."

"I'm sure you will." He smiled his melancholy but very kind smile. "I lost my head for a little while earlier, but I know from experience that nothing bad can happen to a child here. That's the special magic of this place."

Yes, I wanted to believe that, too. But the words Old Stucky had murmured on Christmas Eve and the story of the grand hotel kidnapper were still floating around in the back of my mind. Even Monsieur Rocher had admitted that bad things did sometimes happen at Castle in the Clouds. But I couldn't tell Yegorov that, of course, any more than I could tell him about my theory that the children had been drugged. Perhaps I could encourage everyone to be a bit more vigilant, though, at least, in the unlikely event that this kidnapper really did exist and had his sights set on Dasha.

"I won't let Dasha out of my sight for a moment tomorrow," I said, keeping my tone as light as possible. "And perhaps you could tell your bodyguard to keep a closer eye on her than usual. Children can vanish so quickly."

"Bodyguard?" Viktor Yegorov furrowed his brow.

"Yes, your bodyguard or security guard or whatever you call him?" I looked pointedly toward Room 117.

Viktor Yegorov didn't seem to be following me. "My wife and I are here without bodyguards or any other staff for that matter."

"Er—are you sure?" Again I stared emphatically at the door to Room 117.

"Quite sure." He smiled politely. "That's what's so wonderful about staying at Castle in the Clouds—nobody knows we're here, so we can just be ourselves without having to worry. Officially, we're spending Christmas on our yacht in the Caribbean." He winked at me. "Where my wife would much rather be."

"But . . ." I was confused now. If Mr. Huber from Room 117 wasn't here with the Yegorovs, then who was he here with? And why was he carrying a gun under his coat?

Yegorov nodded in a friendly way as he passed me. "See you tomorrow."

I just stood there in the corridor for a few seconds, deep in thought. And in the back of my mind, a new theory started to take shape.

What if Alexander Huber from Room 117 was the grand hotel kidnapper?

19

The next person I ran into was Tristan Brown—on my way downstairs, this time.

"Agent Sophie!" he exclaimed happily.

"I wish I was," I replied. And it was true. If I'd been Agent Sophie from the FBI, I would have been able to call for backup right now. Or tell my people to run Alexander Huber's photo through our database and compare it with the information on the kidnapping cases. Then I'd take out my handcuffs and my Baretti . . . Berebetta . . . or whatever my pistol was called and arrest the man. And then everyone at Castle in the Clouds would be able to sleep easy in their beds again.

"Is there something wrong, Sophie?" Tristan looked at me keenly. "Have you been crying?"

"No!" I wiped a finger under my eyes. "Is my mascara smudged?"

"It is now." He grinned.

I wasn't really in the mood for joking. "What are you doing here in the south wing anyway?" I asked. "And all alone, without your flock of admirers?"

"Jealous?" He brushed a nonexistent strand of hair back from his smooth, bronzed forehead. His eyes sparkled in amusement.

"Oh yes, dreadfully," I said. "My life is so dull without you. And utterly meaningless."

Tristan sighed. "Yes, those were the days, when I was still a hotel thief and you were a secret agent who kept turning up in the wrong place at the right time. We were a brilliant team, you and I. Until your friend the hotelier's son came on the scene and ruined everything. I felt like a sleazy rich guy who goes around chasing after pretty chambermaids."

I laughed out loud. "Believe me, I felt a lot worse—like a sleazy chambermaid who goes around throwing herself at good-looking guests."

"But he's still your boyfriend?" asked Tristan. I hesitated. True, Ben and I had danced a waltz on the roof terrace and had a few moments together that had felt quite intimate, but if I was being honest we hadn't done anything that went beyond friendship. And the fact that I *thought* about kissing him all the time didn't count.

The longer I hesitated, the more curiously Tristan looked at me. I decided to change the subject completely.

"Have you ever heard of the grand hotel kidnapper?" I asked.

Tristan raised one eyebrow. "Bored with hotel thieves, are you? So it's a kidnapper now?"

"No, seriously." We were still alone on the stairs, but I lowered my voice nevertheless. "The grand hotel kidnapper really does exist, according to . . . er . . ." No, I'd better leave the thriller writer out of this. Otherwise the whole story would seem like it belonged to the realms of fantasy. "According to people in the know. Every few years, he kidnaps a child with rich parents, and demands ransom money and valuables for their safe return."

Tristan looked only moderately interested, so I quickly added: "And it's quite possible, if not highly likely, that he's in the hotel right now planning his next crime."

Tristan's other eyebrow shot up. "Quite possible if not highly likely?"

He both looked and sounded so skeptical that I felt myself

getting annoyed. "Yes, that's what I said," I retorted. "There may not be much evidence yet, but a good secret agent always listens to her instincts. Even if she isn't actually an agent at all. And my instincts tell me—"

I heard footsteps on the stairs and fell silent. It was Ben.

"Oh, great," he said when he saw us.

Tristan let out a sigh. "Yes, *great*. You really do have a knack for timing, hotelier's son."

"Oh, there you are, Ben," I said quickly. I was keen to stop things escalating again the way they had last time. "I was just coming downstairs to find you. Bye, Tristan, nice bumping into you."

"Yeah, *so* nice," Ben said, glaring at Tristan.

Tristan stared back, grinning pretty shamelessly. I pushed past them and made my way down the stairs.

"You mean you're just going to leave me with that explosive information and walk away, Sophie?" Tristan called after me.

"Yes! Anyway, it's top secret." I didn't turn around. They could stand up there staring at each other till the cows came home if they wanted. But after a few seconds, I heard Ben following me.

"What were you talking to him about?" he asked as he caught up with me. "I hate the way he says your name, by the way. As if he was the only one who knows it. What explosive information does he mean?"

"You heard—it's top secret," I said. "Anyway, where shall we go? Straight to the kitchen? What's the soup of the day today? I hope it's minestrone—the last one was amazing, even if Pierre says they only make it to use up all the vegetables they need to get rid of, plus if I don't eat something soon I think I might actually die. I keep seeing all these weird spots in front of my eyes. Sorry I'm so late, by the way. I fell asleep. You were right; I really needed an evening off. Obviously, I'd rather have had a hot shower than a cold one, but it is supposed to be good for the circulation, and—"

"What do I have to do to get you to stop talking?" Ben broke in.

If there was ever a perfect opportunity to say "Kiss me!" this was it. We'd reached the ground floor by this time and were walking across the dimly lit ballroom, which wasn't a bad place for a first kiss, I was sure Delia would agree. But before I could open my mouth, I saw Mr. Huber—aka the grand hotel kidnapper—walking toward us.

It took all my self-control not to squeal out loud and to carry on walking normally even though my knees had suddenly turned to jelly. My face froze, which unfortunately meant I couldn't assume a nonchalant expression.

But Mr. Huber wasn't looking at me; he was brushing snow off the shoulders of his coat as he crossed the room.

"Good evening," said Ben politely, and Mr. Huber nodded to him.

I waited until we were through the double glass doors that separated the ballroom from the lobby. "That was him," I gasped, which sadly took the evening in a very different direction from "Kiss me!"

"Who?" Ben bent to pick up a coat hanger that had fallen on the floor and hung it back on the rail again. He brushed my arm as he did so. The cloakroom by the entrance to the ballroom was housed in a little velvet-lined alcove set into the wall. All it contained, apart from a clothes rail with forty empty coat hangers (they were counted regularly) was a painting of a young lady with her hair piled ostentatiously on her head and a smug, reproachful look on her face. I called her "the frustrated cloakroom attendant" because the coat hangers were always empty—though Fräulein Müller still wiped the velvet down with a damp cloth and dusted the picture frame every week. Perhaps the cloakroom would finally come into its own on the night of the ball. I was glad the young lady in the painting was going to get a bit of excitement at last. Especially since I, like an idiot, decided to answer Ben's question and thus robbed her of the opportunity to become a wonderful backdrop for a first kiss.

"The grand hotel kidnapper," I replied. Ben clearly thought I'd lost the plot and treated me for the rest of the evening like someone on the verge of a nervous breakdown.

Without a word, he led me to the basement, presented me with a huge bowl of soup (cream of leek, unfortunately) and said, "I'm not speaking to you until you've eaten at least a thousand calories."

That wasn't hard. We were the only ones eating at this hour, but the buffet in the staff dining room was still well stocked for anyone who didn't finish work until later or was working the night shift. (The kitchen would even deliver meals to people's rooms in the middle of the night if necessary.) As well as the soup, there was freshly baked bread and little mushroom pies, and at that moment one of Pierre's colleagues walked in with a platter of sliced roast veal.

As if a spell had been broken, I wolfed down the soup followed by two slices of bread and roast veal, a pie, and—just to make sure I met Ben's minimum calorie requirement—a piece of apple tart. Then I leaned back and looked at him defiantly. "And now?"

He hadn't been watching me eat this whole time, of course— he'd devoured a generous helping of food, too, even if he wasn't quite as ravenous as I was.

"Now we wait for your blood-sugar levels to return to normal," he said. "And for you to banish this obsession with the kidnapper to where it belongs: fantasyland." He slid a plate of cream puffs toward me. "I saw Don with his parents in the restaurant just now, and he was absolutely fine. He even stuck his tongue out at me. Don't you think he'd have told his parents if someone had kidnapped him and drugged him?"

"Not necessarily." I twirled a cream puff between my fingers. "My friend Delia's cousin's friend's friend had her gin and tonic spiked in a club, and when she woke up she couldn't even remember having been there."

"So the kidnapper put a drug in Don's and Dasha's gin and tonics, but when they fell asleep he forgot to kidnap them," said Ben drily, and I couldn't help grinning.

"Okay," I conceded. "Perhaps it is all a load of nonsense. But wouldn't it be silly not to even consider the possibility that the grand hotel kidnapper is here in the hotel?"

"Especially when you know it's Mr. Huber from Room 117?"

"There's no need to give me that sarcastic look."

"It's not sarcasm; it's despair," said Ben.

"But listen. Mr. *Huber*"—I made the *quote unquote* gesture as I said it—"doesn't actually work for the Yegorovs at all. They didn't bring a bodyguard! And don't you think it's a bit suspicious that a man traveling alone, with a gun hidden under his jacket, happens to be staying in the room next door to the Panorama Suite? Where the richest people in this hotel and probably the whole world are staying with their little daughter? Don't tell me he's just a hopeless romantic who wants to dance at the New Year's Ball."

"A gun hidden under his jacket?"

"Yes, just ask Monsieur Rocher. I bet you'll believe *him*."

Ben said nothing for a while, and I took a bite out of my cream puff in sheer agitation. "All right then," he said at last. "We should probably keep a closer eye on this Mr. Huber. Monsieur Rocher ought to have said something about the gun."

"So you believe me now?"

He shook his head. "I googled the grand hotel kidnapper just now, just for fun. And yes, there have been various kidnappings from hotels over the past thirty years, but there's no proof it was the same guy every time, like that writer claimed. The press reports all say completely different things, and I didn't find anything about a Van Gogh being demanded as a ransom. So no, I don't believe the writer's story, and I definitely don't believe this mysterious kidnapper is staying here in the hotel."

"So who *is* Mr. Huber, then? A hit man working for the Russian government? Stella Yegorov's secret lover? A private detective who—*oomph*." Ben had stuffed a cream puff into my mouth.

"Please can we talk about something else, Sophie? I really liked you before you started coming out with all these conspiracy theories."

I glared at him, insulted. How dare he lump me in with the kind of people who thought that humanity had been infiltrated by a race of reptiles or that the government was secretly spraying us all with mind-altering drugs.

"I don't even want to kiss you anymore," I said crossly. But I'd forgotten I still had the cream puff in my mouth, so it sounded more like: "Ibomemumwomishooumoor," which Ben must have taken to be a secret language spoken among conspiracy theorists. But what was even worse was that I spat a sizable chunk of cream puff onto Ben's shoulder as I spoke, and I could have sworn it made a little *splat* sound as it landed on his jacket.

I wished the ground could have opened up and swallowed me.

Luckily for me, at that moment a crowd of people came streaming out of the kitchen into the room where we were sitting (once the last dessert had been served upstairs in the restaurant, the chefs at least were allowed to knock off for the night), and I seized the opportunity to make a strategic, if rather cowardly, getaway. Before Ben could say a word, I was through the door and halfway back to my bedroom.

Well, what an end to the evening—the first evening I'd had off in ages. Instead of kissing Ben, I'd spat cream puff on him and run away. Now he was going to think I was not only a conspiracy theorist but disgusting, too.

I'd never be able to walk past the frustrated cloakroom attendant again without wishing I'd kept my theories to myself.

"I'm afraid Cinderella and Prince Charming may have missed the boat," I texted Delia once I'd double-locked my door and thrown myself down on the bed. I didn't even bother turning the light on. "I think he's gone off me."

Delia replied at once. "What a stupid prince. Sounds like he needs a kick up the butt."

"I spat on him," I wrote, and Delia sent back three thumbs-up emojis.

And then I cried a little bit and listened and waited in case Ben came and knocked on my door after all. But he didn't come.

20

All the next day the weather was as foul as my mood. It was barely snowing now—the wind had dropped and it felt slightly warmer—but the hotel was shrouded in thick fog. It was like being surrounded by an obnoxious cloud that was just waiting for its chance to seep in through the revolving doors and rob you of your last memories of any sort of color (like lush-grass green or bright-sky blue).

When Nico, the bellhop, went out to walk Mara Matthäus's dogs and didn't come back, everyone thought he must have strayed too close to the edge of the ravine in the fog. If Old Stucky was to be believed, the ghosts and demons that haunted the mountainside liked luring unsuspecting people off the beaten path; it was a specialty of theirs. Luckily, however, Nico soon turned up. Old Stucky heard the dogs barking on his way to the stables and found the poor bellhop was standing there in the snow, completely disoriented. Nico was convinced he'd wandered miles from the hotel and was going to freeze to death alone in the wilderness, when in fact he'd simply gone around in a big circle and was leaning, without realizing it, against the bank of snow that covered the WELCOME TO A CASTLE IN THE CLOUDS sign.

Naturally, we weren't interested in venturing outside with the children in weather like this, despite Gracie's suggestion that we tie cowbells around everyone's necks. After yesterday, Carolyn and I were not taking any chances. We watched the children like hawks (particularly Don and Dasha). They weren't even allowed to go to the bathroom unsupervised.

This made it even harder than usual to keep them all entertained, but we managed. According to my colleagues, the adults were actually harder work than the children. Monsieur Rocher, who provided the guests with a constant supply of headache pills, sachets of herbal tea, vitamin C capsules, and helpful suggestions, assured everyone that the weather would improve very soon. For New Year's Eve, he even promised clear skies and a view of the fireworks display in the valley below. There weren't usually any fireworks at Castle in the Clouds, but the guests did light sky lanterns (which were biodegradable and made of bamboo and paper, with no wires; my mum would have approved).

But not even the prospect of good weather could cheer the guests up. They had cabin fever from being stuck indoors for so long and were all feeling exceedingly irritable. And they were trying to compensate for their low spirits with special requests. Gretchen's father had forgotten his wedding anniversary, and that morning he'd ordered a bouquet of twenty-one roses for immediate delivery. Don's mother kept asking the staff to make the jackdaws caw more quietly because she had a headache. And the thriller writer sent down to the kitchen for a raw suckling pig, which he said he needed for his lecture, for demonstration purposes. And that was just three examples.

Although none of them deserved it, all of their demands were met (as much as possible, anyway): Gretchen's father got his red roses—not immediately, but after two hours, during which he asked no less than seventeen times whether they'd been delivered yet; the Hugos flew off to the other side of the hotel and stayed there; and somehow, while the head chef's back was turned, we managed to fob the thriller writer off with a cooked chicken, which he grudgingly accepted. Though, as he pointed out, a cooked chicken wasn't going to bleed at all when he used it to demonstrate the methods of the serial killer in his book *The Hashtag Slasher*.

The lecture took place that evening in the music room and, unlike the politician's reading, was very well attended—so well that we had a relatively quiet night down in the spa and Mr. Heffelfinger let me leave early, at half past nine.

Until this point, I'd managed not to run into Ben. I'd given the lobby a wide berth and tried to avoid all the places I usually met him. He wasn't on shift at the moment, so I could venture into the lobby if I wanted and say good night to Monsieur Rocher. On the other hand, perhaps it was better to be safe rather than sorry and go up in the elevator—Ben never took the elevator. I'd spent the whole day thinking about our encounter the night before, and the more I thought about it the worse it seemed. I'd barely known Ben a week. For him, it was probably just a bit of fun, flirting with the intern or with one of the chambermaids during his holidays. And showing her the roof terrace. Anyway, what kind of boy—if he was genuinely interested in a girl—used a cream puff to shut her up? Like I said, there were plenty of other more enjoyable ways of doing that.

I found myself sympathizing even more with Amy, who was finding it harder and harder every day to hide how heartbroken she was about Aiden. Gretchen and Ella had nicknamed her Lovesicky Mickey. I definitely didn't want things to go the same way for me.

The elevator announced its arrival with an asthmatic wheeze. I never felt entirely safe in the elevators, but during my stint as a chambermaid, when I'd had to transport bulky cleaning carts and laundry bags from floor to floor, they'd always worked fine. True, they rattled and juddered in a less than reassuring way, but they did reward you with a melodic *ping* when you reached your chosen floor.

In the basement, one of the kitchen temps got into the elevator with me. She was quite pretty and not much older than I was, although she looked tired and a little sad. As the grille closed, she took off her white cap and undid the top button on her white smock. I'd never seen her before, but now, as she leaned back against the wall of the elevator and sighed, for some reason I felt an immediate connection to her.

Especially when she said quietly: "Love makes fools of us all, doesn't it?"

"Definitely!" I agreed. "Thinking about one person all the time must block up the important bits of your brain."

"You spend years being extra careful, trying not to give your heart to someone, and then one day you realize you've lost it, just like that."

"Exactly!" I nodded vigorously. "And then that Someone doesn't want it. Even though it's lying right at his feet."

The elevator jerked into life.

"Basically you have three options." The stranger tucked a lock of brown hair behind her ear, and I admired her pretty teardrop earrings. "Well, four, if you count the option of leaving your poor bleeding heart lying there in the dirt and crying your eyes out until it stops beating."

"No, that would be stupid."

"The second option would be to pick your heart up and put it back in your chest. And then sew it all up so that you could never lose it again." She looked at me expectantly. I shook my head. That sounded kind of bitter and miserable.

"The third option would be to pick it up, dust it off, and place it lovingly in the man's arms," said the girl.

"Too risky. He might just drop it again. Or chuck it against the wall." I could see it all very clearly in my mind. The thriller writer would certainly have enjoyed the images that were running through my head right now. "Or he might lock it up somewhere along with loads of other hearts that girls had given him."

The elevator made its cheery pinging sound. We'd arrived at the second floor.

As the grille opened, the girl smiled at me in a melancholy way. "Yes, it is a risk. But sometimes it's a risk worth taking."

"And what's the fourth option?" I asked as I stepped out of the elevator. The girl didn't follow me—she must be going up to a higher floor.

"Simple. You leave your heart where it is and pick his up instead." She had to speak very loudly to be heard over the rattle of the closing grille. "That's what you've been forgetting this whole time, Sophie."

I'd got so carried away by the metaphor that I actually looked at the floor expecting to see a heart lying there. When I looked up again, the elevator had gone. Now I couldn't ask the girl her name. And how did she know mine, anyway? Not to mention the fact that she seemed to know about my broken heart.

"There you are," said a voice from behind me. It was Ben, leaning against the door to the staff quarters. Having just visualized him doing such horrible things to my heart, it was easy for me to glare at him. Even though he'd clearly been standing here waiting for me. And he looked pretty cute with his trusting blue eyes, his hands stuffed into his pockets and his hair all ruffled after a long, stressful day.

"What do you want?" I asked testily.

"Just to see how you are," he replied. "You left so suddenly yesterday."

Yes. Because I spat food all over your jacket. (*Splat.* The noise had followed me all the way into my dreams last night.) *And because you called me a conspiracy theorist.*

"I had to go and make myself a tinfoil hat," I said. "I needed it for my conspiracy theorists' meeting with Old Stucky and the thriller writer."

He grinned. "Are you free now? We could go and get something to eat. I need to tell you what I've found out about Mr. Huber in Room 117."

I was torn. On the one hand, that *splat!* was still fresh in my mind—I wasn't sure I could sit across a table from him without feeling self-conscious, let alone eat anything. On the other hand, I really did want to know what he'd found out about Mr. Huber. The decision was taken out of my hands by the four hyenas from Lausanne, who emerged from the elevator at that moment in their uniforms looking—like the kitchen temp—rather exhausted. I thought they'd just walk on by without acknowledging me (they were still punishing me with the silent treatment, which I was very much enjoying), but unfortunately only Hortensia, Camilla, and Ava passed me by, with stupid suggestive grins on their faces.

Whatsername, however, stopped in front of us and smiled sweetly at Ben. "Hey, Benny. Please tell me it worked."

No, please tell her to jog on. *Benny.*

But Ben smiled, too. He reached into his pocket, took out a cell phone, and handed it to Whatsername. "Here you go. Good as new."

Whatsername squealed loudly, then clapped a hand to her mouth and said in a whisper: "You're my hero, Benny! Thank you, thank you, thank you!" And as it gradually dawned on me that he hadn't been waiting here for me but for Whatsername, she went up on tiptoe and kissed him effusively somewhere between his mouth, his nose, and his cheek—though I was pretty sure she'd been aiming for his mouth. "You're the best!"

The worst thing wasn't that she'd kissed him. The worst thing was that Ben had blushed. And not just a little bit, but very noticeably. Like a fricking tomato.

"Ariane," he said. He sounded embarrassed, probably because I was still standing there gawking at them.

But not for long. I felt behind me for the door handle and slipped into the corridor. The last thing I heard was Whatsername's gleeful laughter. Not until I was almost in my room did I realize that perhaps I should go back, scrape my heart off the floor, and put it outside in the snow, where it would freeze solid overnight. That would be option five.

Really, though, all this talk about lost hearts was crap. Again I double-locked the door behind me and threw myself down on the bed just as I had yesterday, without switching the light on. I hadn't lost my stupid heart, and it wasn't lying around on the ground somewhere— no, it was beating wildly in my chest and it hurt terribly.

Right on cue, my phone screen lit up. My mum had sent me a message with a photo of my dad and my brother on a walk. They were standing in a field under the wintry gray sky, smiling into the camera. What shook me wasn't the familiar faces but how green the field was. For the first time since I'd been here, I felt something like homesickness. I was homesick for the lowlands and for my old life.

Something scratched at the door. It was the Forbidden Cat, and when I let her in she jumped straight up onto the bed where she curled into a ball and started purring. I was sure she'd come to comfort me.

21

Amy was crying all night," said Gracie.

"Not all night," Amy shot back. "For half an hour at most. And you shouldn't go around telling everyone about it, you blabbermouth."

"I'm only telling Sophie," pouted Gracie, aggrieved. "She understands."

Yes, and I'd guessed anyway because Amy was wearing sunglasses. I should have done the same, really—not only to hide my eyes, which were swollen from crying, but also because it was very, very sunny today.

That morning, as if by magic, the blanket of clouds had lifted and the sunshine had come pouring through. It fell in dazzling, glittering pools on the snow. After all the gray days we'd just had, this bright sunlight was almost overwhelming.

Even Amy and I couldn't help but be cheered up by it, broken hearts or no broken hearts.

It was the day before the ball, the second-to-last day of the year, and since early that morning the hotel and the grounds had been a hive of activity. A constant stream of delivery vans pulled up loaded with flower arrangements, pallets full of food, and a giant ice sculpture for tomorrow's formal dinner. Old Stucky and Jaromir tried to tackle the neglected snowdrifts that had built up around the hotel; the banks of snow on either side of the cleared paths were now over six feet tall. It was like walking through a snow labyrinth.

On one side of the forecourt was an enormous mound of snow

that Carolyn and I had turned into a slide for the children. They romped about on it all day long, while Amy and I sat off to one side baking little snow cakes with the children who needed a bit of quiet time. We sold the cakes to imaginary customers in our imaginary snow bakery. It was the children's idea of heaven. I couldn't help thinking of what Viktor Yegorov had said: Nothing bad could ever happen at Castle in the Clouds. Today I was inclined to agree with him. I'd never have admitted it to Ben, but perhaps I *had* been too quick to believe in the grand hotel kidnapper. On such a glorious day, with not a cloud in the sky, I found it hard to feel paranoid.

The same could not be said of Grouchy Gordon, however.

"Did you hear about that little snitch of a bellhop?" Pierre had asked me at breakfast. "He only went and told Montfort about the Forbidden Cat."

Everyone was talking about it. Nico, it turned out, had presented the hotelier with photos of the Forbidden Cat and even collected cat hairs as proof. And as if we weren't stressed out enough already, Gordon Montfort had gone around and searched the basement and all the bedrooms in the staff quarters for the Forbidden Cat (or any sign of cat food, or a litter box), accompanied by Nico and Fräulein Müller. Again. I hoped the cat had found a good hiding place. She'd spent all night on my bed, and it wasn't until this morning that she'd slipped out of the window and padded away across the roof. I'd made my bed nice and neatly, but the thought of Ben's dad and Fräulein Müller rifling through the suitcase underneath it and seeing all the balled-up support tights on the shelf I used as a wardrobe was not a pleasant one. I was willing to bet Fräulein Müller kept her tights in neat little piles, with all the edges lined up.

But Gordon Montfort couldn't find even the slightest trace of a cat, which made him quite irate. He yelled at Nico for only having taken photos of the cat instead of catching it; now they'd had to waste precious time searching for it. Instead of the promotion Nico had been hoping for (preferably to a job that didn't require him to wear his little bellhop's hat anymore), he suddenly found himself with no friends. Even his buddy Jonas wasn't speaking to him.

Gordon Montfort's bad mood worsened as the day went on. Nobody was safe from it, not even the children playing outdoors. That afternoon, their happy shouts got on Montfort's nerves so much that he asked Carolyn to take them around to the back of the hotel to play.

Carolyn replied calmly that she couldn't bring herself to spoil the children's fun, but if Mr. Montfort could persuade them to abandon their beloved snow slide then of course she would be happy to take them to play elsewhere. This was very clever of her: Gordon Montfort would never dare upset the children of his VIP guests if he had to do it in person.

So he had no choice but to grit his teeth and put up with the noise—though not without shooting Carolyn plenty of vengeful looks. I guessed he must be standing out here waiting for someone to arrive, otherwise he could have just gone inside for some peace and quiet. Burkhardt Sr. came to chat with him for a while, holding some rolled-up papers—probably blueprints for the golf course. He was making lots of sweeping gestures, at any rate, and drawing imaginary lines in the air with his finger.

My heart sank. What with everything else that was going on, I'd pushed the sale of the hotel to the back of my mind. Today more than ever, I couldn't imagine how anyone could bring themselves to deliberately destroy such a magical place.

"Over there, where that fir tree is, we're putting in a four-story apartment block," said Don, suddenly materializing beside me. He pointed his little plastic sled at the half-moon fir tree.

"Good Lord," I murmured.

"We're only keeping the outside of the hotel," Don went on. I eyed him closely, but for once I couldn't detect any hint of mockery or schadenfreude in his face. "The front bit, anyway. My dad says people don't like this wedding-cake-style architecture anymore."

"Are you even supposed to be talking about this?" I asked, surprised. "I thought it was meant to be a secret?"

"And I thought you and Ben Montfort were so loved up that you already knew the secret?" Don countered, without batting an eyelid.

"Ben and I are not . . . ," I began, but Don rolled his eyes and said, "I really couldn't care less what you are or are not, Sophie Spark." He shoved Gracie against a snowdrift as he walked away, then went whizzing down the slide with a scornful laugh.

Gracie was about to chase after him, but at that moment somebody else attracted her attention. "Look, there's Tristan!" she cried. She hurried toward Tristan and the teenage Barnbrookes, who were tramping over from the car park dressed in full ski gear. Lots of the guests had made the trip to Evolène that morning to go skiing and were now returning to the hotel in dribs and drabs. Although Amy loved skiing, she hadn't gone with them because of Aiden. And because of Ella and Gretchen, of course—who annoyingly looked as stunning in ski gear as they did in everything else.

"I can just imagine the photos on Gretchen's Instagram page. #chairliftselfie, #perfectbobblehatface, #howigetboystocarrymyskis," Amy growled, and fixed her eyes on the ground as Aiden, loaded down with three pairs of skis, trudged past us in the direction of the ski cellar. "I hope he knows *I* don't care that he's trampling all over my heart."

This reminded me of my conversation with the sympathetic kitchen temp last night.

"Perhaps it's all just a big misunderstanding," I said. "Perhaps he hasn't even realized you've given him your heart. Because you put it down behind him secretly without saying a word, instead of placing it lovingly in his arms."

"I asked him to go to the ball with me," Amy hissed.

"I know. But perhaps he thought you were only asking him because you felt sorry for him because he's deaf. Perhaps he thinks that's why you're learning sign language."

"Why would he think something so stupid? He knows me!"

I shrugged. "Everyone thinks stupid things sometimes."

Now Viktor Yegorov came out onto the forecourt. He went to stand beside Gordon Montfort and looked at his watch. They must both be waiting for someone. The seven jackdaws, who'd been circling on the thermals above us for the past few hours, now swooped down onto the awning above the revolving door and started chattering noisily to one another.

Montfort looked up at them irritably. "I hate those ugly creatures," I heard him snarl. "They're like flying rats."

One-Legged Hugo gave an affronted *caaww*, but the others just ignored him and carried on twittering merrily. If they'd paid more attention in my language lessons, they could have left the hotelier utterly gobsmacked by croaking "Quiet, you philistine!" at him. But it turned out they had something even better in store for him. As if at a secret signal they all rose into the air, and something fell from the flurry of black feathers—a thick white glob of something that

242

landed slap-bang on the shoulder of Montfort's jacket. A little bit went on his ear, too.

"Splat," I said with satisfaction, but nobody could hear me above Montfort's loud cursing. He had to make do with quickly wiping his jacket with a tissue, though, because at that moment a dark limousine pulled slowly up the drive and rolled onto the forecourt. Two men got out. Clearly these were the people Yegorov and Montfort had been waiting for. Upstairs, at the window of Room 310 Mr. Von Dietrichstein was watching the whole thing through his camera lens. I hoped very much that he'd managed to get a photo of the bird poo incident.

"Interesting, eh?"

I hadn't realized Tristan had popped up in between me and Amy, and I jumped. "Four men shaking hands?" I said. "Not particularly."

"Not even if one of them has an armored suitcase chained to his wrist?" As always, Tristan sounded deeply amused.

"Oh." Now I saw it, too.

"I bet that famous necklace is in there—the one the Russian lady was given as a wedding present," said Amy. "She's going to wear it to the ball tomorrow."

I looked at her in surprise. Was there anyone in this place who didn't know all about the so-called Smirnovs and their priceless jewelry?

Tristan nodded. "The legendary blue Nadezhda Diamond," he said quietly. "It's still an enormous thirty-five carats, even after being cut. It's a cushion cut, surrounded by twelve flawless diamonds, set in eighteen karat white gold. It once belonged to Catherine the Great, but for decades after the October Revolution it was believed to be lost."

The four men now strode across to the revolving door and disappeared into the lobby one after the other.

"It's said to be cursed," Tristan went on. "Legend has it that the diamond was stolen from a secret temple in Madurai in India in the seventeenth century. It used to be set into a golden statue of the goddess Kali, as the third eye on her forehead."

"How exciting! But how do you know all this?" Amy asked.

Tristan shrugged. "I know pretty much everything about famous jewels—my grandpa told me all these stories when I was very young. You don't mess with the goddess Kali—you'd think the robbers back in the seventeenth century would have known that. After all, Kali wears a skirt made of human arms and holds a sickle and a bowl for catching blood. She's a goddess of death, famed for her powers of destruction, and her task is to maintain the balance of the universe. No wonder her third eye has never brought good luck to anyone."

Amy shuddered. "Well, I certainly wouldn't want to wear it."

"It is beautiful, though," said Tristan, smiling up at Room 310, where Mr. Von Dietrichstein was now closing his window. "And very photogenic."

"And very valuable," I added, having just spotted Mr. Huber from Room 117 crossing the forecourt and following the four men through the revolving door. Where had he sprung from?

"Indeed," said Tristan quietly, "it would fetch the same price on the black market as it would in a legal sale. There are plenty of rich people out there who don't care about the law. They'd do anything to get their hands on a piece like that. And I mean anything."

Oh man. I'd only just managed to get my fears under control and turn my back on my paranoia (and my tinfoil hat)—and now this.

"Stop scaring us," I snapped at Tristan, earning myself a surprised glance from Amy.

And a smug laugh from Tristan. "'Nadezhda' means hope, incidentally," he said, swinging himself gracefully up onto a snowdrift. "And speaking of hope—you do know Aiden's in love with you, don't you, Amy? He's just too proud to tell you. Because he's afraid you might just humor him out of pity." He didn't stay to see Amy's expression change from one of disbelief to one of astonishment to one of pure rapture, but jumped down from the bank of snow, strolled nonchalantly across the forecourt, and disappeared into the hotel.

I didn't see him again for the rest of the day, otherwise I would have thanked him for lifting Amy out of her bleak mood. If Tristan was telling the truth, there was nothing standing in the way of a happy ending for Amy and Aiden.

Well, at least one of us was happy. I was genuinely pleased for Amy.

I, on the other hand, couldn't even walk past Reception without feeling really awkward. It annoyed me that Ben smiled at me so warmly, as if nothing was wrong. But I didn't want him to think I was bothered by what had happened last night. So I smiled back and even gave him a friendly wave before I went upstairs. I'd read somewhere that if you force yourself to smile for one minute, the brain starts producing happy hormones. But I couldn't even manage thirty seconds. Because I *was* bothered by what had happened last night. And I didn't think my body was going to produce any happy hormones ever again.

That was probably why a giant zit had sprouted on my forehead—I discovered it in the bathroom mirror a few minutes later. And to make matters worse, I then cut off a big chunk of my hair to make bangs to hide it. Now I not only had a massive pimple on my forehead, but also a quarter of a set of bangs, which made me look pretty bizarre.

It was the first thing Ben noticed about me when we next met. I popped down to the laundry room to see Pavel before starting my shift in the spa, only to find Ben standing there on a stool, topless, with Pavel pinning up the hem of his black trousers.

"Oh, I didn't expect to see you here," I said unimaginatively—but it was true, because Ben was supposed to still be at work. And at the same time, Ben said: "What happened to your hair?"

We both fell silent, so Pavel kindly took over. "Poor boy is needing tuxedo for tomorrow night, he forget to buy. But good thing about tuxedos: never out of fashion. I just have to make right size. I already pin jacket. He borrow dad's shirt; I make smaller size already. Now only need to iron." He pointed to the white dress shirt that was hanging over the back of the chair. "If you want to help . . . oh, your hair is looking very strange, little Sophie. What you do to it?"

"It's hiding a pimple," I said grumpily, draping the shirt over the ironing board.

"Doesn't mean you have to disfigure yourself," said Ben.

"It's a very big pimple. At least eighteen carats," I replied.

Ben chuckled.

I bent to plug in the iron. "I'm glad you're in such a good mood, *Benny*." I tried to mimic Whatsername's high-pitched voice. And I put on a bit of a lisp as well. "You're my hero, Benny! You're the best!"

Ben stopped chuckling. "I can't help it if other people . . . *like* me," he said. "I fixed her phone, that was all."

"Oh, please be careful with shirt." Pavel frowned anxiously when he saw how roughly I was handling the shirt. "Is only one we have. And ball is tomorrow."

"Yes, yes, okay." I was determined not to mention Gretchen and the waltz. Absolutely determined. "What was it you were going to tell me about Mr. Huber from Room 117?" I asked instead. Jeez, couldn't Ben put a T-shirt on or something? Looking at his bare torso was getting me all flustered, especially when he folded his arms like that across his muscular chest. He must spend all his free time doing push-ups and sit-ups. You didn't get a body like that without working out.

"I was going to tell you last night," he said. "But you ran off."

"I actually got beamed up onto an alien spaceship for a conspiracy theorists' conference." I ran the iron along the hem of the shirt. "So tell me, what did you find out?"

Pavel sighed. "I not like it when you two argue. You should come with me to concert tomorrow. In Jesuit church in Sion. Beautiful choir music. Good for soul. Always I go at New Year. Come back with new strength and full of peace."

"We're not arguing, Pavel. We're just having a discussion. Even if Ben doesn't want to tell me anything and I have to drag it out of him. He probably hasn't found out anything at all—he's been too busy fixing people's phones and being *the best*."

"I *have* found out something, actually," said Ben. "His name is Alexander Huber, and he's forty-three years old—"

"Oh, wow," I broke in sarcastically. I just couldn't help myself. "Just like it says on his booking form? That's some amazing detective work right there."

Ben looked affronted. "If you really want to know, I managed to look at his ID card *and* I made inquiries with the registry office *and* his employer." Just to annoy me, he paused for effect. "I even saw his gun license," he added. "Mr. Huber isn't here to kidnap anyone. He's here because of the Yegorovs' necklace."

Aha! So that was it. "And he just admitted this to you?"

Ben nodded happily. "He was actually very keen to clear up any misunderstanding. He works for an insurance company. To be precise, the insurance company that insures the insurance company Yegorov's necklace is insured with."

It took me a minute to process this.

"The necklace is incredibly valuable." Ben was visibly pleased by my stunned silence. "But Yegorov has insured it for even more than its actual value, just to be on the safe side. So the insurers always want to know exactly where the diamond is. As soon as the necklace leaves its safe at the bank, Yegorov's insurance company has to let *its* insurance company know. And that's the company Mr. Huber works for."

"Sophie. Do not leave iron on fabric," Pavel admonished me.

"But . . . Yegorov doesn't even know this Huber man." I gnawed my bottom lip.

"True. Yegorov doesn't know his insurance company's insurer has sent a man to keep an eye on the necklace," Ben declared. He'd clearly been expecting me to say this and looked thoroughly pleased with himself. "Because it's not unheard of for people to 'lose' their own valuables just to get their hands on the insurance money. It happens more often than you'd think."

"Finished," said Pavel, slapping Ben on the leg.

But Ben didn't move—he just looked triumphantly down at me. "Well, Miss Tinfoil Hat? Any more questions?"

"Yes, actually," I promptly replied. To be honest, I believed his story and I was already starting to change my mind about the kidnapping theory, but Ben's smug tone, his bare chest, and the memory of him and Whatsername whispering sweet nothings to each other last night made it impossible for me to admit it. "Firstly, the necklace only arrived here today, but Mr. Huber's been here for over a week—how do you explain that? And secondly, what was he doing last Saturday poking around in the staff quarters? And thirdly, are you ever going to put some clothes on? Do you think I'm impressed by your naked body?"

Ben jumped hurriedly down from the stool. He'd gone red, though not quite the same shade of tomato red as last night when Whatsername had kissed him.

"Oh no!" said Pavel. "You iron crease into shirt, Sophie!"

"Nobody will see it under that stupid tux anyway." And it served Ben right. I'd done it on purpose.

"The shirt will have to wait a moment, I'm afraid, Sophie," a soft voice broke in, and I looked up in surprise. Monsieur Rocher very rarely left his room, and I'd never seen him down here at this hour before. He was cradling the purring Forbidden Cat in one arm. "You're needed urgently."

"What for?" I was about to ask, when I heard voices approaching down the corridor.

". . . I caught it and put it in a cardboard box and did it up with packing tape. He was supposed to keep it in the concierge's lodge till you came. But you took so long . . ." It was Nico, the traitor, and the testy voice that answered him belonged to none other than Gordon Montfort.

"Are you trying to tell me where I have to be and when, now?"

Montfort blustered. "You're lucky I needed to come down to the basement anyway."

The voices came closer and I realized I had to do something. Monsieur Rocher was looking at me expectantly: When Gordon Montfort came bursting in he was going to find not only the Forbidden Cat but also me, standing next to his half-naked son, scorching his stolen dress shirt with a hot iron.

"But it's true! I swear on my mother's life," Nico wailed.

"I feel sorry for your mother," thundered Montfort. "Back to your post, you useless moron."

I put the iron down, launched myself out into the corridor, and managed to close the door to the laundry room just as Ben's dad strode around the corner. He narrowed his eyes and stared at me, and I was close to flinging myself in front of the door and crying, "Don't hurt them!"

"Ah, there you are. A word, please, Miss . . . er . . . ," he said.

Of course. He must have found cat hairs on my bed. And now he was going to fire me. There could be no doubt about it. At last he'd be rid of the intern who didn't know her place, who'd fallen in love with his son, and who was always causing trouble.

"I was told I'd find you down here." He looked me up and down, and I felt a rising panic.

"You know the Smirnovs, who are staying in the Panorama Suite," he went on. He was wearing a new jacket, one without bird poo on the shoulder. And his voice was relatively friendly. But that could be deceptive, as I well knew.

I nodded tentatively.

"Well, the Smirnovs need a babysitter for little Natasha while they're at the ball tomorrow evening," he went on in a booming voice. "And Mr. Smirnov specifically asked for you, Miss . . . er . . ."

"Spark," I said, flabbergasted.

"It'll be quiet in the spa tomorrow evening, so Mr. Heffelfinger won't need you. I should like you to report to the Panorama Suite tomorrow evening at seven o'clock sharp. In uniform, please."

He made to leave, but then turned back for a second. "You don't happen to have seen Monsieur Rocher around here just now with a cat? Or a cat on its own?"

I shook my head mutely.

"Just as I thought." He tutted as he walked away. I waited until his footsteps had faded on the stairs, then tottered back into the laundry room, trembling. Monsieur Rocher and the Forbidden Cat were gone—they must have escaped through one of the back doors. Pavel had saved the shirt from irrevocable ruin and hung it on a coat hanger. And Ben had put a T-shirt on at last.

I collapsed into a chair, emotionally drained. "Right, where were we? Oh yes—if Mr. Huber is the hotel kidnapper, I need to know. Now." Before I found myself all alone with little Dasha in the Panorama Suite—with Mr. Huber and his gun in the room next door.

Ben rolled his eyes. "Not this hotel kidnapper stuff again. I've explained exactly what . . . oh, I'm sick of this. I'm going back upstairs."

"Yes, go," I said. "I'm sure there are plenty of phones out there that need fixing."

22

She's very tired," said Yegorov, despite the fact that Dasha was currently wide awake, bouncing around on her parents' king-sized bed and shouting my name excitedly. "It doesn't take her long to fall asleep here. I put it down to the mountain air and all that playing in the snow."

I smoothed my perfectly fitted uniform and gave what I hoped was a serene smile. If he thought I was fazed by bouncing children, he was quite mistaken. Especially when there was only one of them.

Dasha tried to do a somersault. Then she said something in Russian that I didn't understand, but I suspected meant something like, "Come on, Sophie, you do a somersault, too."

"She's had her supper and brushed her teeth, and I've read her a bedtime story." Yegorov tugged rather distractedly at his black bow tie. Like all the men this evening, he was wearing a tuxedo, which looked exactly the same as everyone else's even though it had probably cost twenty times as much.

I'd arrived at the Panorama Suite to find, to my great disappointment, that Stella Yegorov had already left. She and her dog were downstairs at the champagne reception, giving the Von Dietrichsteins an exclusive interview. And she was wearing the Nadezhda Diamond. I'd been hoping my babysitting duties would mean I was the first to clap eyes on the famous jewel. Gracie, Amy, Madison, and particularly Mrs. Ludwig had been green with envy when I'd told them, although Mrs. Ludwig was more interested in the dress than the necklace. I'd bumped into her and Mr. Ludwig walking back to their room hand in hand after their afternoon coffee. Mrs. Ludwig had been so excited she hadn't been able to eat her cake, and Mr. Ludwig had seemed a little nervous, too. He practiced his waltz steps in the corridor while Mrs. Ludwig chattered away happily, jumping from one topic of conversation to another. At last, the day she'd been dreaming of for decades had arrived.

When Mrs. Ludwig heard I was going to be spending the evening in the Panorama Suite, her eyes positively shone. "Oh, you lucky thing!" she cried. "That means you'll be the first to see the belle of the ball. What do you think, will she wear a blue dress to match her blue diamond? Although red's usually her color; it suits her so well, with her brown hair. She looks lovely in whatever she wears, not like wrinkly old me . . . I'm rather worried that my dress is too revealing. One ought not show too much cleavage at my age. I don't want to make a fool of myself. The skirt is so long; I'm not used to it, and I can only take tiny little steps. What if I trip and fall over? While I'm dancing, even?"

Mr. Ludwig laid a hand on her arm. "It will all be fine, my beautiful. I'll be waiting for you here at the foot of the stairs, and you'll come floating down them like an angel, I know it. And if anything does go wrong while we're dancing, it'll be because I've stepped on your toes."

Mrs. Ludwig laughed and laid her curly white head on his shoulder for a moment.

These two were just too cute. I hoped that when I was old I'd have someone like Mr. Ludwig by my side, kissing my head fondly.

"The monkey she takes to bed with her is called Alexei," Yegorov instructed me, as Dasha bounced around the bed more energetically than ever. "That's my middle name. He's over there on Dasha's bed.

But I promised her she could sleep in our bed if she likes." He gave a rather sheepish smile. "She usually comes in with us in the middle of the night anyway."

I nodded understandingly. I didn't mind if Dasha wanted to bounce around on the bed for a bit longer, and I was intrigued to find out whether I could actually do a somersault. After Yegorov had gone, of course.

He glanced at his watch. "If you need us for any reason," he said, pointing to the floor, "we'll be just down there in the ballroom."

I nodded again. The ballroom was only a stone's throw from here—out the door, turn right, along the corridor a little way, down the stairs, and there you were. You could hear the music from here, though it was surprisingly faint given that the room was directly above the orchestra gallery. The gala orchestra had been setting up since early that afternoon, and now the strings were tuning up. The ballroom itself was unrecognizable, with the tables around the dance floor all decked out in damask cloths and lavish flower arrangements, with candlesticks on all the tables and the walls. At eight o'clock, 276 ivory candles would be lit and, together with the twelve chandeliers, would bathe the ballroom in golden light. Monsieur Rocher had told me the same amount of candles again were held in reserve, ready to replace the others when they burned out. Two of the waiters had been put on candle-monitoring duty; while handing round the canapés, they would subtly inspect the candlesticks to make sure the wax wasn't dripping and that nothing had caught fire. I didn't envy anyone working in the ballroom this evening. At most I was a little jealous of Gretchen Barnbrooke, who would get to waltz with Ben. She would probably—no, definitely—be looking stunning tonight, in an absolutely beautiful dress. (Gracie and Madison had described it to me in great detail. I couldn't remember what color it was, but I knew it was supposed to be quite exquisite.)

On the other hand—no atmospheric lighting, no string orchestra, no ball gown, *nothing* could top my waltz with Ben on the roof, and whatever had happened afterward, nobody could take that moment away from me. I'd probably still be telling my grandchildren about it when I was a bitter old woman. Oh no, hang on—that wouldn't work, would it? If I was a bitter old woman, I wouldn't have any children or grandchildren. I'd probably have a skinny, grumpy old cat.

Yegorov sighed. "I think I've covered everything, haven't I?"

"Yes, you have." I flashed him my very best Mary Poppins smile. "Dasha and I will be just fine till you get back."

"I'll pop in every so often to make sure you're okay," he said.

"Yes, do. You won't be far away."

"And I could bring a few canapés up for you," he said, fastening both the buttons on his tuxedo and giving his daughter a good-night kiss.

Oh my goodness yes, I bet the canapés were delicious. "No, thank you," I said. Fräulein Müller would have been proud of me. "I've already eaten. Have a lovely evening."

Dasha bounced up and down and shouted something in Russian—presumably, "Go on then, go!" because Yegorov smiled and left the suite at last.

Although I was fairly convinced by now that the grand hotel kidnapper didn't exist, I drew the bolt and put the chain on the door once Yegorov had gone, just in case. My former suspect, Mr. Huber, would be downstairs at the champagne reception right now, staring intently at Stella Yegorov's necklace. She'd probably think he was ogling her boobs or something.

I went around checking that all the windows and doors were locked as Dasha hopped off the bed and went to fetch her monkey and a picture book. It was in Russian, but that didn't matter. We sat next to each other on the bed, looked at the pictures, and took turns telling each other the story in Russian and English. Now and then I got Alexei to make funny little monkey noises, and Dasha giggled with delight.

In the middle of this brilliant performance, the doorbell rang. Not all the rooms had doorbells, only the big suites. This bell buzzed tunelessly, as if there was an unfriendly butler hidden in the wall who wanted to scare off any visitors.

I tiptoed over to the door and looked through the peephole.

Outside stood Mrs. Ludwig in a bathrobe, and even through the peephole I could tell she'd been crying.

I rushed to open the door. "Oh my goodness, what's happened? Shouldn't you be at the champagne reception?"

Mrs. Ludwig sniffled. "Thank goodness you're here, my dear. I just didn't know where to turn."

I grabbed her sleeve, pulled her inside the suite and locked the door again, not forgetting the bolt and chain. "Is there something wrong with Mr. Ludwig?" I asked. Dasha looked anxiously over at us from the bed, but she couldn't understand what we were saying.

"No," said Mrs. Ludwig, dabbing at her nose with the sleeve of her bathrobe. "He's waiting for me downstairs. At the foot of the staircase, just like he promised. But . . ."

"What's the matter, then?" She looked so miserable that I wanted to give her a hug.

"My dress," Mrs. Ludwig sniffed, untying the belt of her bathrobe. "I've tried everything, but I just can't do up this blasted zip on my own."

"Is that all?" I breathed a sigh of relief. I'd been imagining all sorts of nightmare scenarios, beginning with Mr. Ludwig dying of a heart attack (today of all days). "That's easily sorted. Let me have a look." Under the bathrobe, Mrs. Ludwig was wearing a black sequined evening dress with a long zip that was, indeed, very fiddly to do up. The dress was flapping open at the back. As I carefully fastened the zip, I said, "Not even a contortionist would be able to do up a zip like this on their own. I'm not surprised you needed help. There we go! Done. You look like a princess."

Dasha handed Mrs. Ludwig a tissue from the dressing table and chirped something in Russian before climbing back onto the bed and snuggling down among the pillows.

Mrs. Ludwig was beaming again. "What a darling child. And so are you, my dear! I'm so sorry, I completely lost my head. I'm not usually like this."

"I understand. You've been looking forward to this moment for so many years and then your zip goes and gets stuck." I smiled fondly at her. I couldn't wait for Tristan's grandpa to tell her how much the ring on her finger was really worth, though she probably couldn't have been happier than she was right now, even if she knew the ring's true value. "And now you'd better hurry downstairs—Mr. Ludwig is waiting for you."

But Mrs. Ludwig was in no hurry. She looked inquisitively

around the room, wide-eyed, and wandered over to the bed with her bathrobe under her arm. "So this is the Panorama Suite. So spacious. And all those windows . . . But the curtains are the same as in our room. Where's the little doggie?"

"It's gone to spend the evening with the Von Dietrichsteins' pug in Room 310," I said.

"Oh, how lovely." Mrs. Ludwig smiled warmly at Dasha. "My, my, somebody looks sleepy. Are you allowed to sleep in Mama and Daddy's bed? I always used to let my children come in with me, too. Is this your monkey?" She stroked Dasha's curls, then straightened up and took a deep breath, as if plucking up her courage for the big night ahead.

I was about to say something encouraging when there was a knock on the door.

Mrs. Ludwig jumped, startled. "Who's that?"

"No idea," I said, and hurried back over to the peephole. Ben was standing outside, buttoning up his tuxedo.

"It's Ben Montfort," I said as I unlocked the door.

"Goodness gracious." Mrs. Ludwig screwed up the tissue in her hand. "He'll be surprised to see me here. I don't want you to get into trouble for letting me in."

"Oh, he'll understand," I assured her as I opened the door and Ben stepped inside.

"Oh, there you are," he said when he spotted Mrs. Ludwig. "Your husband is pacing up and down at the bottom of the stairs."

"I had a little wardrobe malfunction, but this helpful young lady has put it right for me." Mrs. Ludwig took another deep breath. "I suppose I should go down. Wish me luck!"

I couldn't help it—I gave her a kiss on the cheek. "This is your night," I said. "And you're going to have a wonderful time."

"What was this wardrobe malfunction?" asked Ben once I'd closed the door behind Mrs. Ludwig and locked it.

"The zip on her dress wouldn't do up." I was still feeling quite emotional, and my voice wobbled a little as I spoke. I looked over at the bed and saw Dasha lying on the quilt fast asleep. Her dad had been right; it hadn't taken long. I carefully lifted her head onto the pillow and pulled the quilt over her. "And what can I do for you?" I asked Ben softly.

"I thought I'd pop in and see how you were." He picked up Dasha's monkey, which had fallen on the floor.

"Ah, and I thought you'd just come to show me how good you look in a tux." He really did look the part, and I suddenly felt a bit like Cinderella in my chambermaid's uniform. At least my massive pimple had disappeared overnight. Pavel had dabbed some of Old Stucky's brother-in-law's pear brandy on it; the stuff seemed to work miracles. The spot was completely gone, and I'd also clipped my unflattering quarter-bangs back from my face.

"Thanks," said Ben, blushing slightly. "You look pretty great yourself, Sophie."

Now I couldn't help but grin. "Yes, these support tights are just so stunningly attractive."

"You look great in anything." Ben cleared his throat. "I mean it. You're . . . you're so . . ." He fell silent.

I waited a few seconds, then asked, "Weren't you supposed to be downstairs ages ago? I thought the first waltz would be starting any minute now?"

He nodded. "Yes. But first I just wanted to . . . I wanted to tell you . . ." He went quiet again, and again I waited.

Then the violins started playing in the ballroom below us.

"For goodness' sake," I said. "Whatever you want to tell me, you'd better leave it till later. Your dad is going to kill you if you don't get down there right now."

"Yes," he murmured as he went over to the door and unlocked it. "You're probably right." He turned to me again. "Perhaps I'll pop back again in a little while." And then he hurried off, leaving me none the wiser. But I suddenly felt a whole lot better. I was positively elated as I shut the door again, slid the bolt home, and fastened the chain.

23

Ben wouldn't be late for the first waltz, as I now saw from the digital alarm clock on the nightstand. It was only quarter to eight—the orchestra must just be warming up. Or perhaps the violins had started playing to encourage the guests away from the champagne reception and into the ballroom. It would be another half hour, at any rate, till the ball really got going. I knew when it started because I heard everyone go quiet and Mara Matthäus start speaking into the microphone.

Annoyingly I couldn't hear what she was saying from up here—the ceilings were too thick—but my imagination more than made up for it. And when a booming male voice took over I realized Gordon Montfort must be making his phony speech to the guests, who laughed and applauded despite his hypocrisy. No doubt he'd omitted telling them that this would be the last New Year's Ball in the tradition set by his beloved great-grandparents.

Dasha was sound asleep. She wasn't bothered by the hubbub from downstairs, the sound of the orchestra, or Mara Matthäus's and Gordon Montfort's voices on the microphone. She looked adorable, lying there in the middle of the huge bed, her curly hair slightly ruffled, her little arms outstretched. I'd laid the monkey down beside her, and I would have snuggled up on the other side if this had been my bed—but it wasn't, it belonged to our VIP guests, and if Viktor Yegorov came to look in on us I didn't want him to find me asleep and drooling all over his pillow. So I sat down on the sofa opposite the bed, annoyed that I'd followed Fräulein Müller's rules and left my phone in my room. I could have been messaging Delia right now, instead of dying of boredom. There were a few books on the nightstand on what I presumed was Viktor Yegorov's side of the bed, but they were all in Russian, just like Dasha's picture books.

There was a moment of solemn silence downstairs, and then the horns, flutes, and violins struck up a tune. They were playing the prelude to the "Blue Danube" waltz, soft and full of promise, and I couldn't help picturing the scene: The chandeliers would be casting their brilliant light over the ballroom as Ben led Gretchen out onto the dance floor to the first few strains of the waltz. Now he would be putting his arm around her and looking earnestly into her eyes. And then, as the famous three-four rhythm set in and the music sped up, they would start dancing, spinning around and around, and her beautiful dress would billow out around her and she would smile happily at him—

There was a knock at the door. Quite an urgent-sounding one. And then the doorbell rang. My first thought was that Ben might have abandoned Gretchen in the ballroom midtwirl and come back to see me. But I'd already ruled out the idea by the time I got to the door. It was much more likely to be Viktor Yegorov coming to check on his daughter.

As I looked through the peephole, however, who did I see but Mrs. Ludwig, swinging her sequined evening bag in great agitation?

For goodness' sake! What was it this time? She was supposed to be down in the ballroom right now, dancing the waltz of her life. I was about to unlock the door when, all of a sudden, I was grabbed from behind and dragged away from the door, somebody's hand pressed tight over my mouth.

Until that moment, I'd never known what it was like to get a real shock. Until that moment, to be honest, I'd never known what it was like to be truly scared.

But the worst thing was that I was powerless to do anything other than struggle and flail wildly, which didn't do me much good at all since my captor was a lot stronger than I was. He grasped me firmly from behind and pulled me toward the bathroom, and all I could think was *No! No! Please no!*—which probably didn't even count as a thought.

I could understand now why people peed in their pants when they were scared. I very nearly did it myself.

The attacker dragged me into the bathroom, pressed my back to the door, and switched the light on.

And I saw that it was Tristan. Tristan Brown from Room 211.

"Shh," he said. "Don't be scared, Sophie. It's only me."

But it was a bit late for that. I was half paralyzed with shock and fear.

Tristan gradually loosened his grip on me, but he kept his hand over my mouth and my body pressed against the door.

"You have to listen to me very carefully, Sophie. And trust me." With his free hand, he reached into the pocket of his tux and cursed softly. "Damn, I must have lost my phone on the way in. Okay. We don't have much time. Listen: Outside the door to this suite are the grand hotel kidnappers, and we need to be out of here before they get in." He spoke quietly and with great urgency, and he was nothing like the Tristan I knew—the arrogant, cocky, permanently amused Tristan. This new Tristan seemed almost afraid. "So you need to get the kid into a coat or something, and then we'll all climb out the window and take her somewhere safe. Nod if you understand."

I shook my head. Was he completely insane? There weren't any kidnappers at the door, only Mrs. Ludwig!

Tristan sighed impatiently. "I know this must be very confusing for you, and I wish I'd figured it out sooner, then we wouldn't be in this mess. But I only just found out. Are you going to scream if I take my hand away?"

I shook my head again, and Tristan cautiously removed his hand from my mouth. Even if I'd wanted to scream, I probably couldn't have managed much more than a croak.

"You've made a mistake. That's just Mrs. Ludwig out there." I gasped. "And Mr. Huber showed Ben his gun license. There *is* no grand hotel kidnapper . . ." I ran out of breath.

Tristan grabbed my upper arms with both hands and shook me gently. "There is, I'm afraid. Two of them. And they're right here." He pulled me away from the bathroom door, opened it and peered into the next room. From here, we could see Dasha's curly head on the pillow. "I fell for their hand-holding and that harmless old couple schtick just like everyone else—although the ring did make me a bit suspicious. But even so, who could have guessed they were kidnappers?" He grabbed my hand and led me into the next room.

Meanwhile there was another knock on the door, and Mrs. Ludwig, from the corridor, called in a tearful voice: "Sophie, my dear, is that you?"

She sounded genuinely distraught. And half of me wanted to run to the door and yell for help, tell her I'd been ambushed by a crazy Brit who was coming out with all kinds of madness. But the other half of me was starting to believe Tristan. I wished I had a third half that could tell me which one was right. And that could sit me down and explain everything to me properly.

"I need your help again, Sophie! It's urgent!" cried Mrs. Ludwig.

"Again?" Tristan shook me harder this time. "Sophie? Has Mrs. Ludwig already been in this room?"

I nodded. "Yes, a few minutes ago. Her zip was stuck."

"No!" Tristan let go of me and lurched toward the bed. He tried to wake Dasha, shaking her vigorously. And he cursed over and over again. "They must have drugged her." He started examining Dasha, rolling up her sleeves and lifting the curly hair from the back of her neck. "There," he said, pointing to a reddish patch on her skin. "That must be from a needle."

Oh my God. The memory was so vivid: Mrs. Ludwig leaning lovingly over Dasha, stroking her head . . .

I'd been so stupid.

"The Ludwigs are the grand hotel kidnappers?" I whispered.

Tristan nodded grimly. "It certainly looks like it! The innocent old couple that everyone loves."

"Sophie, my dear?" Mrs. Ludwig knocked on the door again. She sounded less tearful now—almost impatient.

Tristan looked around frantically. "I don't know why she didn't finish you off straightaway and do what she came here to do. She was inside the room, exactly where she wanted to be."

The idea of Mrs. Ludwig "finishing someone off" just sounded so—so wrong. And yet . . . I remembered her taking a deep breath just as we'd heard the knock on the door.

"She left because Ben came to the door," I whispered.

"Then he probably saved your life without even realizing it." Tristan lifted Dasha off the bed. "We'll just have to carry her. Sophie, no!"

I'd moved closer to the door. Not to open it, as Tristan must have feared, but because I'd heard another voice: a quiet, deep voice.

"She's not opening the door," said Mrs. Ludwig.

"Perhaps she's in the bathroom?" said the second voice. It belonged to Mr. Ludwig, and I recognized it at once. "Or perhaps she's been a bad girl and snuck out once the kid was asleep." He laughed softly. "She didn't suspect anything earlier, did she?"

"No, nothing," said Mrs. Ludwig.

She was right. I hadn't suspected anything at all.

The next thing Mr. Ludwig said made me feel positively sick.

"Do you have the master key?" he asked his wife, as matter-of-factly as if he were inquiring about the weather. "I want to be away by the time this waltz finishes. Oh, I miss my old Walther PPK. This Glock is just so tacky and pretentious. Though I do like the silencer."

I sprang back from the door in horror. "They've got a master key," I whispered to Tristan, aghast. "And a gun with a silencer."

Tristan nodded grimly, cradling the drugged little girl in his arms. "They're professionals," he said. "The bolt and chain won't hold them up for more than a few seconds. We'll climb out of the window in the room next door. If we lock the bedroom door, we might be able to buy ourselves a little more time before they realize we're gone. And once we're on the ground, we can fetch help. And I'll explain everything to you properly. Let's just hope they haven't stationed any accomplices outside the building."

"We can't climb out of the window, Tristan. I'm scared of heights. And Dasha is unconscious. We . . . we . . ." I looked around in panic. My eyes fell on the telephone, and I could have wept with relief. Why hadn't we thought of this before? "I'll phone through to the concierge's lodge. Monsieur Rocher will call the police and send help. Mr. Huber can come with his pistol."

From the door to the suite, I heard the scrape of metal on metal. Someone was fumbling around with the lock. It was only now that I heard the music again from downstairs, though it must have been playing the whole time. My brain had tuned it out. The waltz was reaching its crescendo, and I realized that if we shouted for help—from the roof terrace, for example—nobody would hear us. Everyone was downstairs in the ballroom. I could rely on Monsieur Rocher, though. He was bound to be sitting in his room, solid and steadfast as a rock.

My fingers trembled as I dialed the extension for the concierge's lodge, and I wasted precious seconds before I figured out that the phone wasn't working. I whispered "Hello?" into the receiver several times before I thought to check the cable—and found a loose end in my hand.

Somebody had cut the wire.

"Mrs. Ludwig!" So she'd taken care of that, too—she must have done it when I'd let her into the room earlier. I'd probably have collapsed on the floor there and then if Tristan hadn't dragged me through into the next room and locked the door behind us. He lifted Dasha from the bed and draped her over his shoulder. "Come on, Sophie." He clicked his fingers in front of my face. "Don't give up! You can do this."

I wasn't so sure. My fingers were trembling so badly it was all I could do to grab Dasha's sable coat from the coat stand at the end of the bed and dress her in it. Meanwhile, Tristan was pushing a chest of drawers in front of the door. "This whole thing is completely absurd," I murmured as I pulled Dasha's sable hat over her head—the same sable hat I'd once come to fetch from this suite, what felt like forever ago. It was like something from another life.

"We're on the first floor." Tristan tried to reassure me. "It's only sixteen feet to the ground from this window, and the snow's so deep and soft it's better than any mattress. We'll just jump down. You go first, then I'll drop Dasha down to you and I'll follow. And then we'll find somewhere safe to hide."

While he was speaking, he'd already started encouraging me onto the windowsill. The window was open—presumably from when Tristan had climbed into the suite just now. I clung to the window frame, practically hyperventilating.

"This is crazy! We can't just throw a drugged four-year-old out the window." I listened anxiously for noises from the next room.

"Yes, we can. We have to! Just step off the sill—the snow hasn't been cleared down there yet. You'll have a soft landing, I promise you."

And with that, Tristan gave me an almighty shove.

24

Tristan had been right: The snow really was softer than a mattress. But unlike a mattress, it was deep and wet—as I wriggled out of the hole I'd made as I landed, I could feel the melting snow soaking into my tights and trickling into my shoes. But I was more worried about Dasha. I knew I'd never forget the sight of her limp body falling through the air. I'd managed to catch her gently enough that (I hoped) she hadn't hurt herself. But it was six degrees below zero out here, and she didn't have any shoes or tights on. We had to get her somewhere warm. And safe.

I'd thought, naively, that if we made it to the ground alive this nightmare would all be over. But in reality, the danger was far from past. Perhaps the Ludwigs weren't about to launch themselves out of the window after us, but there was no way they were going to just give up and accept that their victim had slipped through their fingers.

No sooner had Tristan landed beside me in the snow, falling softly on his feet like a cat, when he pulled me toward the shelter of the wall and pointed upward in warning. I tried not to breathe. Had the Ludwigs already discovered the open window? Were they standing directly above us right now, looking down? Would they shoot at us if we moved? Or were they on the phone to one of their accomplices, who was setting out in search of us right now and might appear around the corner at any moment? In my mind, I saw the devious kidnapper couple scurrying down the stairs, hand in hand, to intercept us before we could get inside the hotel and raise the alarm.

And getting inside the hotel wasn't going to be as easy as you might think. We'd landed behind the ballroom and we were now standing in the deep snow beneath the arched windows where nobody could see or hear us. The light from the chandeliers streamed out into the night. I felt like someone who'd fallen overboard, floundering helplessly in the dark ocean beside a brightly lit cruise ship. The nearest entrance (the door by the little smoking area outside the spa, where I'd spotted Tristan climbing up the wall last week) was all the way around the other side of the south wing. Or we could go around the east side of the main building to the main door at the front, which I instinctively preferred because it was so busy there—hopefully too busy for the Ludwigs to mount an ambush.

But neither route would be a walk in the park in this deep snow and carrying an unconscious Dasha—especially as we could hardly see a thing. The moon hadn't risen yet and the light from the windows didn't pierce far into the deep darkness surrounding the hotel.

At that moment, however, I had my bright idea about the coal chute. It wasn't exactly an official entrance, but the hatch through which coal had once been emptied into the cellar was easily big enough for a person to fit through, and it was much closer—on the east side of the hotel, where the south wing joined the main building. We only had to battle our way through about a hundred feet of snow to get there. So we set off, sticking close to the wall, and reached the hatch a few minutes later. Although it hadn't been used for a long time, it opened quite easily. I'd been afraid it might have rusted or frozen shut, but it seemed we were in luck.

My knowledge of all the little nooks and crannies of the hotel was now worth its weight in gold. Pavel still hadn't shown me all the secrets of the basement, but I did know that the old coal cellar opened straight into the laundry room. Nobody would think to look for us in there.

Tristan looked around once more, then climbed through the hatch, slid down the chute, and crouched ready to catch Dasha at the bottom. I followed, and as my feet touched the ground and I smelled the musty basement air I let out a sigh of relief.

We'd done it. We were safe!

I felt really bad about Dasha—drugged, thrown out of a window, and now rolled down a coal chute. She'd probably be covered in bruises by tomorrow morning. But at least that was better than being kidnapped.

"Not a bad shortcut," said Tristan approvingly as I flicked the light switch and opened the door to the laundry room. It was a heavy fire door and you could lock it from the other side with a massive bolt. Which, luckily for us, nobody had done.

Unfortunately, though, the laundry room was unusually quiet, dark, and deserted. And now I remembered that Pavel had gone to his New Year's Eve concert in Sion. Tonight of all nights. But after all the panic, it still felt like coming home.

I switched on all the lights in here, too, and I was tempted to turn on some of the washing machines and tumble dryers just to hear the familiar noises of the laundry room. I took Dasha from Tristan and tried to warm up her little feet in my hands. But it was a futile endeavor, because my hands were icy cold, too.

"Do you think the drugs will do her any harm?" I asked anxiously. At least her skin was still a normal color, and her breathing was regular.

The same thing seemed to have occurred to Tristan. He shook his head. "I don't think she'd look like that if the drugs were affecting her," he said, casting a glance around the room.

"So what now?" I asked, imagining us bursting into the ballroom upstairs yelling "Help! Kidnappers!"

Tristan didn't appear to have a plan, either. "Who knows how many accomplices they have? At least down here we're safe," he muttered.

"Perhaps we should all go for a spin in the dryer," I said cheerfully. I was overwhelmed with relief at having survived. It wasn't every day you jumped out of a window, after all. But now, the thousand questions I'd been suppressing during our adrenaline-fueled escape came crowding into my mind.

As I laid Dasha down on a pile of sheets and started rubbing her little feet with a towel, Tristan opened the door to the corridor a crack and peered out. "Is there a phone around here?"

I shook my head. "The closest one is in the kitchen. And there's one in the spa, but that's just as far away. How did you figure out the Ludwigs were the kidnappers, anyway? And how did you time it so well, coming to rescue us? A second later and I'd have let them in." In hindsight, the idea sent a shiver down my spine.

"Yes, it was a close shave." Tristan closed the door again. "I realized too late who the Ludwigs really were. By then they were already on their way to you, so I had no choice but to sneak in through the window. I knew it would be hard to explain the situation to you, which is why I put my hand over your mouth—sorry about that . . ." He grinned wryly. "But I have to say you got your head around it all pretty quickly."

That was definitely not true.

It all seemed so absurd. Ben had spent days trying to convince me there was no grand hotel kidnapper, and eventually I'd come to agree with him. And now it turned out the kidnapper did exist after all. Or rather kidnapp*ers*, plural. And they were the Ludwigs, of all people—my favorite guests. No, I still hadn't got my head around that.

"How did you figure it out?" I asked.

"The ring," said Tristan. "I thought it was weird that someone could wear a ring like that for thirty-five years without realizing, or at least without someone telling them, that it was platinum and not silver. And the stone! It doesn't look anything like a beryl. You don't find pink diamonds of that size and quality at your local jewelry store. Stones like that are incredibly rare. The flea-market story sounded very implausible to me, and my grandpa thought the same. So I took some photos of the ring and Grandpa sent them to . . . well, to a friend. We thought we might have stumbled across a cunning pair of small-time crooks. We never dreamed they could be dangerous kidnappers. But when you asked me about the grand hotel kidnapper the other day, alarm bells started to ring."

"I don't understand." Dasha's feet were nice and warm again now, so I moved onto her hands.

Tristan leaned back against the door. "My grandpa remembered the kidnapping cases immediately because the kidnappers had such an unusual modus operandi—they always asked for valuables as well as cash, and they showed astonishingly good taste. They knew exactly what their victims' parents owned—from jewelry to paintings to a Stradivarius worth millions of euros. It took a while, but eventually we got a message from a friend who'd cross-referenced our photo of the pink diamond with all the information he had on the kidnapping cases. It left us in no doubt: The stone in Mrs. Ludwig's engagement ring was originally part of a brooch belonging to a publisher whose young daughter was abducted from a luxury hotel on Lake Maggiore in 1997."

It took me a few seconds to process this information. "So the ring could be used as evidence against the Ludwigs? What an amazing coincidence that your grandpa is a gemologist and just happens to be staying in the same hotel at the same time as . . . ," I trailed off.

Tristan smiled. "Do you know what's *really* an amazing coincidence? The fact that Stella Yegorov stole the ring in the first place. If she hadn't done that, Mrs. Ludwig wouldn't have had to come up with that story about the flea market, and I'd never have suspected there was something fishy about the pair of them."

"That's a lot of coincidences . . . ," I murmured, cradling Dasha's hand in mine. Tristan had just so happened to know that Stella Yegorov was a kleptomaniac and that was why he'd suspected her of stealing the ring. He just so happened to be able to climb up walls, so it had been easy for him to break into the suite, where not only had there happened to be a window open but also Stella Yegorov happened to have left the ring in the drawer of her nightstand instead of in the safe. And Tristan's grandpa just so happened to have a friend who could access the police database.

No, I wasn't falling for that.

"Grandpa says that coincidences are God's logic." Tristan sighed as if he knew exactly what I was thinking.

"Who are you really, Tristan?" I burst out.

He sighed again. "Have I ever lied to you, Agent Sophie?"

How should I know? There were plenty of times I'd asked him a question and he'd replied with another question—like he'd done just now, for example. Instinctively, I stepped in between him and Dasha on her pile of sheets.

"No, I haven't." Tristan slipped off his tuxedo jacket. "From the moment I met you, I found you charmingly disarming. Or disarmingly charming, if you prefer."

"What are you doing?" I asked, puzzled.

"I'm showing you the truth. Otherwise you'll never believe me." Tristan loosened his elegant black bow tie and started unbuttoning his shirt.

I stared at him, baffled.

"It's no coincidence that Grandpa and I are staying here," he said. "We're here for the Nadezhda Diamond, and when we realized who the Ludwigs were, we thought they might interfere with our plan to steal it."

This had to be some kind of sick joke, surely?

"So you—you really are a hotel thief? And your grandpa, too? You're here to . . . you're actually planning to steal the necklace?" I could hardly get the words out.

"Oh, I've already taken care of the necklace." Tristan ripped open his shirt with a dramatic gesture to reveal his perfectly toned chest. Around his neck was a two-string diamond necklace with a large blue stone in the center, surrounded by smaller jewels.

I had to hold onto Pavel's sewing table to stop myself from falling over.

"Magnificent, isn't it?" Tristan took off the necklace with a practiced movement and held it out to me. "Kali's third eye. See how it glows? As if there was a divine fire at the heart of it. Do you want to put it on?"

I took a step backward. "No, I don't. I want . . ." What did I want, actually? To run away? To call the police? "I want you to tell me none of this is true," I finished, in a whisper.

"Don't worry, Sophie!" Tristan's eyes met mine. "We don't steal things. We just restore them to their rightful owners. This diamond belongs in a secret temple in Madurai, India. That's where it was first used and that's where we're going to take it—back to the goddess Kali. It's not meant for ordinary mortals."

"Are you one of those freaks from one of those wacky cults?" I asked, taking another step backward.

Tristan laughed out loud, and suddenly he looked more like the Tristan I knew: arrogant and amused. He turned the necklace over in his hand and the blue stone sparkled in the light. "Good Lord, no! But I do work for a secret society that . . . well, let's just say it has an interest in righting wrongs. In maintaining balance in the world."

"The Illuminati?" I stammered.

"No. Although . . . some of us might well be Illuminati, too. Listen: nobody's going to miss the diamond. Up there in the ballroom right now, unbeknownst to her, Stella Yegorov is wearing a remarkably realistic replica necklace, and my grandpa is confirming her belief that she's got the most beautiful and expensive diamond in the world hanging around her neck. The man from the insurance company thinks everything is perfectly legit. They'll have no idea it's not genuine until they try and sell it, which hopefully they'll never do. And the smaller diamonds in the forged necklace are equal in quality to these ones. Only the replica blue diamond is made of zirconia, because there's no other diamond like it in the world."

Somewhere in the basement a door slammed, and we both jumped.

"We should probably think about trying to get back to civilization," said Tristan, as if the previous conversation had never happened. "What time is it, do you reckon?"

I had no idea how much time had passed since the moment Tristan had pressed his hand to my mouth in the suite upstairs—given how rapidly events had unfolded, probably not very much.

"Do you think the Ludwigs might have just given up by now?" I asked hopefully. Tristan might be in a secret society, and he might have stolen the necklace, but he'd still saved me and Dasha from the kidnappers.

"I doubt it," he said. "They don't know their cover's blown. They think you've run off with Dasha and are hiding in a corner somewhere, quaking with fear. They're probably dancing a couple of waltzes at the ball while their people come looking for you."

"People? You think they have more than one accomplice?" I said. "You think they have several?" And they probably all had pistols with silencers.

Tristan shrugged. "Or they could be working alone. I wouldn't put it past them."

"But they have no idea you're with us, do they?"

"No." Tristan's face brightened. "How could they? They have no idea that Grandpa and I are onto them or that we know about the engagement ring. They'll assume you and Dasha are alone." He glanced at the little oligarch's daughter, lying on her pile of laundry like in "The Princess and the Pea." "Which means I can just walk straight out of here—they're not going to do anything to me." He smiled at me. "Sorry, I should have thought of that before. It's just that it's the first time I've had to deal with dangerous criminals."

"Oh, you get used to it," I said.

Tristan was already at the door. "I'll go upstairs and tell people about the Ludwigs. Then I'll come back and get you. You'd better stay put."

"And perhaps you could call the police, too, before you come back," I said. "Or is that too big a risk for a hotel thief?"

Tristan held up the necklace. "As I said, we don't call it theft. We call it restoring ill-gotten gains—priceless treasures—to their rightful owners. But if you don't trust me . . ." He came back to stand beside me and before I knew what was happening he'd pressed the necklace into my hand. "Then I'll leave this with you as a security deposit till I get back. Just don't let anyone see it." He looked deep into my eyes and added solemnly: "You and I have a secret now, Agent Sophie. I trust you and you trust me."

I watched, stunned, as he walked to the door. In the doorway he turned back again. "I just hope they believe me upstairs," he said. "Everyone loves the Ludwigs."

"Tell Ben. You can count on him."

Tristan grimaced slightly. "I'll do what I can." And then he was gone.

I stood there beside Pavel's sewing table with an unconscious child in front of me and Kali's third eye in my hand and gasped for breath.

25

O kay. Just stay calm. Don't panic.

I stared at the bottle of Old Stucky's brother-in-law's pear brandy, which was still sitting there on the sewing table, and tried to breathe deeply and evenly. In and out and in and out . . .

Everything was fine. Dasha was warm, her breathing was regular, her pulse was normal, help was on its way.

But what if it wasn't? What if the Ludwigs knew perfectly well that someone had helped me and Dasha escape from the Panorama Suite? What if they'd seen Tristan trudging through the snow with us? Or noticed that he was missing from the ballroom? I was pretty sure Ella Barnbrooke wouldn't have kept quiet about her partner's absence—could the Ludwigs have put two and two together?

And what if nobody believed Tristan's story? What if, while he was upstairs trying to convince everyone, the Ludwigs' accomplices came down to search the basement and found me and Dasha? I could picture it now, the way the Ludwigs would play the innocent victims, holding hands and looking like rabbits in the headlights.

Just staying here and waiting for it all to play out suddenly seemed like a stupid idea—and dangerous, too. I had to try and call for help myself. I had to get to one of the telephones and call Monsieur Rocher. He'd take care of everything, I knew he would.

But first I had to hide Dasha so she'd be safe till I got back. And I knew the perfect place. There was enough room inside Tired Bertha for a whole nursery full of children. I made a little nest of towels for Dasha inside the drum and covered her up with more towels until only her nose and mouth were showing. Then I unplugged the machine, just in case anyone came in wanting to put a wash on.

So. That was sorted. Now I just had to find somewhere to hide the necklace. Unless I did what Tristan had done and wore it next to my chest, hidden under my clothes. The diamond clasp fastened around my neck almost without me having to touch it—it was a truly beautiful piece of craftsmanship. And man, was it heavy. As I tucked Kali's third eye inside my bra, I hoped I wasn't about to become the next victim of her curse.

I opened the door to the corridor a fraction to check the coast was clear. The kitchen and the spa were both about the same distance away, but I decided to make for the kitchen. I thought Mr. Heffelfinger might have closed the spa early, given that everyone was at the ball tonight.

I rounded the first corner very slowly and hesitantly, afraid Mr. Ludwig might be lying in wait with his pistol, but then I decided to run. The quicker I could get to a phone, the sooner this nightmare would be over.

As I turned the next corner, I ran slap-bang into Pierre, who was carrying a huge basket of bread rolls. A few of them fell onto the floor.

"Sophie!" Pierre exclaimed in surprise.

I was so relieved to see him that I almost burst into tears.

"Oh, phew," I cried. "Thank goodness it's you. You haven't seen any—er—suspicious characters lurking around here by any chance, have you?"

"Oh yes, loads of them," said Pierre. "The kitchen's full of suspicious characters. And the head chef is the worst of them. I'm sick and tired of it, I tell you. But after this shift, I've got two days off. And guess what I'm going to do with them?" Only now did he seem to realize there was something wrong with me. He set down his basket. "Good Lord, Sophie, what's up? You look like you've seen a ghost."

If only that was all it was! "Pierre, you have to help me," I burst out. "Someone's trying to kidnap the Russian oligarch's daughter to get the Nadezhda Diamond, and I escaped from the Panorama Suite with her. But they're still after us. They're armed and very dangerous."

The expression on Pierre's face changed from one of solicitude to one of pure disbelief mingled with concern as to my mental state. He tipped his head slowly to one side without taking his eyes off me, and I suddenly realized how Tristan must have felt earlier. Nobody believed a story like this the first time you told it. It was just too much for the brain to process.

"Okay," he said slowly. "So you ran off with the Russian oligarch's daughter because you were being chased by armed kidnappers who want to get their hands on the . . . Nad-something Diamond?"

"I know how it sounds," I broke in. "But I have to get to the kitchen and call Monsieur Rocher and tell him everything. Then he can call the police and fetch Yegorov. Will you help me?"

"Of course I'll help you." Pierre still didn't look entirely convinced, but the little smile of amusement had left his face. He was obviously starting to realize the seriousness of the situation. "Where's the kid now?"

"I left her in the laundry room."

"What? All alone?" Pierre took a deep breath. "Okay. Here's what we'll do: You go back to the kid and wait with her. I'll tell

Monsieur Rocher and call the police. And then I'll get my sharpest knife and come and stand guard outside the laundry room. No one is getting kidnapped on my watch!" Without stopping to pick up his bread basket, he set off at a run. "You can count on me, Sophie!" he called back over his shoulder.

Everything was going to be all right now. I ran back to the laundry room and lifted Dasha out of her nest inside Tired Bertha. Was I imagining it, or did her breathing sound more ragged than it had before? Perhaps there wasn't enough oxygen in the washing machine? I sat down at the sewing table with her and rocked her like a baby. "Not long now—Daddy's on his way," I was saying as the door opened and Pierre came in. He had his knife with him, as promised. It wasn't very big but it was murderously sharp, and if anyone knew how to use it, it was Pierre.

"It's all sorted," he panted, completely out of breath. "Monsieur Rocher is calling the police and letting the Montforts know, and I've told my friend Lucas to hide behind the stairs with a fire extinguisher and give any suspicious characters a good wallop over the head. Oh my goodness, is that the little girl? She's so sweet! Is she asleep? And why are you crying, Sophie?"

I hadn't realized there were tears running down my cheeks. "I'm just so relieved." I sniffled. "Thank you. And you must thank Lucas for me, whoever he is. Everything's going to be okay now. You can't imagine what it's been like."

"Oh, I can." Pierre sat down on Pavel's chair. "That jump out of the window alone must have been terrifying. It must be, what, fifteen, twenty feet?"

"I . . . I didn't tell you we jumped out of the window!" This

282

time the horror rose in me very slowly, as if my stomach was turning inside out in slow motion.

"That's true. You didn't." Pierre shrugged and started carving notches into the tabletop with his knife.

Oh no. Please no. Not again. Not Pierre!

Pierre, who was so kind to the Forbidden Cat and fed it scraps of cold meat. Pierre with his friendly, long-nosed face, whose mischievous grin I looked forward to seeing every morning. Who saved me raspberry cheesecake and gave me milk rolls for the Hugos.

"You didn't call Monsieur Rocher, did you?" I asked flatly. I knew the answer already, but I wanted to hear him say it.

"No," he said brightly. "But I did call somebody else, and they were very pleased to hear that you and the little girl are safe and sound down here in the laundry room." Pierre smiled his mischievous smile. "Dear oh dear, Sophie. What were you thinking? Climbing out of the window like that with a sleeping child. That could have backfired on you very badly. Mrs. Ludwig is fuming, I can tell you. And Mr. Ludwig was ready to give the whole thing up as a bad job."

I looked down at Dasha. I almost wished I was unconscious, too, then at least I wouldn't have been aware of what was going on. If only I'd stayed here in the laundry room . . .

"I'd have found you anyway," said Pierre, uncannily, as if he'd read my mind. "I knew you'd try and get in through the basement somehow—which entrance did you use, out of interest?—and the laundry room is the place you know best." He leaned back and let the knife slide through his fingers with a practiced movement. "What do you think the bread basket's for? I'm going to carry the

283

kid outside in it. And no one will suspect a thing. The head chef conveniently asked me to get rid of all the stale rolls."

And what are you going to do with me? I was about to ask, but on second thought, I realized I didn't want to know the answer. The sight of the knife was enough.

Pierre smiled at me over the pear brandy bottle. "I like you, Sophie, honestly I do. You're a nice girl. But just because I've slipped you a few treats now and then doesn't mean we're friends. You have no idea how the world works. Do you know how much a junior chef earns?" He didn't wait for my reply. "And all the crap we have to put up with? Is it really fair? Some of us spend our whole lives grafting and we can barely make ends meet, while those rich bastards come here on vacation and complain because their soft-boiled egg isn't the perfect shape. No, it's not fair, is it? It's every man for himself in this world, and I'm not about to pass up an offer that could be my ticket out of this hellhole once and for all. I'm sure you understand that, don't you?"

I'd heard what he said, but did I really understand it? Probably not. My mind was racing far too quickly for that. How long was it since he'd told the Ludwigs, and how long would it take them to get down here? And what were they going to do to me? Drug me like Dasha and take me with them so I couldn't tell anyone what had happened? But I was hardly going to fit inside a bread basket, was I? It was more likely they'd shoot me on the spot. Or perhaps Pierre would be called upon to use his knife in return for his share of the money?

I had to fight back. Or at least try to. For Dasha, and for myself. And for my parents. It would break their hearts if I died without going to college. Okay, perhaps that was a little unfair. And this was hardly the time for jokes.

I stared down at Dasha's sweet sleeping face and stood up.

"Don't try anything stupid, Sophie." Pierre stood up, too, toying with the knife in his hand.

"I just want to lay her down over there," I said, pointing to the pile of laundry she'd been lying on before.

Pierre nodded. "All right. And then you sit straight back down again, okay?"

"Okay." Like someone who'd abandoned all hope I shuffled over to the laundry pile and carefully laid Dasha down on it. I had no idea what I was going to do, but I had to do something. And I had to do it now.

As I turned around, the light started flickering. And not just one light, but every single bulb in that huge room, all flickering at the same time. Then one of the washing machines suddenly jolted into life. I could have sworn Tired Bertha was the only machine that made a noise like that, but I'd definitely unplugged her earlier.

"What the hell . . . ?" Pierre leapt past me toward the machines, his knife at the ready.

This was my chance. I grabbed the bottle of pear brandy and brought it down as hard as I could on Pierre's head. It didn't break, as I'd expected, but my blow was so forceful that I lost my grip on the bottle and it rolled away across the floor as if it felt insulted. Pierre fell forward onto his knees. He wasn't out cold, unfortunately, just slightly stunned.

Damn it, the man must have a thick skull! And he was still clutching his knife.

I looked hastily around and grabbed the nearest object at hand: the iron.

Pierre staggered to his feet. I knew I mustn't give him time to recover, so I grabbed the iron by the plug and swung it hard against Pierre's shins. I'd read somewhere that the shinbone is the most frequently fractured bone in the body and one of the most excruciatingly painful places you can hit someone.

And this seemed to be true, especially if you happened to hit them with a very heavy metal iron by swinging it through the air like a dog on a leash. Pierre cried out and fell to his knees again. This time he dropped his knife. There was even a rip in one of his trouser legs where the iron had caught it.

Tired Bertha, or whichever machine had been imitating her noises, was silent now and the lights had stopped flickering.

Slowly and painfully, snorting with rage, Pierre tried to haul himself to his feet by holding onto the rotary iron. Unusually, Pavel had switched the machine off with a piece of laundry still in it. In this case, it was a fifteen-foot-long damask table runner from one of the tables in the restaurant. Two thirds of the runner, which was a good two feet wide, was hanging out of the machine waiting to be ironed.

I didn't waste any time thinking or calculating: I picked up the end of the fabric, looped it around Pierre as quickly as I could and fed it into the mangle on the other side. Then I flicked the switch to ON and jumped backward. Pierre didn't even have time to blink before he found himself being squeezed against the mangle by the fabric. And once the mangle had swallowed something, she wasn't going to spit it out again in a hurry. Pierre's wildly flailing arms couldn't quite reach the switch.

"You witch!" he yelled as he realized he was trapped, harnessed to the most powerful rotary iron on the market. (Or it had been when the hotel had first bought it, anyway.) "I'll kill you!"

"Not if the mangle kills you first," I said.

I gave the knife another kick, just to be on the safe side, and it slid underneath the nearest folding machine.

"We'll be off, then," I said, lifting Dasha up off her pile of laundry. "I got in through the coal cellar; I can get out that way, too. Give my love to the Ludwigs!"

Pierre roared something very rude that even Gracie would have drawn the line at.

What I'd said about the coal cellar, of course, had been a red herring. I was actually planning to escape via the ski cellar—the steep coal chute might have been an excellent way in, but it would be much more difficult to climb out of. Especially with an unconscious child in my arms. The good thing was that Pierre couldn't see which way I'd gone because he was stuck facing the wall and he couldn't turn his head 180 degrees. Not that he even attempted it—he was too busy trying to stop the machine from flattening him.

I almost let out a triumphant shout. But Dasha and I weren't out of the woods yet.

As I was about to slip through the archway that separated the laundry room from the ski cellar, something damp brushed past my head and I stood still, startled. Which was a good thing, too, because at that moment I looked through the glass window in the door to the outer staircase and saw the shadow of something moving. A moment later the door opened.

I managed to dive around the corner just in time and squash myself and Dasha in behind the cupboard where the ski wax was kept. I stood stock-still, hoping nobody would spot us in the half darkness. In the laundry room, Pierre was still cursing loudly, and now there was a woman's voice, too. Mrs. Ludwig must have arrived. And Mr. Ludwig had come in through the back door. Very clever. A couple of seconds later and I would have run straight into his arms.

But as it was he hurried toward the sound of the yelling without so much as a glance in our direction.

I heaved a sigh of relief. I had two options now. To try and escape with Dasha through the ski cellar or . . .

I heard the mangle being switched off. "She got out through the coal cellar." Pierre sounded incredibly angry. "You need to go that way."

I lowered Dasha to the floor and laid her down gently with her head on a feather duster. Then I tiptoed back into the laundry room, scuttling between the machines to keep out of sight. One day I'd have to thank Fräulein Müller for insisting that all the staff wear shoes with extra-quiet soles. From my hiding place behind a tower of tumble dryers, I saw Pierre heading for the coal cellar, the Ludwigs' curly white heads close behind him.

"If she's still in the chute, she's mine," I heard Pierre say.

"Clever little thing, isn't she?" That was Mr. Ludwig. He was the last of the three to step inside the coal cellar. And he had a pistol in his hand, the sight of which made me hesitate for a moment.

I knew it was reckless, but if it worked I'd have killed three birds with one stone. So I took a deep breath, darted out of my hiding place and ran toward them as silently as I could.

Only six feet left. Three. One.

Then I was at the coal cellar door. I pushed it gingerly and felt it move, very slowly, inch by inch, until . . . *squeak!* The hinge had made a noise.

The Ludwigs spun round. Pierre already had his head inside the coal chute. Mr. Ludwig raised his revolver.

No, no, no. I hadn't gotten this far to give up now. I heard a plopping sound from somewhere, like a cork being pulled out of a champagne bottle, but I shoved the door closed with the last of my strength, leaned my whole weight against it, and shot the massive bolt home.

I'd done it.

Only now did I notice the stabbing pain in my shoulder. When I put my hand to it, I felt something wet. It took me a second to realize I'd been shot. My hand was red with my own blood.

Mr. Ludwig had been right—the silencer really did work.

26

So there I stood, exhausted, in the snow, as the distant sound of violins drifted toward us from the ballroom. Around my neck was a thirty-five-carat diamond that didn't belong to me, and in my arms was a sleeping child who didn't belong to me, either.

Somewhere along the way I'd lost a shoe.

"Oh my God, Sophie, you're bleeding." That was Tristan.

"Pierre's my friend." Perhaps it was the shock, but for a moment I couldn't remember how I'd gotten here or where Tristan had suddenly appeared from. All I knew was that I'd managed to stagger back into the ski cellar and pick Dasha up. I'd heard Pierre and the Ludwigs ranting and raving in the coal cellar behind the fire door, and wondered whether a door like that was bulletproof as well as fireproof. And how long it would take them to climb up the coal chute.

No matter. I was exhausted. If only I hadn't been in so much pain I would have fallen asleep already.

"I'm so sorry. I would have been here sooner but that stupid Ella girl came running after me and made a scene. She wouldn't leave me alone." As he spoke, Tristan was trying frantically to examine me, but without much success. It was too dark, for one thing, and for another thing he wasn't a doctor. He was a . . . hmm, what was he exactly? "And then just as I was about to head down the stairs into the laundry room I saw a guy with a pistol . . . So I came in through the ski cellar, and I saw the trail of blood and followed it. Where were you headed?"

I had no idea. I must have just started walking without knowing where I was going, and now here we were standing beside the half-moon fir tree, halfway to the stables. Perhaps I'd instinctively wanted to crawl in underneath the tree and hide, like the twin boys I'd looked after on my first day on childcare duty. What were their names again?

"Ashley and Jeremy. Or something like that. All their clothes were white." It was weird—my voice sounded completely different from normal. As if it was coming from somewhere outside of me and didn't belong to me anymore. "All white! Can you imagine? Perhaps they're going to be dentists when they grow up. Or chefs. Though that ruins your character."

"Oh my God, Sophie! How much blood have you lost?" Tristan seemed to be trying to destroy his shirt. He'd pulled it out of his trousers and was now tearing at it with all his might, cursing as he did so.

The music in the ballroom grew more energetic.

Why was the orchestra still playing, actually? Shouldn't everyone be running around calling Dasha's name by now? And perhaps my name too from time to time? "Why are they still in there dancing with Gretchen while I have to lock the kidnappers in the coal cellar?" I looked up at Tristan. "Did you forget to raise the alarm, Tristan?"

"No! I told my grandpa. And Monsieur Rocher the concierge. Help is on its way. Monsieur Rocher called the police straightaway, but I didn't want to wait. I wanted to get back to you. And if Ella hadn't delayed me . . ."

"You should have told Ben. I told you to tell him." By now I couldn't manage anything more than a mumble. "But it doesn't matter," I murmured. "I just want to sleep. And so does Dasha. Though she just did this really weird twitching thing. It must be nice and cozy under the fir tree, you can come with us if you like. No one will find us there. As long as we don't giggle." I stared at the tree. "But the snow's a bit deep. You don't have a shovel with you, by any chance?" I closed my eyes. Maybe I could sleep standing up. I just had to make sure I didn't drop Dasha. I had to hold onto her very, very tightly.

"Sophie! Don't fall asleep!" Tristan had finally succeeded in ripping his shirt into pieces and now he wrapped one of the strips around my upper arm. The sharp pain took my breath away for a moment. "Come on, you've made it this far. We can't give up now. We've got to get out of here."

"You go on without me. You can take Dasha and the diamond, I'll stay here and sleep for a bit. And I'll come and find you when I'm . . . back to normal."

Tristan shook me gently. "You have to pull yourself together," he said. And then he kissed me. Quite fiercely, almost desperately. He took my head in both his hands and pressed his lips against mine.

The effect was similar to that of Old Stucky's brother-in-law's pear brandy. The kiss burned itself into my body and filled me with new warmth.

"I've been wanting to do that ever since the first time I saw you," he whispered as he let me go.

"Okay! Okay! I'm awake!" I exclaimed. And it was true. I'd never been more awake in my life. "Let's get out of here."

"Yes—the sooner, the better." Tristan smiled, relieved. "If I can follow the trail of blood, other people can, too."

And a voice I'd never heard before replied: "Quite right."

You had to be kidding me. I was starting to get well and truly sick of this.

"Stay right where you are. Either of you move a muscle and I'll shoot." From behind the nearest snowdrift, a figure had emerged from the shadows and now stepped into the light. Well, to say "light" was a bit generous, but the moon had risen by now and together with the Christmas lights in the half-moon fir tree it was just about bright enough to see the man standing in front of us. He was a stranger, of medium height, and wearing black leather gloves—which for some reason scared me more than the pistol he had trained on us. It too was fitted with a silencer. Perhaps Mr. Ludwig had bought a double pack of them to save money.

With his other hand, the man was holding a phone to his ear. "I've got them. Down by the parking lot, where that big tree is. You were right; they're not alone. They've got this boy in a tux with them. Right now? Here? Okay." He slipped the phone into his pocket.

Right here and now what? Was he going to shoot us?

"Listen, I don't know how much money they've offered you but whatever it is, I can offer you more," said Tristan.

"Yes—we've got the necklace. The real one," I added. If I'd had my hands free I would have ripped my uniform off and dazzled him with the Nadezhda Diamond.

"You rich people are all the same when you're in trouble. I know when someone's trying to make a fool of me." The man took a step toward us, and now we could see his face more clearly. He looked so . . . ordinary. "Sorry, but I've got a reputation to keep up. I'm the hit man on this job." And without a moment's hesitation he aimed the gun straight at Tristan's head. "Nothing personal, kiddo."

"Listen," Tristan began—and then suddenly everything happened at once.

The killer's gloved finger was on the trigger when, out of nowhere, a ski came flying through the air and hit him in the back of the head. With a wild yell, somebody came running at our attacker from behind and shoved him hard.

It took me a second to realize this somebody was Ben, and another to realize that the gun had actually gone off. The bullet had grazed Tristan's ear. Judging by his cursing, it must have hurt like hell.

Ludwig's hit man didn't fall over, but staggered forward toward the fir tree, still with the gun in his hand. If he turned around now, it was all over. I hugged Dasha closer to me, knowing I couldn't hold on to her much longer. Damn it, why couldn't luck be on our side for once? I really did feel we'd earned it.

The killer had steadied himself by now. He straightened up under the tree, turned around—and suddenly a gust of wind must have blown through the snow-laden branches, though strangely enough I wasn't aware of any breeze. The branches trembled and a huge chunk of snow slipped off and landed on the man, who fell to his knees. But that wasn't all. Now more and more of the branches had started drooping toward the ground, and suddenly all the snow that had collected in the needles of the enormous tree slid off at the same time and fell to the ground. It collapsed onto the man like an avalanche, completely burying him. You couldn't even see the top of his head.

Ben, Tristan, and I stumbled backward, staring in disbelief at the huge mound of snow.

"He won't be getting out of there anytime soon," said Ben with great satisfaction. He lifted Dasha out of my arms, which by now were starting to seize up. "Oh my God, you're bleeding!"

I knew I should answer him, but I just couldn't get the words out. Tristan came to my rescue.

"You've only just realized that? I thought you'd found us by following the trail of Sophie's blood." Tristan was clutching his ear. Blood dripped through his fingers onto the snow. "Oh, great, now I'm bleeding, too. Damn it, I don't understand how there can be hit men with guns running around all over the place and nobody doing anything about it! Why hasn't anyone come to help us?"

"*I* came," said Ben, rather indignantly. "Just in time to stop you getting shot, actually, you ungrateful bastard. And I would've come sooner if I'd had even the slightest idea what was going on here." He looked around and took a deep breath. "Christ, nobody knew you were out here! Everyone thought you were in the basement; they all went down there. Monsieur Rocher took his walking stick, and my uncle took a stapler."

"Oh, brilliant," said Tristan.

"And I would've gone down there, too, if I hadn't run into this girl who told me to come out to the half-moon fir tree," said Ben. "She must be one of the kitchen temps, though I've never seen her before."

"How interesting," said Tristan sarcastically, but the sarcasm died in his throat all of a sudden as we heard the sound of footsteps. It was *them*.

They were walking toward us from the forecourt, crunching across the snow without even trying to be quiet.

"There's the fir tree." That was Mrs. Ludwig. And then Pierre, panting: "That's handy—now we won't have so far to walk to the car." Mr. Ludwig said nothing; he was probably too busy stroking his gun.

If the paths hadn't been obscured by massive snowdrifts, we would have seen them coming. But they would have seen us, too. At least this way we had a chance.

"We should split up," Ben whispered. "You go that way, Tristan, and they'll follow your trail of blood, and Sophie and I will take Dasha to the stables. Let the blood drip."

To my astonishment, Tristan nodded and slipped away, bent double, along the circular path that Old Stucky had cleared yesterday. I didn't think it was the best idea—the path led straight into the deserted woods—but Ben was already ushering me toward the stables. I could run a bit faster now that I didn't have to carry Dasha, but because I only had one shoe on and my shoulder was killing me, it was still a struggle. And though we tried not to make any noise, the snow crunched beneath our feet. (I only crunched on every second footstep, because of my missing shoe.) At last, however, we made it to the stables, and Ben flung open the door and almost pushed me inside. How he was managing to carry Dasha one-handed was a mystery to me—it looked like he had a giant doll clamped firmly under one arm. Still, she was better off with Ben than with the Ludwigs.

As he closed the door, I freed Dasha from his iron grip and checked to make sure she was still breathing. She was. She was surprisingly unscathed, actually, although she had a bit of blood from my wound smeared on her cheek and we'd lost the sable hat somewhere along the way. And her little feet were icy cold.

Jesty and Vesty snorted happily. They were standing together in a large stall, poking their heads out curiously over the partition. I surveyed the stables. There were plenty of hiding places here: the hayloft at the top of the steep staircase; the tack room full of nooks and crannies; and all the chests, crates, blankets, and feed bags piled up along the walls. But what good was the best hiding place against a gun that could shoot through a crate, a plank of wood—a horse, even? Nevertheless, I laid Dasha down on a chest in the far corner of the stables and covered her with a horse blanket. Then I looked around for a weapon. A pitchfork was no match for a gun, of course, but it was better than nothing.

In the meantime, Ben had opened the door to the stall—I had no idea what he was planning. Perhaps he was going to ride one of the horses straight at the Ludwigs and trample them underfoot.

Standing there by the door in his tuxedo, with his tousled hair and fierce expression and a metal sign in his hand that read NO SMOKING IN THE STABLES, he was the most wonderful sight I'd ever seen.

"Do you think Tristan will be able to lure them off the scent?" he asked. "Things are going to get pretty hairy now he's got all three of them on his tail."

"Since when did you care about Tristan?"

"I don't. I hate him," said Ben. "But unfortunately I can't kill him because he saved your life."

I couldn't help grinning. That was possibly a bit of an exaggeration. But by persuading me to jump out of the window, Tristan had at least saved me from getting a reputation as the world's most irresponsible babysitter. Technically, all the other stuff had only happened *because* he'd rescued me.

"I should have been the one to come and save you," said Ben

despairingly. "And instead I spent the whole time arguing with you, telling you there was no kidnapper and you were crazy to think there was."

This was true.

Ben looked at me earnestly. "What I was going to say to you before, but I freaked out . . . I . . . Sophie, I've fallen in love with you. You're the funniest, cleverest, bravest, and most wonderful girl I've ever met. And just now, when Monsieur Rocher told me you were in danger, I regretted not telling you that. Because I was afraid I'd never get another chance."

My eyes filled with tears. I would have liked to throw down my pitchfork, run over to Ben, and kiss him.

But I couldn't, because now we heard footsteps outside. And somebody muttering instructions.

"It was nice knowing you," I said under my breath, not knowing whether my voice would carry to where Ben stood. But he heard me.

"I'm sorry it took me so long to find you," he replied, also in a whisper.

Just in time to die with me, I thought.

Then there was a knock at the stable door. A very polite, civilized knock. "Sophie? Are you in there, my dear?" It was crazy, but Mr. Ludwig's voice still sounded like that of a sweet little old man. Was he alone? Who was with him? Pierre or his wife? Or had the hit man finally managed to extricate himself from the pile of snow?

"If you weren't so stubborn, Sophie, you'd be fast asleep on the bed in the Panorama Suite right now," said Mr. Ludwig jovially. "True, you'd have got in trouble for raiding the minibar and drinking yourself into a stupor while little Dasha ran away and hid, the way she's done once before, but that would have been a small price to pay compared to what's going to happen to you now."

At last, it was all starting to make sense! The day Don and Dasha had gone missing, it was the Ludwigs who'd drugged them and hidden them in the music room so that tonight, when they kidnapped Dasha for real, everyone would think she'd just run off to play hide-and-seek. It wouldn't even occur to people that she could have been kidnapped, because they'd all assume she was hiding somewhere just like she had before. And they'd have found me, the drunken baby-sitter, lying asleep in the corner of the Panorama Suite. The Ludwigs would have bought themselves plenty of time to escape.

A plan as simple as it was evil. And they would have pulled it off, too, if the thriller writer hadn't happened to start researching the grand hotel kidnapper and mentioned it to me.

What was it Tristan's grandpa had said? Coincidences are all part of God's plan?

Ben and I exchanged a glance. He'd obviously made the connection, too, because he gave me an apologetic smile.

"Don't you think it's time you gave up?" asked Mr. Ludwig softly. "You're not going to achieve anything by being so obstinate. Why make things difficult for yourself? Just give us the child, and nothing will happen to you."

Ben shook his head silently, and Jesty snorted.

"Think of the child," said Mr. Ludwig. "Think of what you've put the poor little thing through."

I'd gone through pretty much the entire spectrum of human emotions by this time, but this terrible rage, this righteous anger that I felt now, was new. This was all so incredibly unfair. I didn't want to die yet. Not without having had my first kiss with Ben. And a second kiss, and a third one . . .

"And I think *you'd* better give up, Mr. Ludwig, or whatever your real name is," I called. "The police are on their way, and we've told them everything. You should get out of here while you still can."

Mr. Ludwig laughed out loud. "Very well then—we'll have to do this hard way." I heard two oddly muffled thuds, and it took me a second to realize they were gunshots. Mr. Ludwig was shooting through the lock. Then the stable door flew open. "What a shame you didn't take the opportunity to escape through the back door," he remarked. "Too late now."

In the tack room, I remembered now, there was another way in and out of the stables that we'd completely forgotten about. The realization gripped me like an icy fist. Then Mr. Ludwig burst in through the door and Ben ran at him with a wild shout—the same wild shout as when he'd attacked the hit man. Only this time he was engaged in a hopeless battle against a pistol, and he was armed only with a NO SMOKING sign. I spun around, but it was too late. Mrs. Ludwig was standing behind me, and the last thing I saw was her lunging toward me with a needle in her hand.

27

When I woke up, the first thing I saw was a wall full of books. And then Monsieur Rocher's kind face.

"Am I dead?" I asked.

He shook his head. "Oh, no. Although there are people who imagine heaven is a library."

I realized now what a stupid question it was. The wound on my shoulder was throbbing, my foot hurt, and I was still wearing my chambermaid's uniform, though one of the sleeves was missing. I was comfortably ensconced on a pile of velvet cushions in one of the big upholstered window seats in the hotel library. Outside the window it was dark, so it must still be nighttime. The curtains had been half drawn, probably to give me some privacy, but I could hear voices, laughter, and the clink of glasses, as if there was still a party going on somewhere. It sounded as though the corridors, the foyer, and the bar were all full of people.

Someone had tended to my wound, and there was a white dressing on my upper arm. The wound had bled so much that I could hardly believe all it needed was this little bandage.

"The bullet just grazed your arm: painful, but not serious," Monsieur Rocher explained. "I managed to convince the paramedics not to take you to the hospital—I thought you'd prefer to be here with us when you woke up. Mr. Montfort told us to bring you here to the library. I suppose he didn't like the idea of people seeing your dingy little bedroom when they came to visit you. You're the woman of the hour, you know—everyone is impatient for you to wake up.

The thriller writer insists that the arrest of the grand hotel kidnappers was entirely due to his powers of deduction, but we all know who the real heroine of the story is." He smiled at me over the top of his glasses.

"Where are Ben and Dasha?" I tried to sit up. "And Tristan and the Ludwigs? And Pierre?"

Monsieur Rocher eased me softly back into the cushions. "Oh, I'm so sorry! I should have told you that first. The Ludwigs, Pierre, and their accomplices are all in police custody. Ben is just fine. He's been sitting with you holding your hand for hours. I think he may have had a little cry. Young Dasha woke up two hours ago, and the doctor says she's in very good shape. Her father shed a few tears, too. And young Mr. Brown had to have stitches in the wound in his ear. I don't think he cried, but he did come to check on you several times. He and his grandfather are flying back to London today."

My hand leapt to my chest. The stolen diamond necklace was still there. I'd have known without having to feel for it, to be honest—it lay so heavy on my chest that I could hardly forget it. I was frankly amazed to find I could be shot and drugged and treated by paramedics and manage to hide the world's most valuable necklace under my uniform through it all, but it appeared that I could!

No wonder Tristan had come to check on me multiple times . . .

"What time is it?" I asked.

"Almost half past one," said Monsieur Rocher. "But in all the commotion we forgot to see in the new year and light the sky lanterns. The New Year's Ball has never finished so early. The police cars and ambulances have only just left."

"But no one seems to have gone to bed." I cocked my head toward the bar, where most of the party-type noises were coming from.

"Oh, no! Hardly anyone has gone to sleep. Everyone's in a state of great excitement. And curiosity. You must have lots of questions, too."

Yes. And the most pressing one was how Ben and I had got out of the stables alive.

In our panicked state, as it turned out, we'd forgotten about a lot more than just the back door in the tack room. It hadn't crossed our minds that Old Stucky might be in the vicinity, and we hadn't stopped to wonder what effect a pair of pistol-toting men might have on two horses in an open stall.

Old Stucky had come to check in on the horses one last time before he went to bed. He said a little voice in his head had told him to. And as he approached the stables, he saw that both of the Ludwigs—or "tha moarst earvul creechers Ol' Stucky's ever come acrorse," as he called them—were in the process of breaking open the lock. This made him very angry indeed. And although he was a small, frail old man, he was still more than capable of defending his territory.

"When ye mek Ol' Stucky mad, he gets rearly mad," he told the police later. "Better ta learve well aloon."

And the same clearly applied to the horses. Perhaps Jesty was just impatient for a well-earned rest or perhaps she was living up to her name: Either way, the kick she gave Mr. Ludwig could certainly be described as a "grand gesture." Before he could pull the trigger on his gun, Mr. Ludwig was catapulted at least six feet into the air. He then crashed into the wall and slid to the floor, where Old Stucky walloped him over the head with a feeding trough. And anything else he could lay his hands on that was even remotely suitable for walloping someone over the head with.

I would have loved to have seen this, but by that time Mrs. Ludwig had already knocked me out. She didn't have a gun, but she had several more of those needles, and now she pulled one out and brandished it like a knife at Ben. After his opponent had been unexpectedly vanquished by the horse and Old Stucky, Ben had come charging toward Mrs. Ludwig with his NO SMOKING sign. But seeing me unconscious made him so angry that he tossed the sign aside, picked up the pitchfork, and drove Mrs. Ludwig back against the wall with it—assisted by Vesty, who clearly also wanted a role in this drama. Mrs. Ludwig realized she'd lost and, because she couldn't expect any more help from her husband, dropped the needle, and resorted to begging for mercy.

"I'll let Ben tell you what happened next," said Monsieur Rocher, standing up. "But first I'm going to make you a cup of tea. You need to get your strength up. And Madame Cléo brought you these wonderful truffles. She had made them for the ladies in Room 303, but they said your need was greater than theirs."

It was a strange feeling to be lying on these velvet cushions in the library waiting for Ben to come and see me, and being treated like a VIP guest. An extra pillow was soon tucked under my knees and another behind my back, and Pavel brought up a cashmere blanket from the laundry room and wrapped it around me. He, too, was crying a little. He couldn't believe someone had tried to shoot me in the laundry room tonight of all nights, when he hadn't been there. And he cried even more when he heard that Tired Bertha had provided a temporary hiding place for little Dasha.

"You see, and everyone say she useless." He kissed me on both cheeks before he left (I decided to break it to him gently the next day about the role the mangle had played in proceedings) and promised to pass on my thanks to Old Stucky. It seemed the tough little man had saved my and Ben's lives. Along with Jesty and Vesty, to whom I would definitely be giving two extra carrots tomorrow.

No sooner had Pavel left than Gracie, Amy, and Madison arrived with a plate of sliced fruit (it went untouched, though—we had Madame Cléo's truffles, after all) and bombarded me with questions. I had to admit that our adventure made for an exciting tale: kidnappers lurking outside the door with guns and syringes like the wolf in "The Three Little Pigs"; then me and Tristan jumping out of the window with Dasha, fleeing through the snow, and sliding down the chute into the coal cellar. It was the stuff of a bestseller. And I hadn't even told them the whole story yet—the most exciting part was yet to come.

Gracie was quite offended that the Ludwigs hadn't chosen her as their kidnapping victim. While Gracie lamented her dull fate, Amy told me how she'd spoken to Aiden and cleared up all the misunderstandings between them. And even if she hadn't told me, I'd have guessed it from her beaming smile and her shining eyes. Aiden, leaning against the library door waiting for Amy, looked just as happy.

Ella and Gretchen, on the other hand, were both extremely miffed. Tristan hadn't turned up to the ball at all, and Ben had been so distracted the entire time that he'd caused a pileup on the dance floor during the waltz, bringing down not only Gretchen but also the Swiss politician and her husband. They'd all ended up in a heap on the floor. Madison had taken a photo of the disaster and secretly posted it to Gretchen's Instagram account, with the hashtags #theglamourneverstops #groggygretchen #bluedanubewaltz.

Now I was looking forward to talking to Ben even more. But still he didn't come. Instead, Don came strolling in. He, like Gracie, should have been in bed a long time ago, but tonight was far too exciting a night for that. He'd seen the police taking away the gloved hit man with his own eyes. The Ludwigs' violent accomplice hadn't been able to free himself from the snowdrift in the end—the fire department had had to come and dig him out. The half-moon fir tree had done a very thorough job. Amazingly, he'd escaped with nothing worse than a mild case of hypothermia.

"Is it true you took on three people and a gun on your own, and won?" asked Don.

"Only briefly," I said modestly. "But yes—I locked them in the coal cellar."

Don nodded approvingly. "Perhaps you're not the worst babysitter in the world, Sophie Spark."

Yes, perhaps I wasn't. And perhaps Don wasn't the sneakiest child in the world—there had to be worse kids than him. A few. If you looked really hard.

Even Gordon Montfort paid me a visit in my window seat. He clearly wanted it to look as if he was concerned for my welfare. He asked how I was feeling and praised my "quick-wittedness," as he called it. I'd never known him to be so friendly. But I quickly realized all he really wanted to do was make sure my parents weren't going to sue him. He probably didn't think his insurance would cover an underage intern jumping out of the window, getting shot, and being injected with a sedative while on duty.

I assured him my parents wouldn't breathe a word of what had happened that night—for their own sake, if no one else's—and he withdrew, greatly relieved.

Then I asked Amy to help me up. Before anyone else drifted in as if by chance (when the only face I really wanted to see was Ben's),

I urgently needed to go to the bathroom. Amy, Gracie, and Madison escorted me to the "powder room," as Fräulein Müller called the ladies' toilets off the lobby. There was a crowd of guests gathered nearby, waiting to go outside and light sky lanterns, and the three Barnbrooke girls—sensing how embarrassed I was at having to walk past all these people—tried their best to shield me from prying eyes. I was still wearing my uniform with the missing sleeve, and I only had one shoe on. In the bar, someone was playing Beethoven's "Ode to Joy" on the piano.

"Look, there's Tristan!" cried Gracie. "Oh, he's changed his clothes. That's a shame. Just now he was wearing this ripped shirt with blood all over it. Madison really wanted to take a photo of him and Ella, but Ella didn't want to be in it."

Tristan was standing beside his grandpa, leaning back against one of the pillars in the lobby and smiling at me. His ear was hidden under a thick bandage, but he still looked superhot. He was the most attractive man I'd ever seen.

And kissed. Well, technically it had been the other way around. *He'd* kissed *me*. Although strictly speaking, it hadn't been a proper kiss, more a means of resuscitating me. And it felt like forever ago. As if it had happened to another girl, in another life.

I thought about the fantastic tale Tristan had told me down in the laundry room. That he wasn't a thief; that he and his grandpa worked for a secret society that restored things to their rightful places. And I decided the story was so absurd that it just might be true. After all, Tristan had always told me the truth, hadn't he?

I decided it was time to return the necklace, so that the goddess Kali could get her third eye back at last and the balance of the universe could be restored. I could've dragged Tristan into another alcove or a cupboard or something to hand it over, like in the old days, but now I had a better idea.

"Can you lend me your cat hat, Gracie?" I asked when we got to the powder room. Gracie plucked her beloved hat eagerly off her head and held it out to me, and she didn't even bat an eye when I took it and hurried into one of the cubicles. I removed the necklace, wrapped it in several layers of toilet paper—the paper in the powder room was lovely and soft and thick—and tucked it inside the hat.

"I've got a job for you," I said as I came out of the cubicle. "I need you to carry a secret cat-hat message to Tristan Brown. It might be a bit dangerous, though."

"Oh yes," said Gracie, and Madison cried, "I want to go, too!"

"Okay. You can both go. It's very important that nobody but Tristan sees inside this hat. Gracie, you give it to him and tell him Agent Sophie sends her best wishes and says bon voyage. And then Madison, you say, 'long live the balance of the universe.' Do you think you can remember that?"

They both nodded eagerly and disappeared through the door in great excitement. I stayed with Amy, who was considerate enough not to ask any questions. In the mirror—which was enormous, with a magnificent golden frame—I saw I looked pretty much like my normal self, and nowhere near as bad as I'd feared. Amy still took a little comb out of her evening bag, though, and tidied up my hair a bit.

Tristan and his grandpa were gone from the lobby when we came out of the bathroom, and for a moment I felt a little stab of disappointment in my chest. Gracie and Madison, beaming widely, told us the handover had gone off without a hitch.

"He said to tell you that . . . What was it again, Agent Madison?"

"That the third eye sees everything and that the universe thanks

Agent Sophie," said Madison. "And that you should leave your window open if the hotelier's son turns out to be an idiot."

"Whatever that means," said Gracie.

"Hmm," said Amy, sounding exactly like Monsieur Rocher.

We returned to the library, and I settled happily back into my nest on the window seat. Next door in the bar, everyone was singing "Auld Lang Syne," and outside on the terrace the sky lanterns were being laid out ready for the guests to come and light them.

"You're awake." Viktor Yegorov was standing in the doorway.

"How's Dasha?" I asked.

"She's fine." Viktor Yegorov came a few steps closer. He was much paler than usual and had dark circles under his eyes. "Thanks to you. I know I said nothing bad could ever happen to anyone in this hotel, and perhaps that's true, ultimately." He bent over me and took my hand. "But now I know why. It's not the hotel that's magic; it's the people who work here. How can I ever thank you? You risked your own life to save my daughter's."

"I did have help, though," I said, pretending not to see the tears running down his cheeks. "From Tristan and Ben and . . . I don't know if I'd call it magic, but . . ." I thought of the lights that had flickered on and off in the laundry room. And the wet thing that had brushed past my face when I was about to enter the ski cellar. And all that snow falling off the half-moon fir tree . . . "On second thought, maybe I would," I murmured.

Viktor Yegorov had let go of my hand now and was staring out of the window into the darkness. "I have to tell you—when I last stayed at Castle in the Clouds, many years ago when I was hardly more than a child myself, I was in despair," he said quietly. "I'd decided I didn't want to live any longer. But . . . this place and the people here—they saved me. They stopped me from taking my own life, and they gave me the courage to go on living. I'll never forget what you did for my daughter today. I'd like to do something to express my gratitude. So if there's anything I can do for you, just say the word. Money is no object."

He wiped the tears from his eyes and smiled at me.

I found myself in a quandary. On the one hand, I'd just helped relieve him of a necklace worth millions of euros. But on the other hand, it had been stolen not for me but for the goddess Kali, and with any luck, Yegorov would never realize he'd lost it.

"If you want this place to stay the way it is, there is something you can do for me," I said slowly. "Well, not for me exactly, but for all of us here. How would you feel about a new business venture?"

"Go on," said Yegorov, suddenly listening very intently. His smile widened.

"It's supposed to be a secret, but the hotel is up for sale. You'd have to outbid another potential buyer, though."

Yegorov laughed. "That happens to be my speciality," he said. "Consider it done."

And I did. Burkhardt might have a suitcase full of dirty money and know every trick in the book, but he couldn't compete with a Russian oligarch. His plans for apartment buildings and golf shops turned to dust the moment Yegorov strode decisively out of the library.

And then, at last, Ben arrived.

He was slightly out of breath as he burst into the library. "I'm sorry I took so long," he said.

"Did you have to fix someone's phone?"

He grinned. "No. I was talking to the police. And I found this."

He brought a hand out from behind his back and presented me with my missing shoe. "It was lying on the stairs down to the ski cellar. Shall we see if it fits you, Cinderella?"

"Why thank you, Your Highness." I stretched my foot out toward him. "Delia will be delighted. Even if it's not a glass slipper, just one of Fräulein Müller's extra-comfortable work shoes with extra-quiet soles."

"It fits you like a glove." Ben grinned at me. "Now we can go outside, light a sky lantern, and make a wish." He pointed through the window onto the terrace. "Look, there are the Yegorovs with Dasha." Yegorov was holding his little girl in his arms. She looked adorable, her curly head tipped back and her eyes wide as she gazed into the sky. The events of the past few hours clearly hadn't done her any harm.

"My wish is that the Ludwigs stay behind bars for the rest of their lives," I said. "Oh, that reminds me—do the police know about Mrs. Ludwig's so-called engagement ring being part of the ransom from another kidnapping?"

"What? The ring with the pink stone? The one the oligarch's wife stole and you stole back?"

I nodded. Eventually I'd tell Ben the truth about all this, but perhaps not today. "The police can use it to convict her for that crime, too."

Ben looked at me in dismay. "No they can't, I'm afraid. You see . . ." And then he told me everything that had happened in the stables after he'd picked up the pitchfork and driven Mrs. Ludwig back against the wall.

Mrs. Ludwig had suddenly looked very small and frail, and she'd opened her eyes wide and begged him not to hurt her. It was all a terrible misunderstanding, she said, and he was scaring her.

And then she'd started crying, telling him she was so dreadfully sorry for all of this.

"I was livid—because of her, you were lying unconscious on the ground. She'd put you through hell. But I couldn't hit a whimpering old lady. Even if she is evil incarnate. So I did something very childish. I took her beloved engagement ring off her finger and chucked it out the door into the snow; I wanted to do something to make her suffer. She immediately stopped crying and started cursing like mad. You wouldn't believe the swear words that old lady knows!"

"You threw the ring away?"

Ben nodded contritely. "I didn't know it was evidence."

"As well as being worth about three million euros," I said.

"What?!" Ben exclaimed. "Well in that case, we'll go out first thing tomorrow morning and look for it, even if we have to dig up every square inch of snow. But we don't need the ring as evidence. They've confessed to everything. And Pierre and that man in the gloves are going to give statements, too—that'll give the police everything they need. Come on." He held out his hand. "Let's go out and join the others. We don't want to miss the sky lanterns."

I stood up. It had gone very quiet in the bar—even the pianist was taking a break. Suddenly, the light of the chandelier went out with a soft sigh and the candles in the windows burned brighter. But I didn't need that to know we'd wasted too much time already. I went over to Ben and put my arms around his neck. Like me, he seemed to feel that the sky lanterns could wait. With a quiet sigh, he pulled me close and kissed me, passionately and tenderly.

Tristan's kiss outside in the snow might have been the most exciting kiss I'd ever had in my life, but this one was the sweetest. It just felt right.

A FEW MONTHS LATER

September was my favorite time of year in the mountains. The light was so beautifully soft, and a sort of golden haze lay over the green of the mountain pastures, fir trees, and ferns. Castle in the Clouds looked more magnificent than ever.

On my way back from the stables, where I'd popped in to feed Jesty and Vesty, I stood still for a moment to take in the sight of the hotel in all its glory. A year ago today, I'd seen it for the first time—tomorrow I'd officially have been working at Castle in the Clouds for a whole year. Nobody had told me anything, but from the way Ben and Monsieur Rocher fell silent midconversation when I approached, and the way Pavel kept trying to change the subject, I'd guessed they were planning something to mark the occasion. I'd just have to pretend I wasn't expecting anything and act totally surprised.

The dramatic events of New Year's Eve felt like a lifetime ago—hardly anyone at the hotel ever mentioned them now. (Apart from Old Stucky, who never tired of telling people, with a fervent gleam in his eye, about how he'd repeatedly walloped that evil Mr. Ludwig over the head—"A boshed him rond tha heed wi' the hoarses' harrniss.") Mrs. Ludwig's so-called engagement ring had never been seen again, though we'd searched high and low for it. We'd hoped it would turn up when the snow melted, but there was no sign of it. The Ludwigs had retracted their confessions on the advice of their lawyers, but there'd been more than enough evidence to convict them and send them to prison. It turned out they hadn't even been intending to kidnap Dasha at first—they'd set their sights on Don and his father's suitcase of dirty money. It was only when they realized that the Smirnovs were actually the Yegorovs and that one of the most valuable pieces of jewelry in the world was within their grasp that they'd decided to scrap their original plan and abduct Dasha instead. Who knew—they might have pulled off yet another kidnapping plot if their greed hadn't gotten the better of them. Either way, the case was now closed once and for all, and the Ludwigs were languishing in jail. Yegorov gave me a hug every time he visited the hotel to see how the renovation work was going, and every time he hugged me he got a bit tearful. It must have been his Russian temperament.

Yegorov had kept his promise, you see, and invested in Castle in the Clouds. Gordon Montfort had been reluctant at first, but he'd soon realized he'd be able to strike a much better (and more legal) deal with Yegorov than with his old mate Burkhardt, and since money trumped friendship every time for a man like Montfort, he had quickly come around to the idea. He'd officially signed over his share of Castle in the Clouds to Ben and withdrawn from the day-to-day running of the hotel. Now Ben was one of the managing directors, along with Yegorov and Gutless Gilbert. We'd last seen Gordon Montfort in March, when he'd told us he was splitting up with his girlfriend in Sion and moving to Frankfurt to be with Mara Matthäus. They seemed pretty serious about each other. So serious that they'd just announced they were getting married next spring, and wanted to have their wedding at Castle in the Clouds. The renovation work should be finished by then. Yegorov was very keen to preserve the old-fashioned charm of the hotel, but he'd put a lot of money into refurbishing the building—not only "front of house" but everywhere, right down to the tiniest little attic room.

Last week, the scaffolding around the building had come down and, from the outside at least, everything looked pristine.

The biggest changes to Castle in the Clouds were taking place in the basement—specifically in the spa, which now had a new terrace with loungers and a big outdoor pool. The former cold storage room was being converted into a steam room. Mr. Heffelfinger was in seventh heaven. Yegorov had put him in charge of redesigning the spa area, and Stella Yegorov had made lots of suggestions as to the various additions and adaptations she felt to be indispensable. It wasn't just that she had to spend a lot of time here now. The spa also had to meet the expectations of her rich and famous friends from all over the world who would now be coming here on holiday. We'd already taken countless reservations for the coming year, and we'd been fully booked for the winter holidays since April. To our great surprise, the Burkhardts had booked the Large Tower Suite again. I was actually looking forward to seeing Don Jr., would you believe. But I was even more excited to see the Barnbrookes again, especially Gracie, Madison, and Amy, whom I wrote to regularly. Gracie and Madison were now learning karate and both wanted to join the Secret Service when they grew up.

Sometimes I wondered whether Tristan and his grandpa and the people from the secret society they worked for really had taken the diamond back to the Indian temple. The balance of the universe was definitely restored up here at Castle in the Clouds, at any rate. Fräulein Müller was still smoking a secret cigar at her window every night; Pavel, Monsieur Rocher, and Old Stucky were still playing scat every third Tuesday in the laundry room; the head chef was still yelling at his staff; and Madame Cléo was still stuffing us full of carbs.

The only one missing was Jaromir. It turned out he'd been working undercover for a Czech investigative agency that was trying to build a case against Burkhardt for money laundering. Burkhardt owned several incinerators and waste-processing plants in the Czech Republic, and was suspected of doing various dodgy deals there. Jaromir and Mr. Huber, the insurance company agent (who, had he but known it, had failed rather spectacularly to do his job) knew each other from their days at Interpol, where they'd both worked years ago. That was why Huber had been looking for Jaromir in the staff quarters on the morning I'd first seen Tristan. They'd both agreed not to reveal each other's true identities. But since Burkhardt was no longer going to be using Castle in the Clouds to launder his dirty money, Jaromir's presence here was no longer required. We'd been very sad to see him go—undercover agent or not, he was the best caretaker the hotel had ever had. He'd promised to come back and visit with his family someday.

Luckily for Mr. Huber, there was a good chance the Yegorovs would never realize their necklace had been swapped for an excellent fake. Stella Yegorov loved the necklace now more than ever. She was convinced she had personally broken the curse of the Nadezhda Diamond.

I came through the revolving door and wandered across the lobby, nodding to Denise at Reception, stroking the Forbidden Cat—who wasn't technically "forbidden" anymore—and arranging with Monsieur Rocher to meet for a cappuccino at four o'clock that afternoon.

Upstairs in my room, I opened the windows wide and waited for the seven Hugos. I no longer lived in my little attic room—like all the other rooms in the south wing, it was being renovated. Instead I lived next door to Ben in Room 210. It was a corner room with a balcony. To the south, I had a view of the valley and the twelve-thousand-foot-high mountains, and to the west I could see my old friend the half-moon fir tree. I was already looking forward to lighting a fire in the fireplace when it got colder.

I sometimes missed my little bedroom and the old water pipe. Perhaps I would move back in there over the winter holidays and free up Room 210 for guests for a little while—after all, it was one of the nicest rooms in the hotel. Ben wanted to put my parents and my little brothers, who were coming to visit us that autumn, in the Large Tower Suite. He was a bit nervous about meeting my parents—he was afraid they wouldn't like him. But I told him he had nothing to worry about.

Delia had come to visit as soon as she'd finished her exams and, although the hotel was still a building site, she'd liked it so much she said she wished she could cancel her year as an au pair in America. She was now sending me lots of hilarious messages from Wyoming.

There was just one thing that was still puzzling me and Ben. And it was to do with the kitchen temp I'd had that memorable conversation with in the elevator, the one about the human heart. It was the same girl who'd stopped Ben running down to the basement on New Year's Eve and had sent him out to the half-moon fir tree instead. Ben remembered her teardrop earrings very clearly. And the rest of his description matched my memory of her, too. The weird thing was that nobody else seemed to know who she was. No one in the kitchen had ever seen a girl like the one we described, and

Ben—who wanted to thank her for helping us—went through all the personnel files without finding any details on her. It was as if she'd never existed. I was tempted to believe we might have had the pleasure of meeting the Lady in White.

A cawing sound brought me out of my reverie. As usual, it hadn't taken long for the seven Hugos to land on the windowsill and start tucking into the milk roll crumbs. They still hadn't learned to speak, unfortunately, but Kleptomaniac Hugo had gotten so tame that he even let me pet him.

When the milk roll was all gone, the birds took flight one after the other: first Suspicious Hugo, then Melancholy Hugo, Hopping Hugo, Chubby Hugo, Unbelievably Greedy Hugo, One-Legged Hugo, and finally Kleptomaniac Hugo. But just as I was about to shut the window, Kleptomaniac Hugo flew back onto the windowsill and hopped toward me with his head on one side. He was holding something shiny in his beak, and looking quizzically at me.

I put my hand out and he placed the glittering object carefully on my palm with a proud coo. For a second, I didn't realize what it was—but then I let out a gasp. The platinum was pure silvery white, and the pink stone sparkled as if it was brand new.

So it had finally been found. And things had come full circle at last.

Kleptomaniac Hugo had brought back Mrs. Ludwig's lost engagement ring.

I couldn't wait to tell Ben.

© Olivier Favre

KERSTIN GIER

is the author of the Silver trilogy (*Dream a Little Dream*, *Dream On*, and *Just Dreaming*) and the *New York Times*–bestselling Ruby Red trilogy (*Ruby Red*, *Sapphire Blue*, and *Emerald Green*), which has been translated into twenty-five languages.

KERSTINGIER.COM/EN

"Gier has created a smart heroine who loves a good mystery and has her wits about her."

—*Publishers Weekly* on the Silver trilogy

"Plot twists, dream make-out sessions, a touch of humor, and a scary culmination make for a thoroughly enjoyable read."

—*School Library Journal* on the Silver trilogy

★ "Adventure, humor, and mystery all have satisfying roles here."

—*Booklist*, starred review, on the Ruby Red trilogy